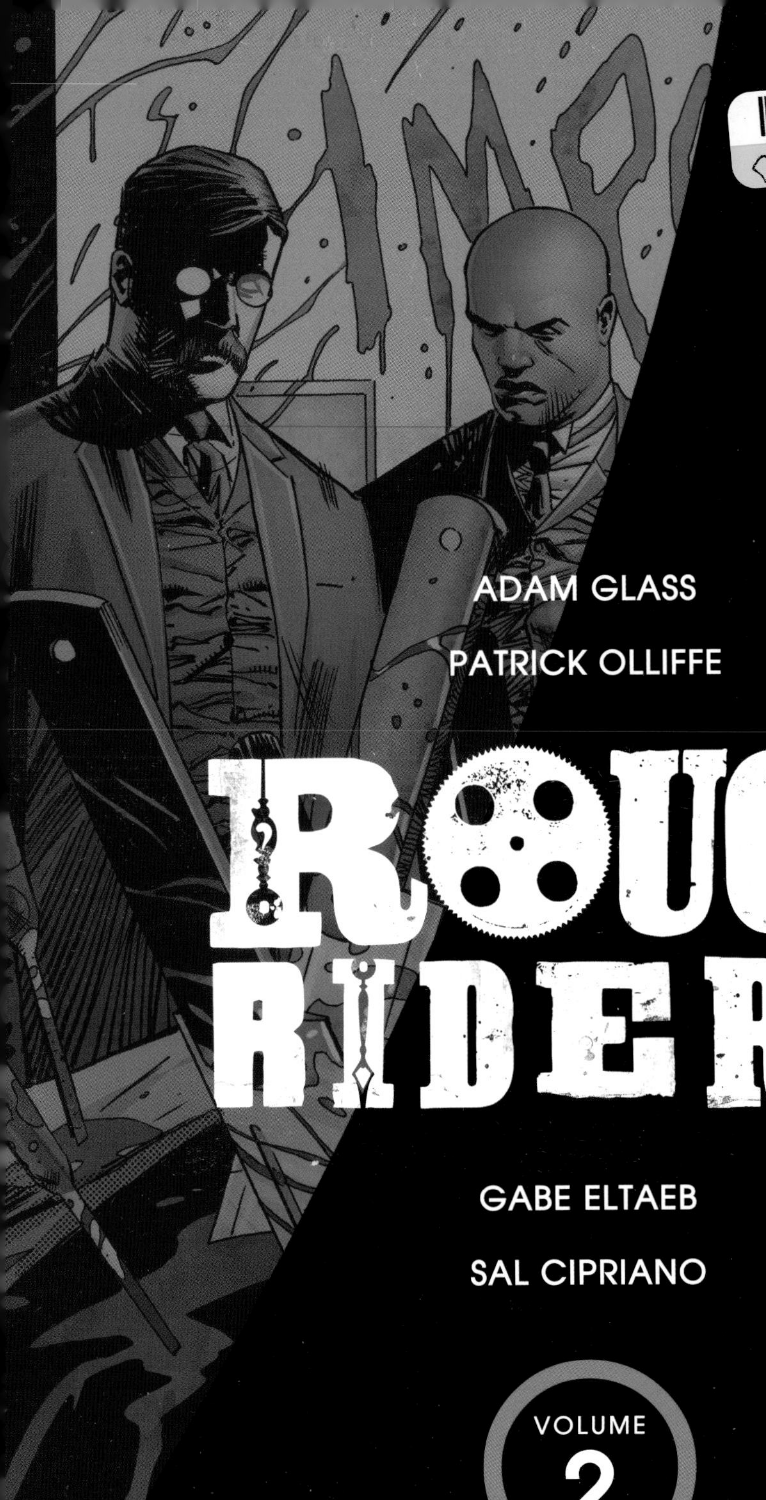

ADAM GLASS

PATRICK OLLIFFE

ROUGH RIDERS

GABE ELTAEB

SAL CIPRIANO

VOLUME
2

RIDERS ON THE STORM

AFTERSHOCK™

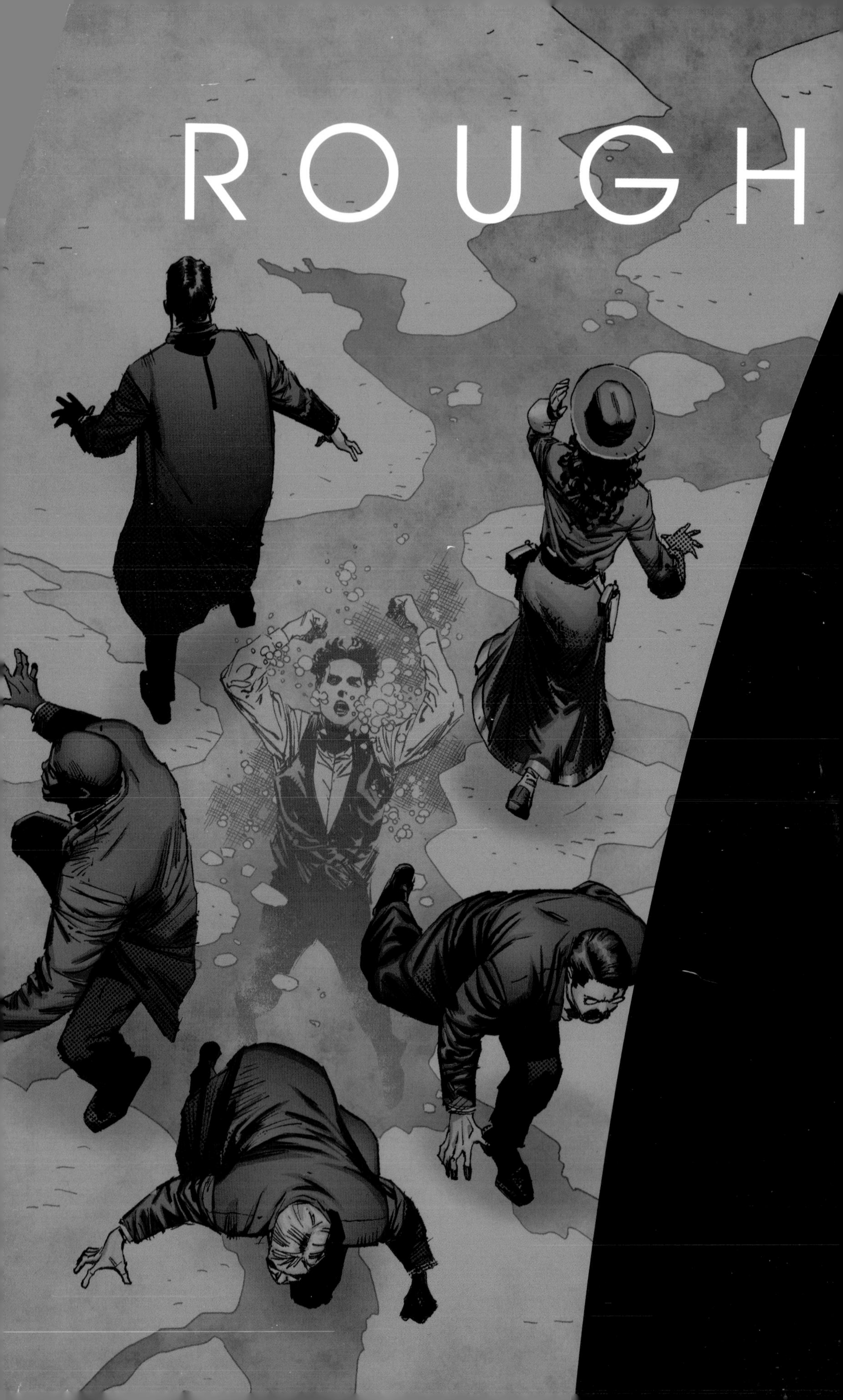
ROUGH

RIDERS
VOLUME 2
RIDERS ON THE STORM

ADAM GLASS creator & writer

PATRICK OLLIFFE artist

GABE ELTAEB colorist **SAL CIPRIANO** letterer

PATRICK OLLIFFE & **GABE ELTAEB** front & original series covers

PATRICK OLLIFFE & **GABE ELTAEB** variant covers

TOM MULLER logo designer

JOHN J. HILL book designer

MIKE MARTS editor

AFTERSHOCK

MIKE MARTS - Editor-in-Chief • JOE PRUETT - Publisher/ Chief Creative Officer • LEE KRAMER - President
JAWAD QURESHI - SVP, Investor Relations • JON KRAMER - Chief Executive Officer • MIKE ZAGARI - SVP, Brand
JAY BEHLING - Chief Financial Officer • STEPHAN NILSON - Publishing Operations Manager
LISA Y. WU - Retailer/Fan Relations Manager • ASHLEY WYATT - Publishing Assistant

AfterShock Trade Dress and Interior Design by JOHN J. HILL • AfterShock Logo Design by COMICRAFT
Original series production by CHARLES PRITCHETT • Proofreading by DOCTOR Z.
Publicity: contact AARON MARION (aaron@fifteenminutes.com) &
RYAN CROY (ryan@fifteenminutes.com) at 15 MINUTES
Special thanks to TEDDY LEO & LISA MOODY

AFTERSHOCKCOMICS.COM Follow us on social media 🐦 📷 f

INTRODUCTION

"Could we get a sketch of Teddy Roosevelt?" When I contacted Mike Marts about possible projects, I didn't expect that to be the "character" I was in the running for. I've worked with Mike at both Marvel and DC, and I've put together a career of mostly super hero action projects, so I was expecting the same genre of titles from the then very new AfterShock comics. So I was a little surprised, but very happy with what I was hearing from Mike about this series. A period piece? Teddy Roosevelt, Harry Houdini, Annie Oakley, Thomas Edison and Jack Johnson, all teaming up to have a crazy adventure that involved conspiracies, aliens and steampunk technology? That sounded awesome! And it was, and it has been!

Being able to draw these characters and stories in not one, but now two series has been more than I initially hoped for! I love history and historical fiction, so it's been great to get the chance to not only draw these famous faces, but to also illustrate the real historical elements that Adam expertly weaves in to his scripts. One of my favorite examples is from the first series where Teddy Roosevelt, in the hopes of recruiting Annie Oakley to his cause, shows her the letter she had written to President McKinley offering her abilities in the service of her country just before the Spanish American War. I was able to find an image of the actual letter she wrote and did my best to approximate it in the book. How cool is that?! There are plenty more examples like that spread throughout both the first ROUGH RIDERS series and ROUGH RIDERS: RIDERS ON THE STORM. Makes my job easy.

I have been lucky to work with some very talented inkers over the course of my career, but felt that on a project like ROUGH RIDERS I needed to ink my own work. I had an idea of what the look for series should be and thought that my being in control of both pencils and inks was the best way to achieve that look. I'm very grateful that Mike was on board with letting me give it a shot. It's allowed me to connect with the project even more than I expected it would.

This project has been a high point in my career, due in no small part to the super talented guys I get to work with. Adam Glass, what can I say? He's the guy who dreamed all this craziness up in the first place! He writes such compelling stories that I find I read the scripts like a fan first—can't wait to see what happens next! And he's great to work with, too! Can't beat that! Gabe Eltaeb and I worked together briefly on *Barb Wire* and I was very excited to have the chance to work with him again on ROUGH RIDERS. He brings the pages to life; he's as responsible for the look of ROUGH RIDERS as I am. Love getting to see the final lettered pages, and Sal Cipriano does an awesome job, even when I occasionally don't leave him enough room in the panels! Sorry, Sal. Of course, Mike Marts and AfterShock were the ones who put us all together. Glad they did, we're all fans of not only this project but of each other—doesn't always work that way, but it's nice when it does.

Guess my Teddy Roosevelt sketch did the trick!

8

"THE BIG BURN"

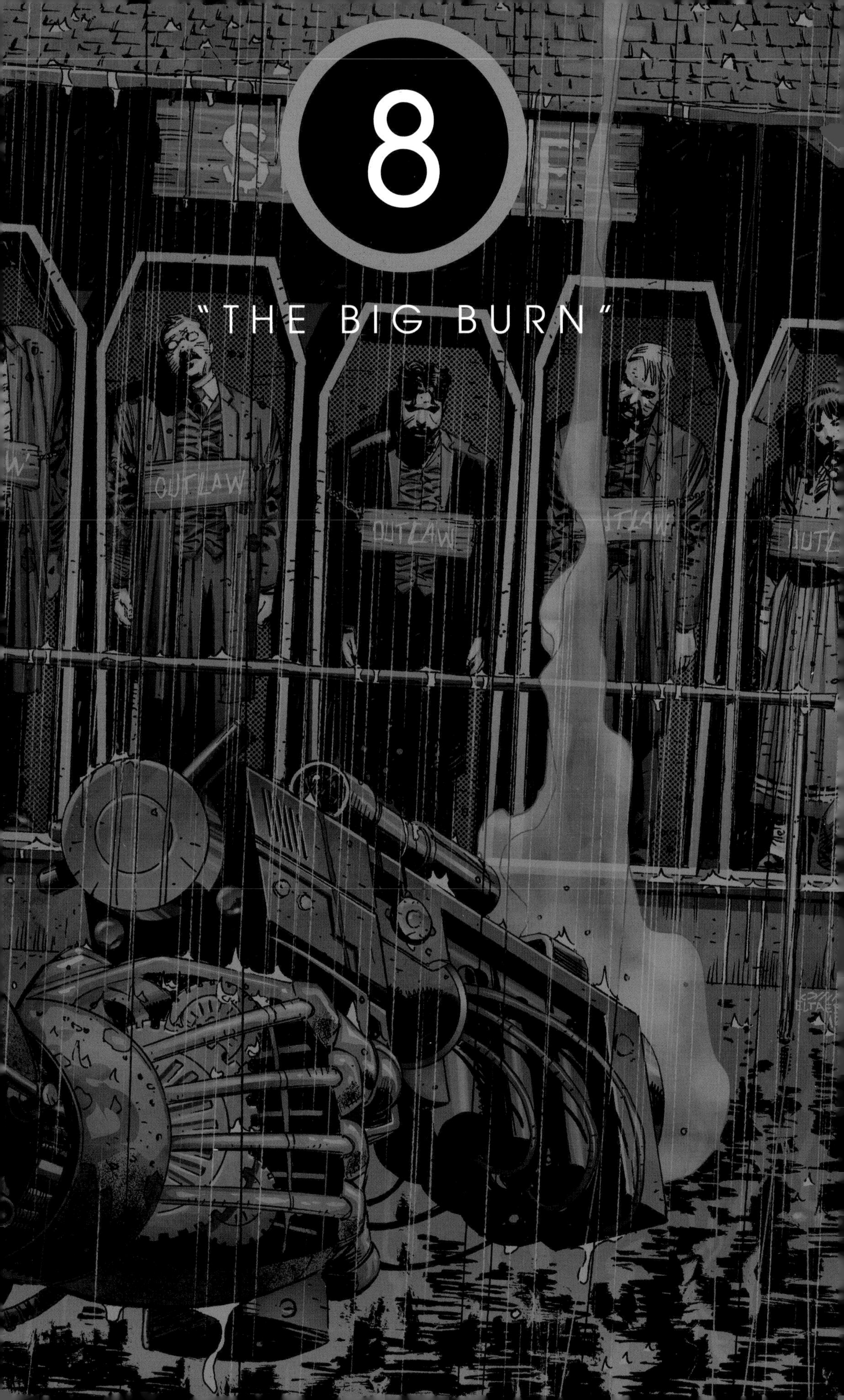
OUTLAW
OUTLAW

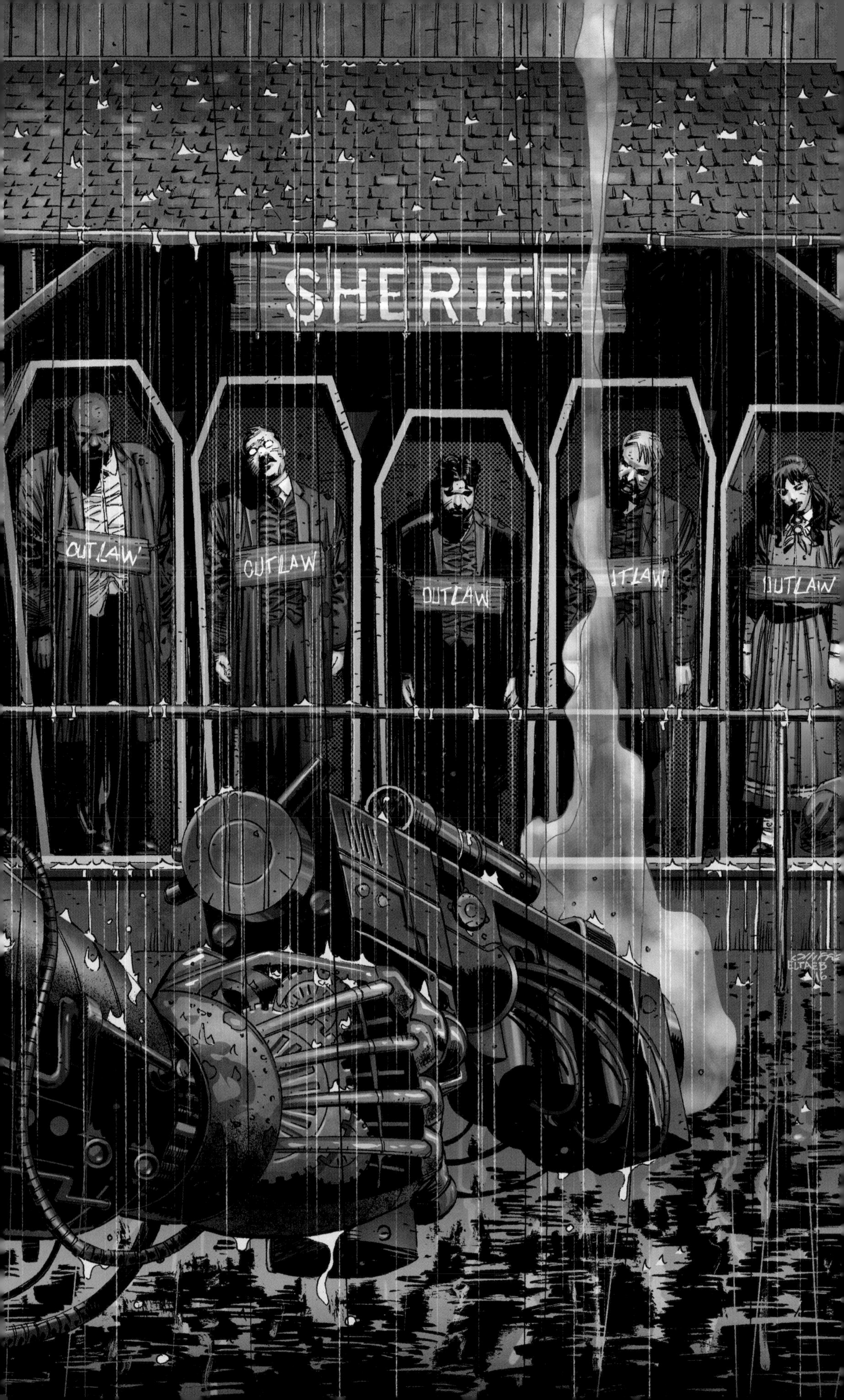
SHERIFF
OUTLAW
OUTLAW
OUTLAW
OUTLAW

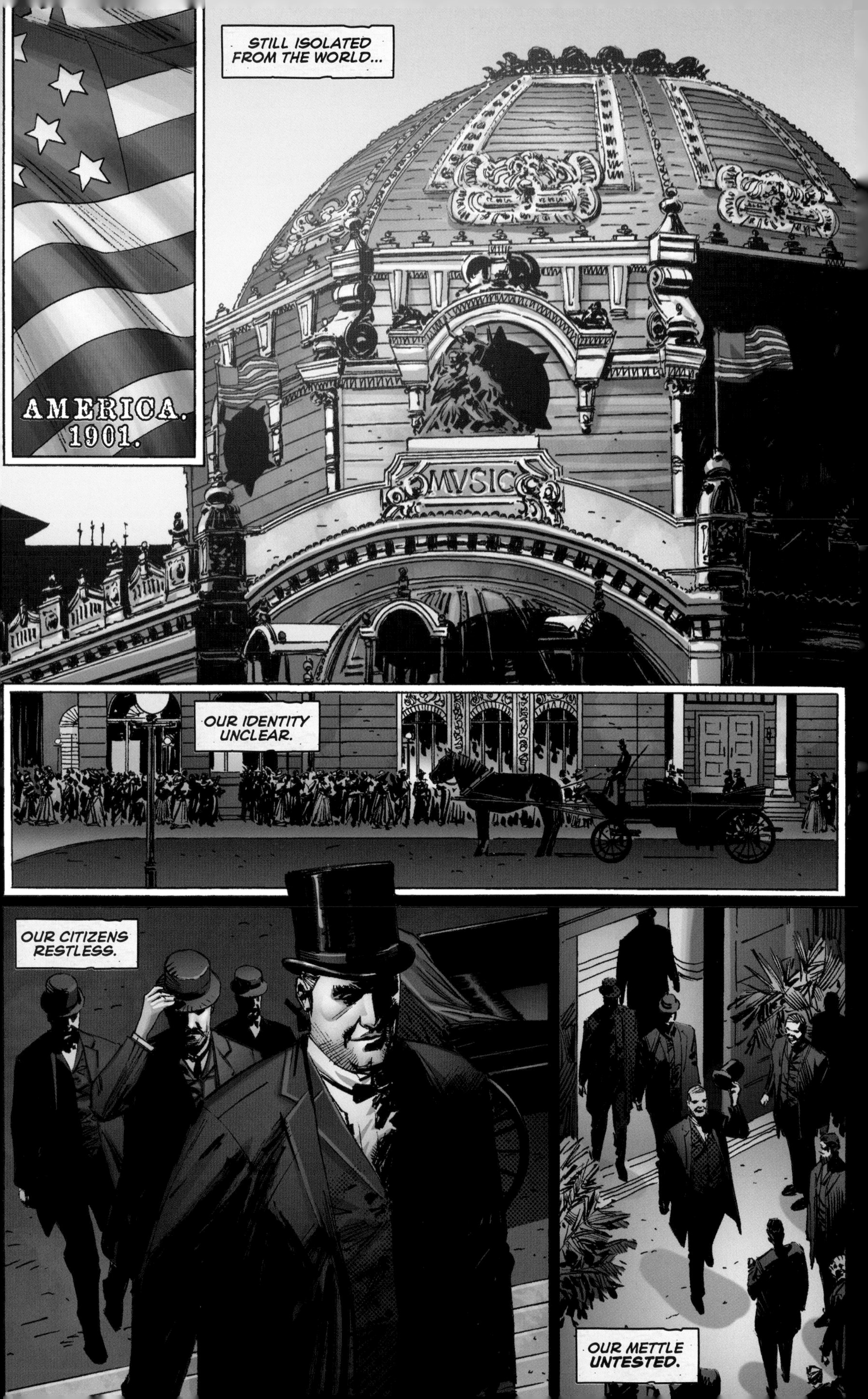
AMERICA.
1901.
STILL ISOLATED FROM THE WORLD...
MVSIC
OUR IDENTITY UNCLEAR.
OUR CITIZENS RESTLESS.
OUR METTLE UNTESTED.

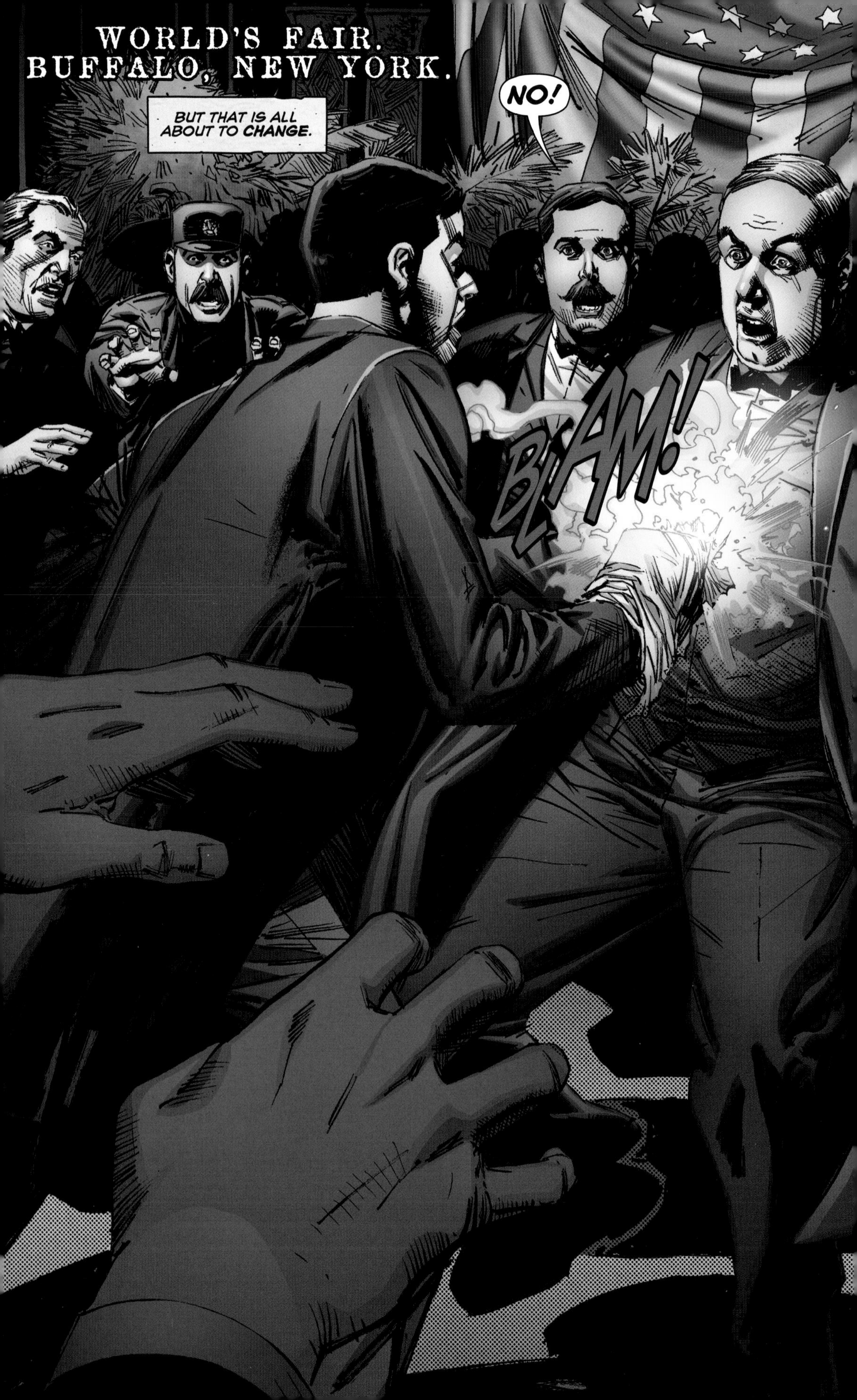
WORLD'S FAIR.
BUFFALO, NEW YORK.
BUT THAT IS ALL ABOUT TO CHANGE.
NO!
BLAM!

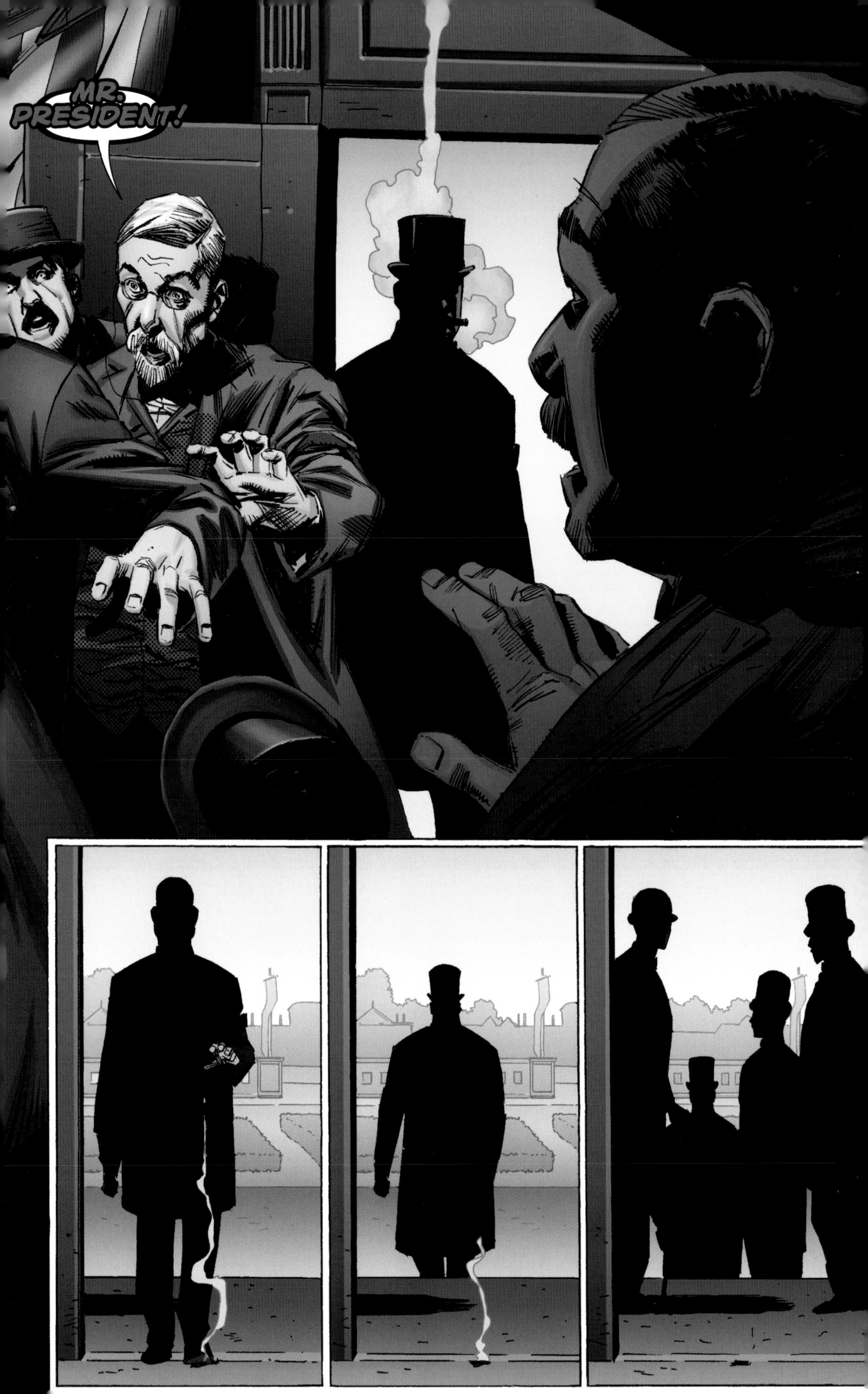
MR. PRESIDENT!

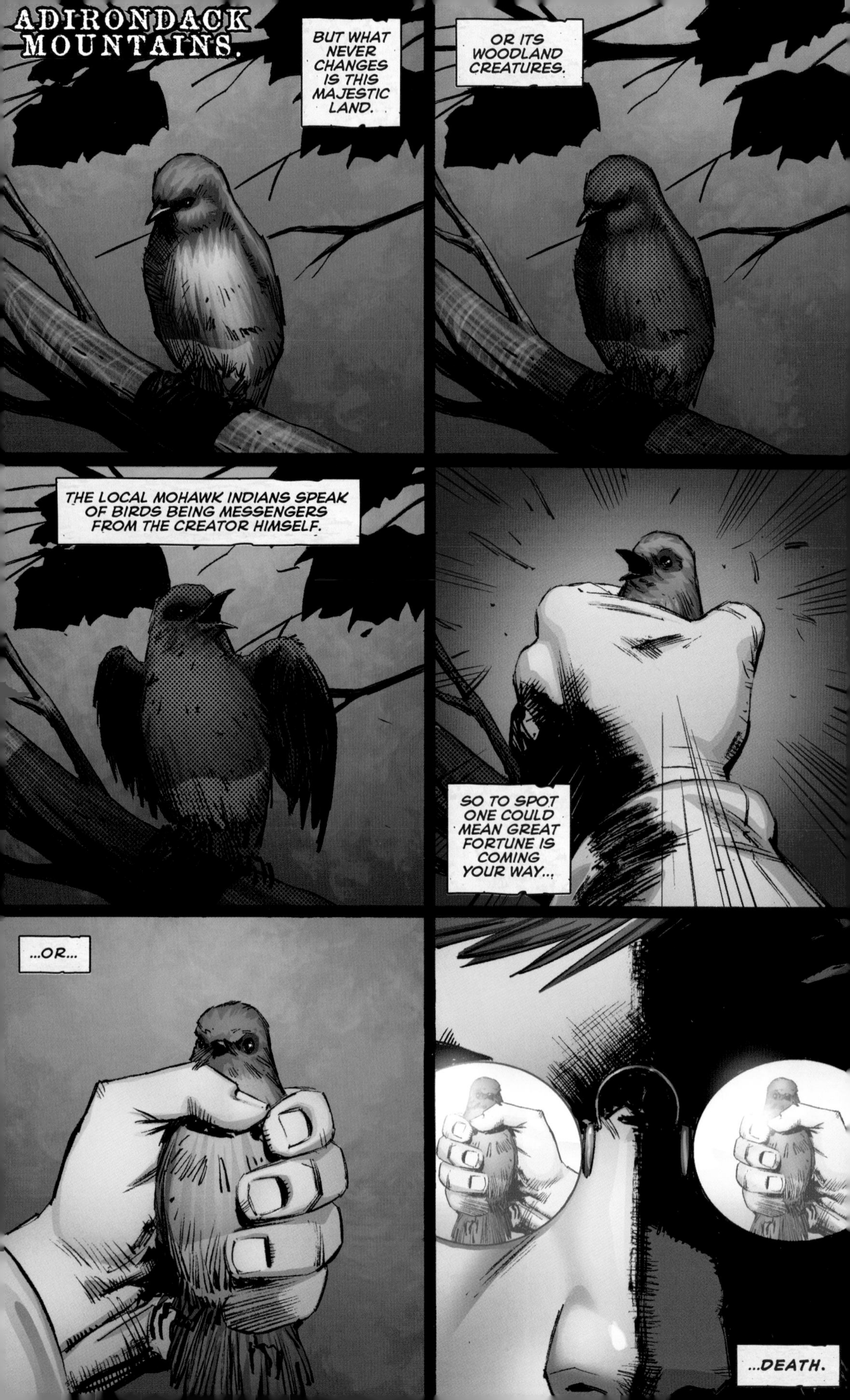
ADIRONDACK MOUNTAINS.
BUT WHAT NEVER CHANGES IS THIS MAJESTIC LAND.
OR ITS WOODLAND CREATURES.
THE LOCAL MOHAWK INDIANS SPEAK OF BIRDS BEING MESSENGERS FROM THE CREATOR HIMSELF.
SO TO SPOT ONE COULD MEAN GREAT FORTUNE IS COMING YOUR WAY...
...OR...
...DEATH.

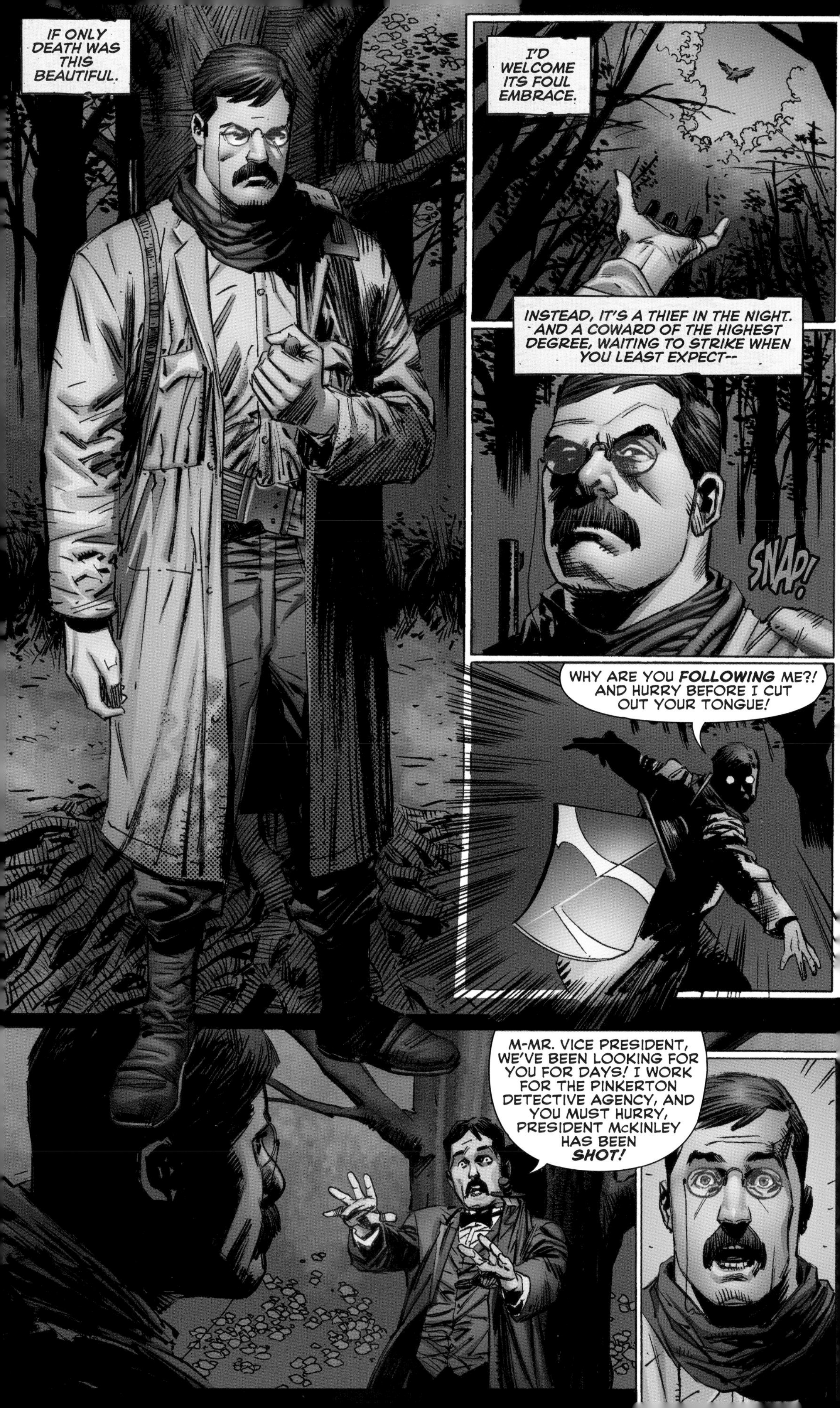
IF ONLY DEATH WAS THIS BEAUTIFUL.
I'D WELCOME ITS FOUL EMBRACE.
INSTEAD, IT'S A THIEF IN THE NIGHT. AND A COWARD OF THE HIGHEST DEGREE, WAITING TO STRIKE WHEN YOU LEAST EXPECT--
SNAP!
WHY ARE YOU FOLLOWING ME?! AND HURRY BEFORE I CUT OUT YOUR TONGUE!
M-MR. VICE PRESIDENT, WE'VE BEEN LOOKING FOR YOU FOR DAYS! I WORK FOR THE PINKERTON DETECTIVE AGENCY, AND YOU MUST HURRY, PRESIDENT McKINLEY HAS BEEN SHOT!

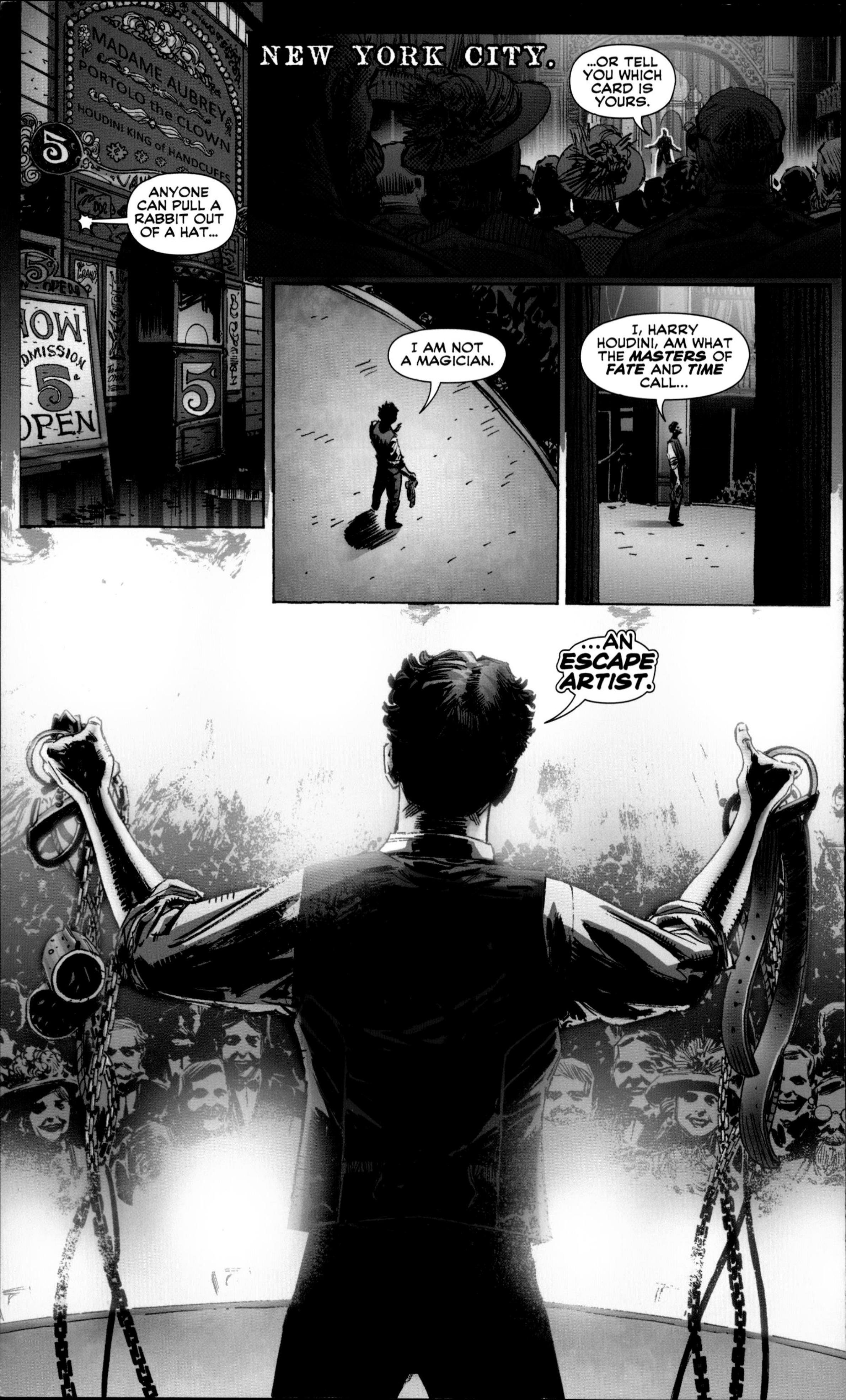
NEW YORK CITY.
MADAME AUBREY
PORTOLO the CLOWN
HOUDINI KING of HANDCUFFS
ANYONE CAN PULL A RABBIT OUT OF A HAT...
...OR TELL YOU WHICH CARD IS YOURS.
NOW
ADMISSION 5¢
OPEN
I AM NOT A MAGICIAN.
I, HARRY HOUDINI, AM WHAT THE MASTERS OF FATE AND TIME CALL...
...AN ESCAPE ARTIST.

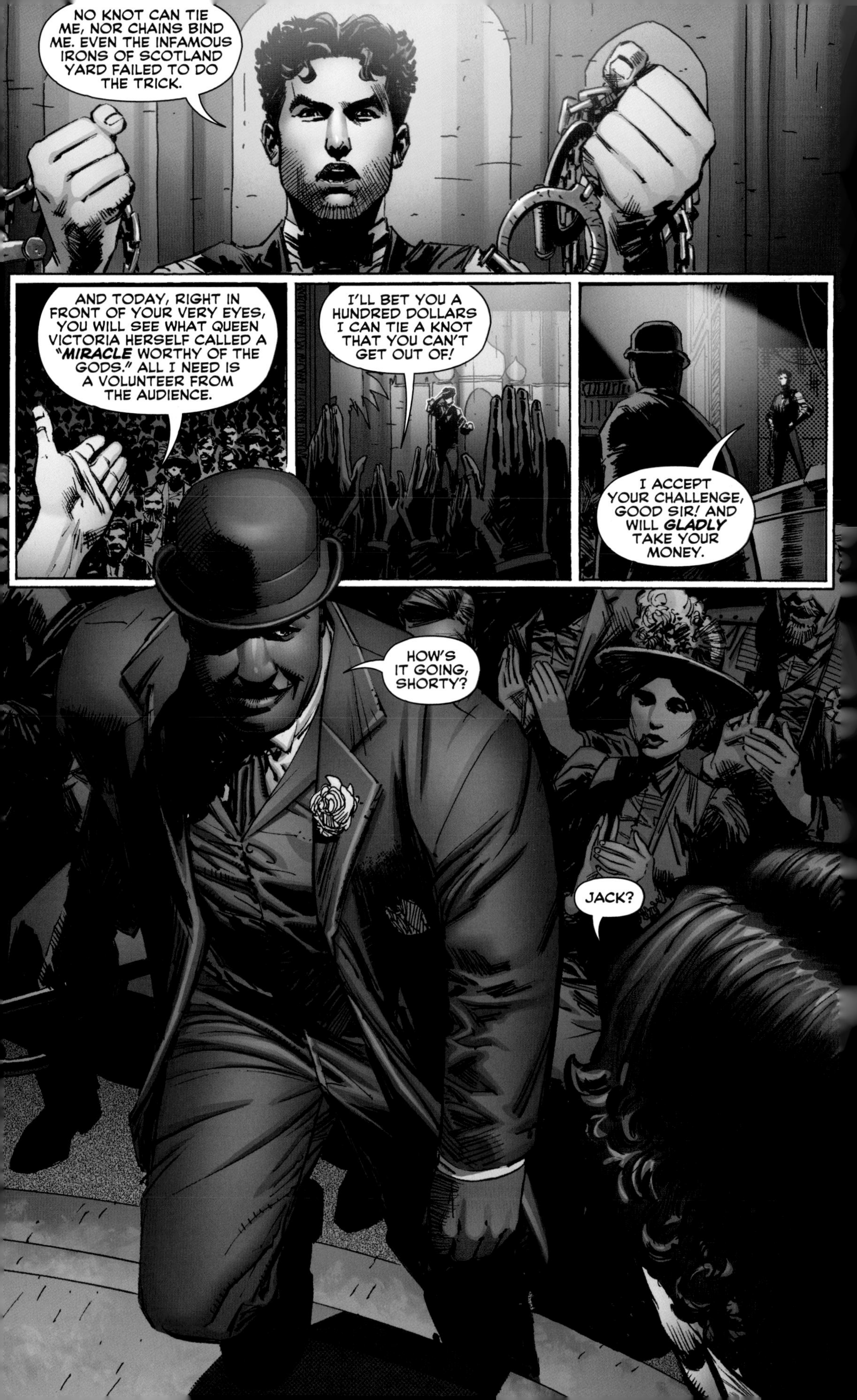
NO KNOT CAN TIE ME, NOR CHAINS BIND ME. EVEN THE INFAMOUS IRONS OF SCOTLAND YARD FAILED TO DO THE TRICK.
AND TODAY, RIGHT IN FRONT OF YOUR VERY EYES, YOU WILL SEE WHAT QUEEN VICTORIA HERSELF CALLED A "*MIRACLE* WORTHY OF THE GODS." ALL I NEED IS A VOLUNTEER FROM THE AUDIENCE.
I'LL BET YOU A HUNDRED DOLLARS I CAN TIE A KNOT THAT YOU CAN'T GET OUT OF!
I ACCEPT YOUR CHALLENGE, GOOD SIR! AND WILL *GLADLY* TAKE YOUR MONEY.
HOW'S IT GOING, SHORTY?
JACK?

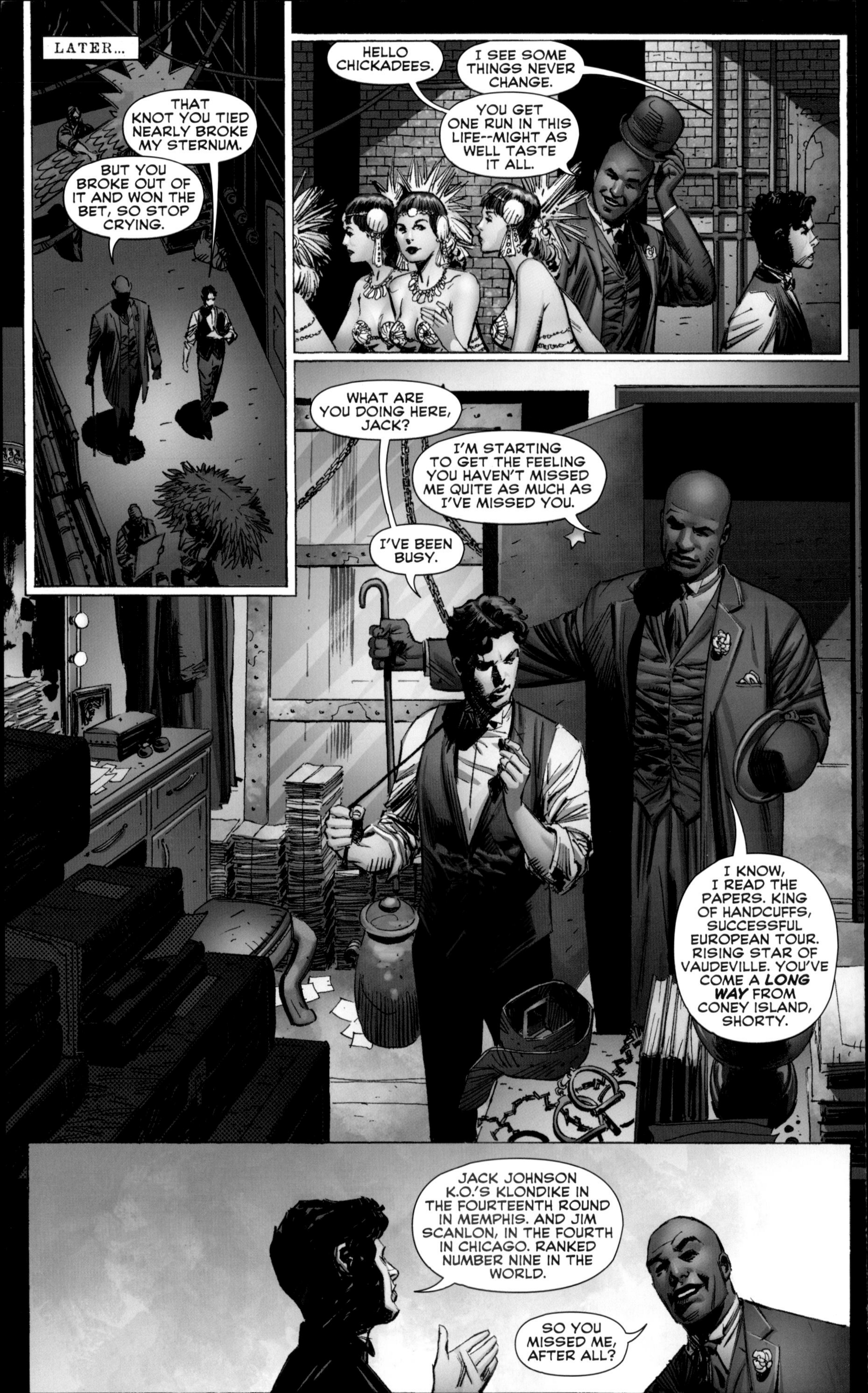
LATER...
THAT KNOT YOU TIED NEARLY BROKE MY STERNUM.
BUT YOU BROKE OUT OF IT AND WON THE BET, SO STOP CRYING.
HELLO CHICKADEES.
I SEE SOME THINGS NEVER CHANGE.
YOU GET ONE RUN IN THIS LIFE--MIGHT AS WELL TASTE IT ALL.
WHAT ARE YOU DOING HERE, JACK?
I'M STARTING TO GET THE FEELING YOU HAVEN'T MISSED ME QUITE AS MUCH AS I'VE MISSED YOU.
I'VE BEEN BUSY.
I KNOW, I READ THE PAPERS. KING OF HANDCUFFS, SUCCESSFUL EUROPEAN TOUR. RISING STAR OF VAUDEVILLE. YOU'VE COME A ***LONG WAY*** FROM CONEY ISLAND, SHORTY.
JACK JOHNSON K.O.'S KLONDIKE IN THE FOURTEENTH ROUND IN MEMPHIS. AND JIM SCANLON, IN THE FOURTH IN CHICAGO. RANKED NUMBER NINE IN THE WORLD.
SO YOU MISSED ME, AFTER ALL?

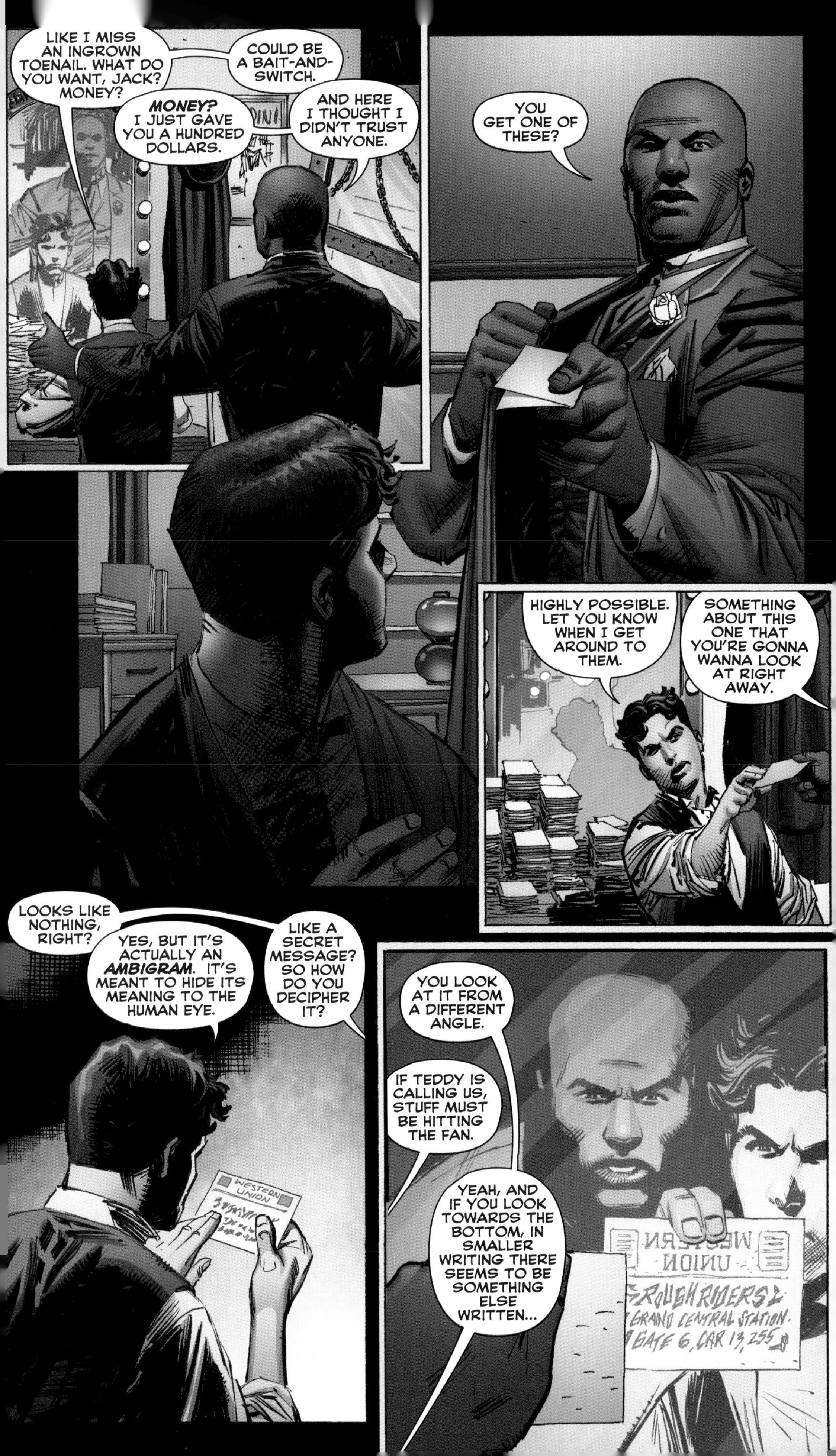
LIKE I MISS AN INGROWN TOENAIL. WHAT DO YOU WANT, JACK? MONEY?
COULD BE A BAIT-AND-SWITCH.
MONEY? I JUST GAVE YOU A HUNDRED DOLLARS.
AND HERE I THOUGHT I DIDN'T TRUST ANYONE.
YOU GET ONE OF THESE?
HIGHLY POSSIBLE. LET YOU KNOW WHEN I GET AROUND TO THEM.
SOMETHING ABOUT THIS ONE THAT YOU'RE GONNA WANNA LOOK AT RIGHT AWAY.
LOOKS LIKE NOTHING, RIGHT?
YES, BUT IT'S ACTUALLY AN **AMBIGRAM**. IT'S MEANT TO HIDE ITS MEANING TO THE HUMAN EYE.
LIKE A SECRET MESSAGE? SO HOW DO YOU DECIPHER IT?
WESTERN UNION
YOU LOOK AT IT FROM A DIFFERENT ANGLE.
IF TEDDY IS CALLING US, STUFF MUST BE HITTING THE FAN.
YEAH, AND IF YOU LOOK TOWARDS THE BOTTOM, IN SMALLER WRITING THERE SEEMS TO BE SOMETHING ELSE WRITTEN...
ROUGHRIDERS
GRAND CENTRAL STATION.
GATE 6, CAR 13,255

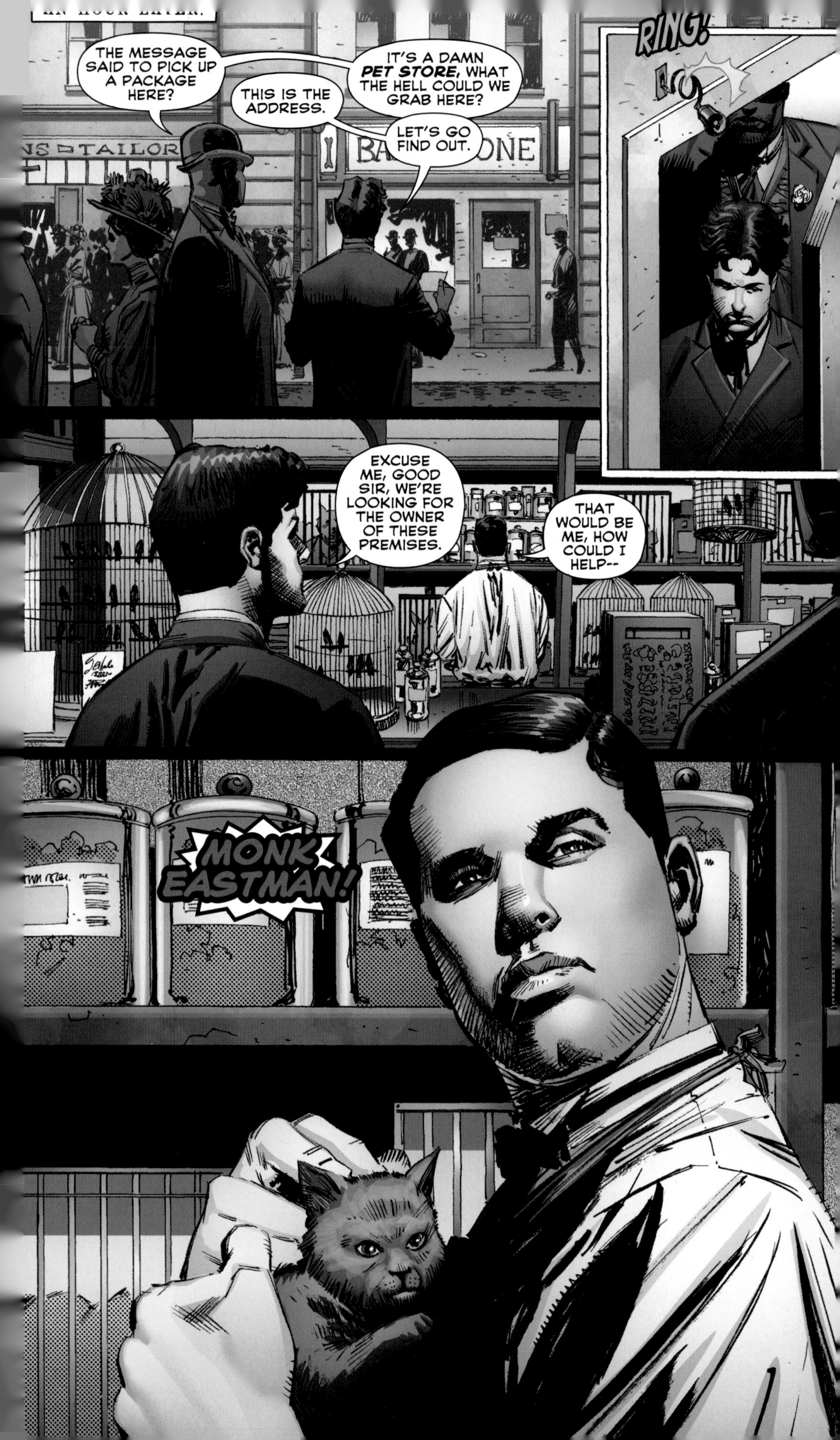
THE MESSAGE SAID TO PICK UP A PACKAGE HERE?
IT'S A DAMN **PET STORE,** WHAT THE HELL COULD WE GRAB HERE?
THIS IS THE ADDRESS.
LET'S GO FIND OUT.
RING!
EXCUSE ME, GOOD SIR, WE'RE LOOKING FOR THE OWNER OF THESE PREMISES.
THAT WOULD BE ME, HOW COULD I HELP--
MONK EASTMAN!

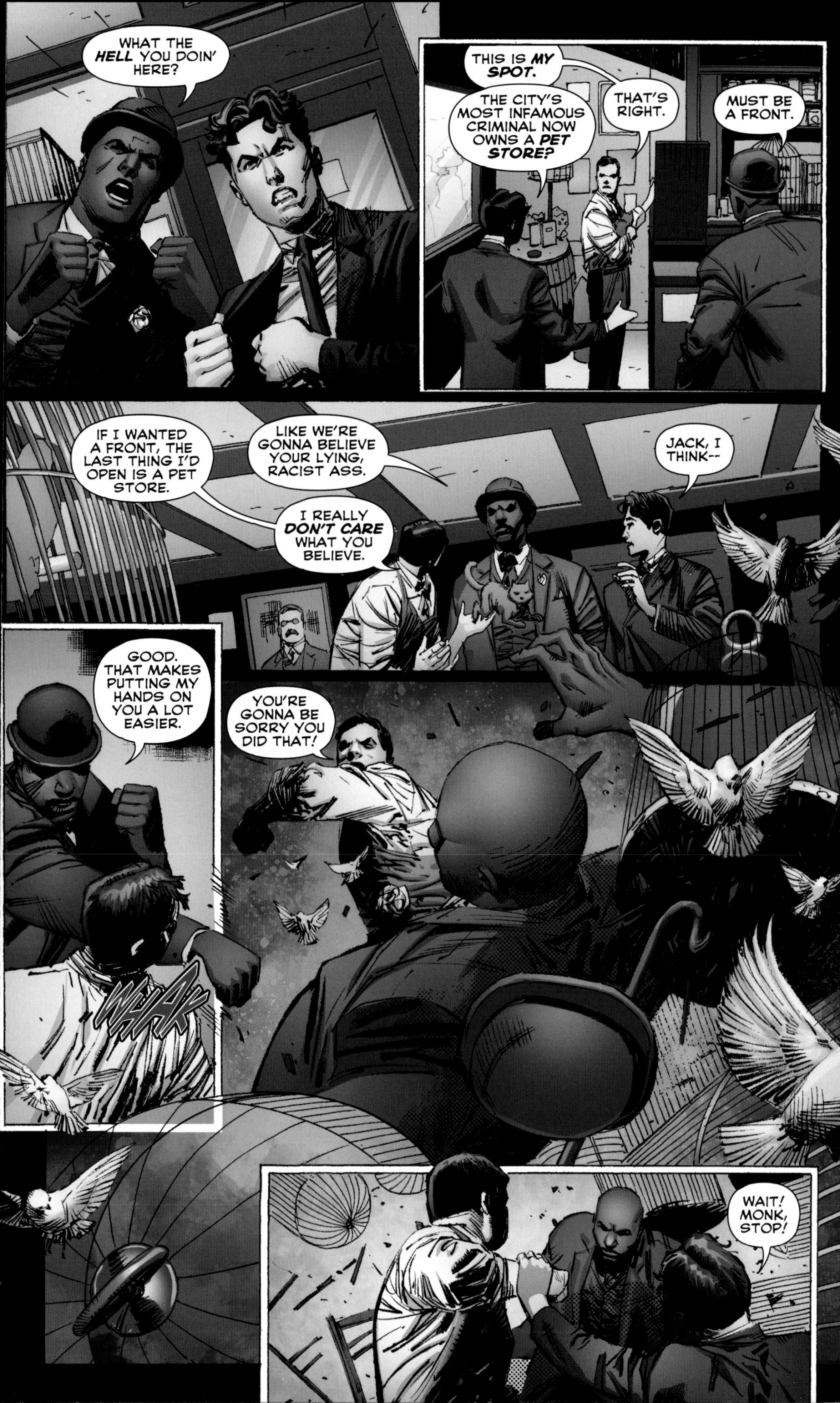

WHAT THE HELL YOU DOIN' HERE?
THIS IS MY SPOT.
THE CITY'S MOST INFAMOUS CRIMINAL NOW OWNS A PET STORE?
THAT'S RIGHT.
MUST BE A FRONT.
IF I WANTED A FRONT, THE LAST THING I'D OPEN IS A PET STORE.
LIKE WE'RE GONNA BELIEVE YOUR LYING, RACIST ASS.
I REALLY DON'T CARE WHAT YOU BELIEVE.
JACK, I THINK--
GOOD. THAT MAKES PUTTING MY HANDS ON YOU A LOT EASIER.
YOU'RE GONNA BE SORRY YOU DID THAT!
WAIT! MONK, STOP!

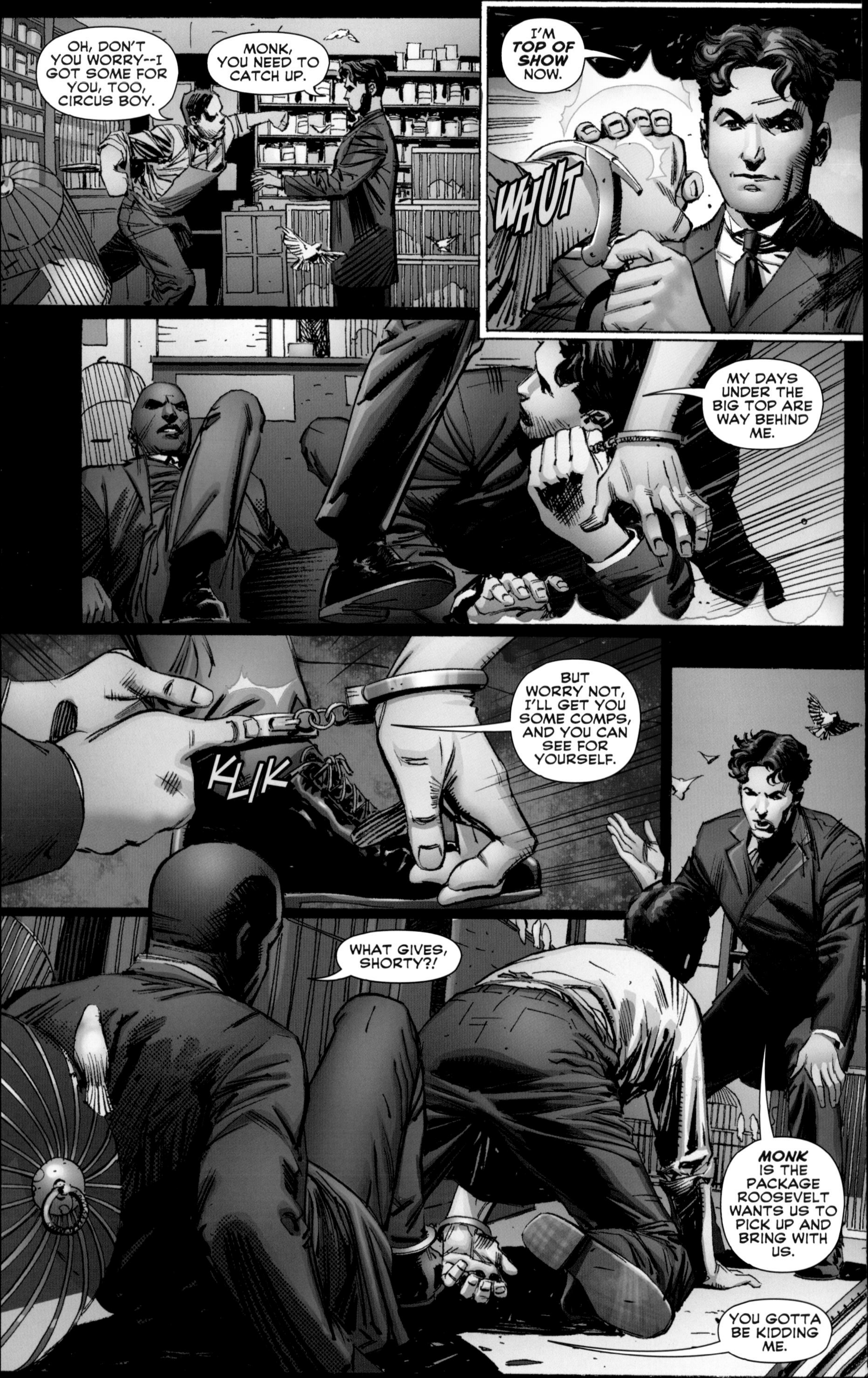
OH, DON'T YOU WORRY--I GOT SOME FOR YOU, TOO, CIRCUS BOY.
MONK, YOU NEED TO CATCH UP.
I'M *TOP OF SHOW* NOW.
WHUT
MY DAYS UNDER THE BIG TOP ARE WAY BEHIND ME.
KLIK
BUT WORRY NOT, I'LL GET YOU SOME COMPS, AND YOU CAN SEE FOR YOURSELF.
WHAT GIVES, SHORTY?!
MONK IS THE PACKAGE ROOSEVELT WANTS US TO PICK UP AND BRING WITH US.
YOU GOTTA BE KIDDING ME.

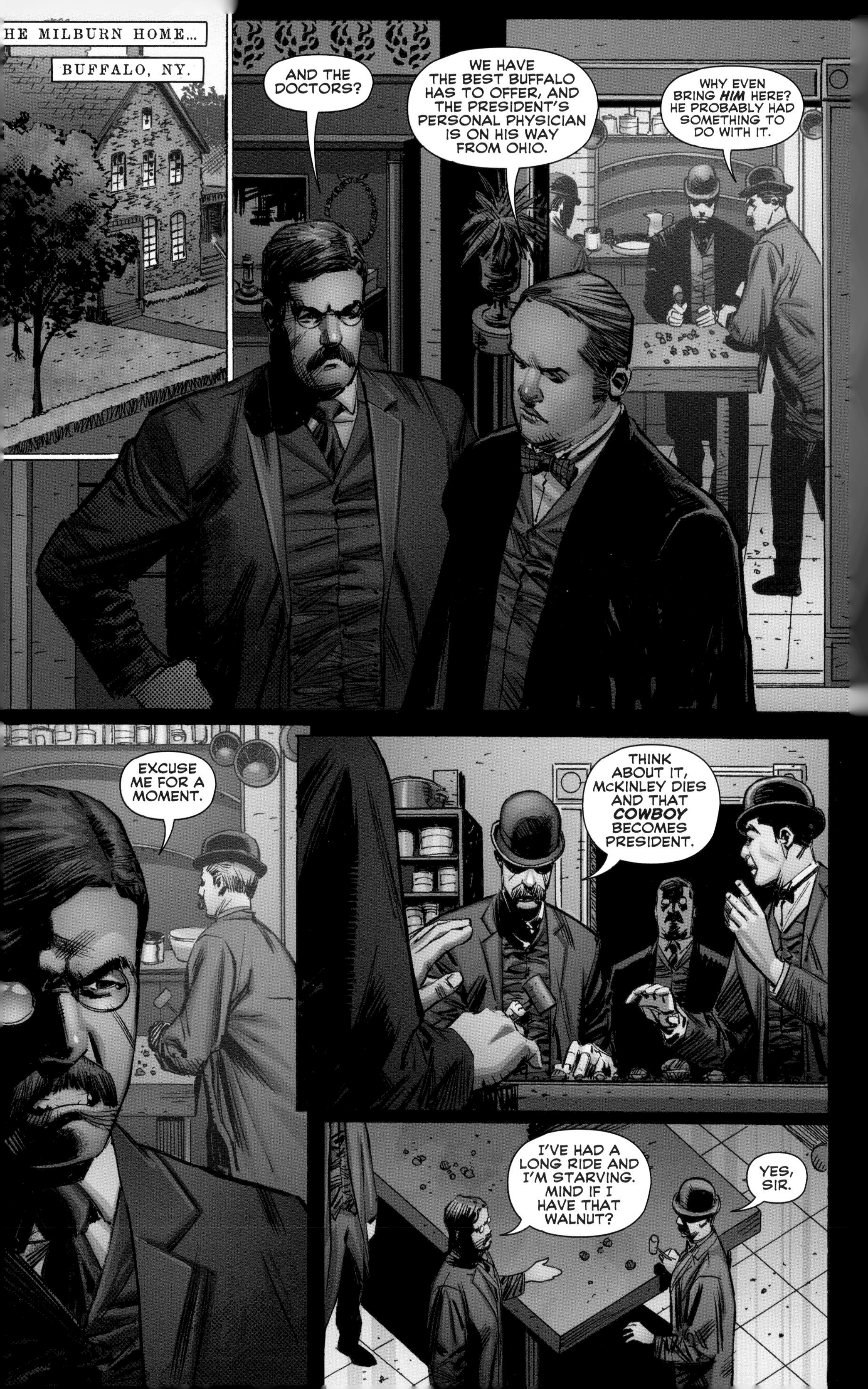
HE MILBURN HOME...
BUFFALO, NY.
AND THE DOCTORS?
WE HAVE THE BEST BUFFALO HAS TO OFFER, AND THE PRESIDENT'S PERSONAL PHYSICIAN IS ON HIS WAY FROM OHIO.
WHY EVEN BRING HIM HERE? HE PROBABLY HAD SOMETHING TO DO WITH IT.
EXCUSE ME FOR A MOMENT.
THINK ABOUT IT, McKINLEY DIES AND THAT COWBOY BECOMES PRESIDENT.
I'VE HAD A LONG RIDE AND I'M STARVING. MIND IF I HAVE THAT WALNUT?
YES, SIR.

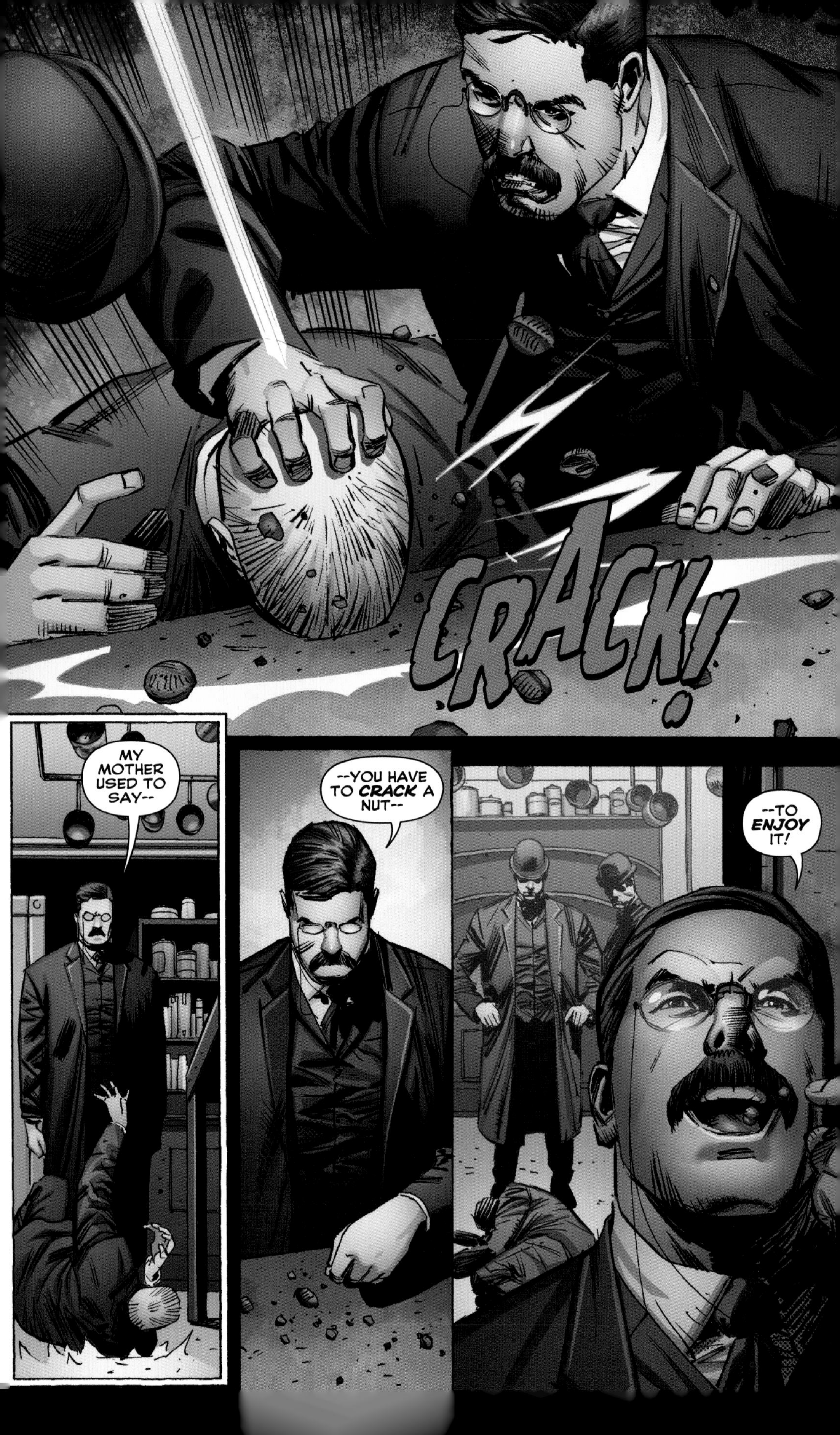
CRACK!
MY MOTHER USED TO SAY--
--YOU HAVE TO CRACK A NUT--
--TO ENJOY IT!

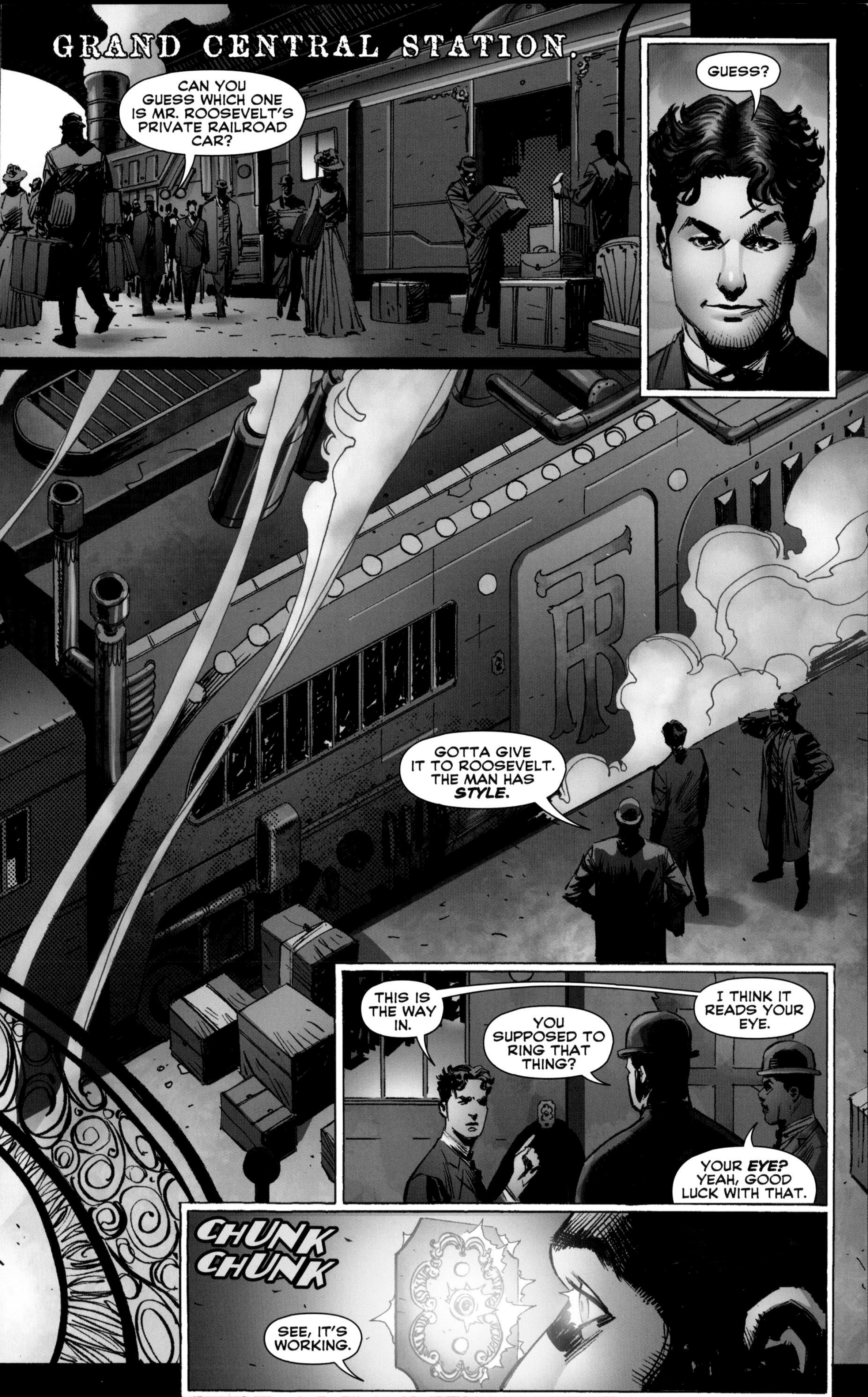

GRAND CENTRAL STATION.
CAN YOU GUESS WHICH ONE IS MR. ROOSEVELT'S PRIVATE RAILROAD CAR?
GUESS?
GOTTA GIVE IT TO ROOSEVELT. THE MAN HAS STYLE.
THIS IS THE WAY IN.
YOU SUPPOSED TO RING THAT THING?
I THINK IT READS YOUR EYE.
YOUR EYE? YEAH, GOOD LUCK WITH THAT.
CHUNK CHUNK
SEE, IT'S WORKING.

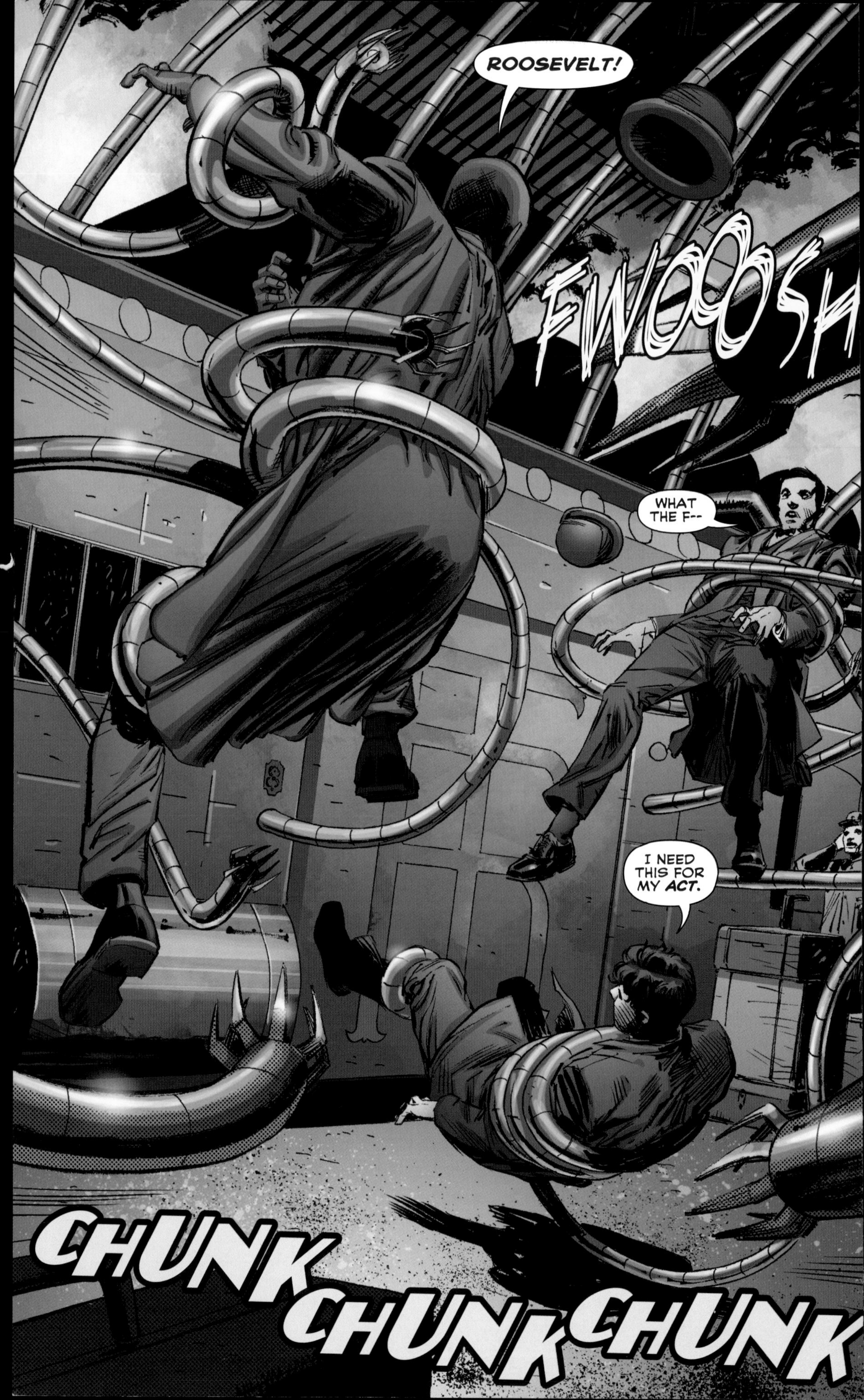
ROOSEVELT!
FWOOOSH
WHAT THE F--
I NEED THIS FOR MY ACT.
CHUNK CHUNK CHUNK

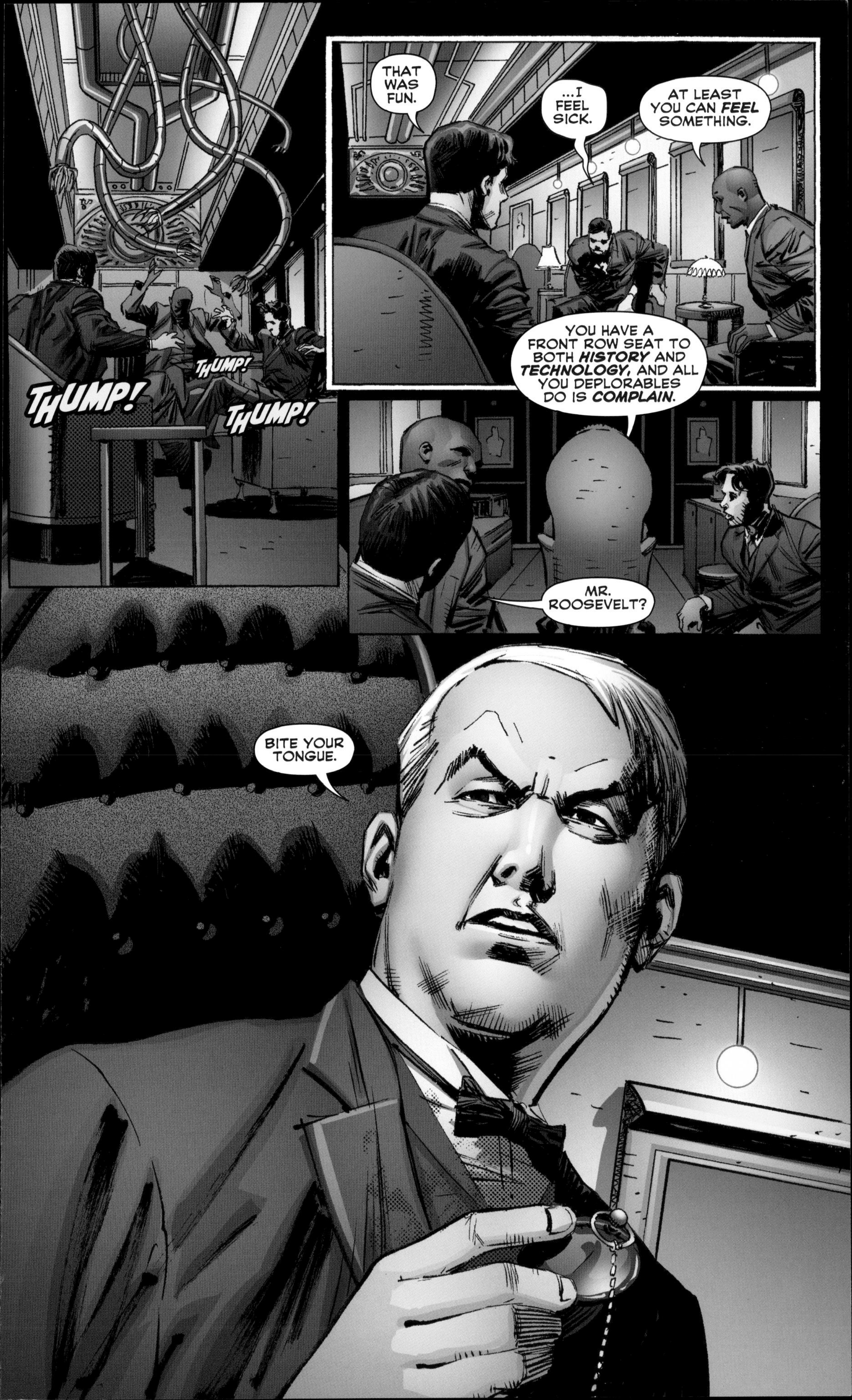
THUMP!
THUMP!
THUMP!
THAT WAS FUN.
...I FEEL SICK.
AT LEAST YOU CAN FEEL SOMETHING.
YOU HAVE A FRONT ROW SEAT TO BOTH HISTORY AND TECHNOLOGY, AND ALL YOU DEPLORABLES DO IS COMPLAIN.
MR. ROOSEVELT?
BITE YOUR TONGUE.

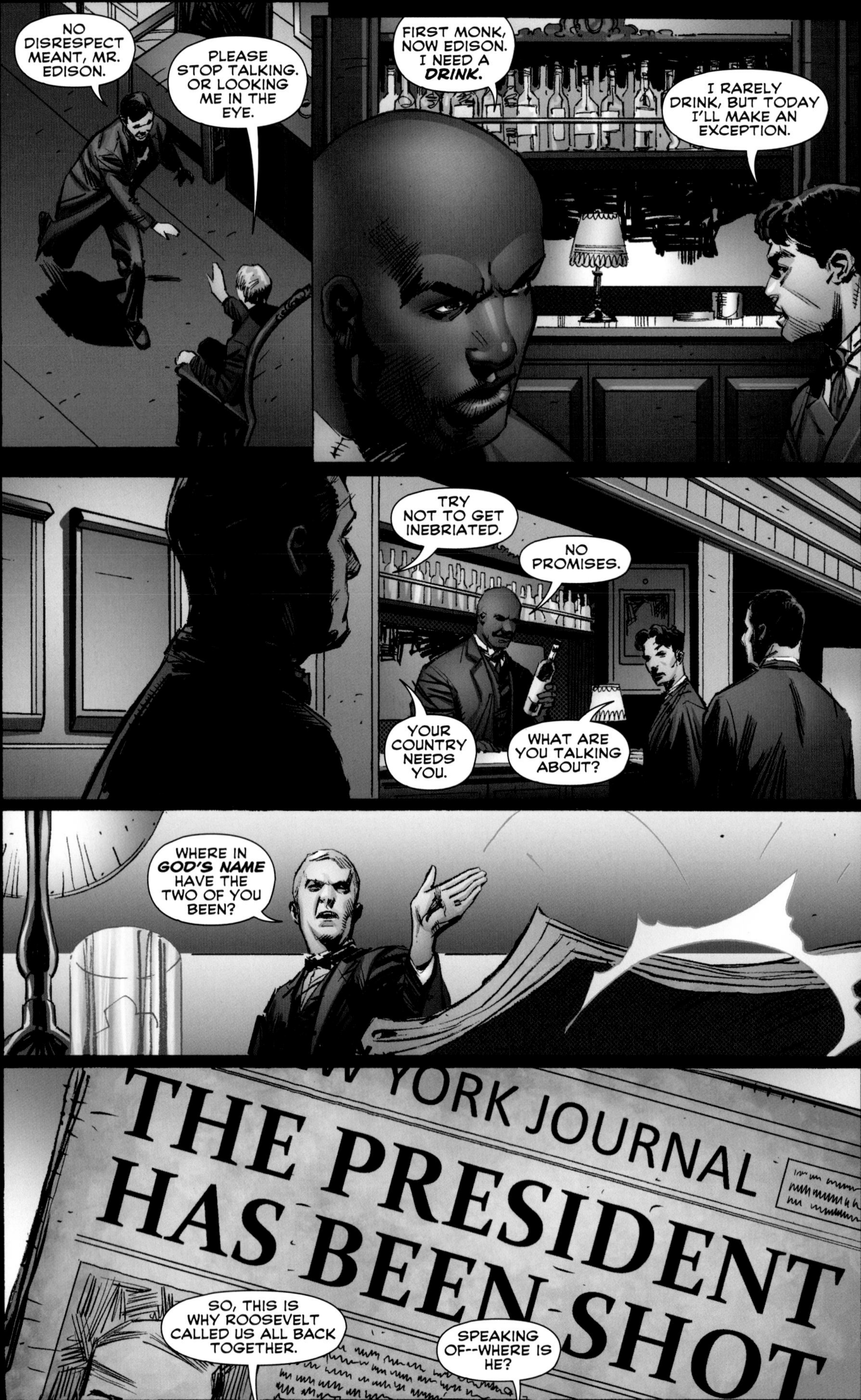
NO DISRESPECT MEANT, MR. EDISON.
PLEASE STOP TALKING. OR LOOKING ME IN THE EYE.
FIRST MONK, NOW EDISON. I NEED A DRINK.
I RARELY DRINK, BUT TODAY I'LL MAKE AN EXCEPTION.
TRY NOT TO GET INEBRIATED.
NO PROMISES.
YOUR COUNTRY NEEDS YOU.
WHAT ARE YOU TALKING ABOUT?
WHERE IN GOD'S NAME HAVE THE TWO OF YOU BEEN?
YORK JOURNAL
THE PRESIDENT HAS BEEN SHOT
SO, THIS IS WHY ROOSEVELT CALLED US ALL BACK TOGETHER.
SPEAKING OF--WHERE IS HE?

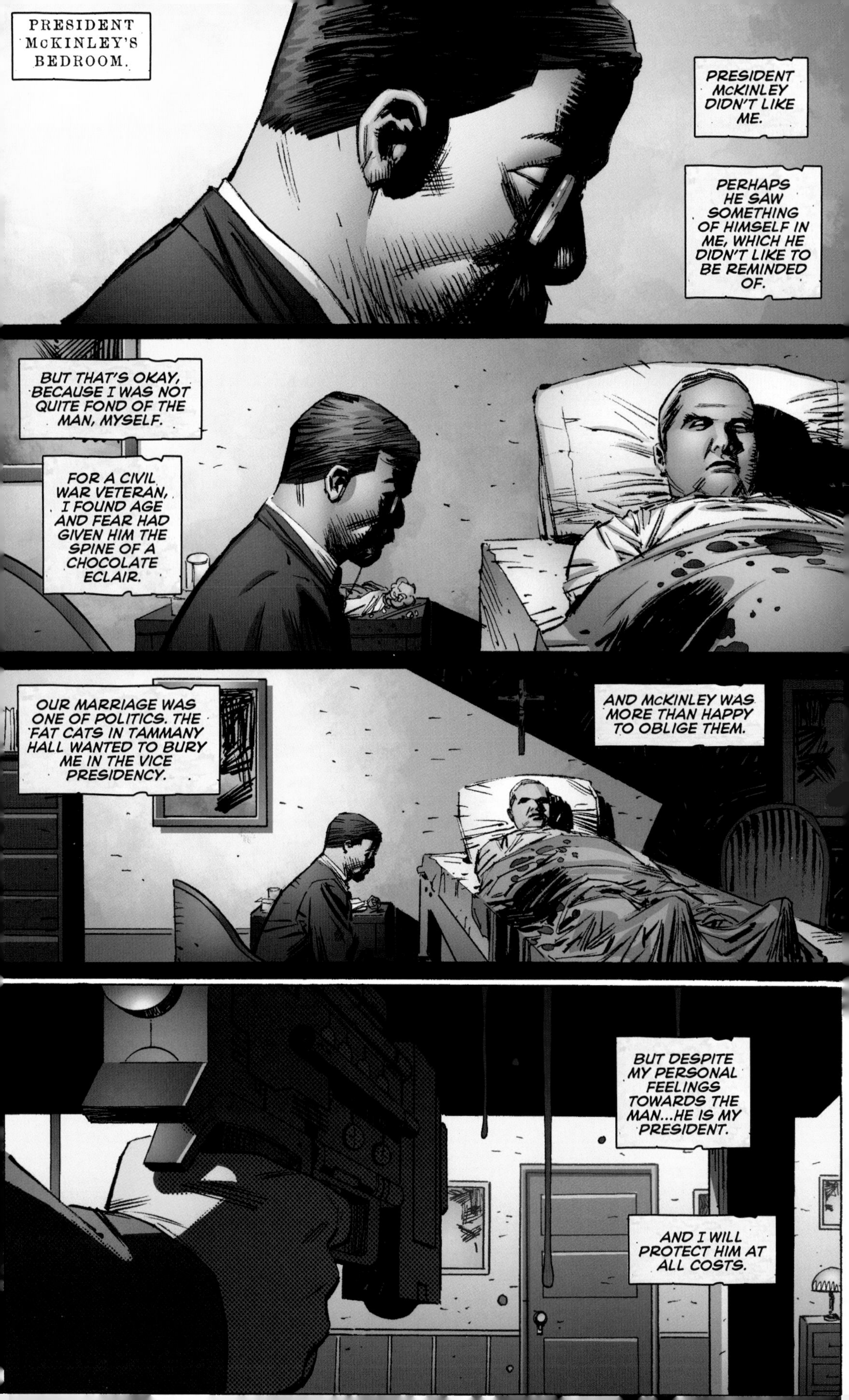
PRESIDENT McKINLEY'S BEDROOM.
PRESIDENT McKINLEY DIDN'T LIKE ME.
PERHAPS HE SAW SOMETHING OF HIMSELF IN ME, WHICH HE DIDN'T LIKE TO BE REMINDED OF.
BUT THAT'S OKAY, BECAUSE I WAS NOT QUITE FOND OF THE MAN, MYSELF.
FOR A CIVIL WAR VETERAN, I FOUND AGE AND FEAR HAD GIVEN HIM THE SPINE OF A CHOCOLATE ECLAIR.
OUR MARRIAGE WAS ONE OF POLITICS. THE FAT CATS IN TAMMANY HALL WANTED TO BURY ME IN THE VICE PRESIDENCY.
AND McKINLEY WAS MORE THAN HAPPY TO OBLIGE THEM.
BUT DESPITE MY PERSONAL FEELINGS TOWARDS THE MAN...HE IS MY PRESIDENT.
AND I WILL PROTECT HIM AT ALL COSTS.

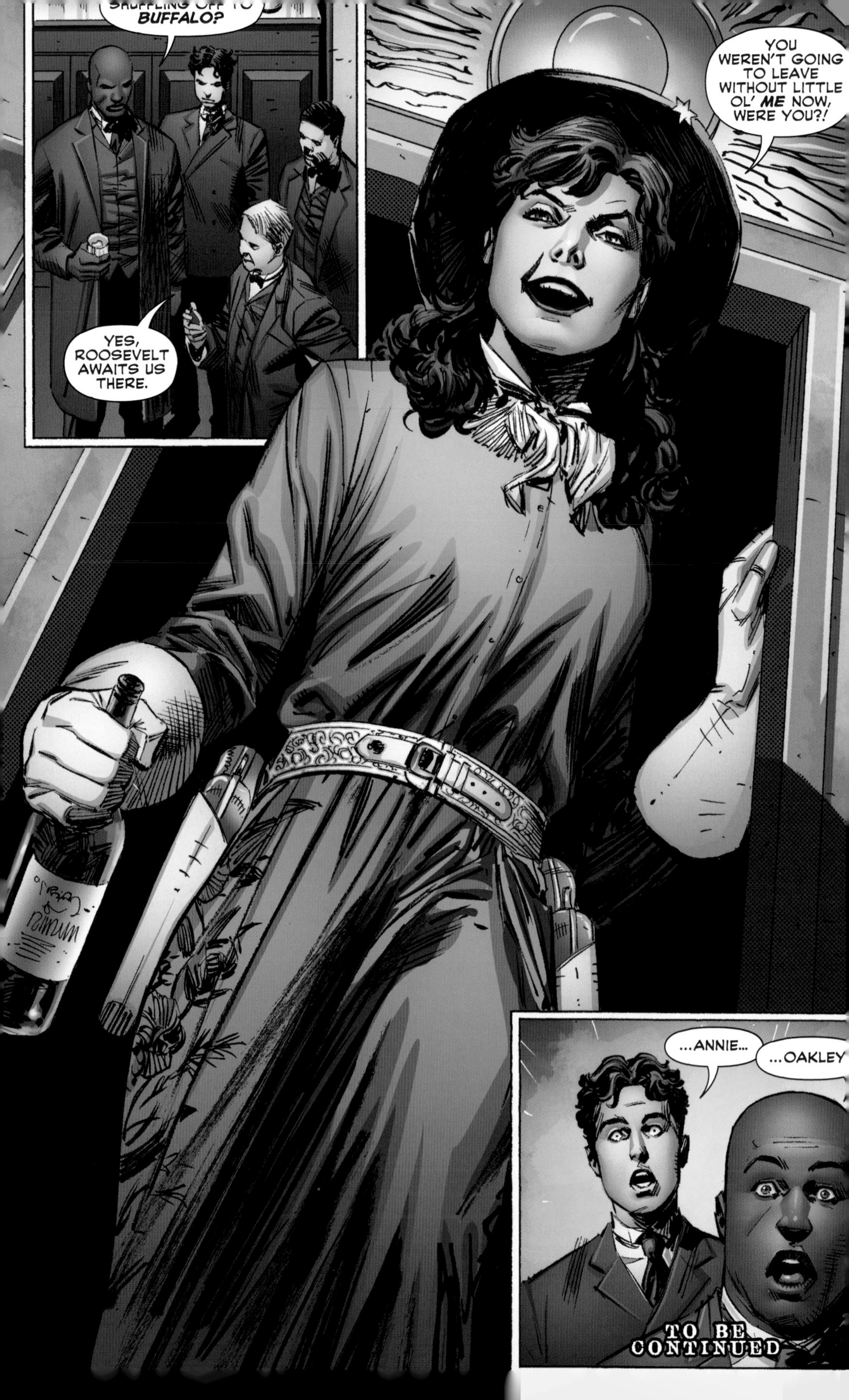
SHUFFLING OFF TO BUFFALO?
YES, ROOSEVELT AWAITS US THERE.
YOU WEREN'T GOING TO LEAVE WITHOUT LITTLE OL' ME NOW, WERE YOU?!
...ANNIE...
...OAKLEY
TO BE CONTINUED

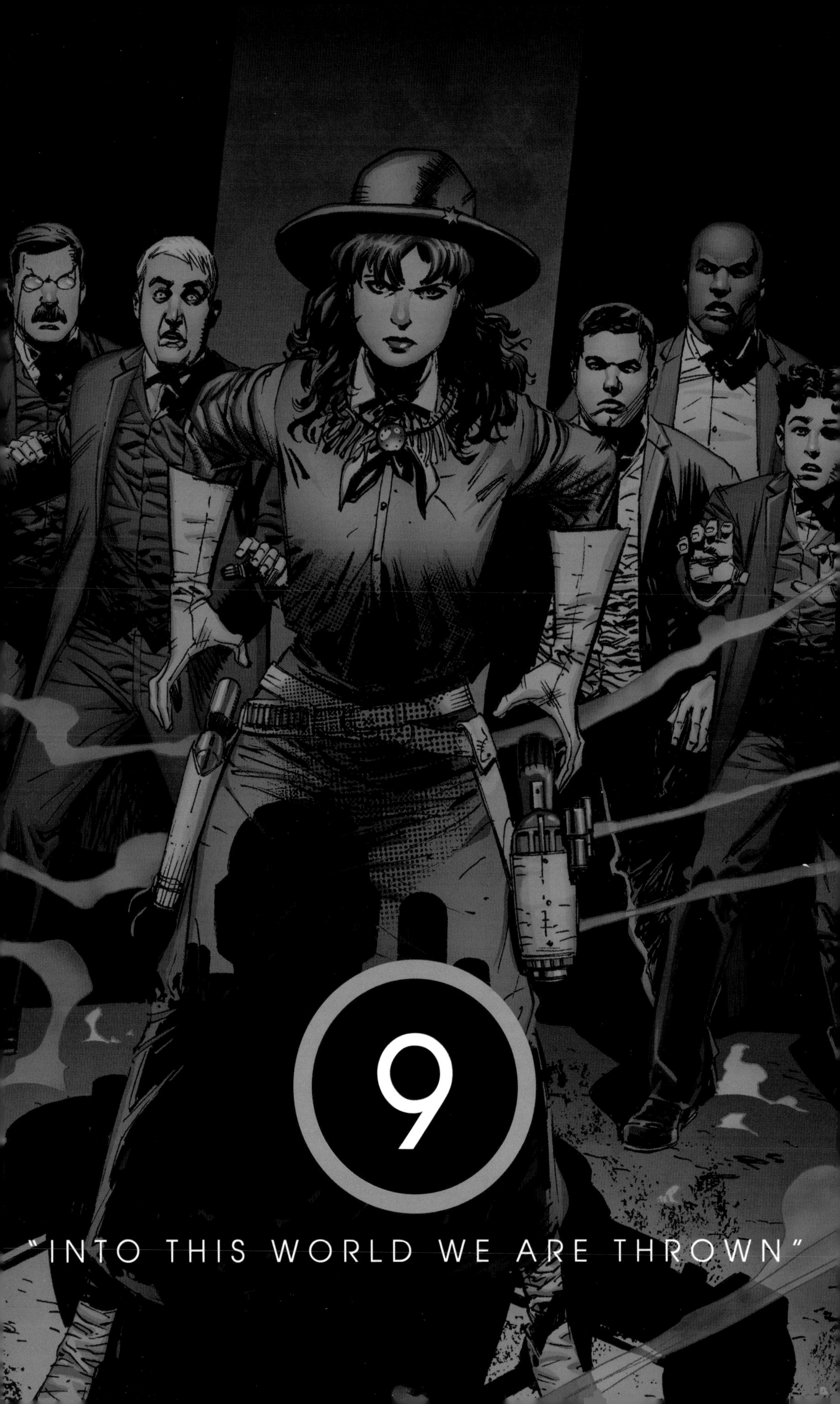

9

“INTO THIS WORLD WE ARE THROWN”

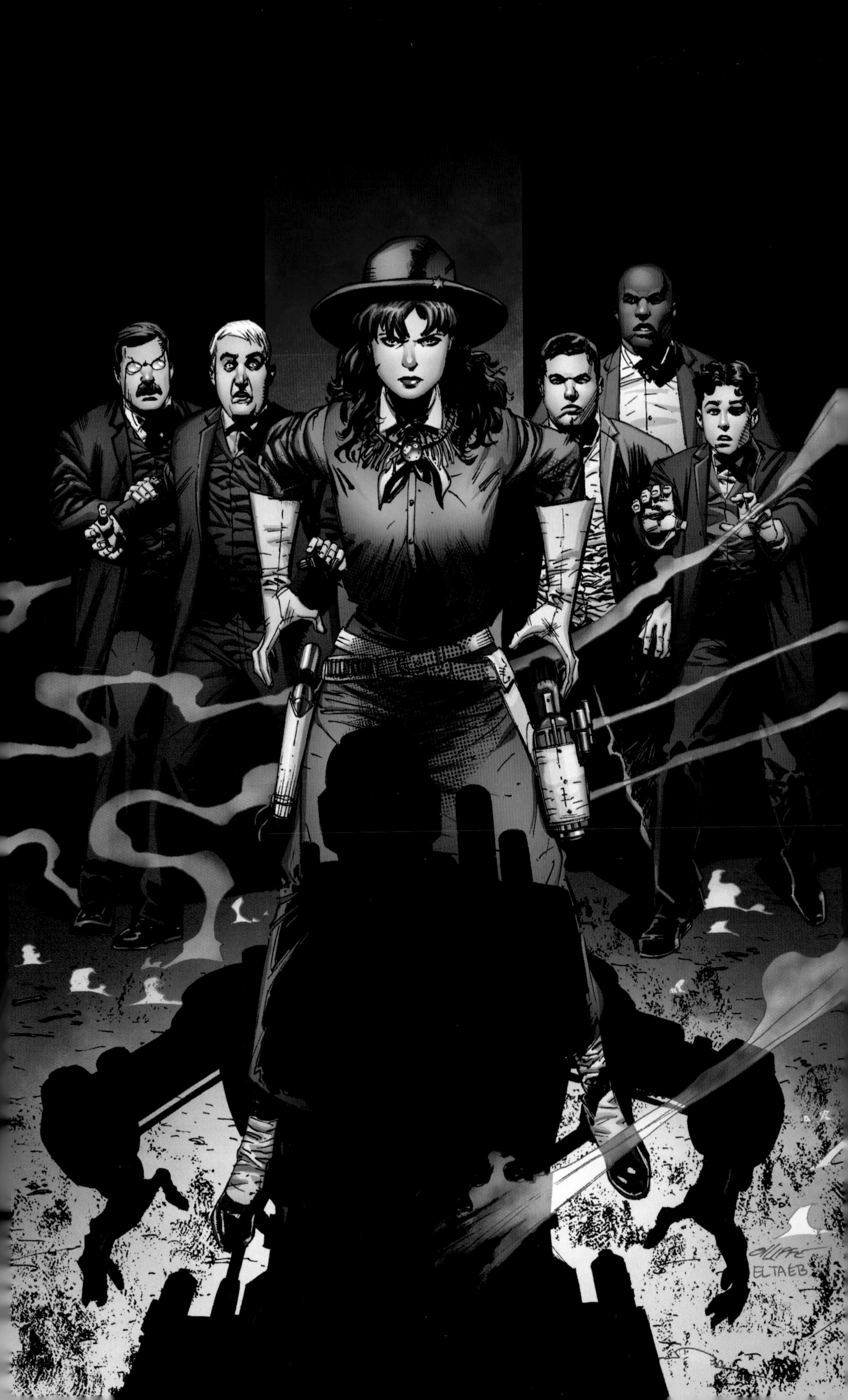

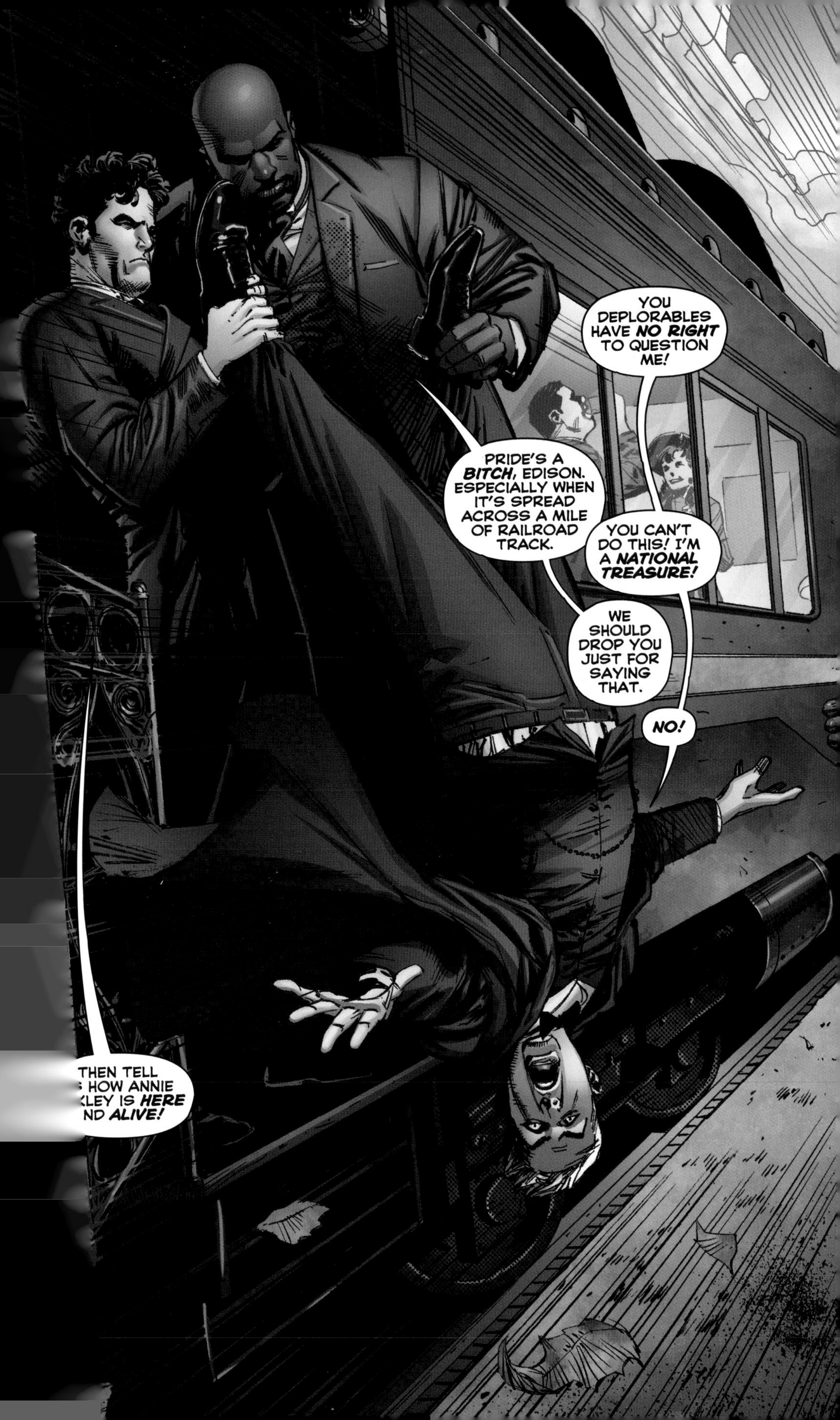
YOU DEPLORABLES HAVE NO RIGHT TO QUESTION ME!
PRIDE'S A BITCH, EDISON. ESPECIALLY WHEN IT'S SPREAD ACROSS A MILE OF RAILROAD TRACK.
YOU CAN'T DO THIS! I'M A NATIONAL TREASURE!
WE SHOULD DROP YOU JUST FOR SAYING THAT.
NO!
THEN TELL HOW ANNIE KLEY IS HERE ND ALIVE!

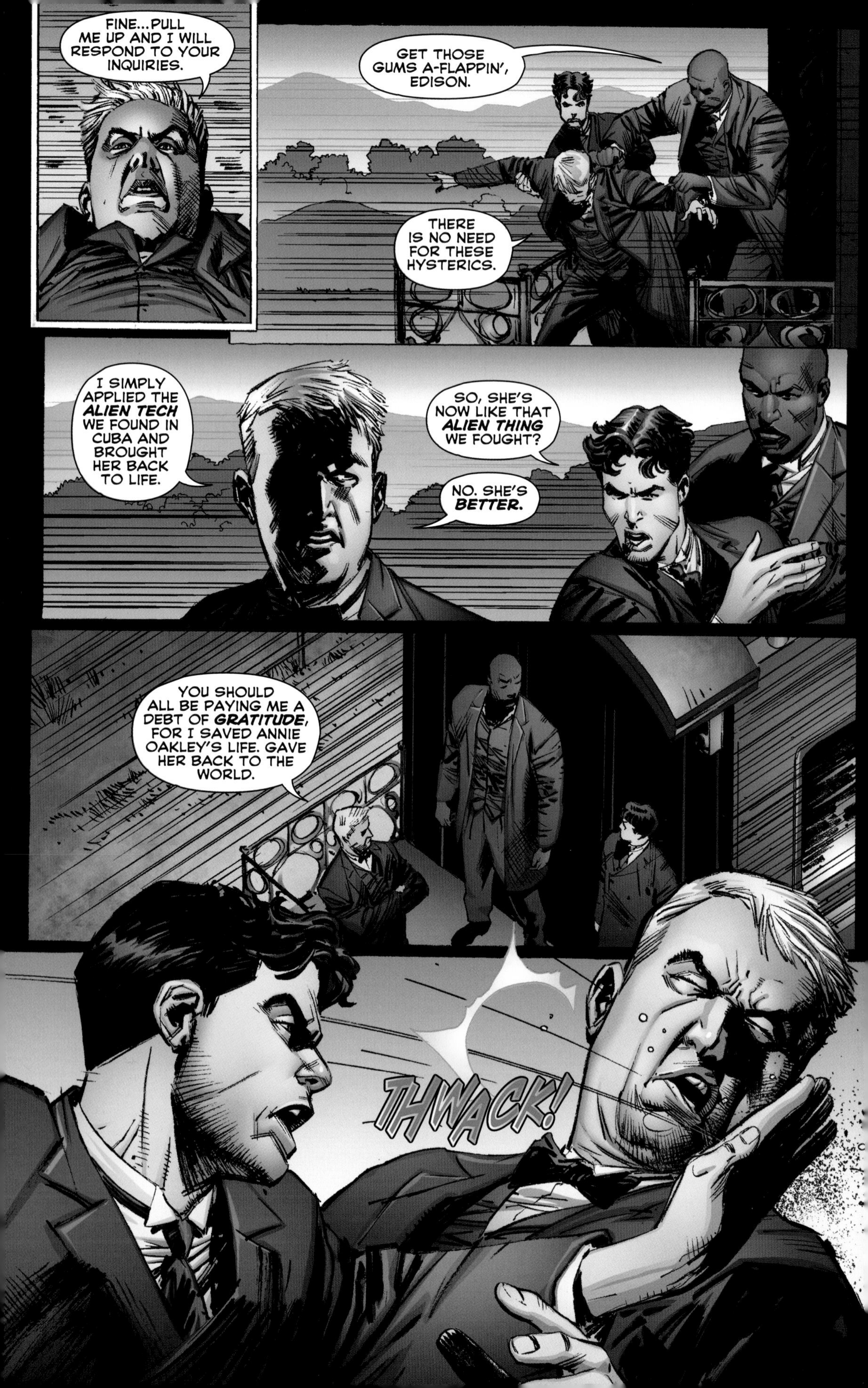
FINE...PULL ME UP AND I WILL RESPOND TO YOUR INQUIRIES.
GET THOSE GUMS A-FLAPPIN', EDISON.
THERE IS NO NEED FOR THESE HYSTERICS.
I SIMPLY APPLIED THE ALIEN TECH WE FOUND IN CUBA AND BROUGHT HER BACK TO LIFE.
SO, SHE'S NOW LIKE THAT ALIEN THING WE FOUGHT?
NO. SHE'S BETTER.
YOU SHOULD ALL BE PAYING ME A DEBT OF GRATITUDE, FOR I SAVED ANNIE OAKLEY'S LIFE. GAVE HER BACK TO THE WORLD.
THWACK!

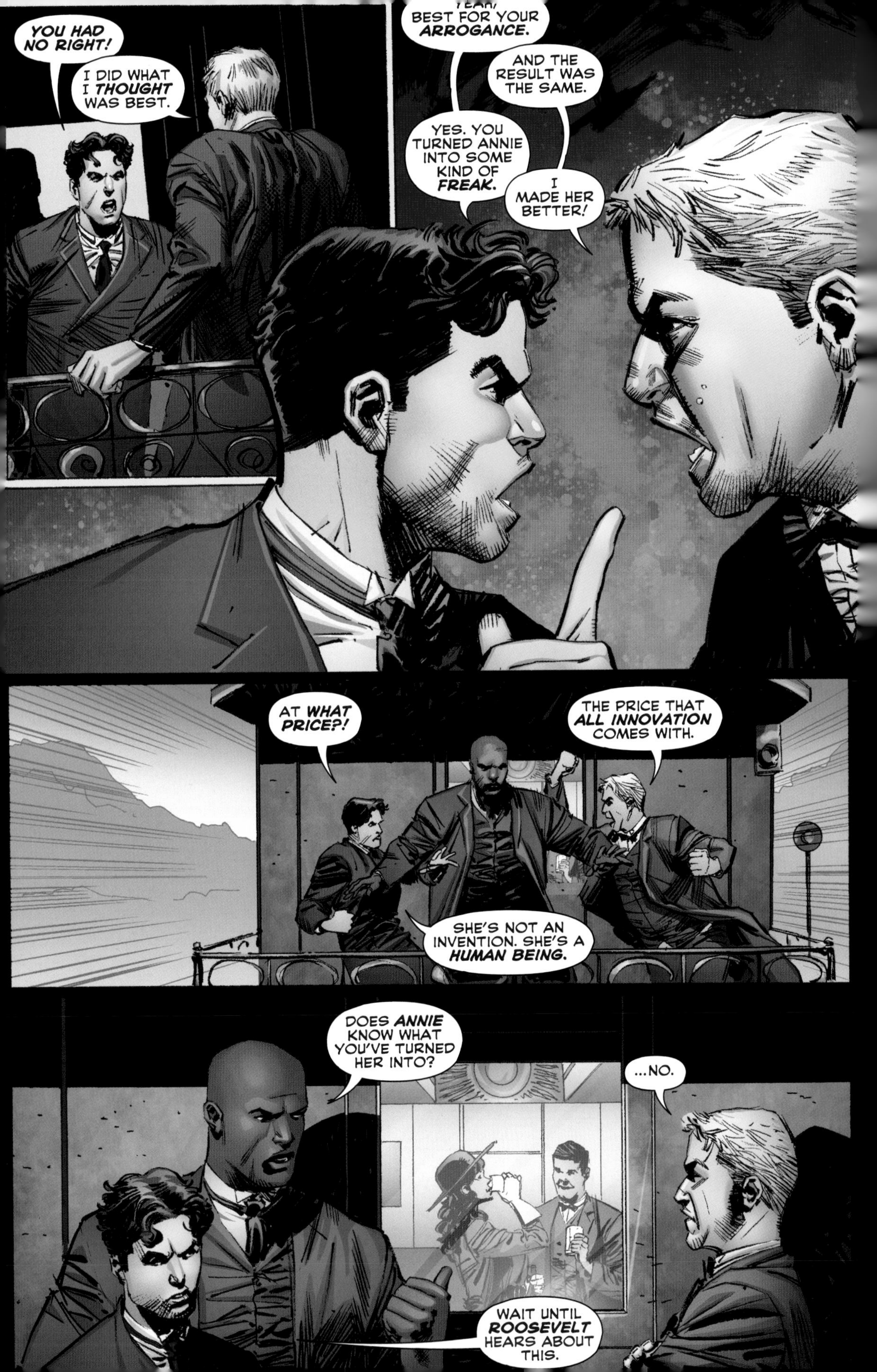
YOU HAD NO RIGHT!
I DID WHAT I THOUGHT WAS BEST.
BEST FOR YOUR ARROGANCE.
AND THE RESULT WAS THE SAME.
YES. YOU TURNED ANNIE INTO SOME KIND OF FREAK.
I MADE HER BETTER!
AT WHAT PRICE?!
THE PRICE THAT ALL INNOVATION COMES WITH.
SHE'S NOT AN INVENTION. SHE'S A HUMAN BEING.
DOES ANNIE KNOW WHAT YOU'VE TURNED HER INTO?
...NO.
WAIT UNTIL ROOSEVELT HEARS ABOUT THIS.

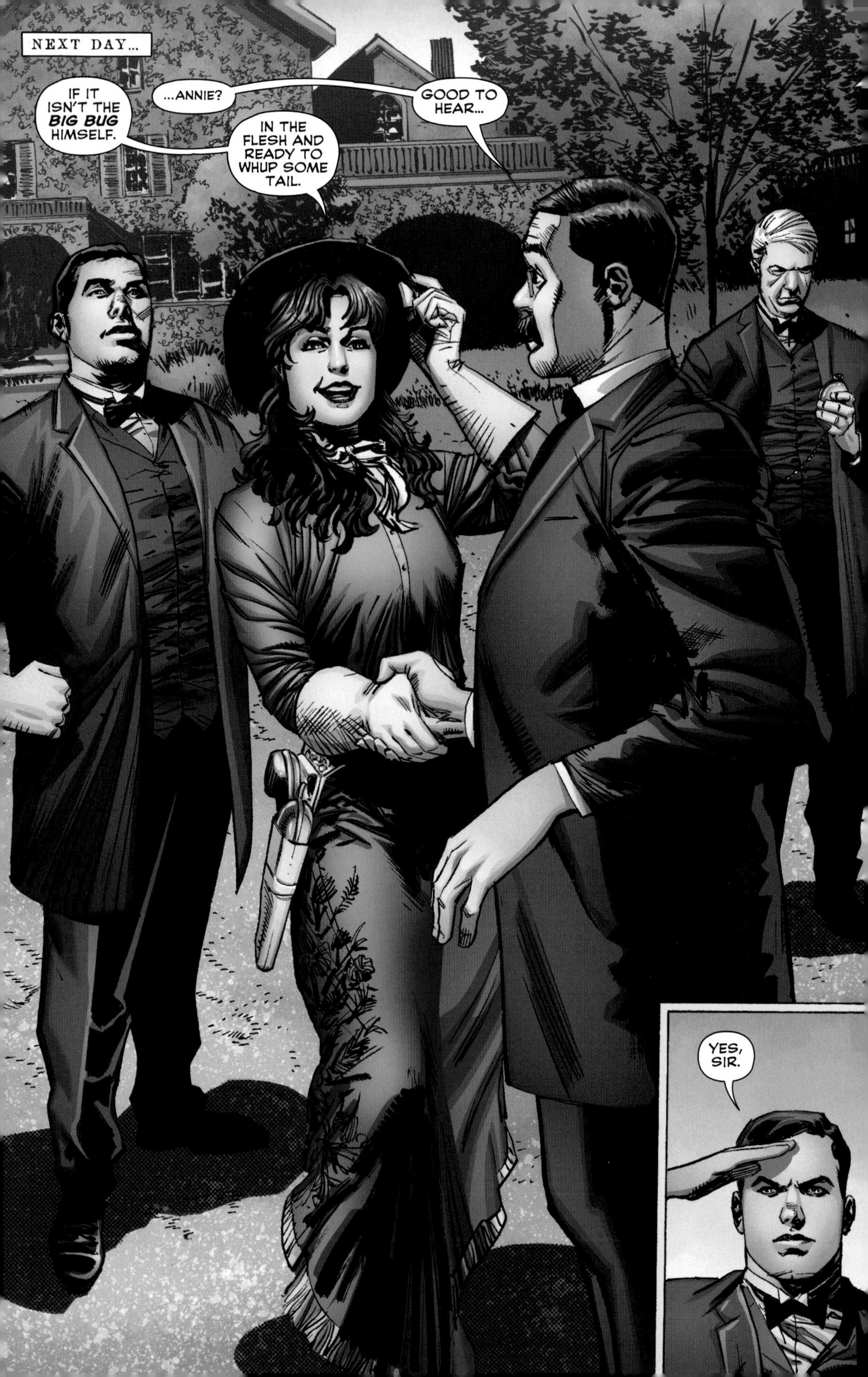
NEXT DAY...
IF IT ISN'T THE ***BIG BUG*** HIMSELF.
...ANNIE?
IN THE FLESH AND READY TO WHUP SOME TAIL.
GOOD TO HEAR...
YES, SIR.

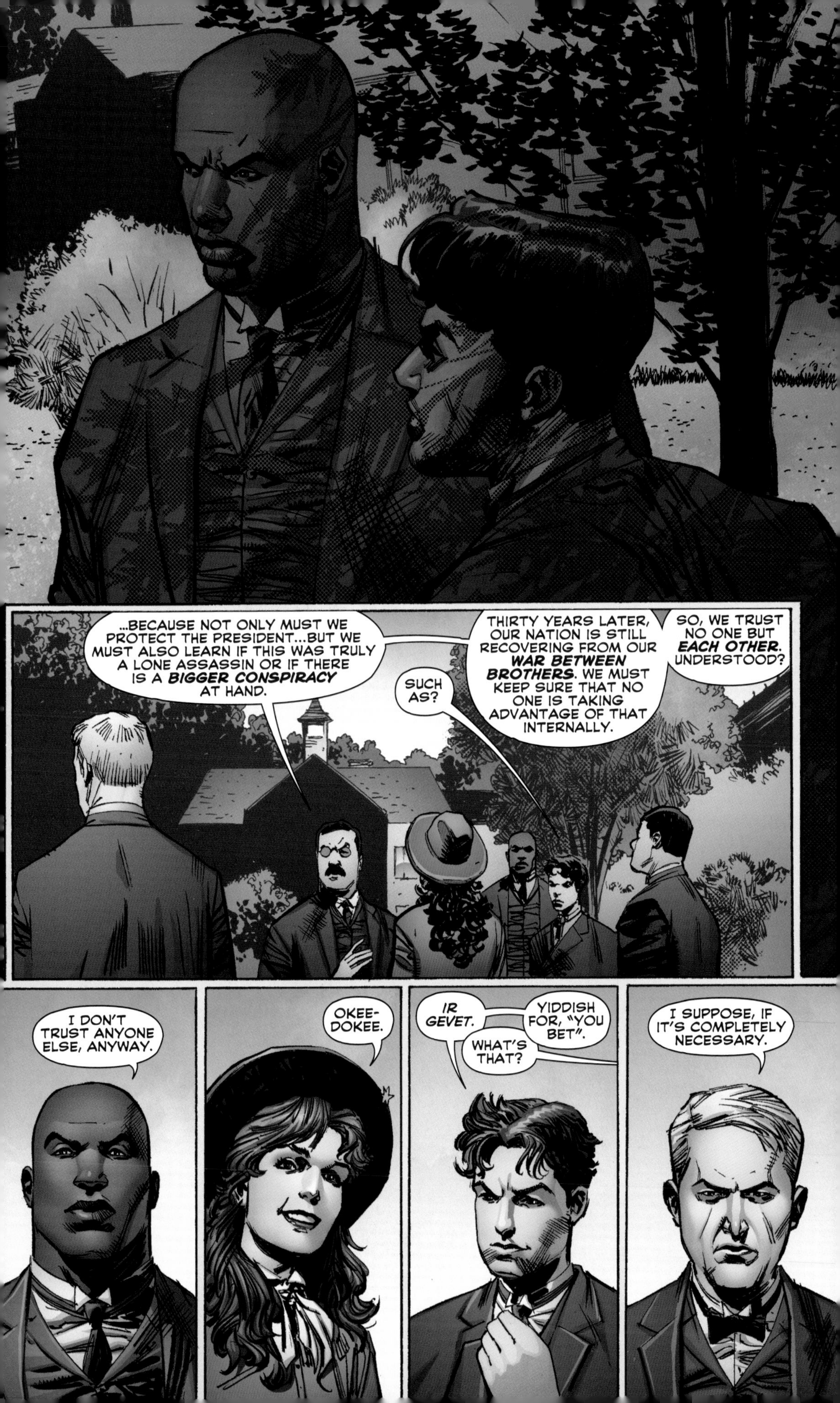

...BECAUSE NOT ONLY MUST WE PROTECT THE PRESIDENT...BUT WE MUST ALSO LEARN IF THIS WAS TRULY A LONE ASSASSIN OR IF THERE IS A *BIGGER CONSPIRACY* AT HAND.
SUCH AS?
THIRTY YEARS LATER, OUR NATION IS STILL RECOVERING FROM OUR *WAR BETWEEN BROTHERS*. WE MUST KEEP SURE THAT NO ONE IS TAKING ADVANTAGE OF THAT INTERNALLY.
SO, WE TRUST NO ONE BUT *EACH OTHER*. UNDERSTOOD?
I DON'T TRUST ANYONE ELSE, ANYWAY.
OKEE-DOKEE.
IR GEVET.
WHAT'S THAT?
YIDDISH FOR, "YOU BET".
I SUPPOSE, IF IT'S COMPLETELY NECESSARY.

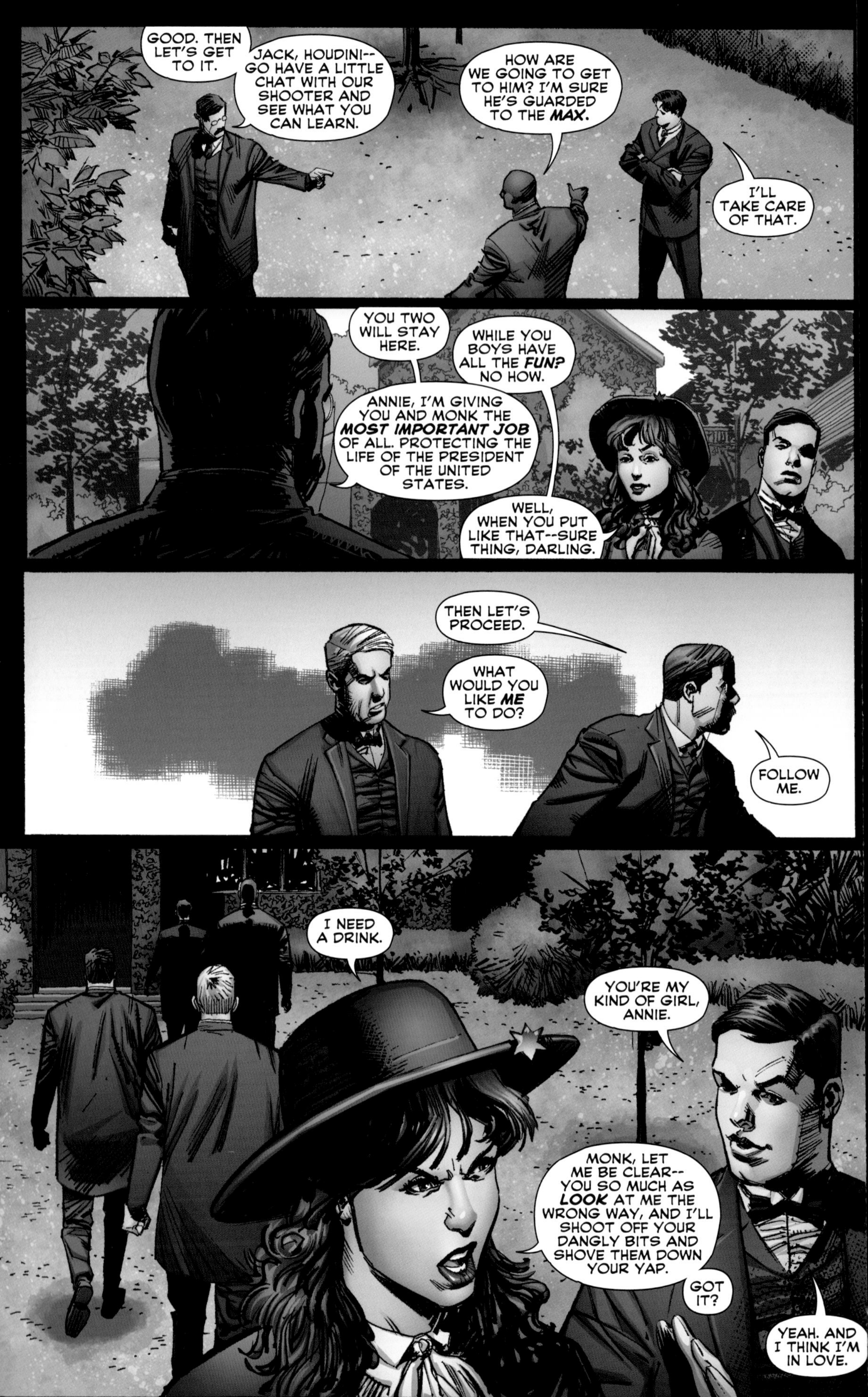
GOOD. THEN LET'S GET TO IT.
JACK, HOUDINI--GO HAVE A LITTLE CHAT WITH OUR SHOOTER AND SEE WHAT YOU CAN LEARN.
HOW ARE WE GOING TO GET TO HIM? I'M SURE HE'S GUARDED TO THE ***MAX.***
I'LL TAKE CARE OF THAT.
YOU TWO WILL STAY HERE.
ANNIE, I'M GIVING YOU AND MONK THE ***MOST IMPORTANT JOB*** OF ALL. PROTECTING THE LIFE OF THE PRESIDENT OF THE UNITED STATES.
WHILE YOU BOYS HAVE ALL THE ***FUN?*** NO HOW.
WELL, WHEN YOU PUT LIKE THAT--SURE THING, DARLING.
THEN LET'S PROCEED.
WHAT WOULD YOU LIKE ***ME*** TO DO?
FOLLOW ME.
I NEED A DRINK.
YOU'RE MY KIND OF GIRL, ANNIE.
MONK, LET ME BE CLEAR--YOU SO MUCH AS ***LOOK*** AT ME THE WRONG WAY, AND I'LL SHOOT OFF YOUR DANGLY BITS AND SHOVE THEM DOWN YOUR YAP.
GOT IT?
YEAH. AND I THINK I'M IN LOVE.

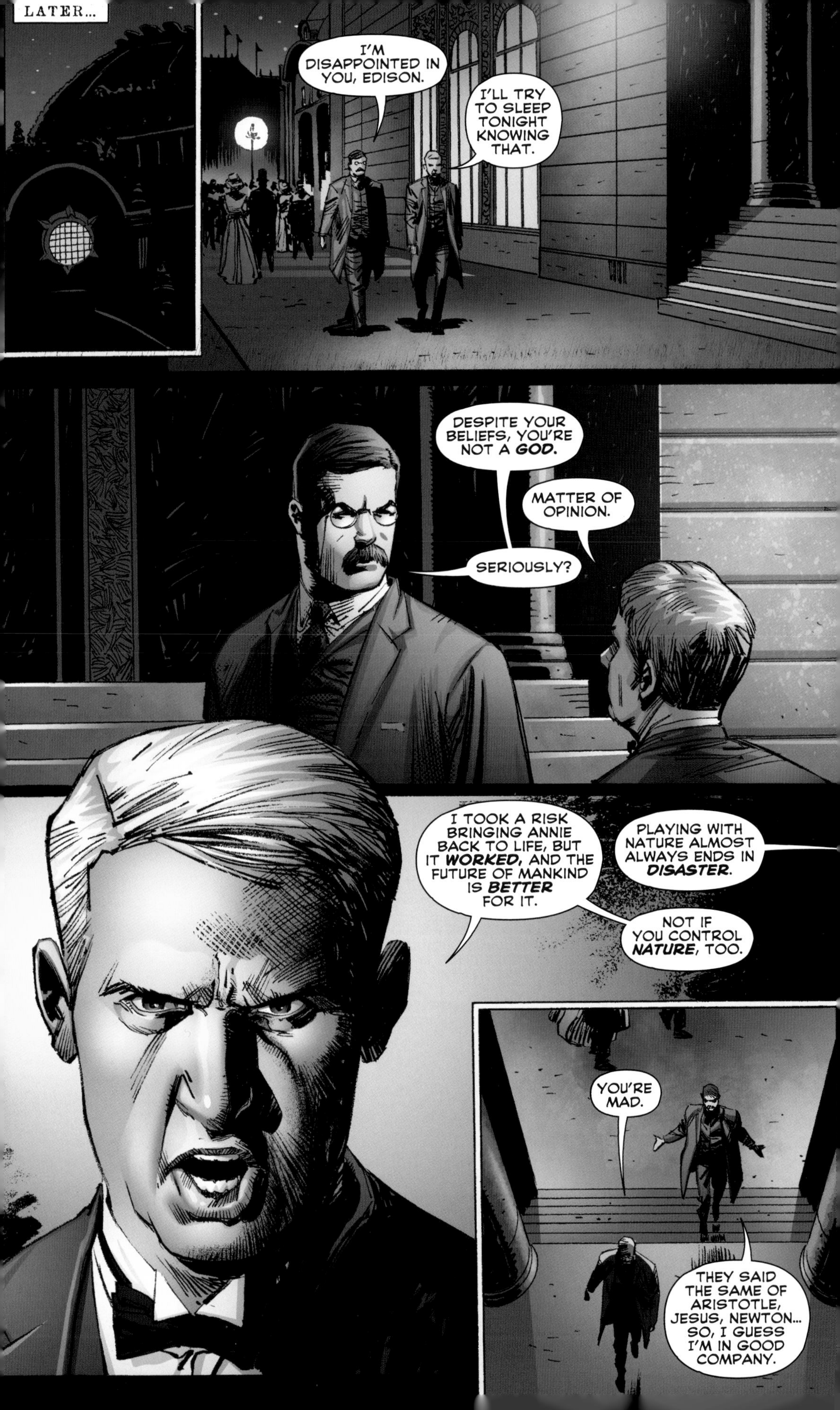
LATER...
I'M DISAPPOINTED IN YOU, EDISON.
I'LL TRY TO SLEEP TONIGHT KNOWING THAT.
DESPITE YOUR BELIEFS, YOU'RE NOT A GOD.
MATTER OF OPINION.
SERIOUSLY?
I TOOK A RISK BRINGING ANNIE BACK TO LIFE, BUT IT WORKED, AND THE FUTURE OF MANKIND IS BETTER FOR IT.
PLAYING WITH NATURE ALMOST ALWAYS ENDS IN DISASTER.
NOT IF YOU CONTROL NATURE, TOO.
YOU'RE MAD.
THEY SAID THE SAME OF ARISTOTLE, JESUS, NEWTON... SO, I GUESS I'M IN GOOD COMPANY.

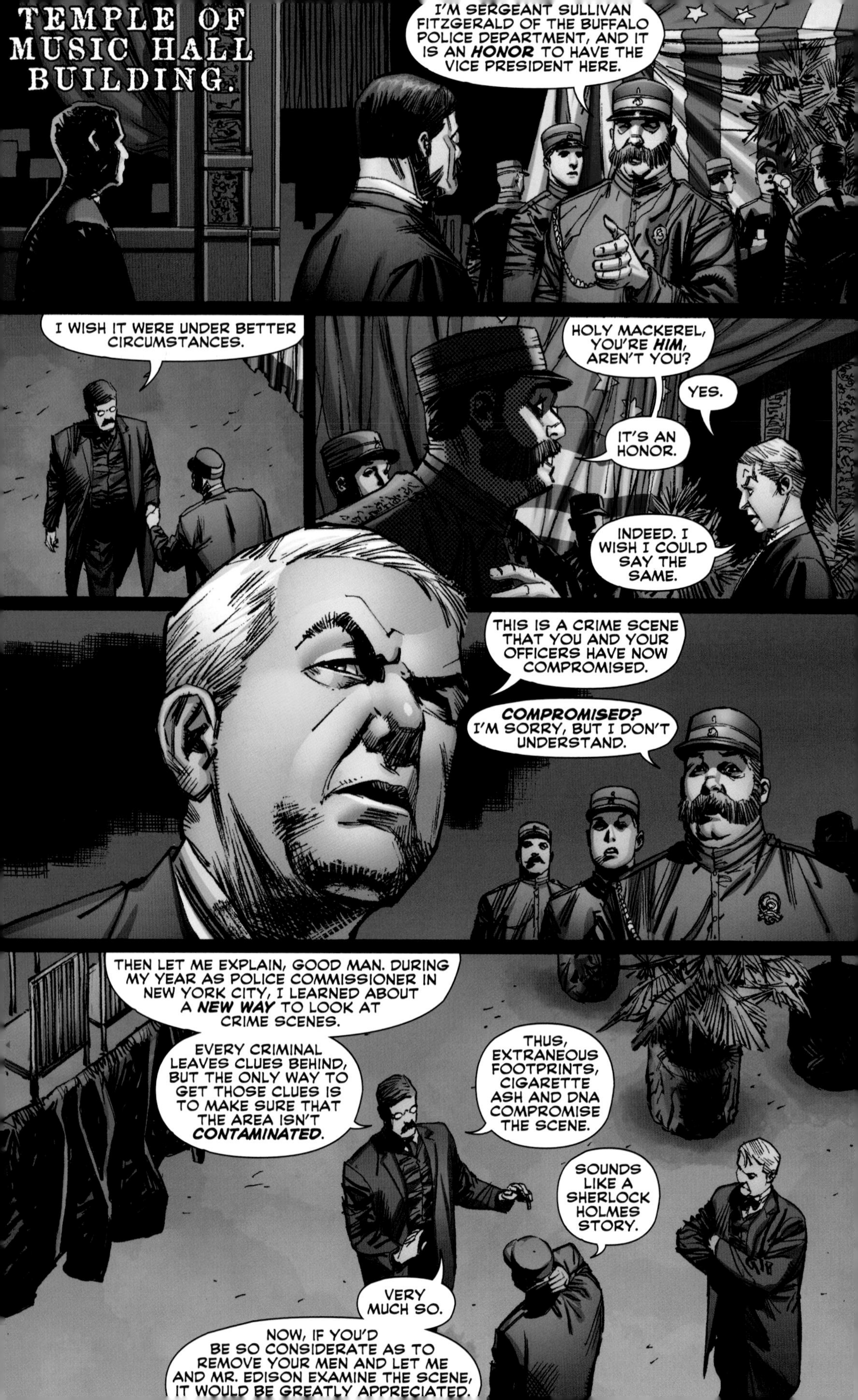
TEMPLE OF MUSIC HALL BUILDING.
I'M SERGEANT SULLIVAN FITZGERALD OF THE BUFFALO POLICE DEPARTMENT, AND IT IS AN HONOR TO HAVE THE VICE PRESIDENT HERE.
I WISH IT WERE UNDER BETTER CIRCUMSTANCES.
HOLY MACKEREL, YOU'RE HIM, AREN'T YOU?
YES.
IT'S AN HONOR.
INDEED. I WISH I COULD SAY THE SAME.
THIS IS A CRIME SCENE THAT YOU AND YOUR OFFICERS HAVE NOW COMPROMISED.
COMPROMISED? I'M SORRY, BUT I DON'T UNDERSTAND.
THEN LET ME EXPLAIN, GOOD MAN. DURING MY YEAR AS POLICE COMMISSIONER IN NEW YORK CITY, I LEARNED ABOUT A NEW WAY TO LOOK AT CRIME SCENES.
EVERY CRIMINAL LEAVES CLUES BEHIND, BUT THE ONLY WAY TO GET THOSE CLUES IS TO MAKE SURE THAT THE AREA ISN'T CONTAMINATED.
THUS, EXTRANEOUS FOOTPRINTS, CIGARETTE ASH AND DNA COMPROMISE THE SCENE.
SOUNDS LIKE A SHERLOCK HOLMES STORY.
VERY MUCH SO.
NOW, IF YOU'D BE SO CONSIDERATE AS TO REMOVE YOUR MEN AND LET ME AND MR. EDISON EXAMINE THE SCENE, IT WOULD BE GREATLY APPRECIATED.

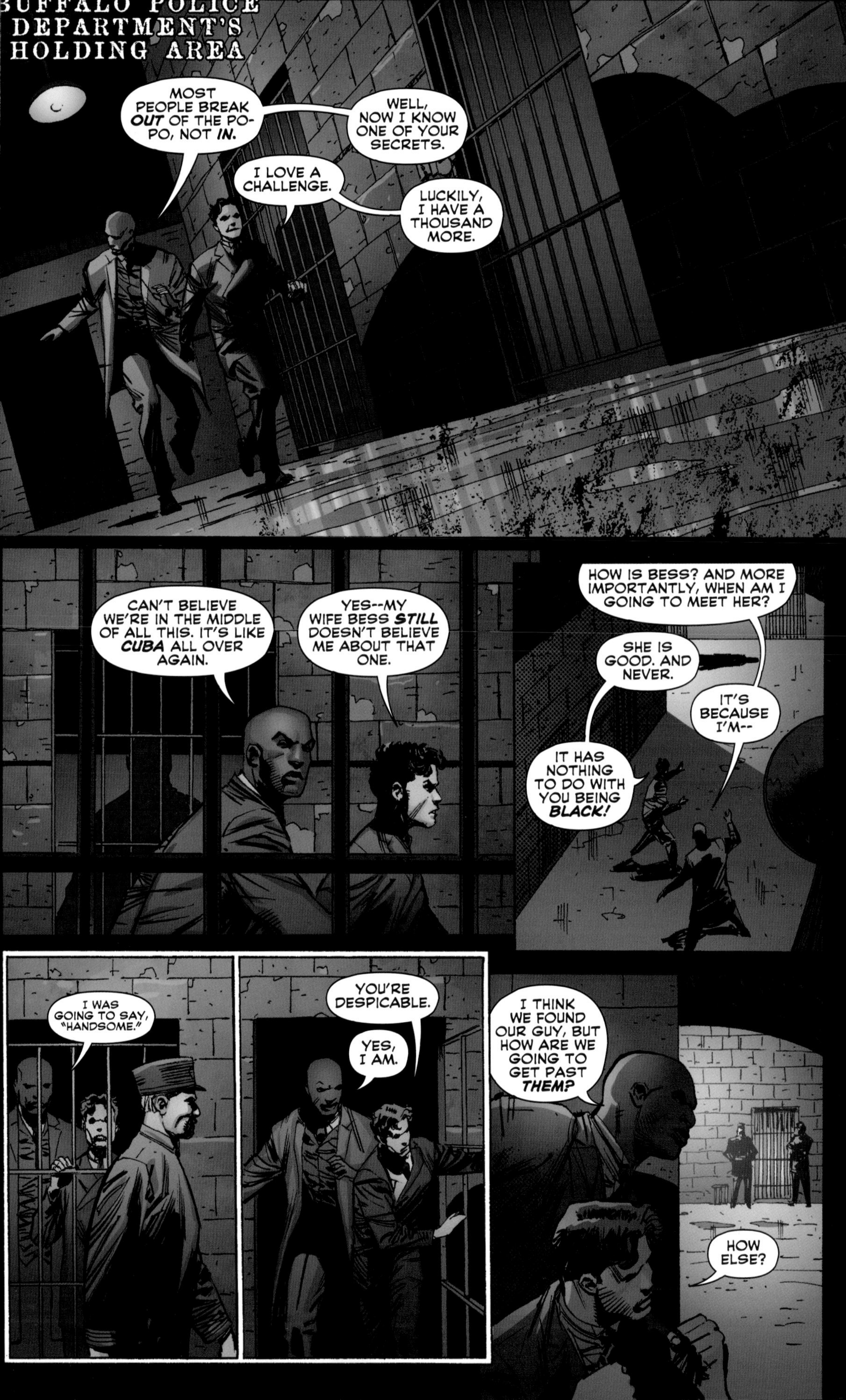
BUFFALO POLICE DEPARTMENT'S HOLDING AREA
MOST PEOPLE BREAK OUT OF THE PO-PO, NOT IN.
WELL, NOW I KNOW ONE OF YOUR SECRETS.
I LOVE A CHALLENGE.
LUCKILY, I HAVE A THOUSAND MORE.
CAN'T BELIEVE WE'RE IN THE MIDDLE OF ALL THIS. IT'S LIKE CUBA ALL OVER AGAIN.
YES--MY WIFE BESS STILL DOESN'T BELIEVE ME ABOUT THAT ONE.
HOW IS BESS? AND MORE IMPORTANTLY, WHEN AM I GOING TO MEET HER?
SHE IS GOOD. AND NEVER.
IT'S BECAUSE I'M--
IT HAS NOTHING TO DO WITH YOU BEING BLACK!
I WAS GOING TO SAY, "HANDSOME."
YOU'RE DESPICABLE.
YES, I AM.
I THINK WE FOUND OUR GUY, BUT HOW ARE WE GOING TO GET PAST THEM?
HOW ELSE?

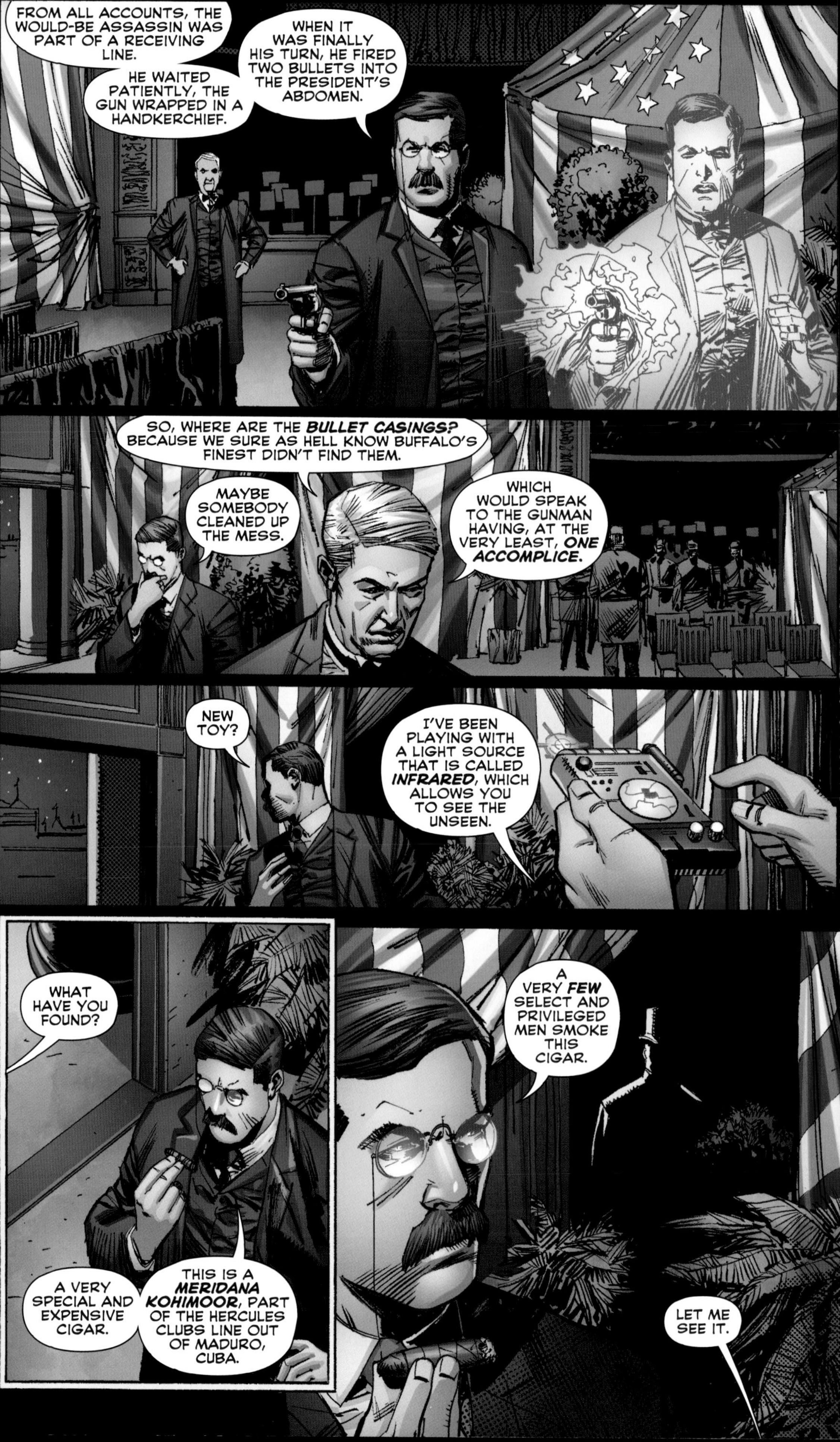
FROM ALL ACCOUNTS, THE WOULD-BE ASSASSIN WAS PART OF A RECEIVING LINE.
HE WAITED PATIENTLY, THE GUN WRAPPED IN A HANDKERCHIEF.
WHEN IT WAS FINALLY HIS TURN, HE FIRED TWO BULLETS INTO THE PRESIDENT'S ABDOMEN.
SO, WHERE ARE THE BULLET CASINGS? BECAUSE WE SURE AS HELL KNOW BUFFALO'S FINEST DIDN'T FIND THEM.
MAYBE SOMEBODY CLEANED UP THE MESS.
WHICH WOULD SPEAK TO THE GUNMAN HAVING, AT THE VERY LEAST, ONE ACCOMPLICE.
NEW TOY?
I'VE BEEN PLAYING WITH A LIGHT SOURCE THAT IS CALLED INFRARED, WHICH ALLOWS YOU TO SEE THE UNSEEN.
WHAT HAVE YOU FOUND?
A VERY SPECIAL AND EXPENSIVE CIGAR.
THIS IS A MERIDANA KOHIMOOR, PART OF THE HERCULES CLUBS LINE OUT OF MADURO, CUBA.
A VERY FEW SELECT AND PRIVILEGED MEN SMOKE THIS CIGAR.
LET ME SEE IT.

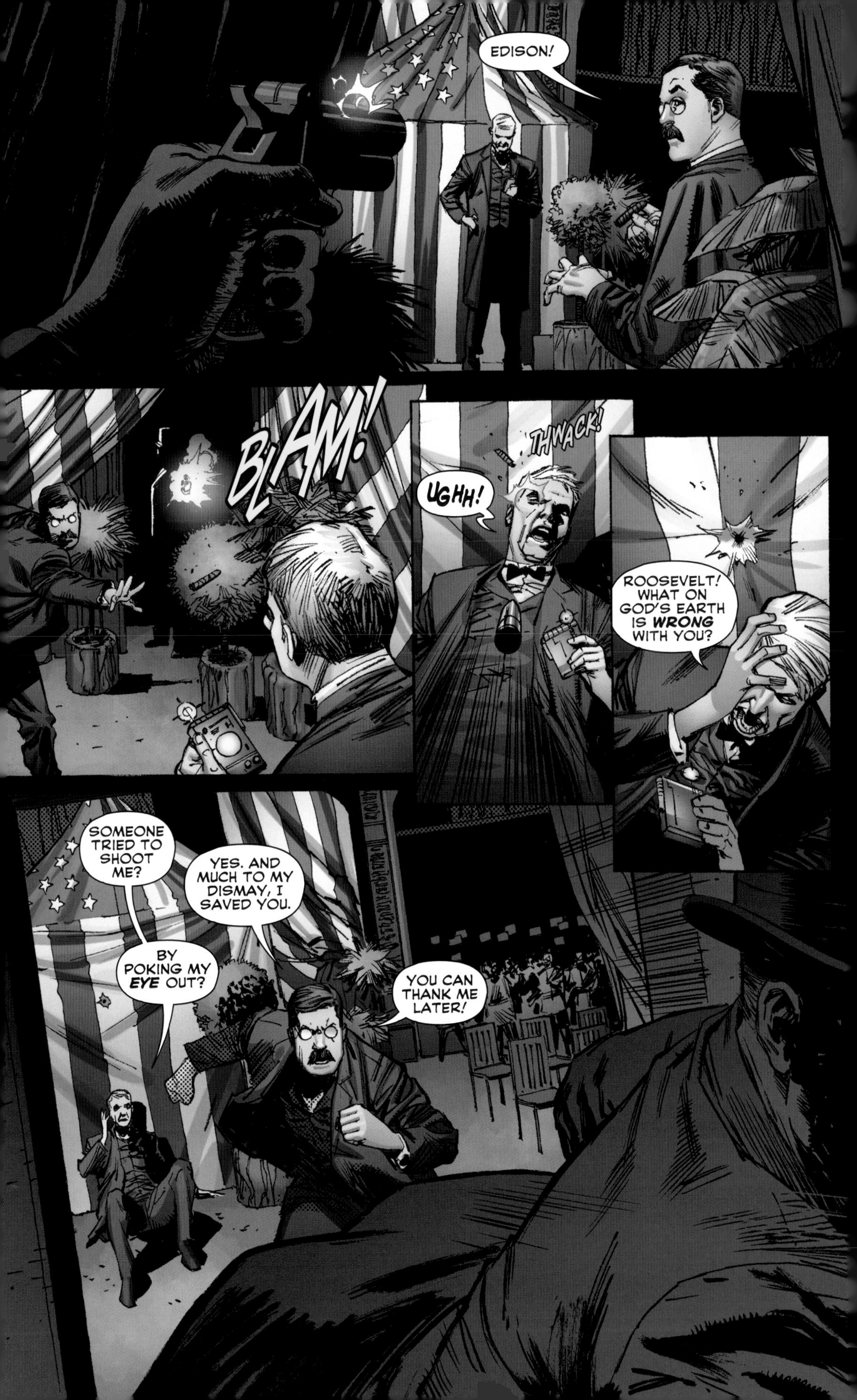
EDISON!
BLAM!
THWACK!
UGHH!
ROOSEVELT! WHAT ON GOD'S EARTH IS **WRONG** WITH YOU?
SOMEONE TRIED TO SHOOT ME?
YES. AND MUCH TO MY DISMAY, I SAVED YOU.
BY POKING MY **EYE** OUT?
YOU CAN THANK ME LATER!

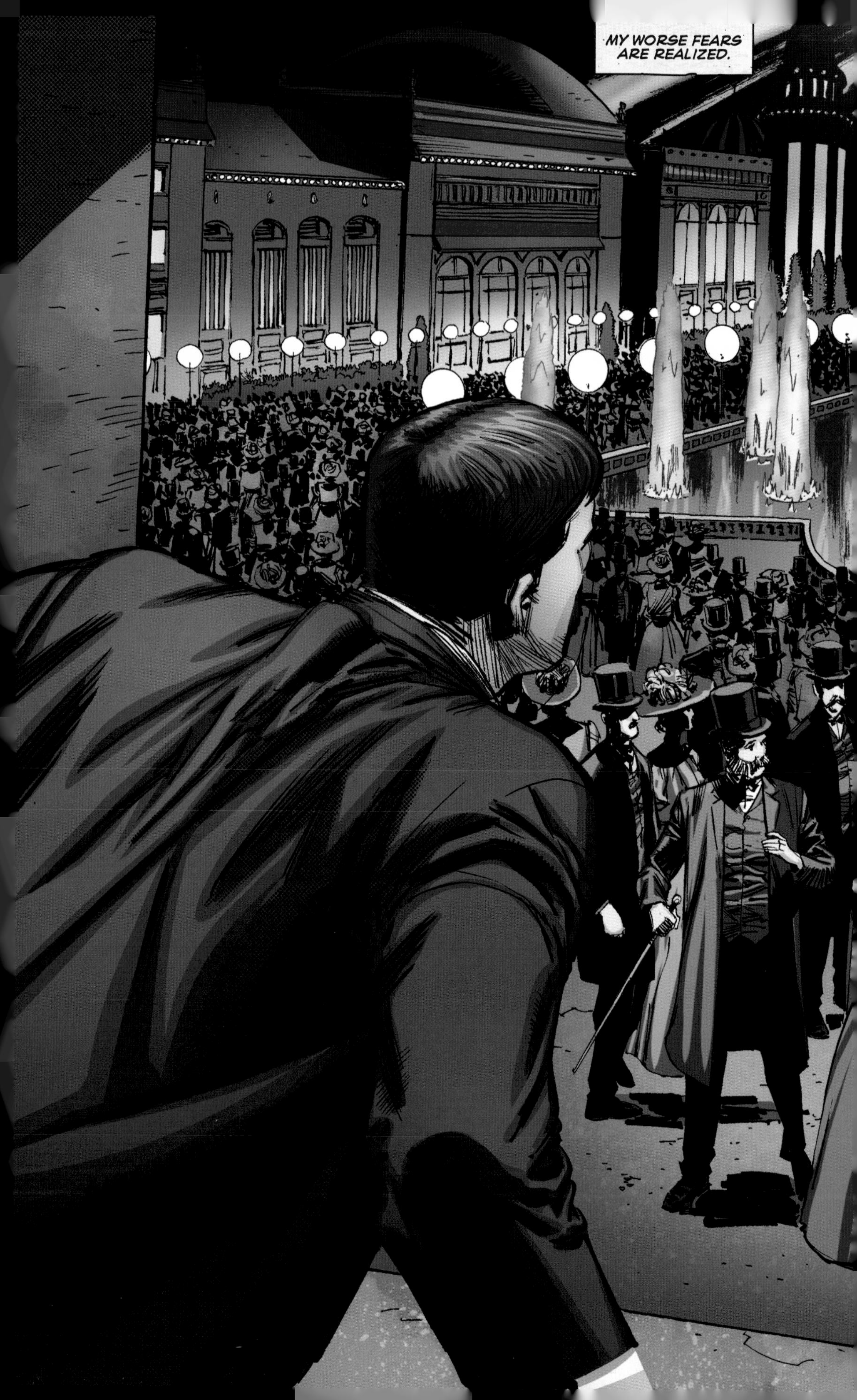
MY WORSE FEARS ARE REALIZED.

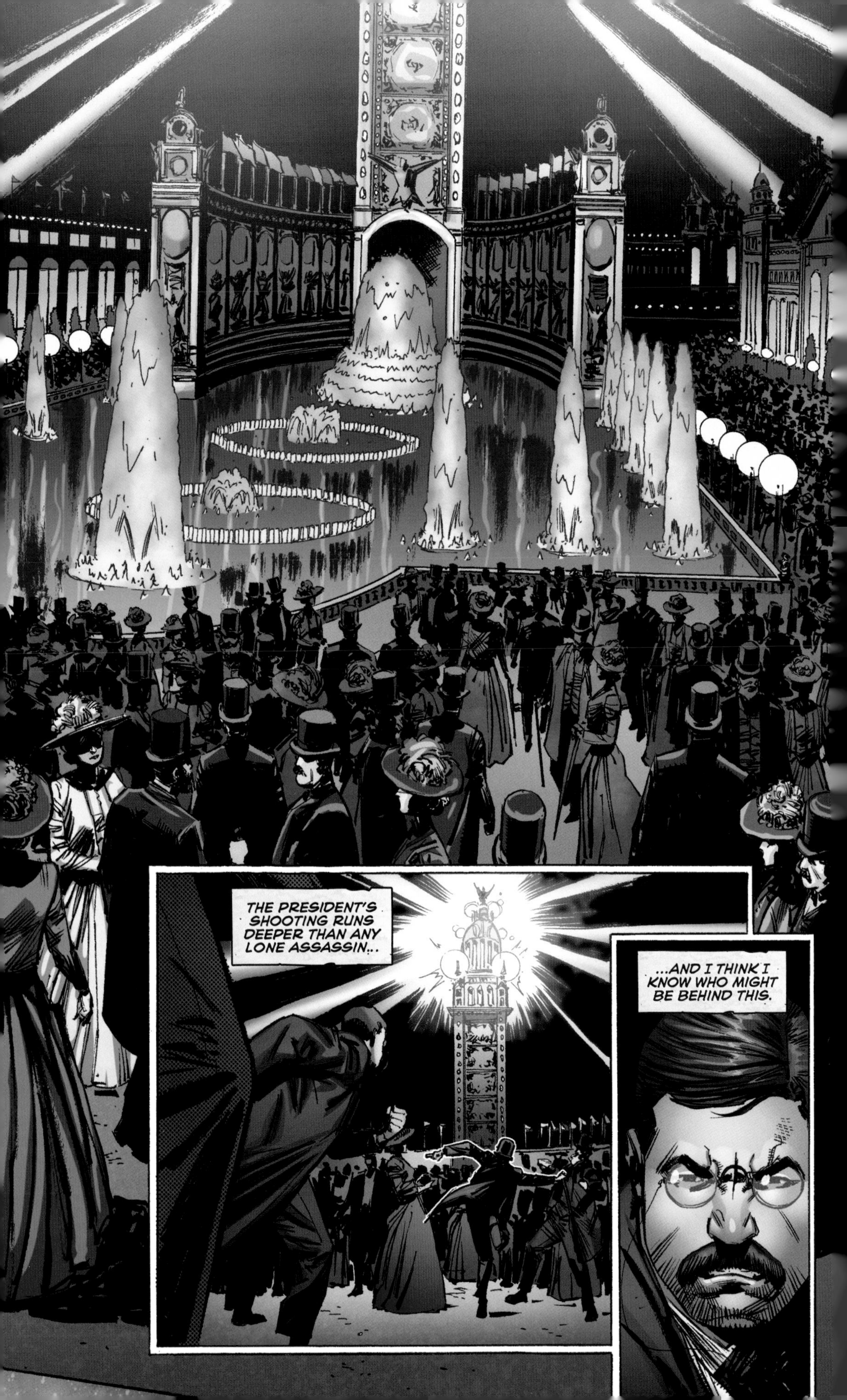
THE PRESIDENT'S SHOOTING RUNS DEEPER THAN ANY LONE ASSASSIN...
...AND I THINK I KNOW WHO MIGHT BE BEHIND THIS.

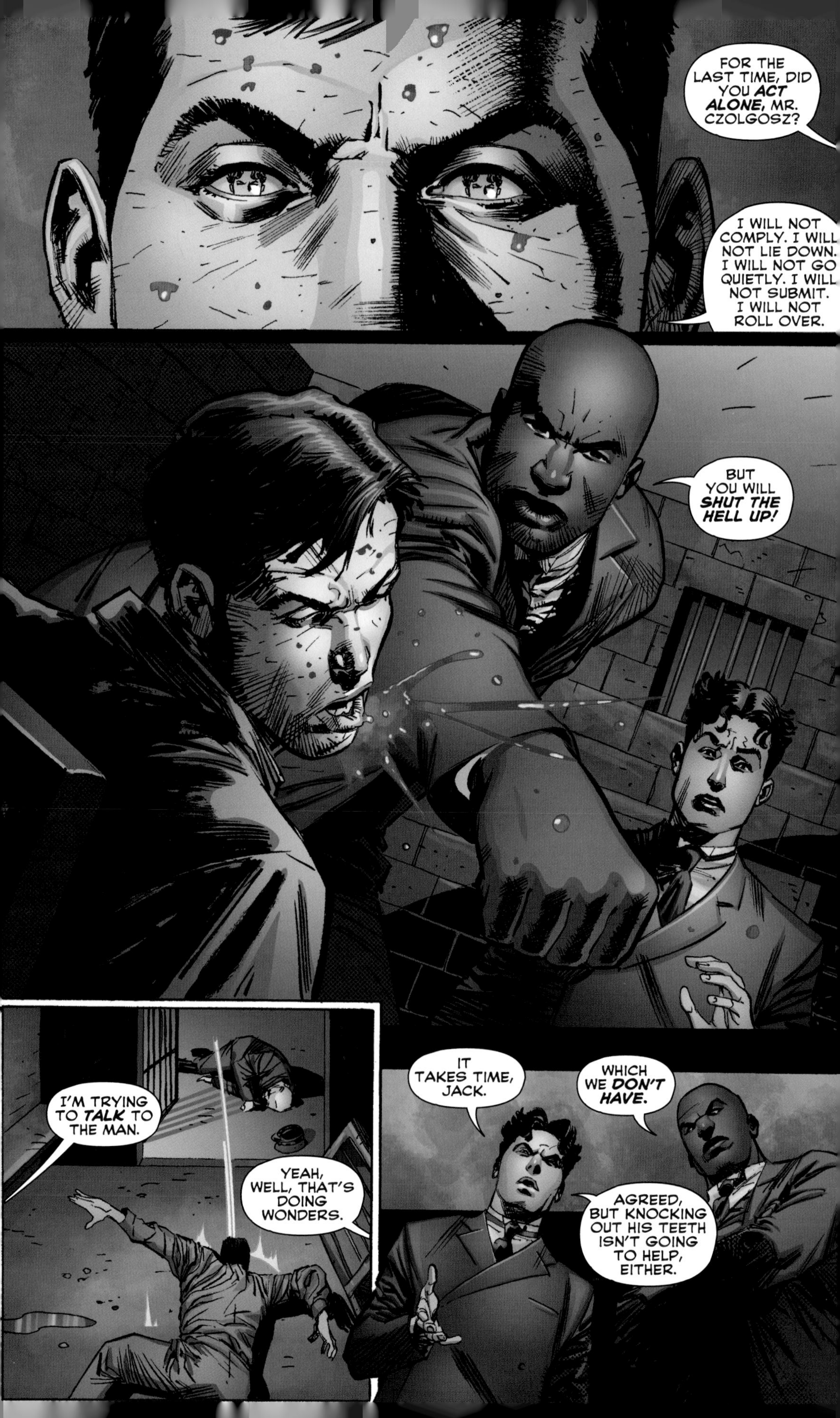

FOR THE LAST TIME, DID YOU ***ACT ALONE***, MR. CZOLGOSZ?
I WILL NOT COMPLY. I WILL NOT LIE DOWN. I WILL NOT GO QUIETLY. I WILL NOT SUBMIT. I WILL NOT ROLL OVER.
BUT YOU WILL ***SHUT THE HELL UP!***
I'M TRYING TO ***TALK*** TO THE MAN.
YEAH, WELL, THAT'S DOING WONDERS.
IT TAKES TIME, JACK.
WHICH WE ***DON'T HAVE.***
AGREED, BUT KNOCKING OUT HIS TEETH ISN'T GOING TO HELP, EITHER.

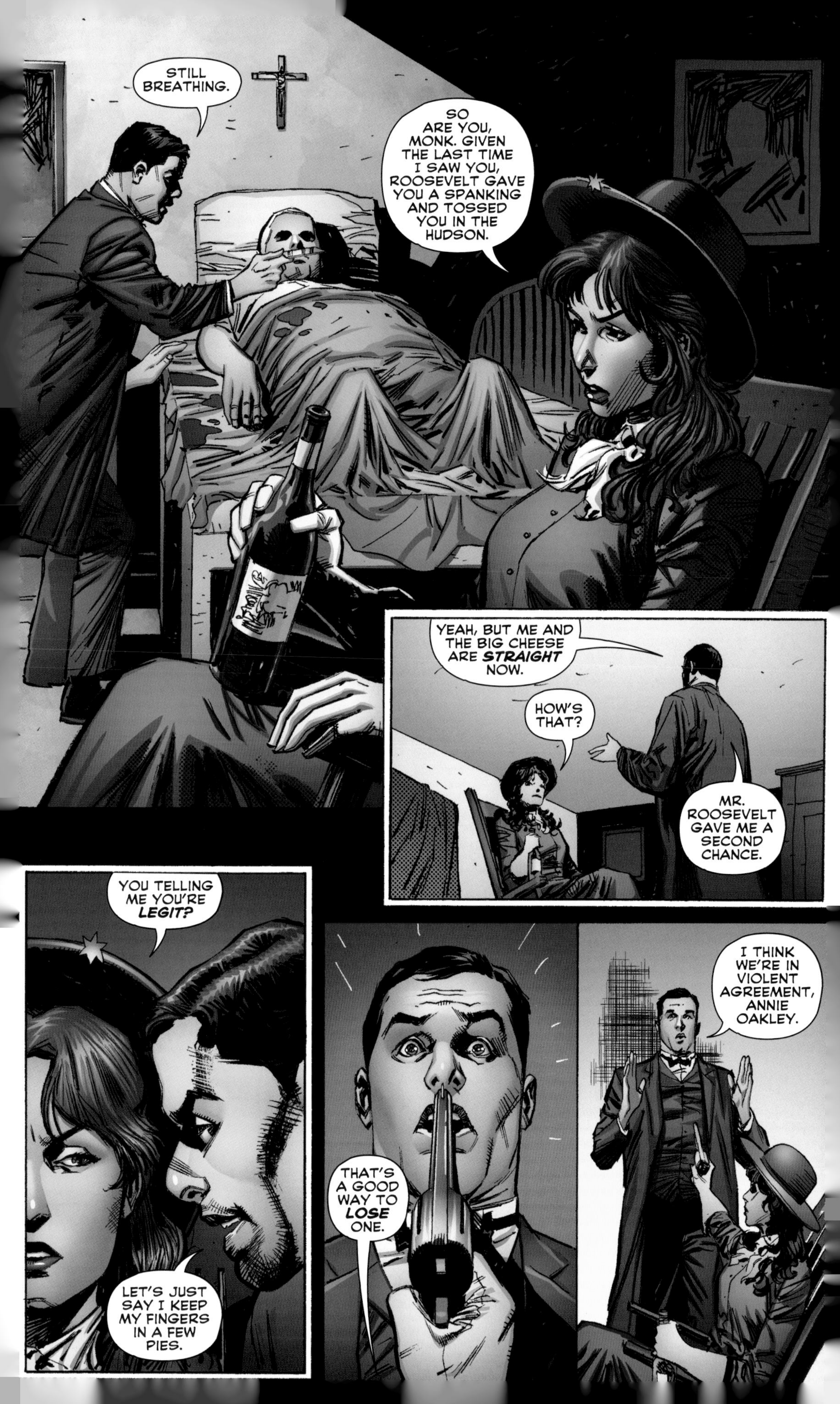
STILL BREATHING.
SO ARE YOU, MONK. GIVEN THE LAST TIME I SAW YOU, ROOSEVELT GAVE YOU A SPANKING AND TOSSED YOU IN THE HUDSON.
YEAH, BUT ME AND THE BIG CHEESE ARE STRAIGHT NOW.
HOW'S THAT?
MR. ROOSEVELT GAVE ME A SECOND CHANCE.
YOU TELLING ME YOU'RE LEGIT?
LET'S JUST SAY I KEEP MY FINGERS IN A FEW PIES.
THAT'S A GOOD WAY TO LOSE ONE.
I THINK WE'RE IN VIOLENT AGREEMENT, ANNIE OAKLEY.

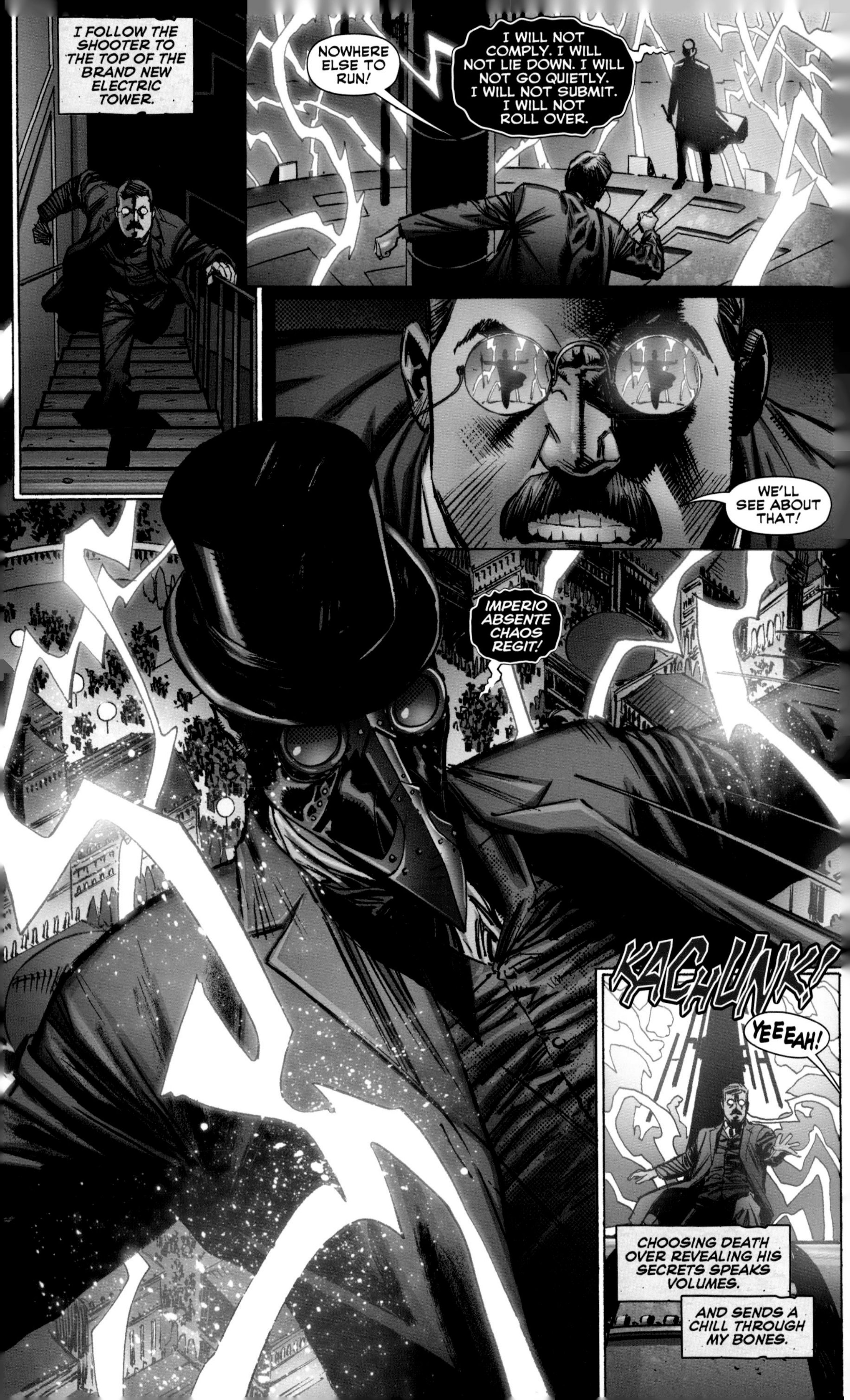
I FOLLOW THE SHOOTER TO THE TOP OF THE BRAND NEW ELECTRIC TOWER.
NOWHERE ELSE TO RUN!
I WILL NOT COMPLY. I WILL NOT LIE DOWN. I WILL NOT GO QUIETLY. I WILL NOT SUBMIT. I WILL NOT ROLL OVER.
WE'LL SEE ABOUT THAT!
IMPERIO ABSENTE CHAOS REGIT!
KACHUNK!
YEEEAH!
CHOOSING DEATH OVER REVEALING HIS SECRETS SPEAKS VOLUMES.
AND SENDS A CHILL THROUGH MY BONES.

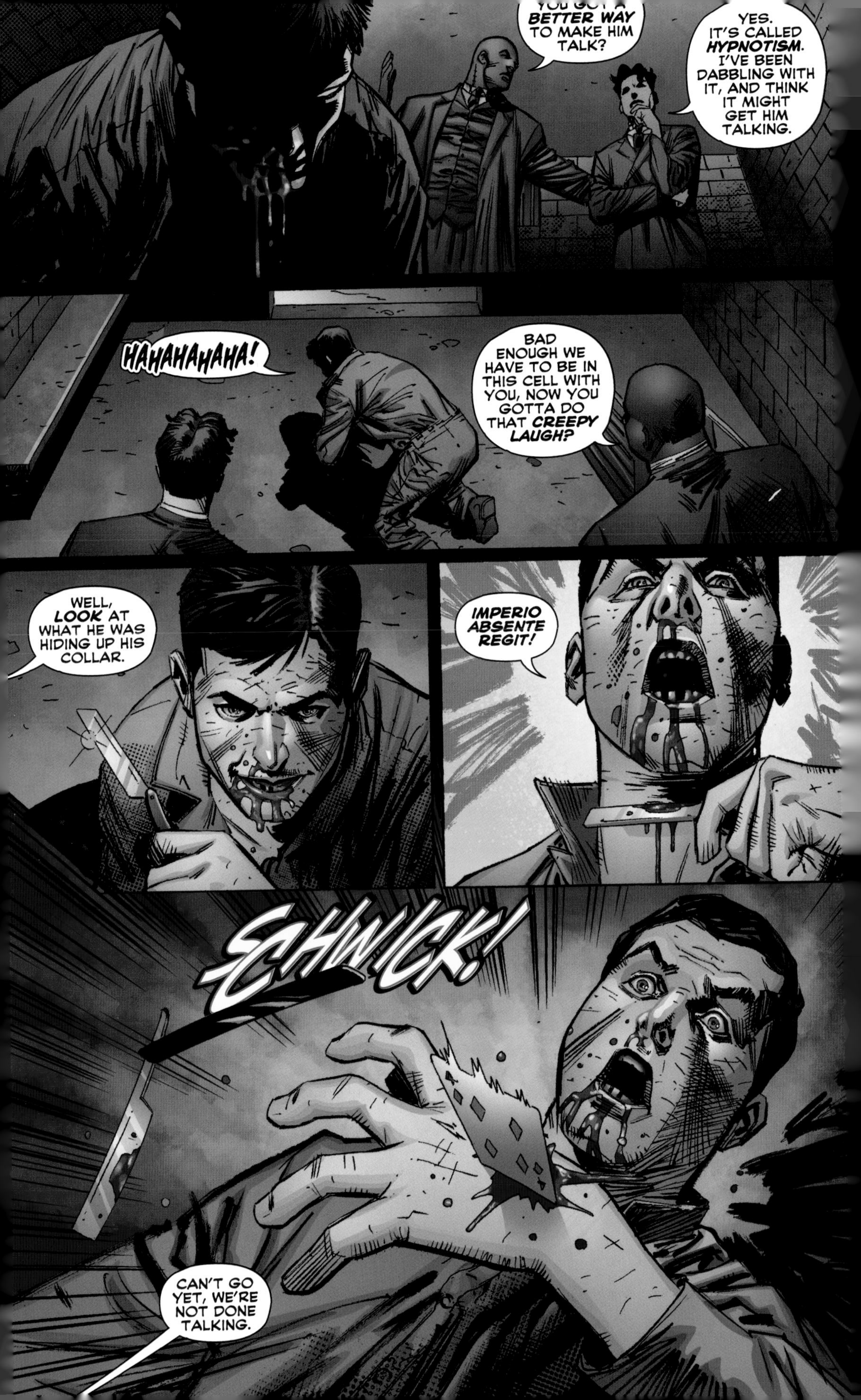
BETTER WAY TO MAKE HIM TALK?
YES. IT'S CALLED HYPNOTISM. I'VE BEEN DABBLING WITH IT, AND THINK IT MIGHT GET HIM TALKING.
HAHAHAHAHA!
BAD ENOUGH WE HAVE TO BE IN THIS CELL WITH YOU, NOW YOU GOTTA DO THAT CREEPY LAUGH?
WELL, LOOK AT WHAT HE WAS HIDING UP HIS COLLAR.
IMPERIO ABSENTE REGIT!
SCHWICK!
CAN'T GO YET, WE'RE NOT DONE TALKING.

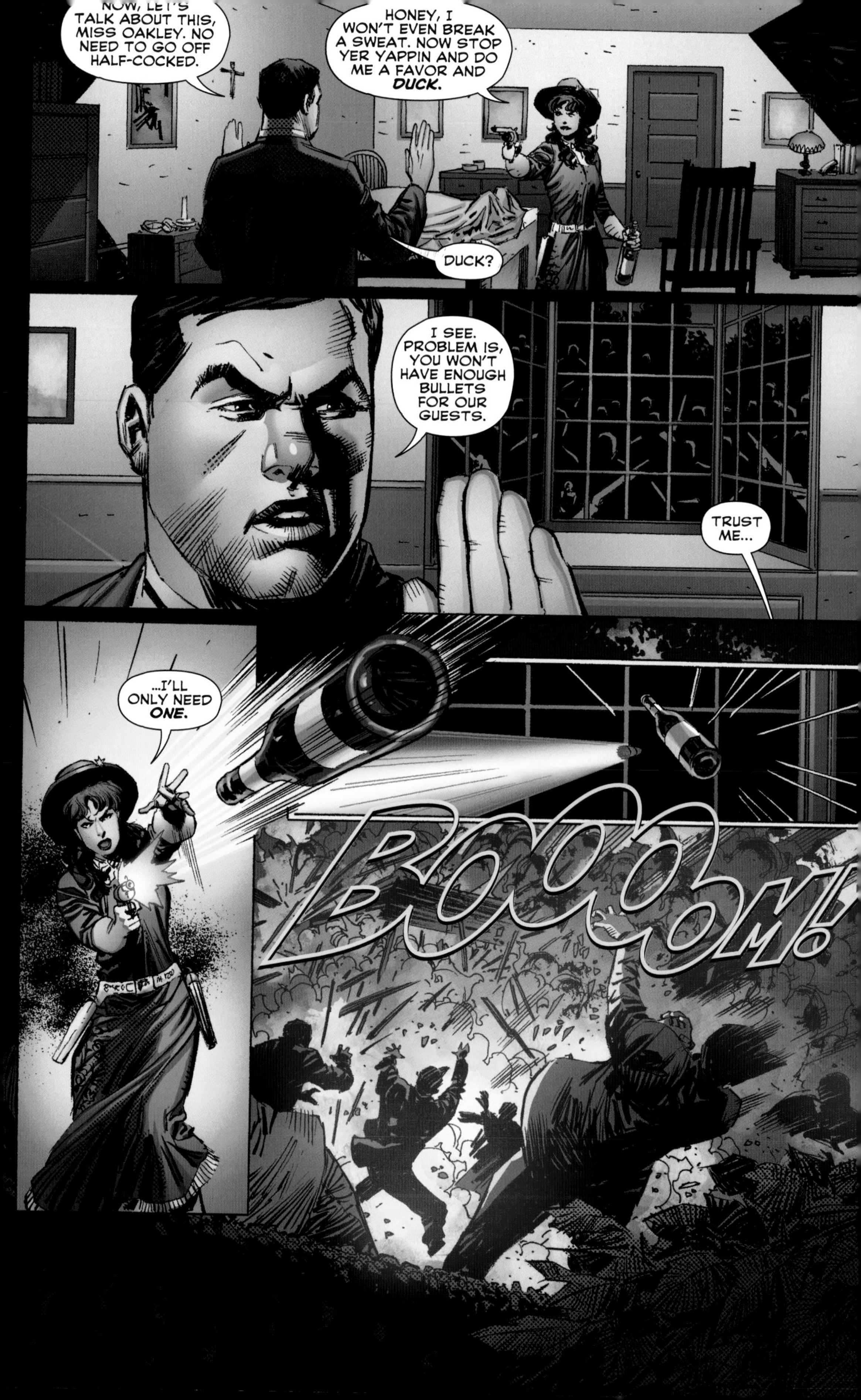
NOW, LET'S TALK ABOUT THIS, MISS OAKLEY. NO NEED TO GO OFF HALF-COCKED.
HONEY, I WON'T EVEN BREAK A SWEAT. NOW STOP YER YAPPIN AND DO ME A FAVOR AND **DUCK.**
DUCK?
I SEE. PROBLEM IS, YOU WON'T HAVE ENOUGH BULLETS FOR OUR GUESTS.
TRUST ME...
...I'LL ONLY NEED **ONE.**
BOOOOM!

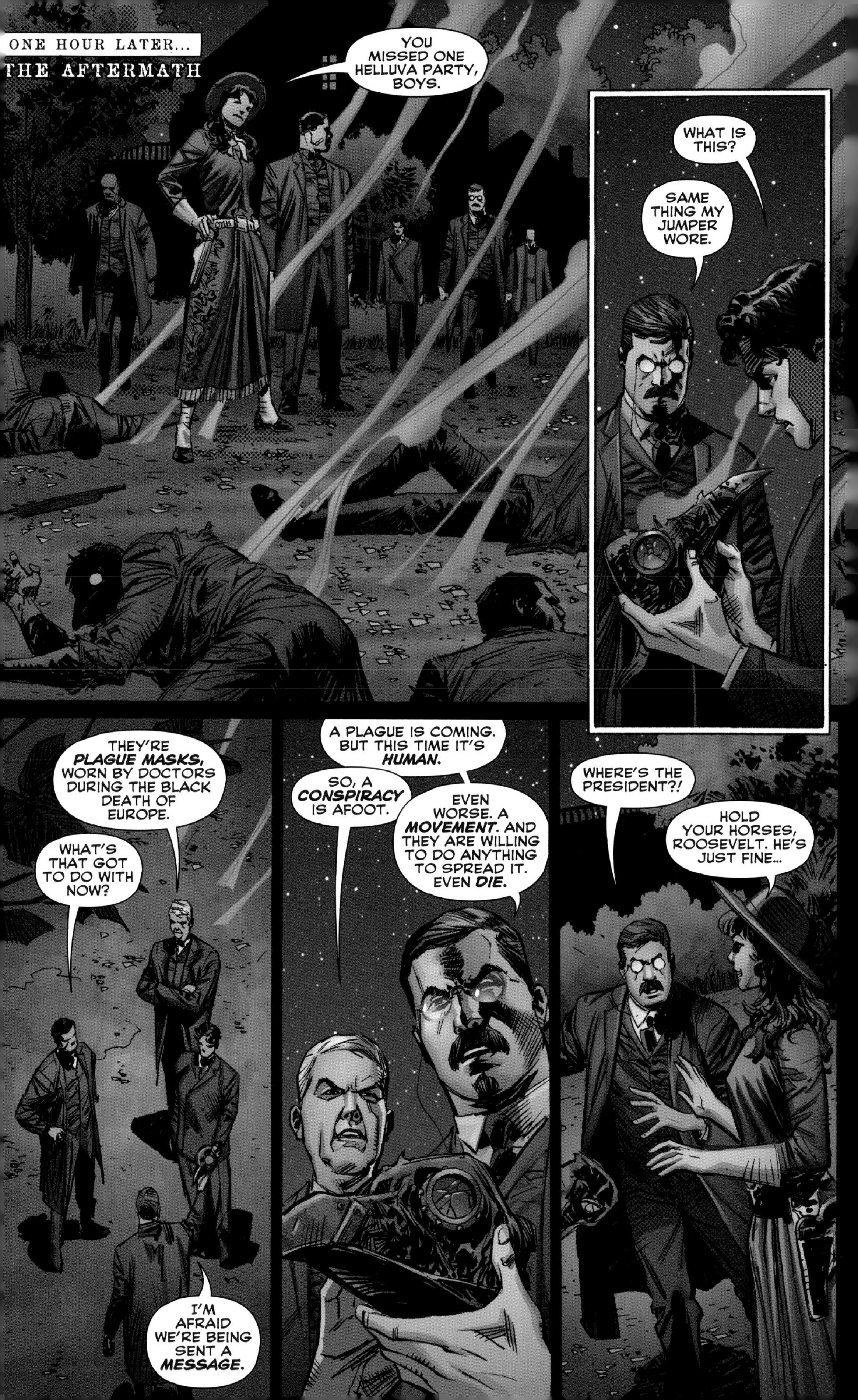
ONE HOUR LATER...
THE AFTERMATH
YOU MISSED ONE HELLUVA PARTY, BOYS.
WHAT IS THIS?
SAME THING MY JUMPER WORE.
THEY'RE PLAGUE MASKS, WORN BY DOCTORS DURING THE BLACK DEATH OF EUROPE.
WHAT'S THAT GOT TO DO WITH NOW?
I'M AFRAID WE'RE BEING SENT A MESSAGE.
A PLAGUE IS COMING. BUT THIS TIME IT'S HUMAN.
SO, A CONSPIRACY IS AFOOT.
EVEN WORSE. A MOVEMENT. AND THEY ARE WILLING TO DO ANYTHING TO SPREAD IT. EVEN DIE.
WHERE'S THE PRESIDENT?!
HOLD YOUR HORSES, ROOSEVELT. HE'S JUST FINE...

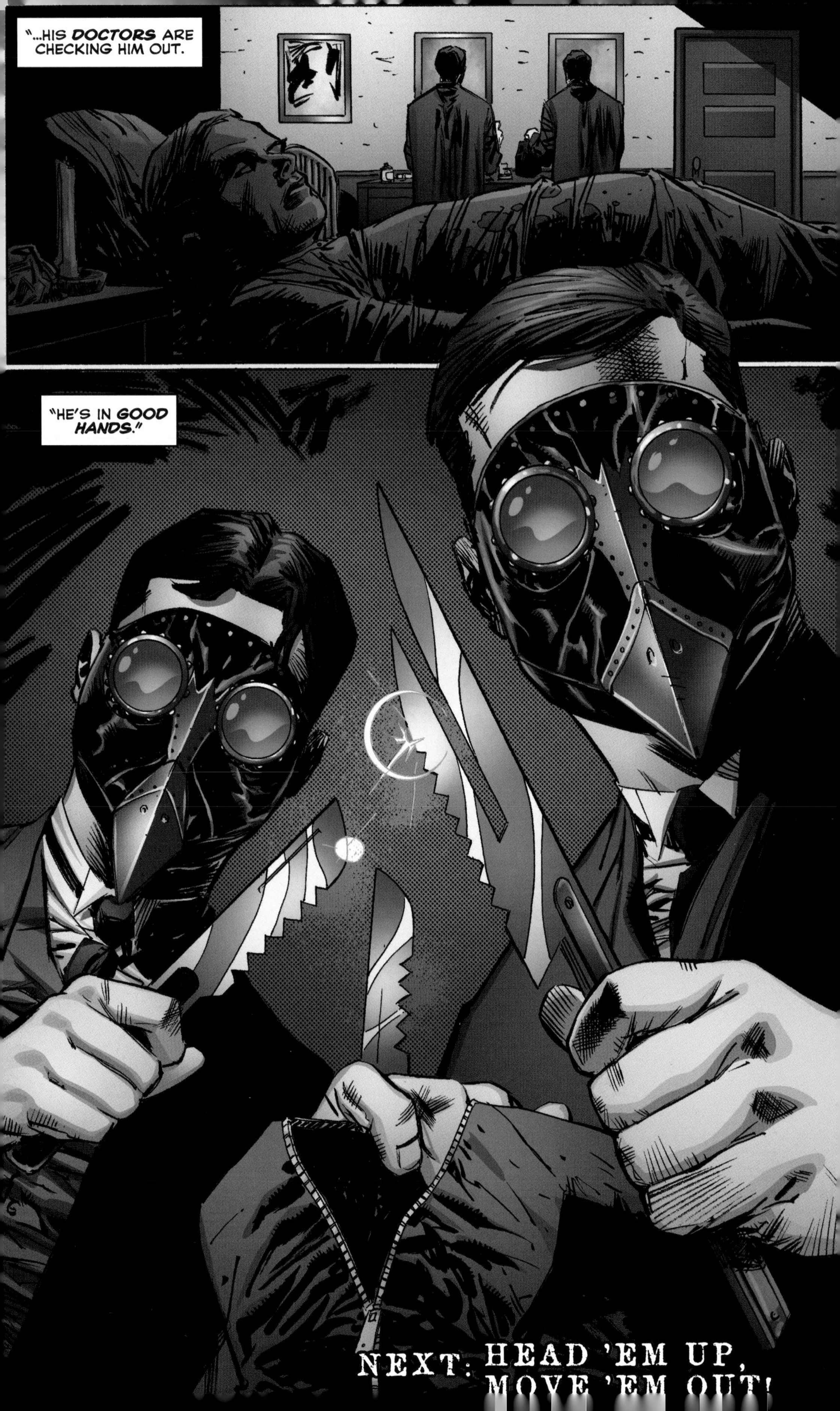
"...HIS DOCTORS ARE CHECKING HIM OUT.
"HE'S IN GOOD HANDS."
NEXT: HEAD 'EM UP, MOVE 'EM OUT!

10

"HEAD `EM UP, MOVE `EM OUT!"

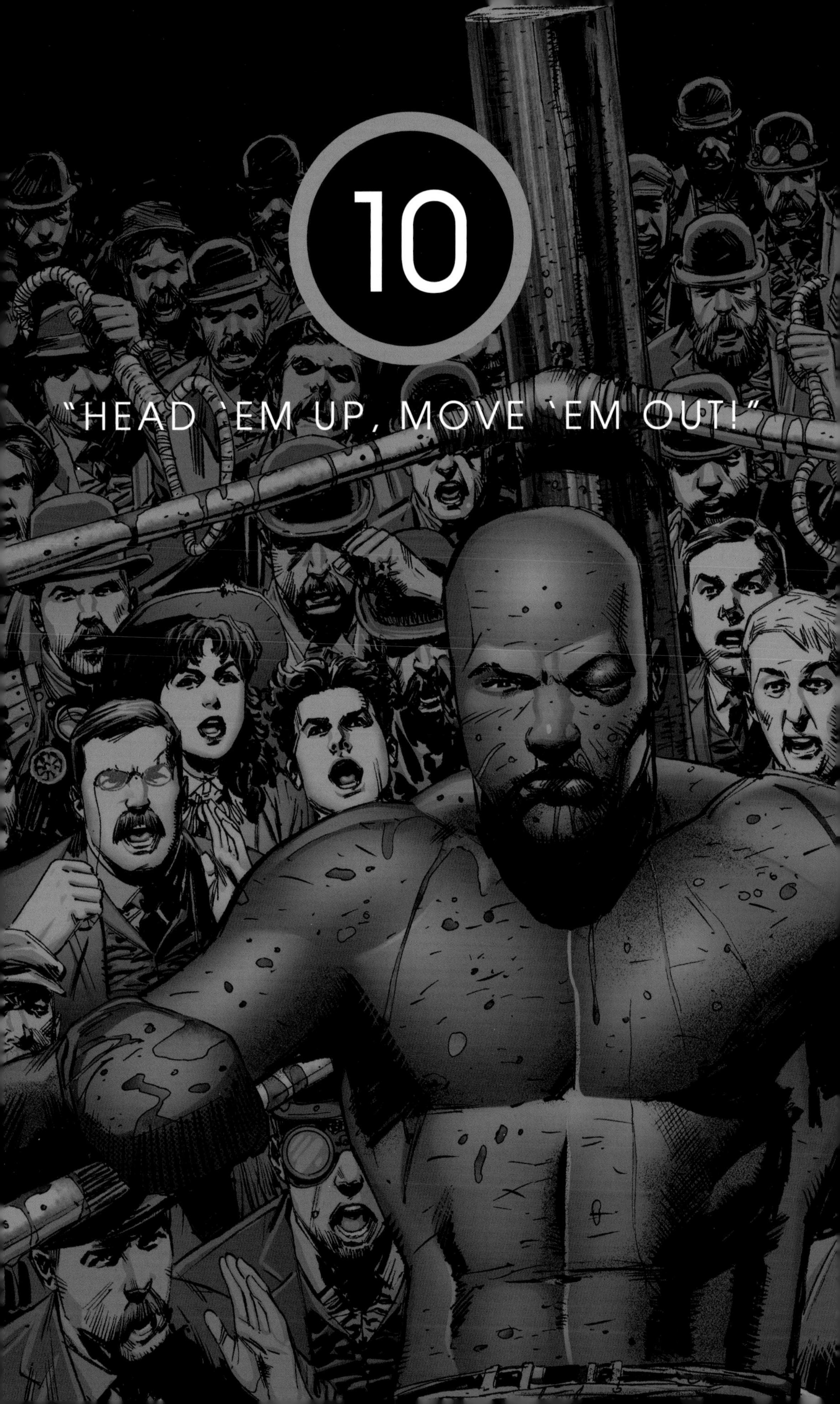

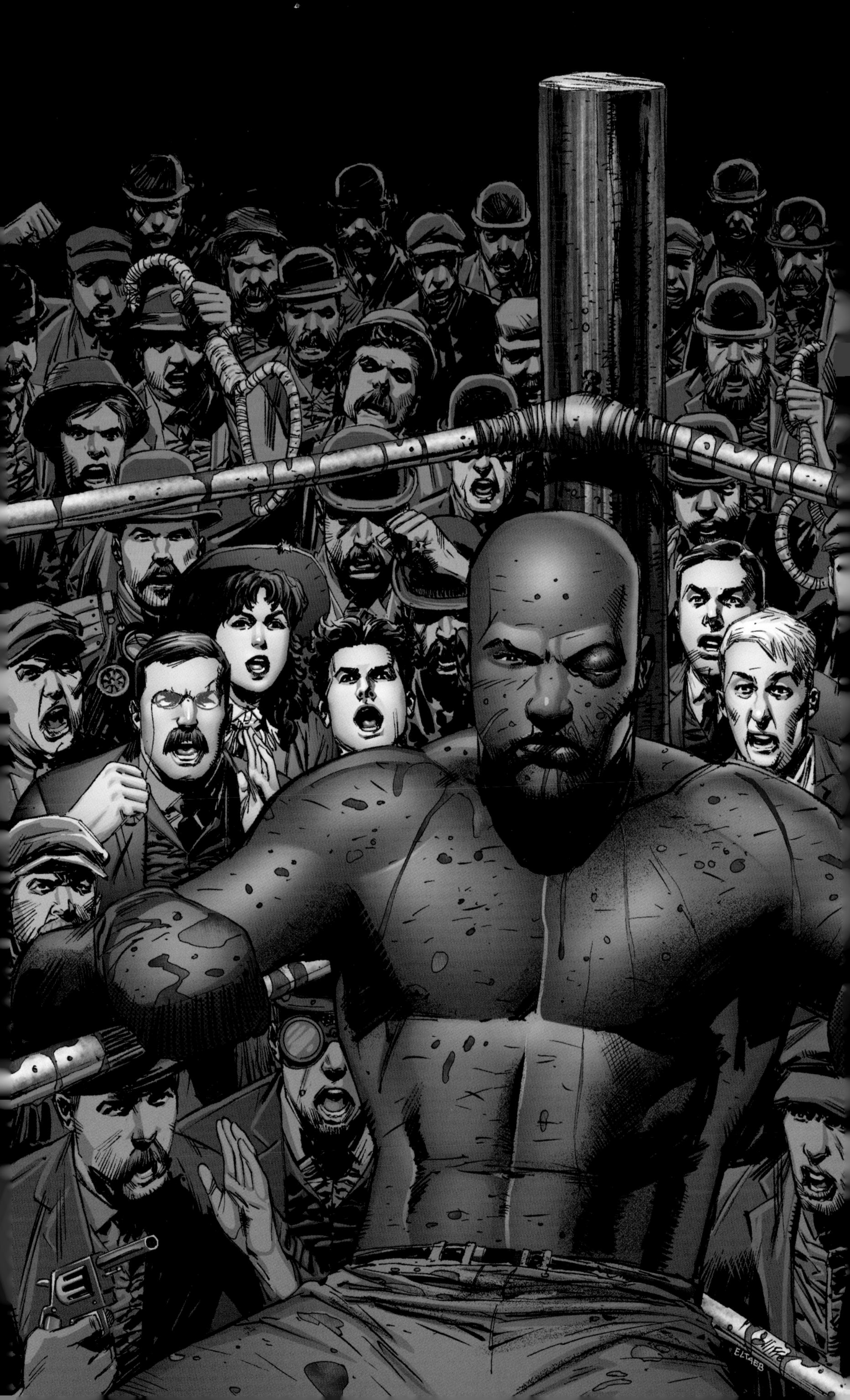

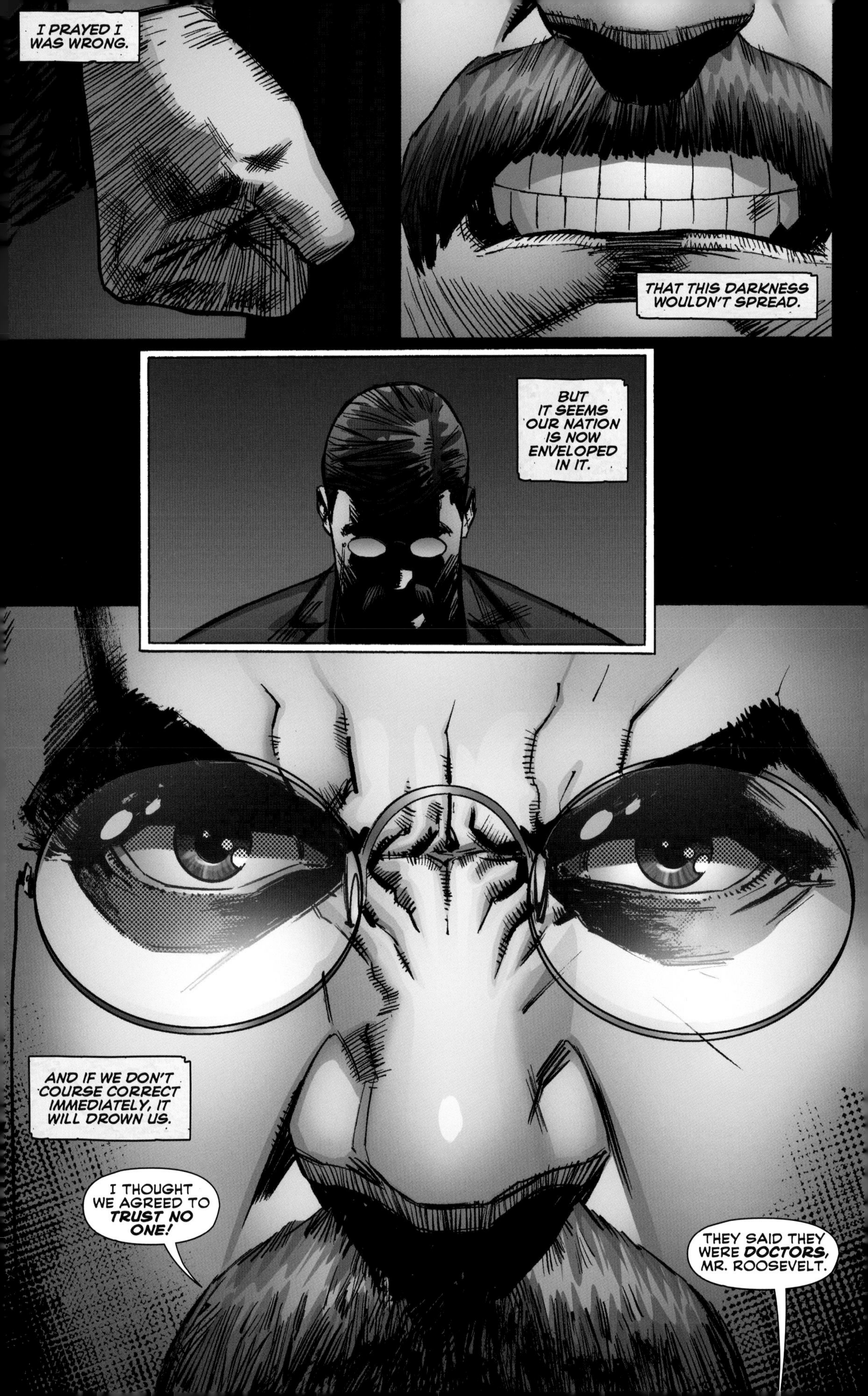

I PRAYED I WAS WRONG.
THAT THIS DARKNESS WOULDN'T SPREAD.
BUT IT SEEMS OUR NATION IS NOW ENVELOPED IN IT.
AND IF WE DON'T COURSE CORRECT IMMEDIATELY, IT WILL DROWN US.
I THOUGHT WE AGREED TO TRUST NO ONE!
THEY SAID THEY WERE DOCTORS, MR. ROOSEVELT.

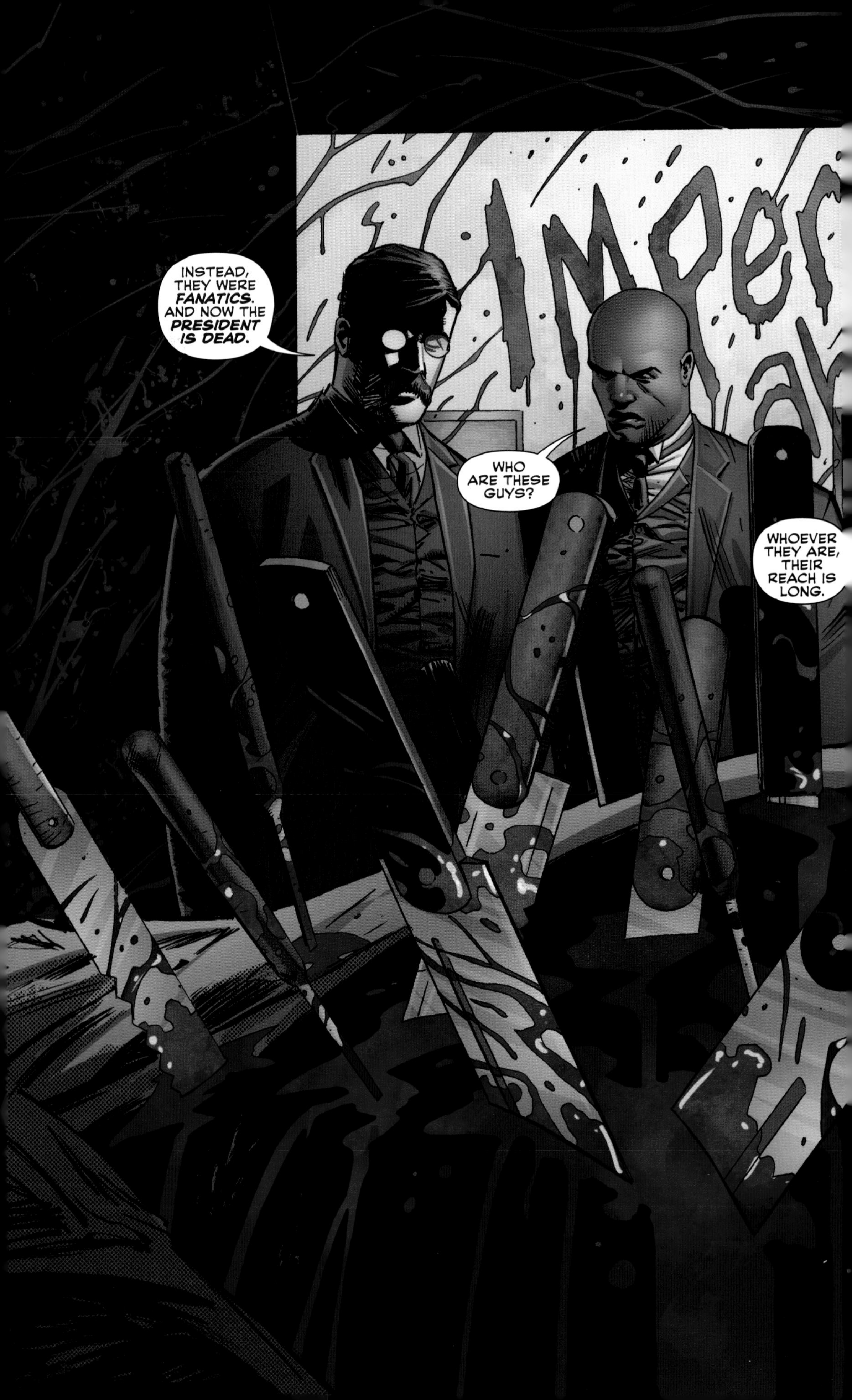
INSTEAD, THEY WERE *FANATICS*. AND NOW THE *PRESIDENT IS DEAD*.
WHO ARE THESE GUYS?
WHOEVER THEY ARE, THEIR REACH IS LONG.

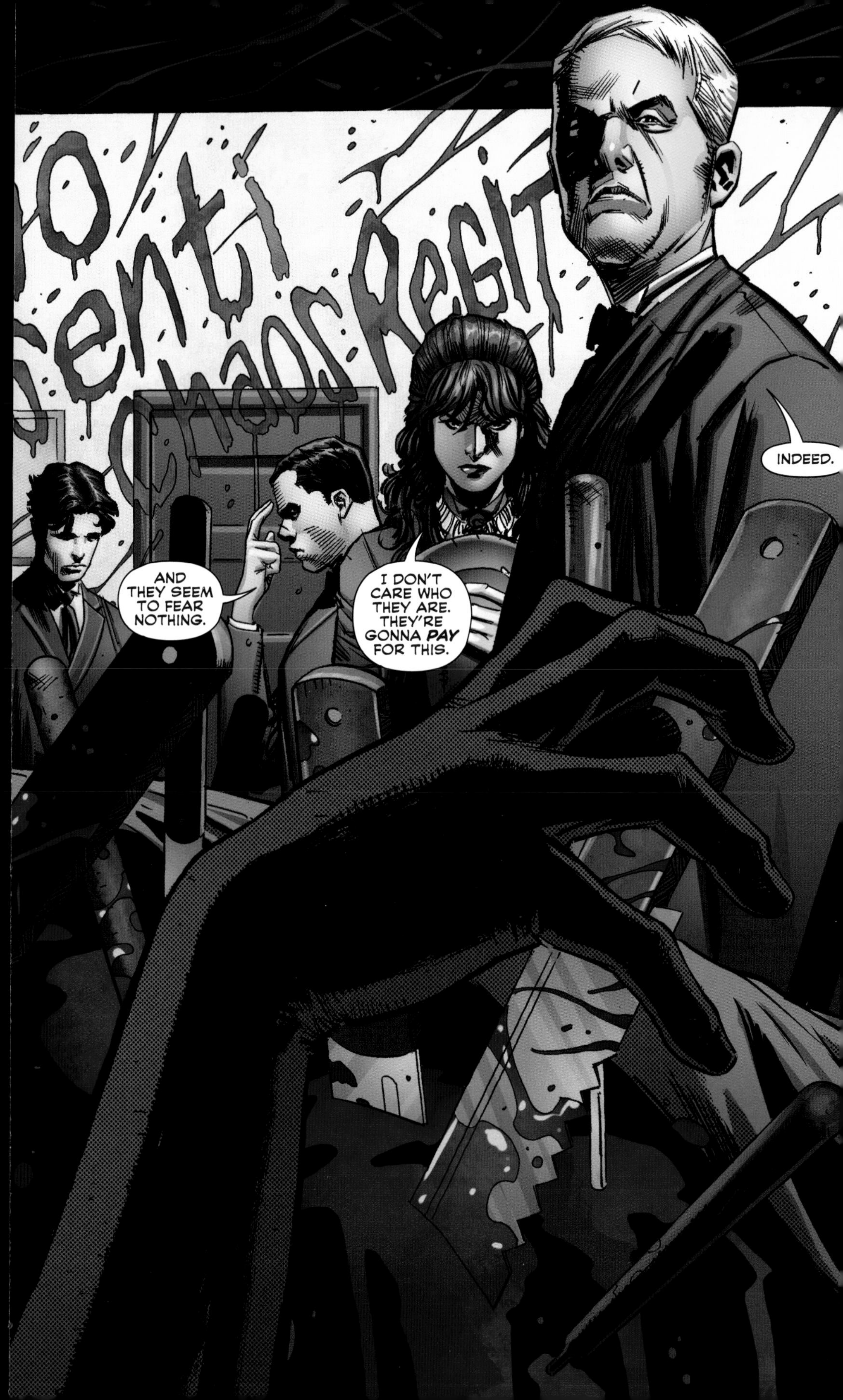

Chaos Regit
AND THEY SEEM TO FEAR NOTHING.
I DON'T CARE WHO THEY ARE. THEY'RE GONNA **PAY** FOR THIS.
INDEED.

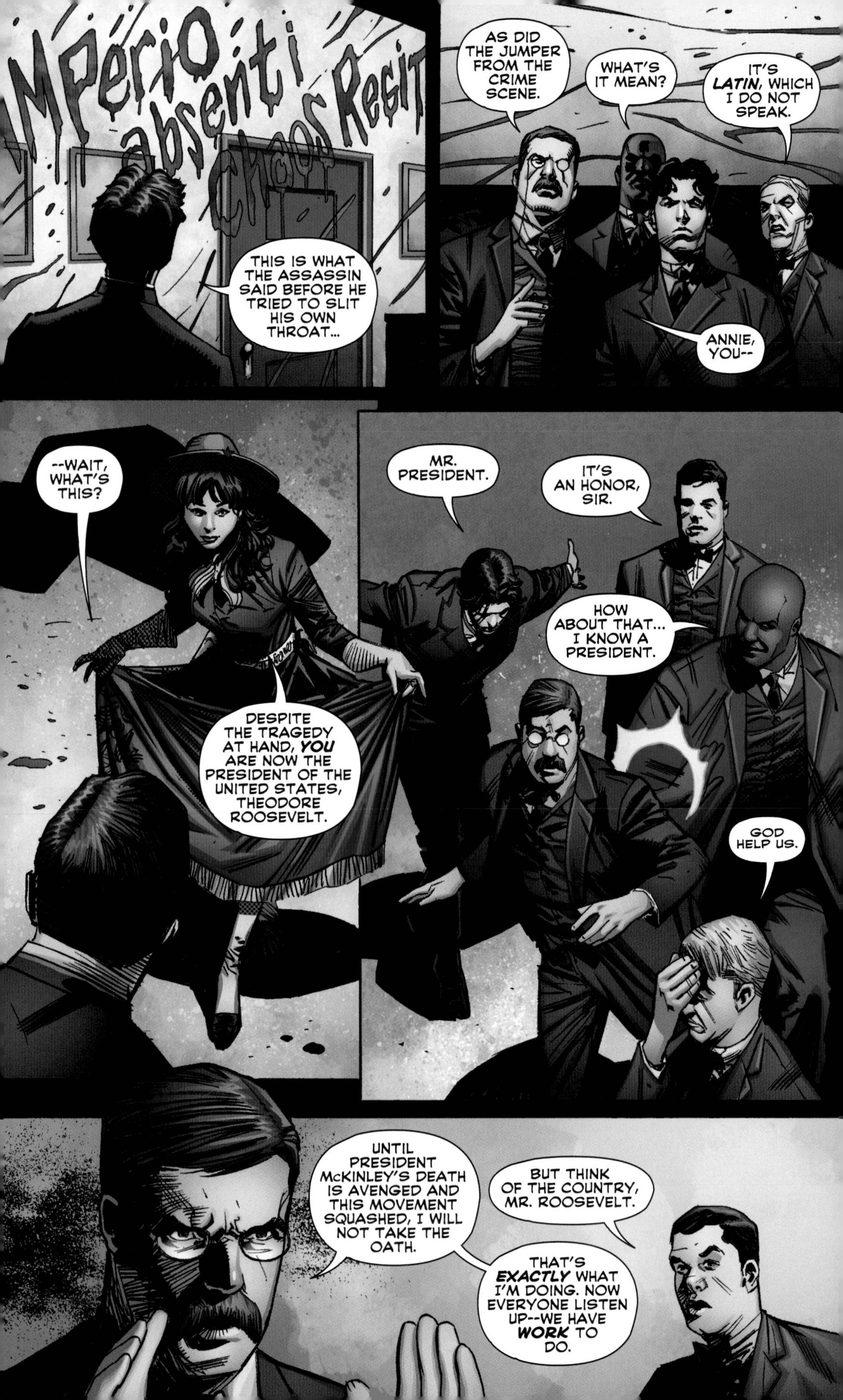

Imperio absenti Chaos Resit
THIS IS WHAT THE ASSASSIN SAID BEFORE HE TRIED TO SLIT HIS OWN THROAT...
AS DID THE JUMPER FROM THE CRIME SCENE.
WHAT'S IT MEAN?
IT'S LATIN, WHICH I DO NOT SPEAK.
ANNIE, YOU--
--WAIT, WHAT'S THIS?
DESPITE THE TRAGEDY AT HAND, YOU ARE NOW THE PRESIDENT OF THE UNITED STATES, THEODORE ROOSEVELT.
MR. PRESIDENT.
IT'S AN HONOR, SIR.
HOW ABOUT THAT... I KNOW A PRESIDENT.
GOD HELP US.
UNTIL PRESIDENT McKINLEY'S DEATH IS AVENGED AND THIS MOVEMENT SQUASHED, I WILL NOT TAKE THE OATH.
BUT THINK OF THE COUNTRY, MR. ROOSEVELT.
THAT'S EXACTLY WHAT I'M DOING. NOW EVERYONE LISTEN UP--WE HAVE WORK TO DO.

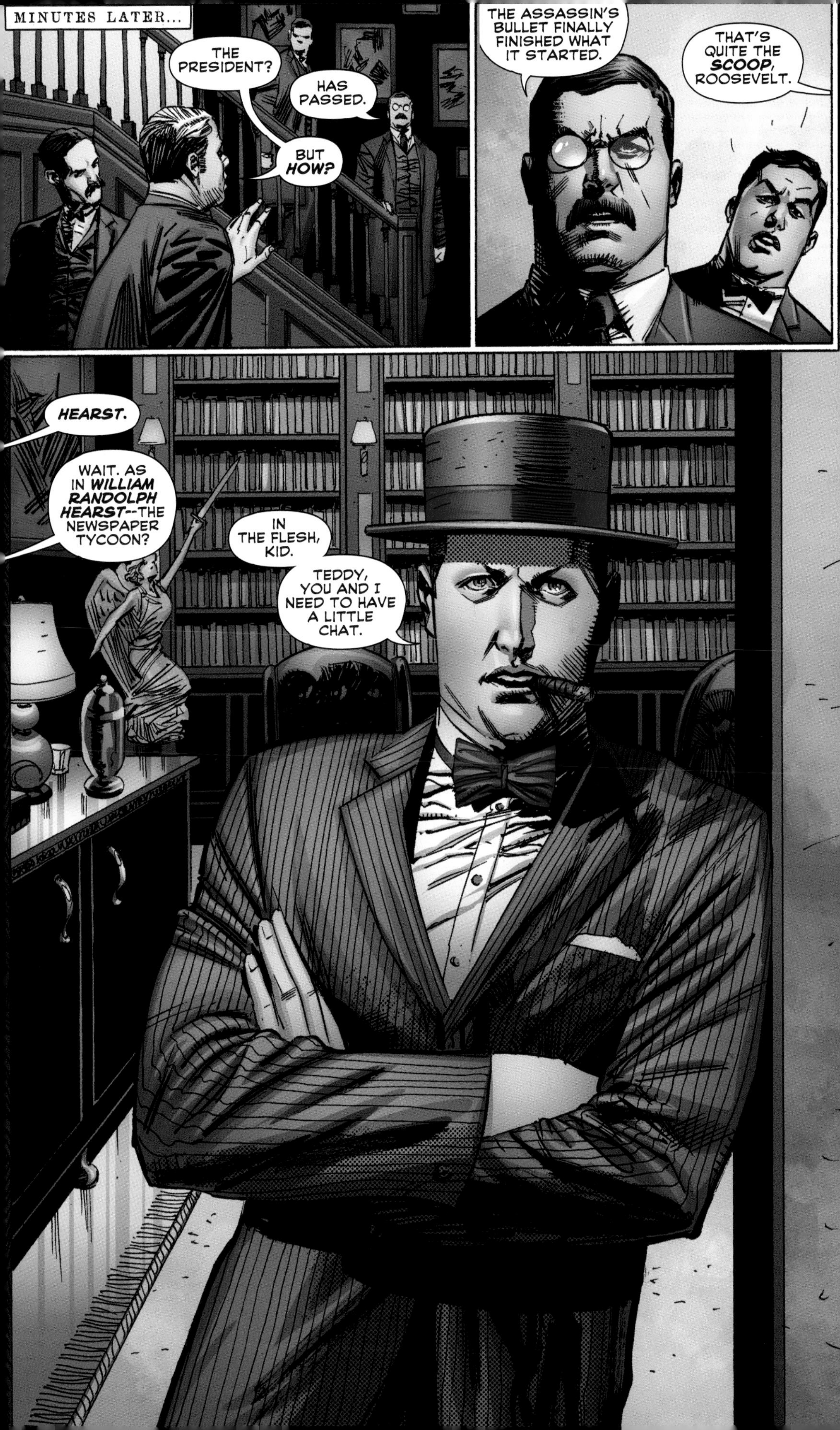

MINUTES LATER...
THE PRESIDENT?
HAS PASSED.
BUT HOW?
THE ASSASSIN'S BULLET FINALLY FINISHED WHAT IT STARTED.
THAT'S QUITE THE SCOOP, ROOSEVELT.
HEARST.
WAIT. AS IN WILLIAM RANDOLPH HEARST--THE NEWSPAPER TYCOON?
IN THE FLESH, KID.
TEDDY, YOU AND I NEED TO HAVE A LITTLE CHAT.

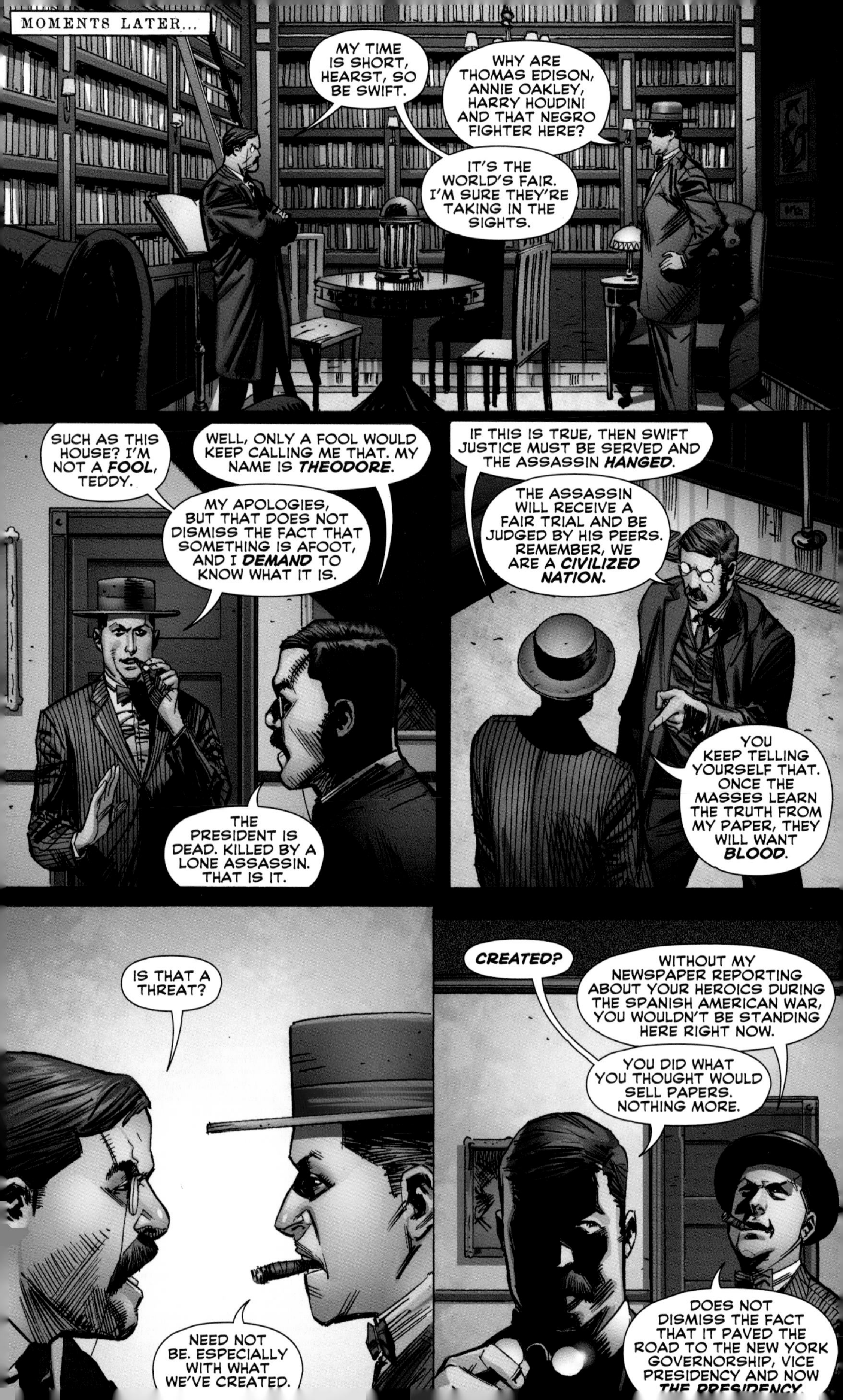
MOMENTS LATER...
MY TIME IS SHORT, HEARST, SO BE SWIFT.
WHY ARE THOMAS EDISON, ANNIE OAKLEY, HARRY HOUDINI AND THAT NEGRO FIGHTER HERE?
IT'S THE WORLD'S FAIR. I'M SURE THEY'RE TAKING IN THE SIGHTS.
SUCH AS THIS HOUSE? I'M NOT A FOOL, TEDDY.
WELL, ONLY A FOOL WOULD KEEP CALLING ME THAT. MY NAME IS THEODORE.
MY APOLOGIES, BUT THAT DOES NOT DISMISS THE FACT THAT SOMETHING IS AFOOT, AND I DEMAND TO KNOW WHAT IT IS.
THE PRESIDENT IS DEAD. KILLED BY A LONE ASSASSIN. THAT IS IT.
IF THIS IS TRUE, THEN SWIFT JUSTICE MUST BE SERVED AND THE ASSASSIN HANGED.
THE ASSASSIN WILL RECEIVE A FAIR TRIAL AND BE JUDGED BY HIS PEERS. REMEMBER, WE ARE A CIVILIZED NATION.
YOU KEEP TELLING YOURSELF THAT. ONCE THE MASSES LEARN THE TRUTH FROM MY PAPER, THEY WILL WANT BLOOD.
IS THAT A THREAT?
NEED NOT BE. ESPECIALLY WITH WHAT WE'VE CREATED.
CREATED?
WITHOUT MY NEWSPAPER REPORTING ABOUT YOUR HEROICS DURING THE SPANISH AMERICAN WAR, YOU WOULDN'T BE STANDING HERE RIGHT NOW.
YOU DID WHAT YOU THOUGHT WOULD SELL PAPERS. NOTHING MORE.
DOES NOT DISMISS THE FACT THAT IT PAVED THE ROAD TO THE NEW YORK GOVERNORSHIP, VICE PRESIDENCY AND NOW THE PRESIDENCY.

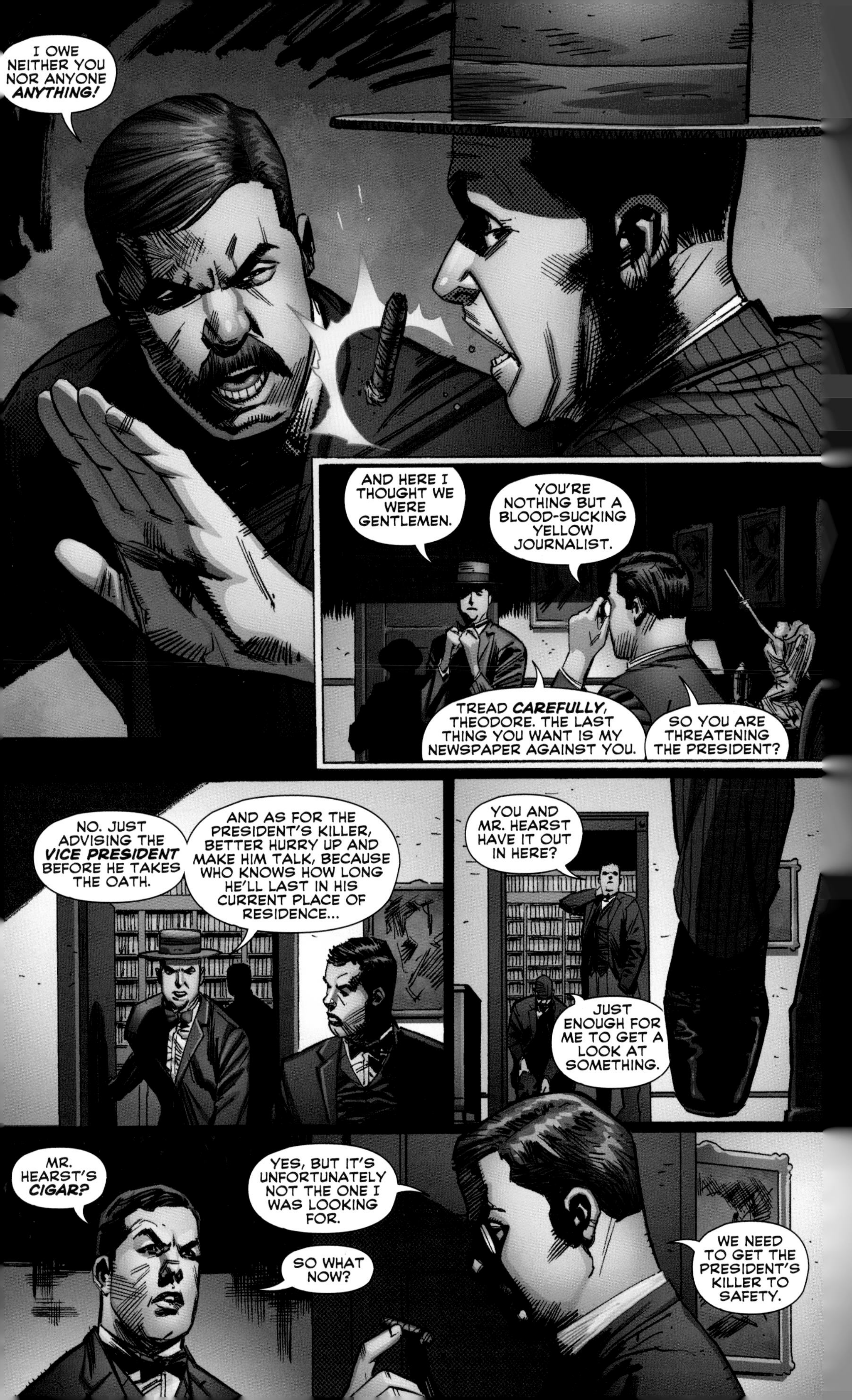
I OWE NEITHER YOU NOR ANYONE *ANYTHING!*
AND HERE I THOUGHT WE WERE GENTLEMEN.
YOU'RE NOTHING BUT A BLOOD-SUCKING YELLOW JOURNALIST.
TREAD *CAREFULLY*, THEODORE. THE LAST THING YOU WANT IS MY NEWSPAPER AGAINST YOU.
SO YOU ARE THREATENING THE PRESIDENT?
NO. JUST ADVISING THE *VICE PRESIDENT* BEFORE HE TAKES THE OATH.
AND AS FOR THE PRESIDENT'S KILLER, BETTER HURRY UP AND MAKE HIM TALK, BECAUSE WHO KNOWS HOW LONG HE'LL LAST IN HIS CURRENT PLACE OF RESIDENCE...
YOU AND MR. HEARST HAVE IT OUT IN HERE?
JUST ENOUGH FOR ME TO GET A LOOK AT SOMETHING.
MR. HEARST'S *CIGAR?*
YES, BUT IT'S UNFORTUNATELY NOT THE ONE I WAS LOOKING FOR.
SO WHAT NOW?
WE NEED TO GET THE PRESIDENT'S KILLER TO SAFETY.

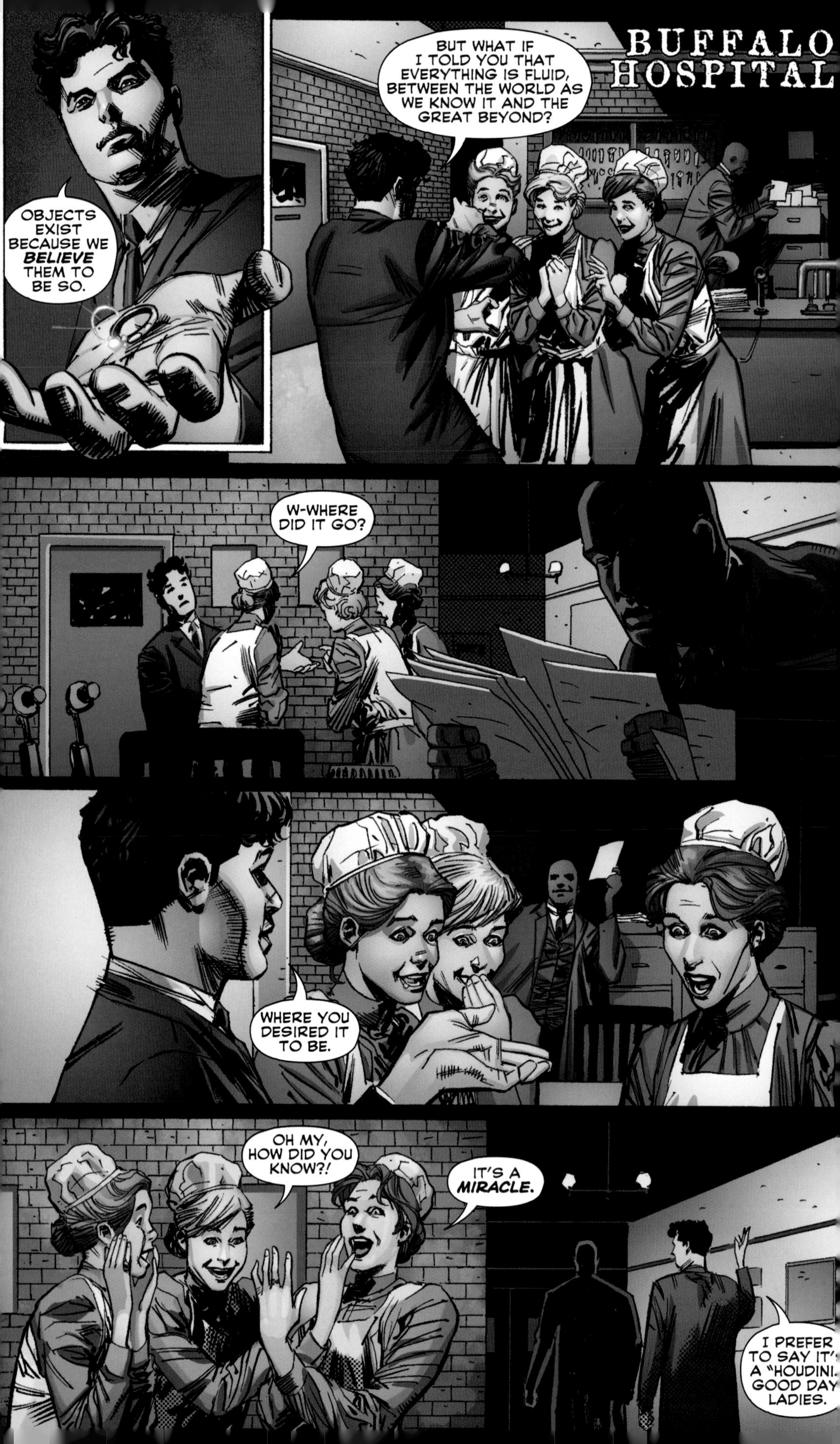
BUFFALO HOSPITAL
OBJECTS EXIST BECAUSE WE *BELIEVE* THEM TO BE SO.
BUT WHAT IF I TOLD YOU THAT EVERYTHING IS FLUID, BETWEEN THE WORLD AS WE KNOW IT AND THE GREAT BEYOND?
W-WHERE DID IT GO?
WHERE YOU DESIRED IT TO BE.
OH MY, HOW DID YOU KNOW?!
IT'S A *MIRACLE*.
I PREFER TO SAY IT' A "HOUDINI GOOD DAY LADIES.

HOLY CROSS CATHOLIC CHURCH...

THEY SURE LOVE THEIR STAINED GLASS WINDOWS.

FIRST TIME IN A CATHOLIC CHURCH?

NAW, BUT THIS IS THE BIGGEST ONE FOR SURE.

MAY I HELP YOU?

EXCUSE ME. WHAT AN HONOR TO HAVE SOMEONE OF YOUR STATURE IN OUR HOUSE OF GOD.

YES, OF COURSE. BUT I DON'T LIKE MAKING A *BIG DEAL* ABOUT IT. SO--

MISS ANNIE OAKLEY, IT IS A *TRUE BLESSING* TO MEET YOU IN PERSON!

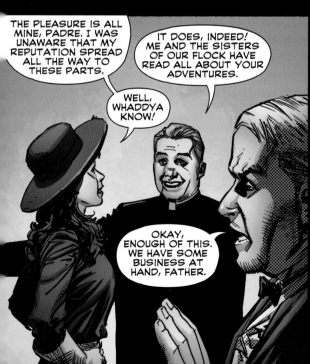

THE PLEASURE IS ALL MINE, PADRE. I WAS UNAWARE THAT MY REPUTATION SPREAD ALL THE WAY TO THESE PARTS.

IT DOES, INDEED! ME AND THE SISTERS OF OUR FLOCK HAVE READ ALL ABOUT YOUR ADVENTURES.

WELL, WHADDYA KNOW!

OKAY, ENOUGH OF THIS. WE HAVE SOME BUSINESS AT HAND, FATHER.

ANYTHING TO HELP THE LEGENDARY ANNIE OAKLEY.

THANKS, PADRE. IS THEIR ANYPLACE PRIVATE WE CAN SPEAK?

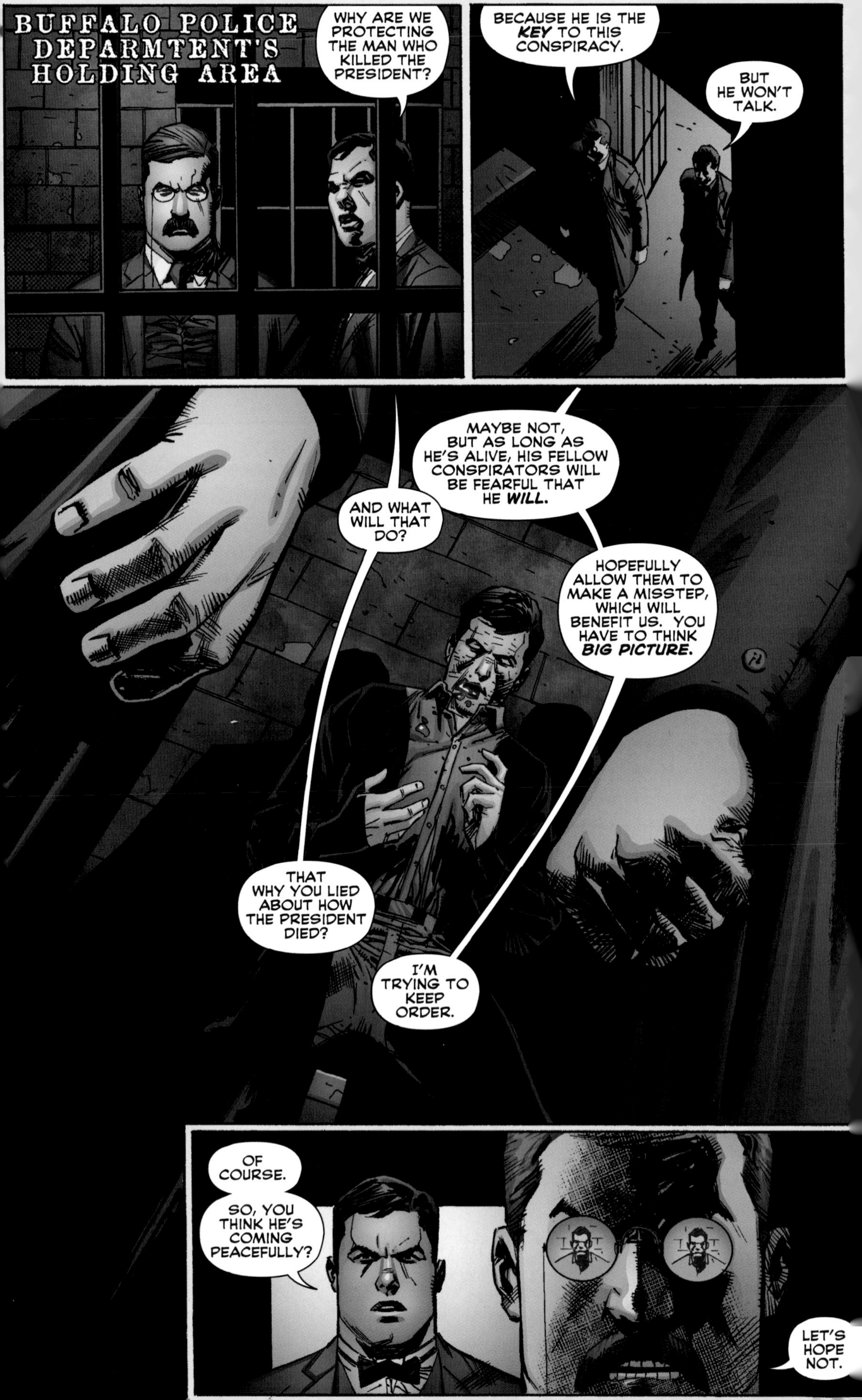
BUFFALO POLICE DEPARMTENT'S HOLDING AREA
WHY ARE WE PROTECTING THE MAN WHO KILLED THE PRESIDENT?
BECAUSE HE IS THE KEY TO THIS CONSPIRACY.
BUT HE WON'T TALK.
MAYBE NOT, BUT AS LONG AS HE'S ALIVE, HIS FELLOW CONSPIRATORS WILL BE FEARFUL THAT HE WILL.
AND WHAT WILL THAT DO?
HOPEFULLY ALLOW THEM TO MAKE A MISSTEP, WHICH WILL BENEFIT US. YOU HAVE TO THINK BIG PICTURE.
THAT WHY YOU LIED ABOUT HOW THE PRESIDENT DIED?
I'M TRYING TO KEEP ORDER.
OF COURSE.
SO, YOU THINK HE'S COMING PEACEFULLY?
LET'S HOPE NOT.

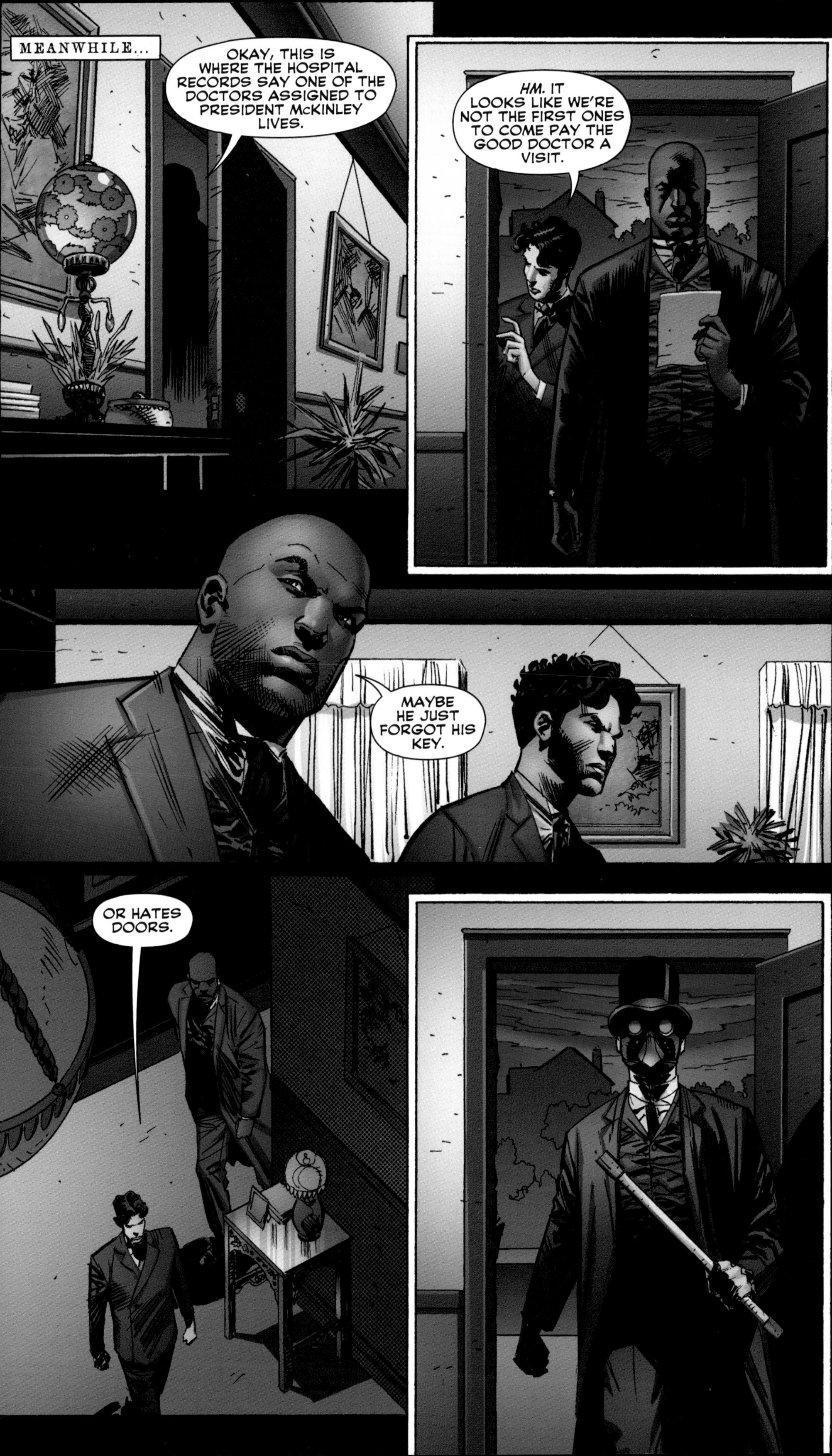
MEANWHILE...
OKAY, THIS IS WHERE THE HOSPITAL RECORDS SAY ONE OF THE DOCTORS ASSIGNED TO PRESIDENT McKINLEY LIVES.
HM. IT LOOKS LIKE WE'RE NOT THE FIRST ONES TO COME PAY THE GOOD DOCTOR A VISIT.
MAYBE HE JUST FORGOT HIS KEY.
OR HATES DOORS.

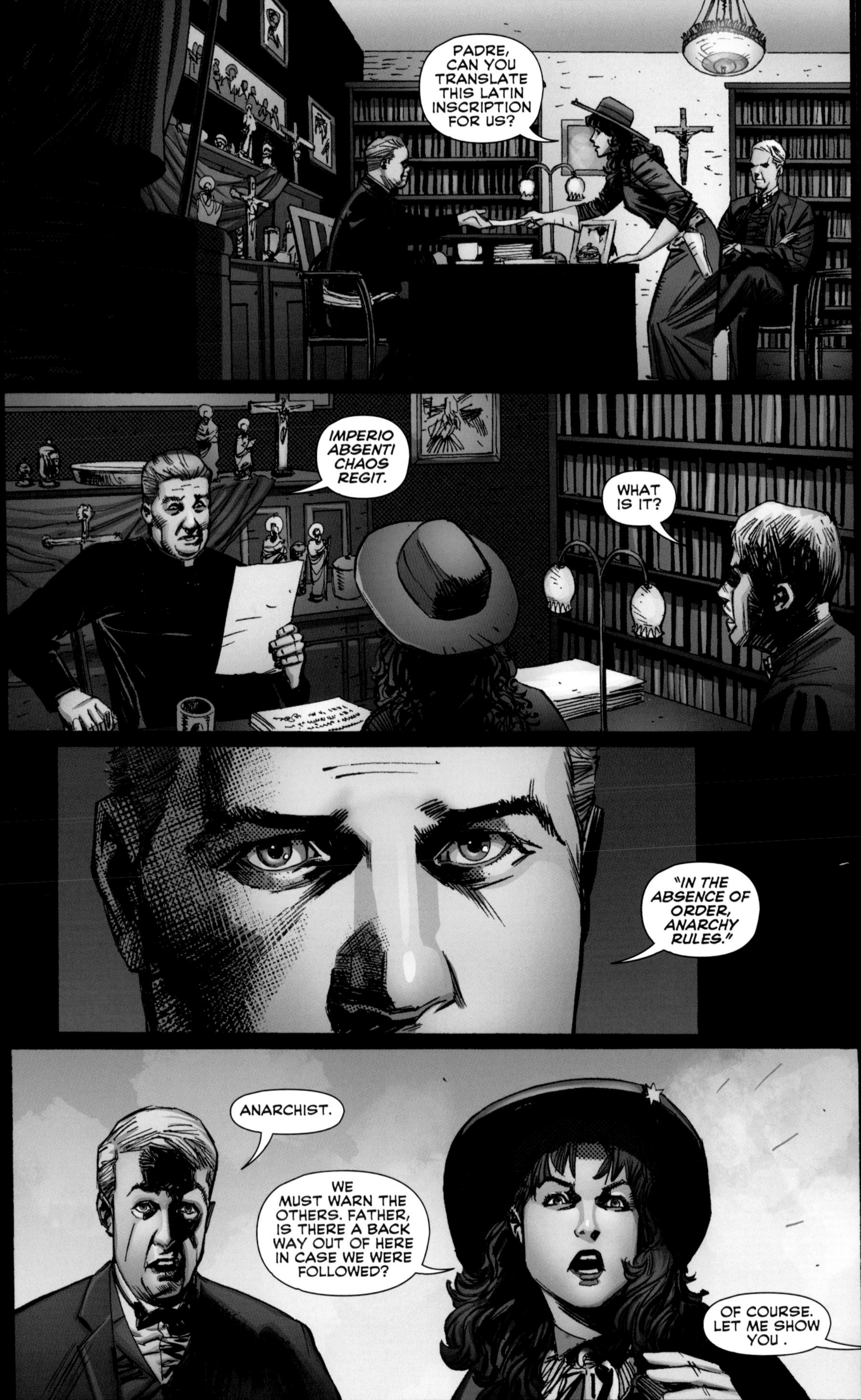
PADRE, CAN YOU TRANSLATE THIS LATIN INSCRIPTION FOR US?
IMPERIO ABSENTI CHAOS REGIT.
WHAT IS IT?
"IN THE ABSENCE OF ORDER, ANARCHY RULES."
ANARCHIST.
WE MUST WARN THE OTHERS. FATHER, IS THERE A BACK WAY OUT OF HERE IN CASE WE WERE FOLLOWED?
OF COURSE. LET ME SHOW YOU .

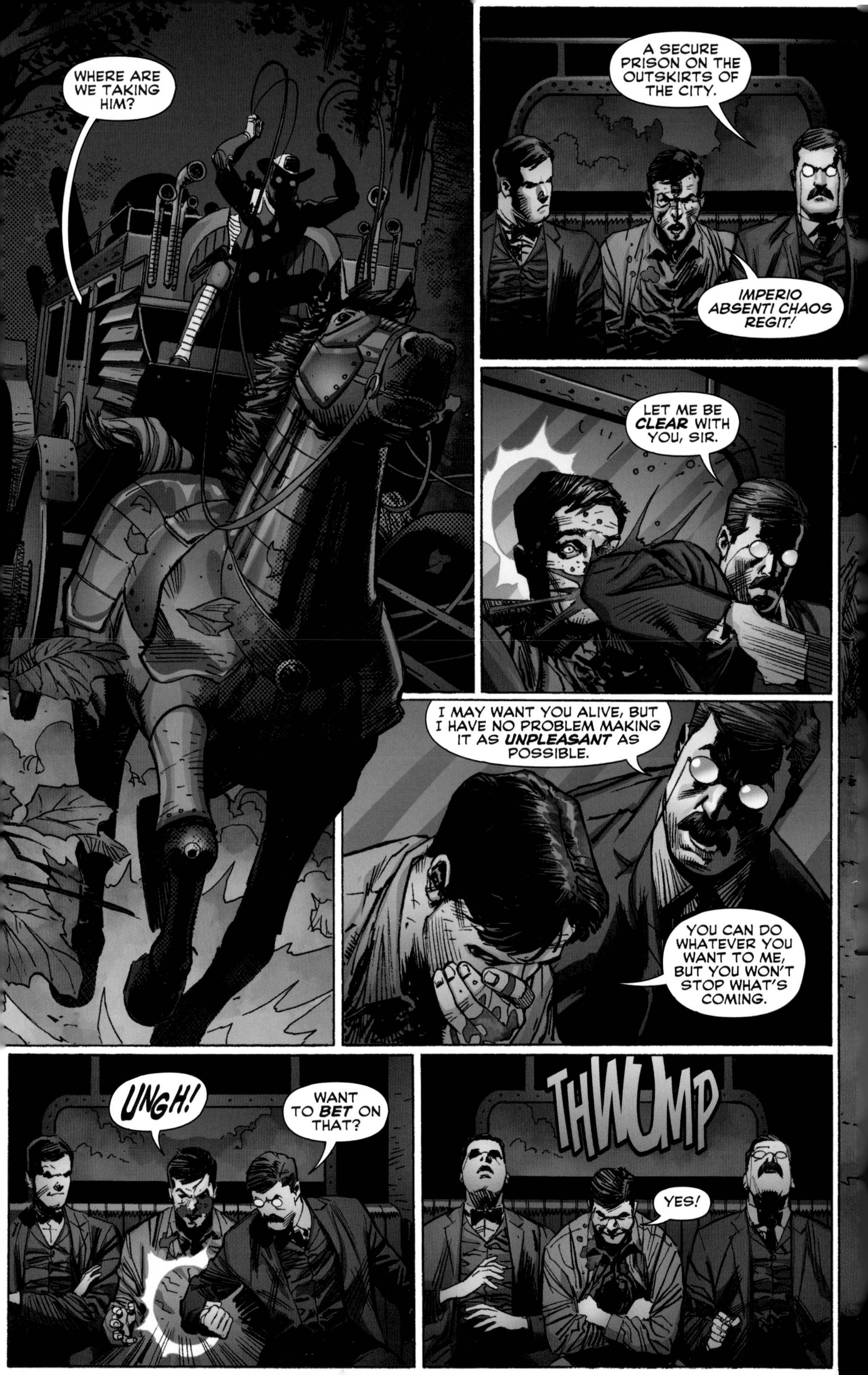
WHERE ARE WE TAKING HIM?
A SECURE PRISON ON THE OUTSKIRTS OF THE CITY.
IMPERIO ABSENTI CHAOS REGIT!
LET ME BE CLEAR WITH YOU, SIR.
I MAY WANT YOU ALIVE, BUT I HAVE NO PROBLEM MAKING IT AS UNPLEASANT AS POSSIBLE.
YOU CAN DO WHATEVER YOU WANT TO ME, BUT YOU WON'T STOP WHAT'S COMING.
UNGH!
WANT TO BET ON THAT?
THWUMP
YES!

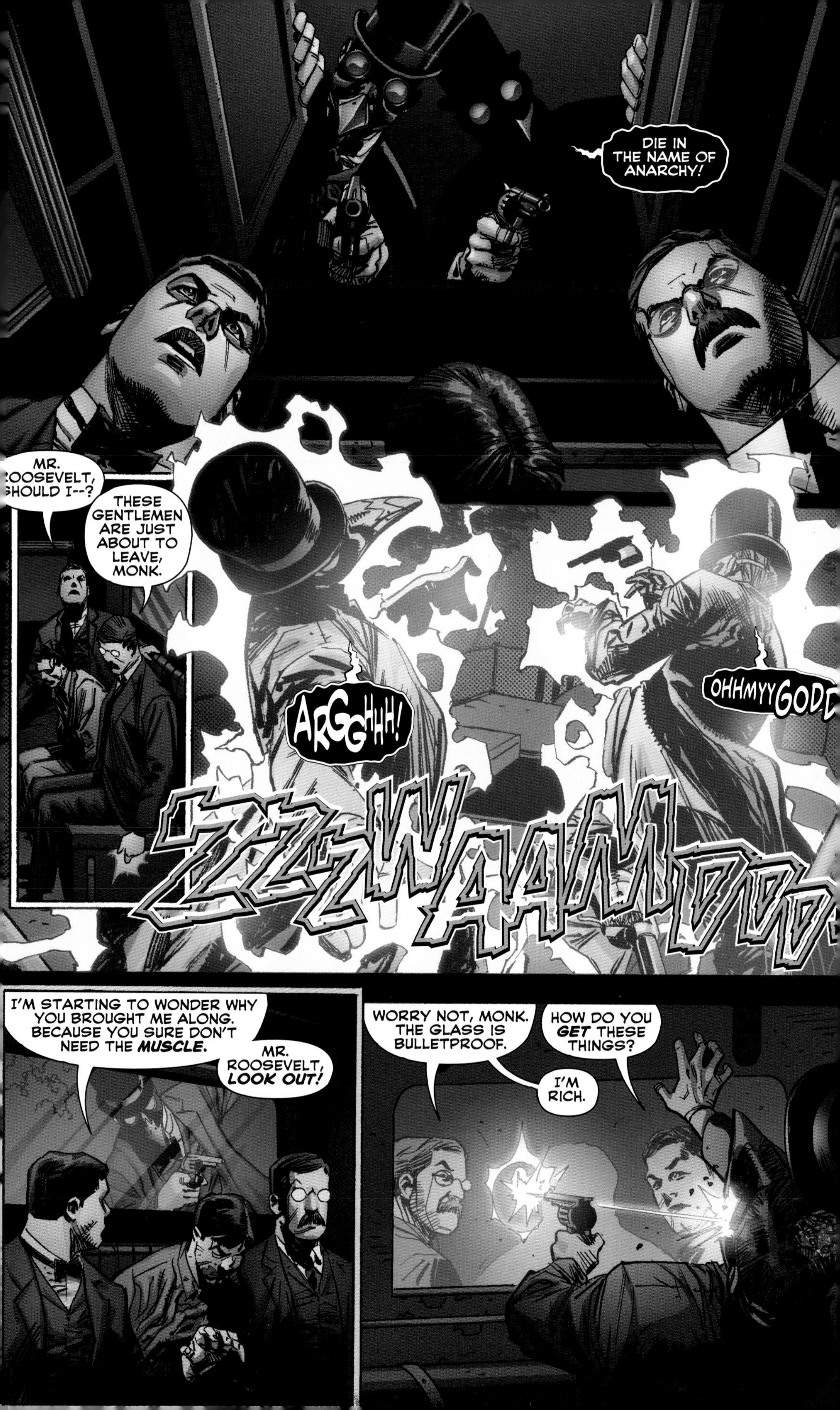
DIE IN THE NAME OF ANARCHY!
MR. ROOSEVELT, SHOULD I--?
THESE GENTLEMEN ARE JUST ABOUT TO LEAVE, MONK.
ARGGHHH!
OHHMYYGODD
ZZZWAAMDDD
I'M STARTING TO WONDER WHY YOU BROUGHT ME ALONG. BECAUSE YOU SURE DON'T NEED THE *MUSCLE*.
MR. ROOSEVELT, *LOOK OUT!*
WORRY NOT, MONK. THE GLASS IS BULLETPROOF.
HOW DO YOU *GET* THESE THINGS?
I'M RICH.

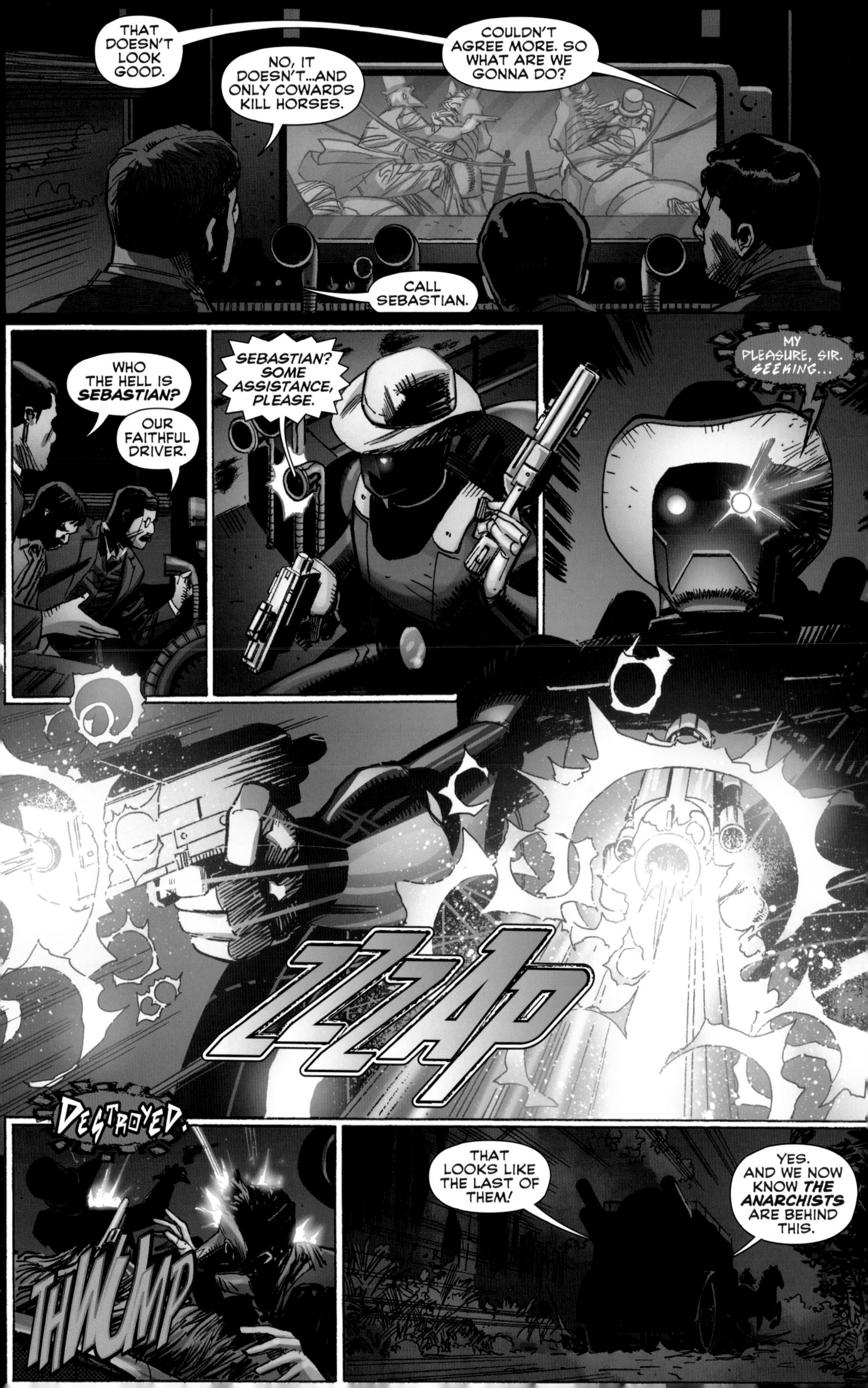
THAT DOESN'T LOOK GOOD.
NO, IT DOESN'T...AND ONLY COWARDS KILL HORSES.
COULDN'T AGREE MORE. SO WHAT ARE WE GONNA DO?
CALL SEBASTIAN.
WHO THE HELL IS SEBASTIAN?
OUR FAITHFUL DRIVER.
SEBASTIAN? SOME ASSISTANCE, PLEASE.
MY PLEASURE, SIR. SEEKING...
ZZZAP
DESTROYED.
THWUMP
THAT LOOKS LIKE THE LAST OF THEM!
YES. AND WE NOW KNOW THE ANARCHISTS ARE BEHIND THIS.

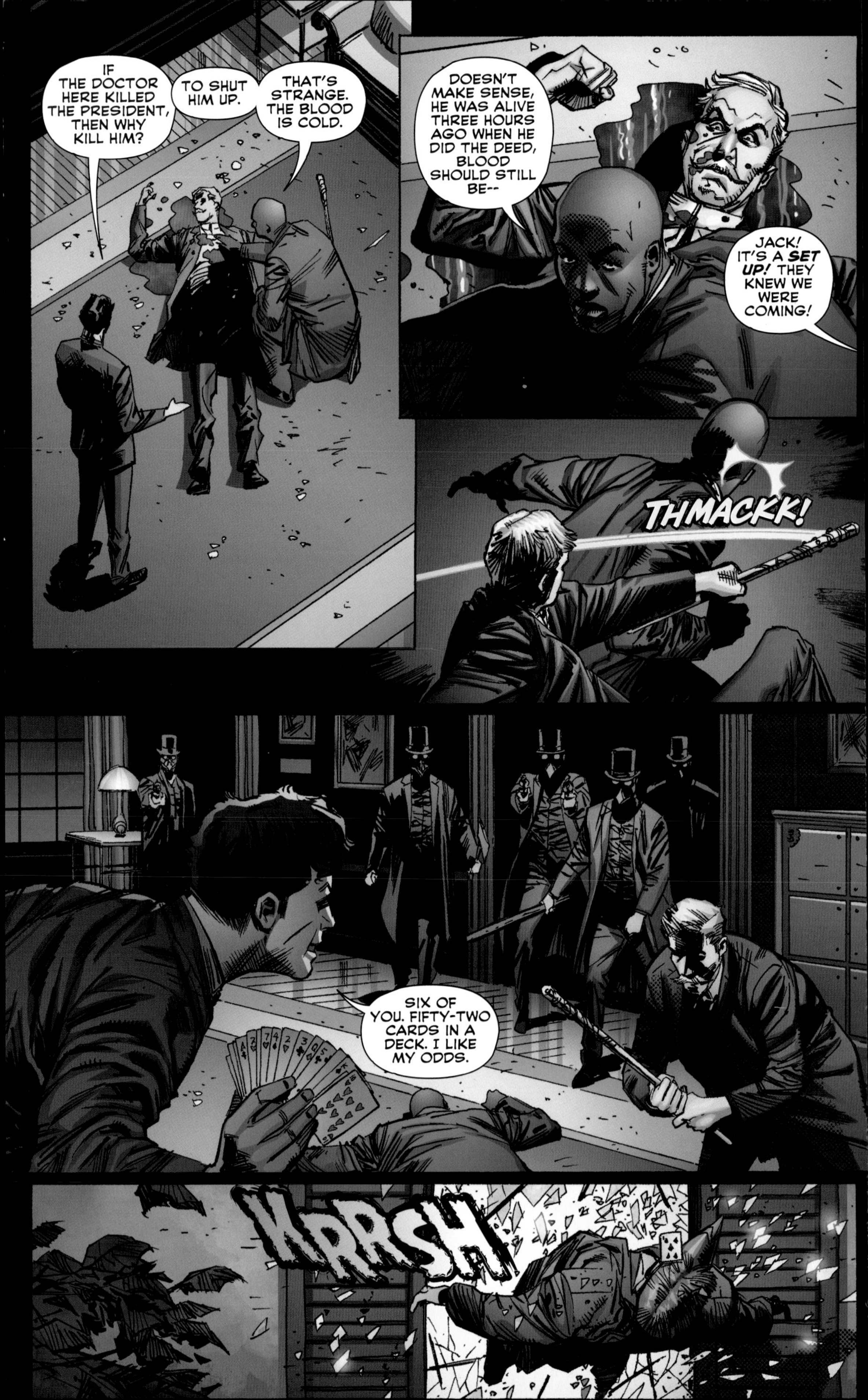

IF THE DOCTOR HERE KILLED THE PRESIDENT, THEN WHY KILL HIM?
TO SHUT HIM UP.
THAT'S STRANGE. THE BLOOD IS COLD.
DOESN'T MAKE SENSE, HE WAS ALIVE THREE HOURS AGO WHEN HE DID THE DEED, BLOOD SHOULD STILL BE--
JACK! IT'S A **SET UP!** THEY KNEW WE WERE COMING!
THMACKK!
SIX OF YOU. FIFTY-TWO CARDS IN A DECK. I LIKE MY ODDS.
KRRSH

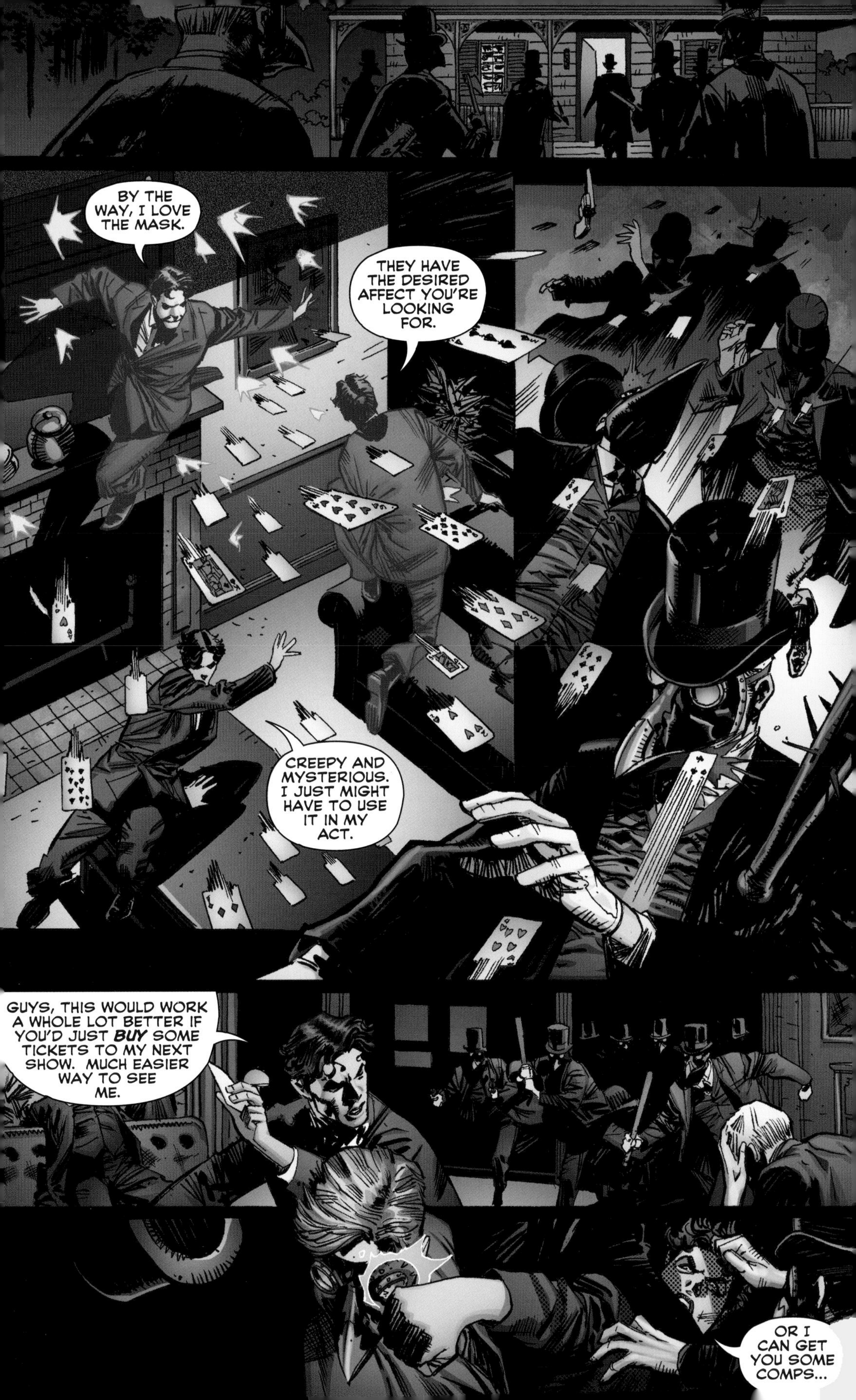
BY THE WAY, I LOVE THE MASK.
THEY HAVE THE DESIRED AFFECT YOU'RE LOOKING FOR.
CREEPY AND MYSTERIOUS. I JUST MIGHT HAVE TO USE IT IN MY ACT.
GUYS, THIS WOULD WORK A WHOLE LOT BETTER IF YOU'D JUST *BUY* SOME TICKETS TO MY NEXT SHOW. MUCH EASIER WAY TO SEE ME.
OR I CAN GET YOU SOME COMPS...

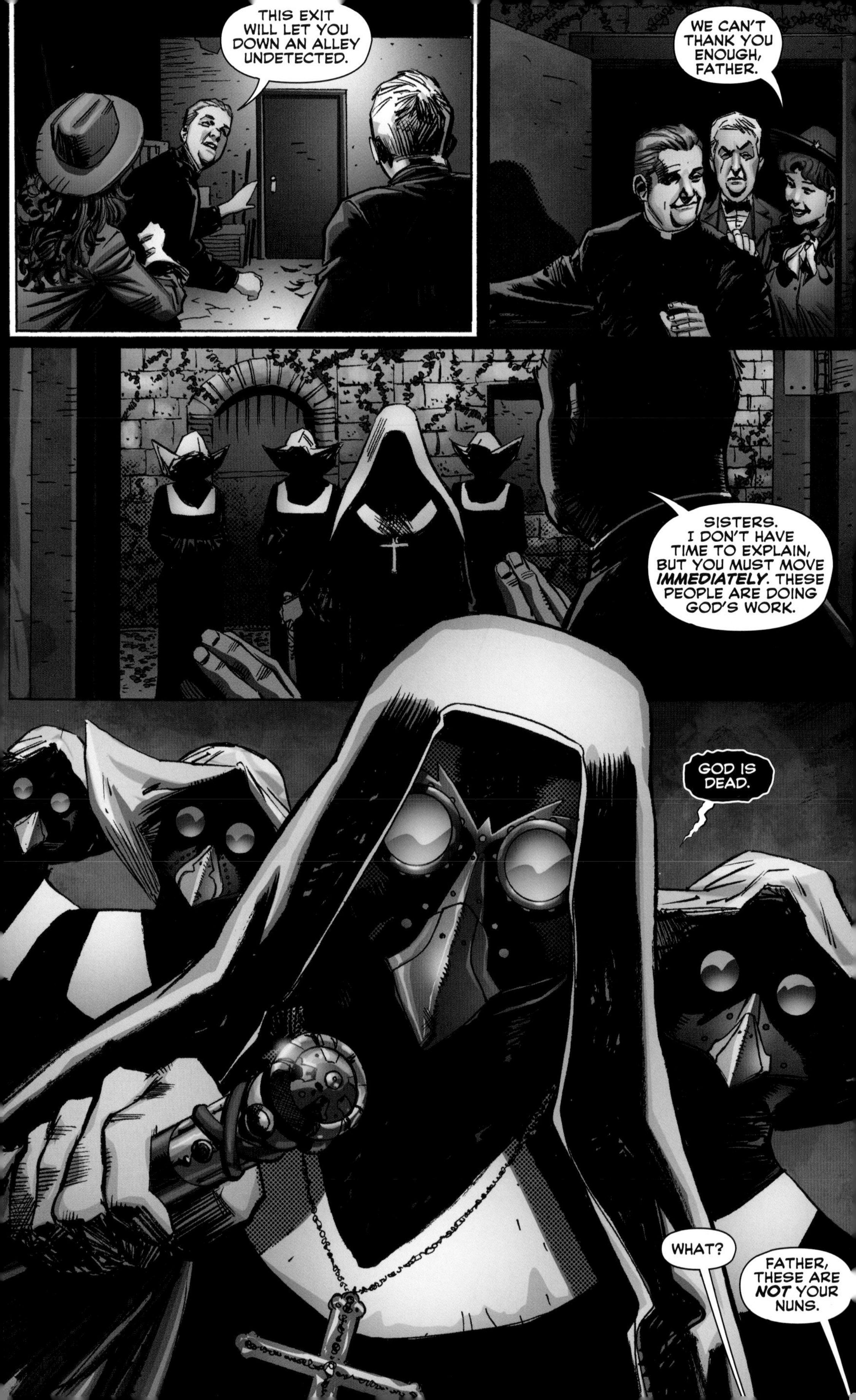
THIS EXIT WILL LET YOU DOWN AN ALLEY UNDETECTED.
WE CAN'T THANK YOU ENOUGH, FATHER.
SISTERS. I DON'T HAVE TIME TO EXPLAIN, BUT YOU MUST MOVE *IMMEDIATELY*. THESE PEOPLE ARE DOING GOD'S WORK.
GOD IS DEAD.
WHAT?
FATHER, THESE ARE *NOT* YOUR NUNS.

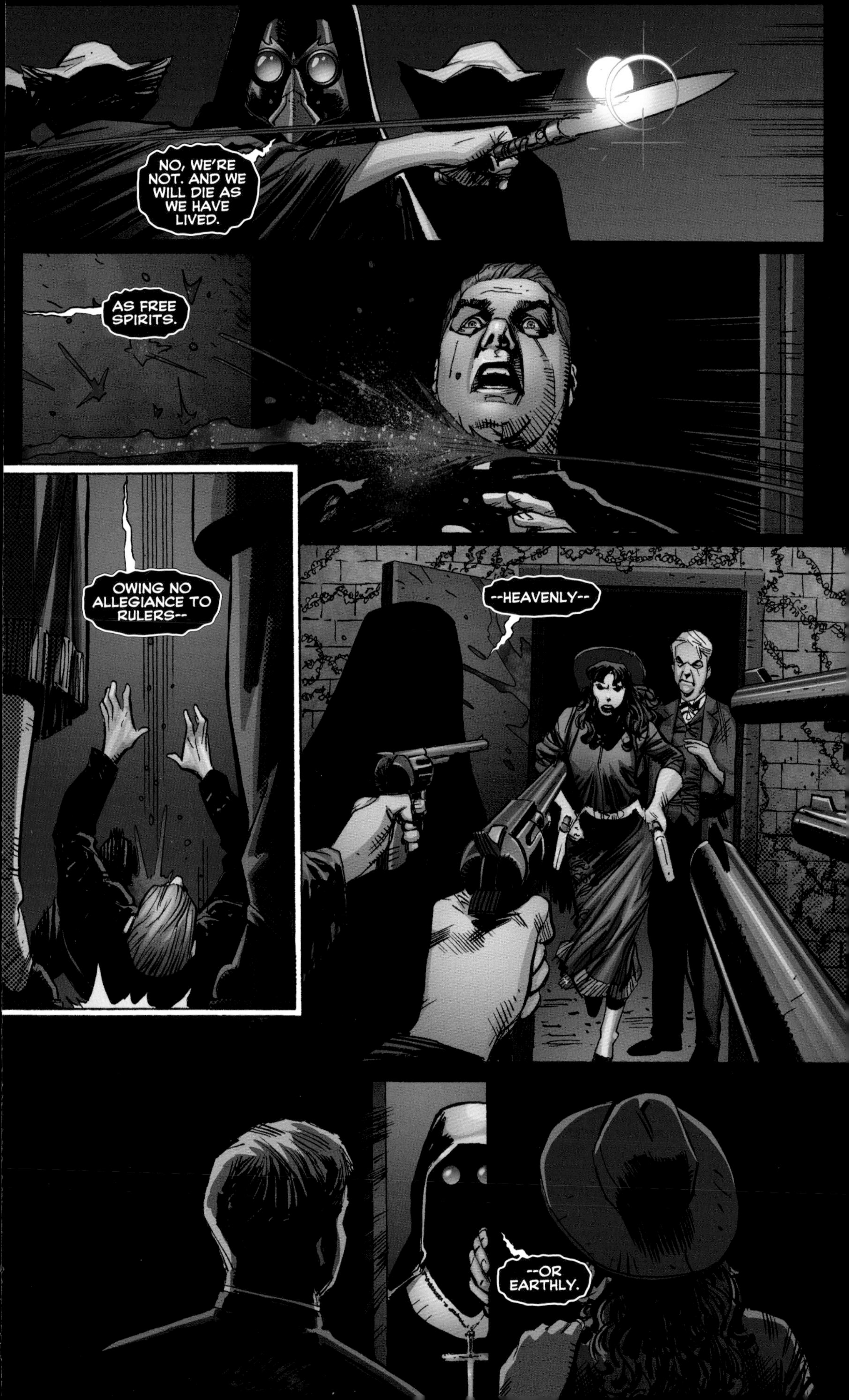
NO, WE'RE NOT. AND WE WILL DIE AS WE HAVE LIVED.
AS FREE SPIRITS.
OWING NO ALLEGIANCE TO RULERS--
--HEAVENLY--
--OR EARTHLY.

YOU CANNOT BUY THE REVOLUTION.
YOU CANNOT MAKE THE REVOLUTION.
YOU CAN ONLY...
...BE...
...THE REVOLUTION!
TO BE CONTINUED!

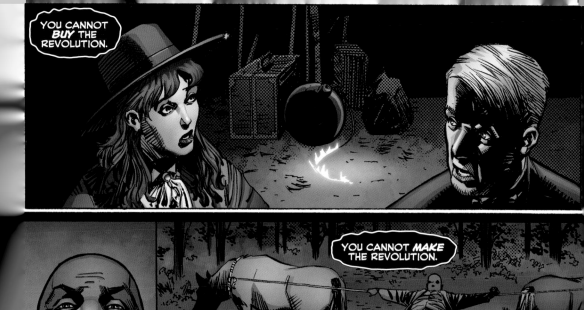

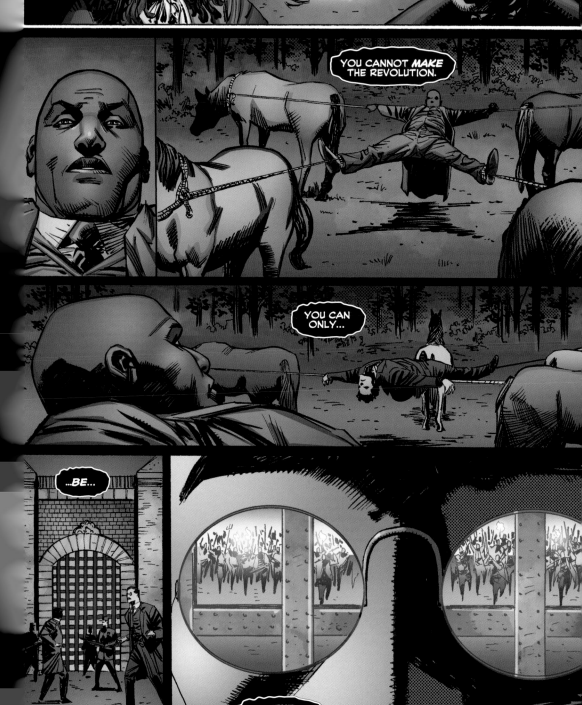

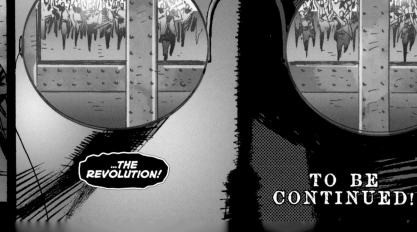

11

"KNOW YOUR ENEMIES"

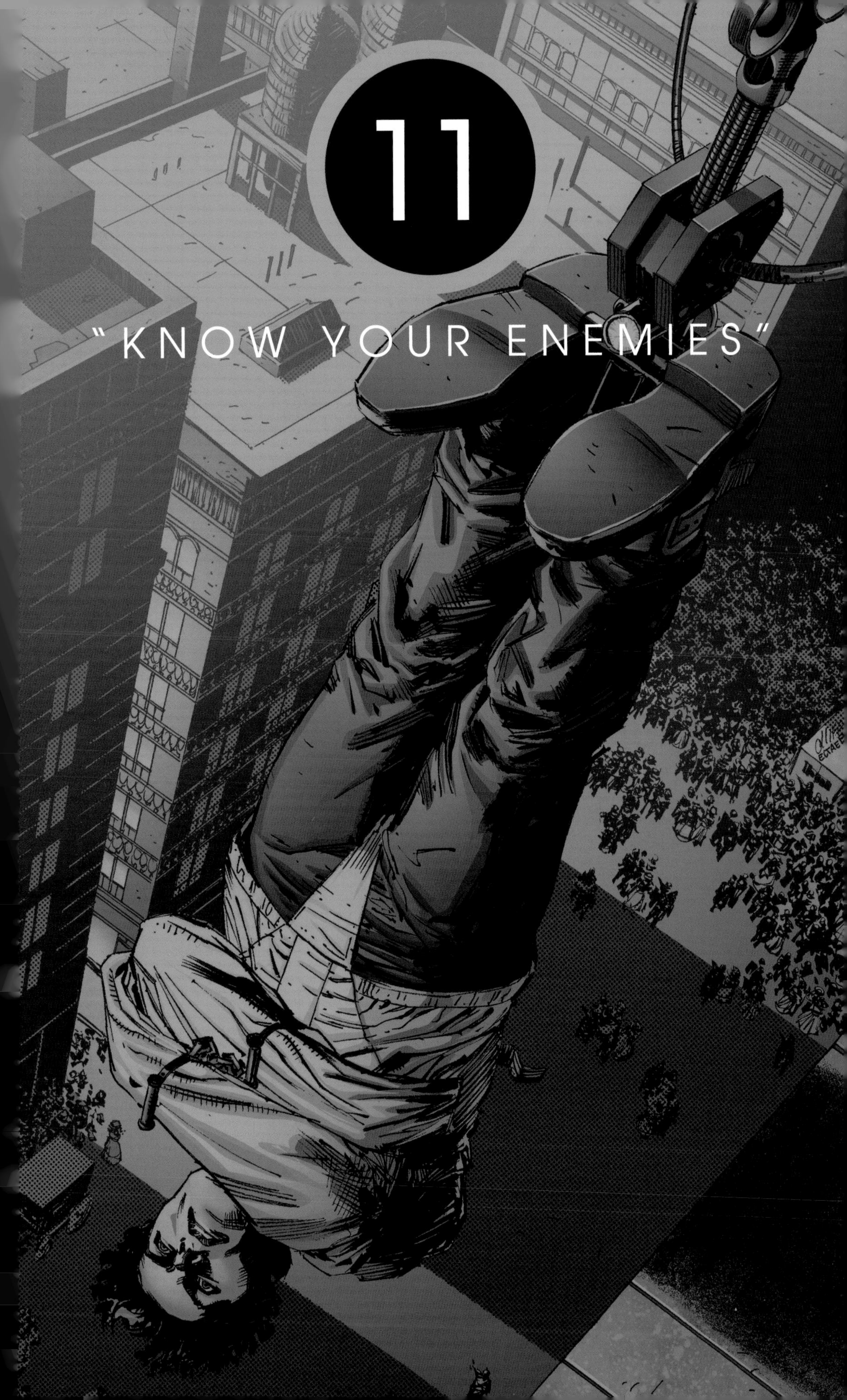

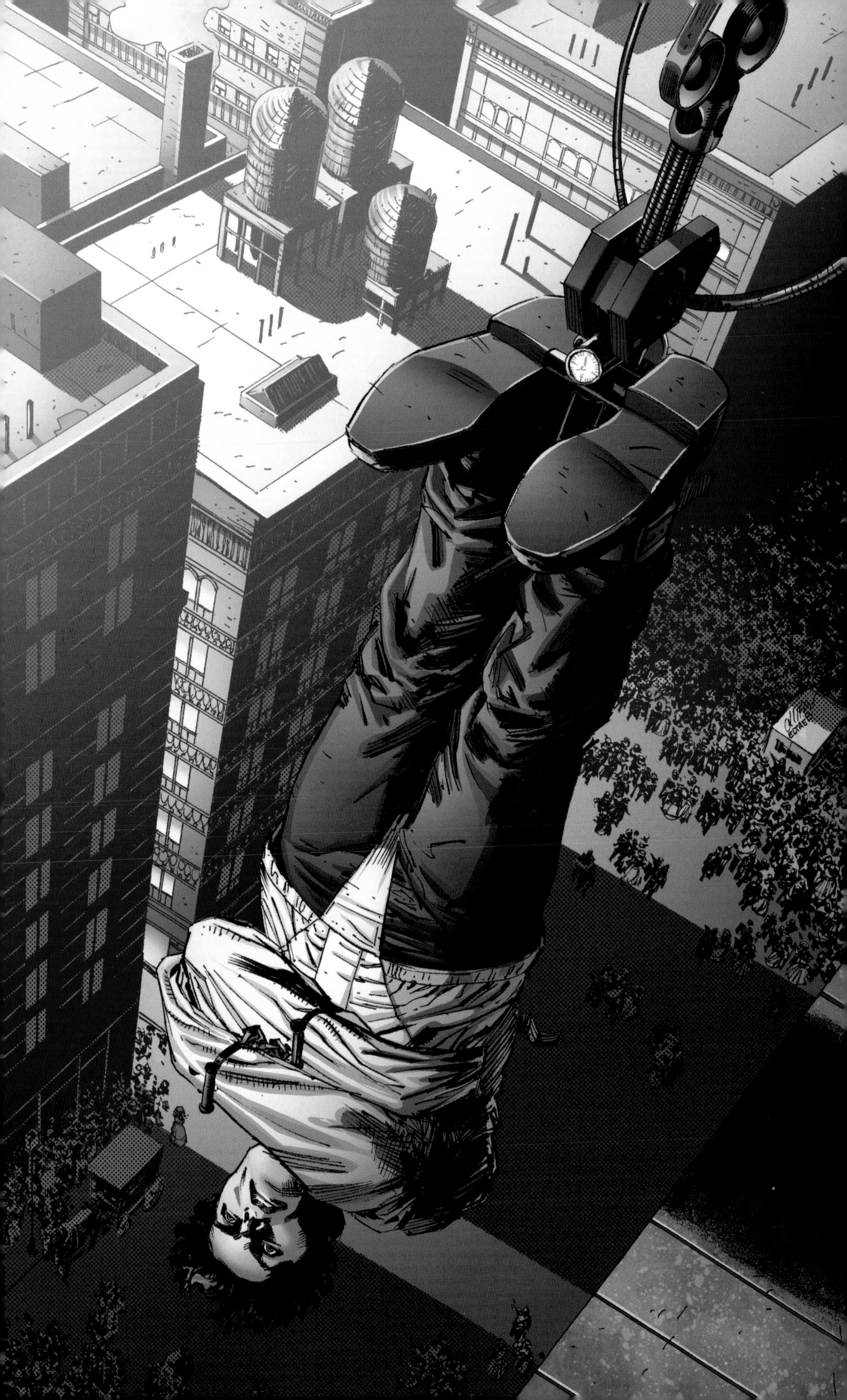

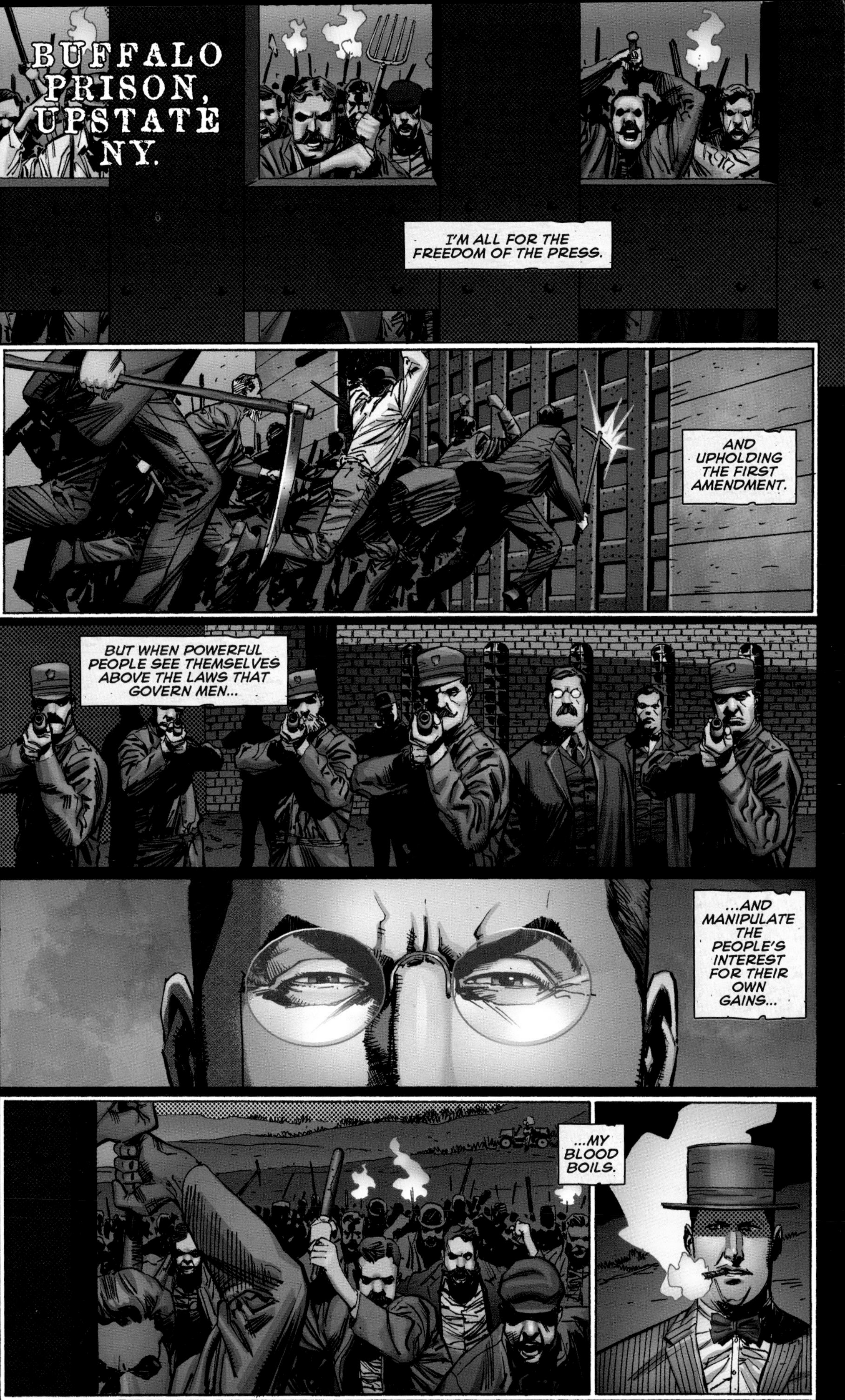
BUFFALO PRISON, UPSTATE NY.
I'M ALL FOR THE FREEDOM OF THE PRESS.
AND UPHOLDING THE FIRST AMENDMENT.
BUT WHEN POWERFUL PEOPLE SEE THEMSELVES ABOVE THE LAWS THAT GOVERN MEN...
...AND MANIPULATE THE PEOPLE'S INTEREST FOR THEIR OWN GAINS...
...MY BLOOD BOILS.

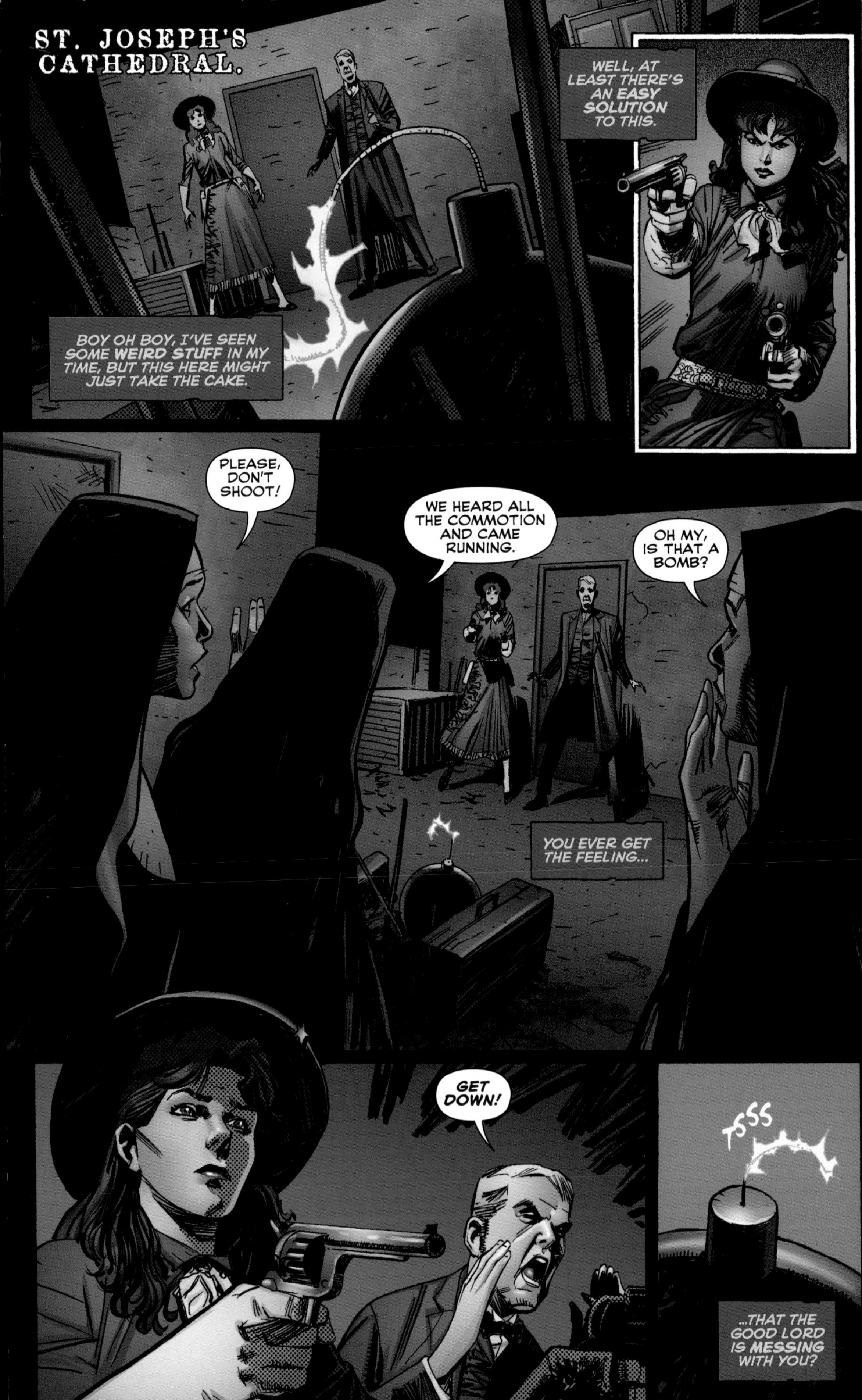

ST. JOSEPH'S CATHEDRAL.
BOY OH BOY, I'VE SEEN SOME WEIRD STUFF IN MY TIME, BUT THIS HERE MIGHT JUST TAKE THE CAKE.
WELL, AT LEAST THERE'S AN EASY SOLUTION TO THIS.
PLEASE, DON'T SHOOT!
WE HEARD ALL THE COMMOTION AND CAME RUNNING.
OH MY, IS THAT A BOMB?
YOU EVER GET THE FEELING...
GET DOWN!
TSSS
...THAT THE GOOD LORD IS MESSING WITH YOU?

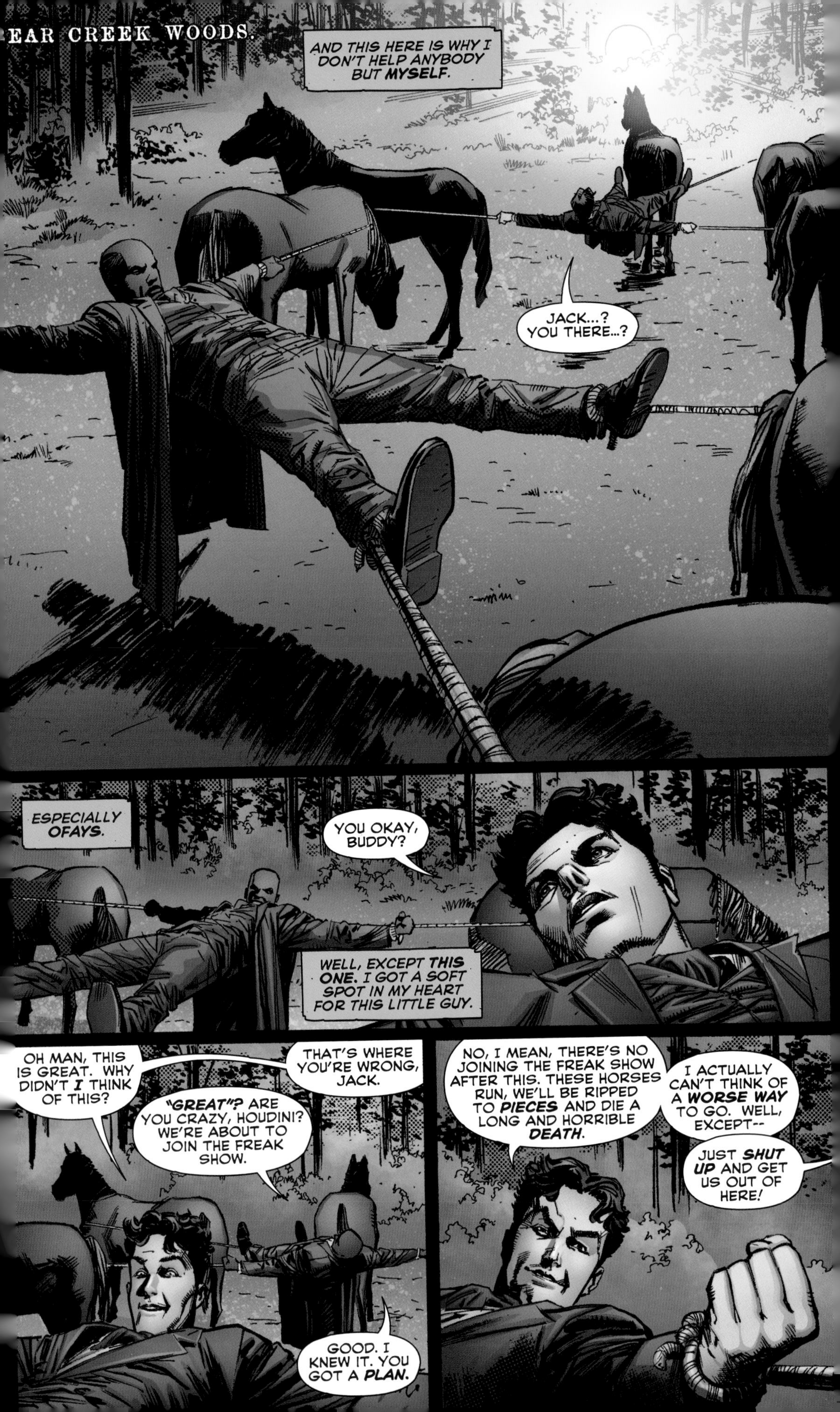
EAR CREEK WOODS.
AND THIS HERE IS WHY I DON'T HELP ANYBODY BUT MYSELF.
JACK...? YOU THERE...?
ESPECIALLY OFAYS.
YOU OKAY, BUDDY?
WELL, EXCEPT THIS ONE. I GOT A SOFT SPOT IN MY HEART FOR THIS LITTLE GUY.
OH MAN, THIS IS GREAT. WHY DIDN'T I THINK OF THIS?
"GREAT"? ARE YOU CRAZY, HOUDINI? WE'RE ABOUT TO JOIN THE FREAK SHOW.
GOOD. I KNEW IT. YOU GOT A PLAN.
THAT'S WHERE YOU'RE WRONG, JACK.
NO, I MEAN, THERE'S NO JOINING THE FREAK SHOW AFTER THIS. THESE HORSES RUN, WE'LL BE RIPPED TO PIECES AND DIE A LONG AND HORRIBLE DEATH.
I ACTUALLY CAN'T THINK OF A WORSE WAY TO GO. WELL, EXCEPT--
JUST SHUT UP AND GET US OUT OF HERE!

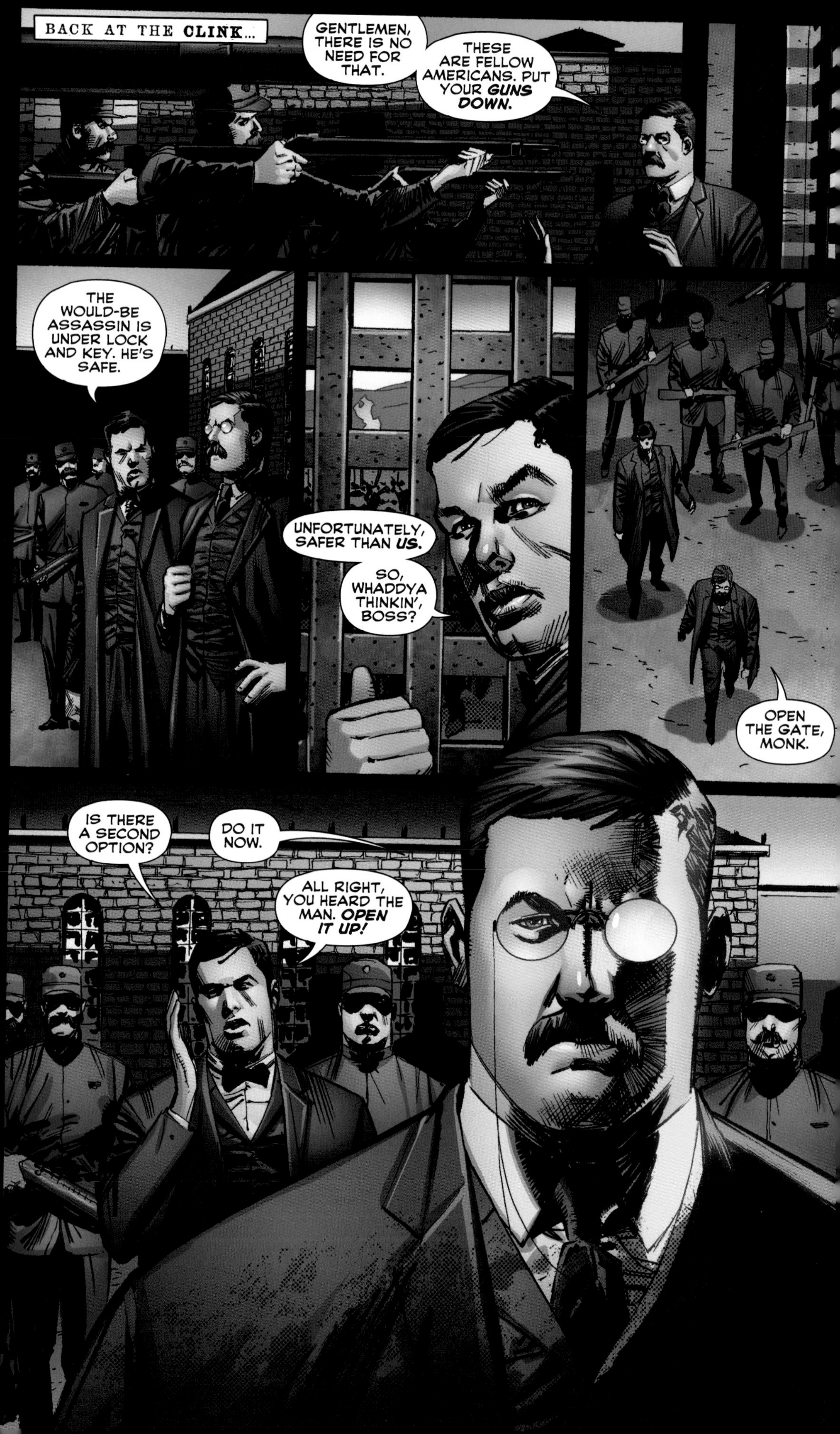
BACK AT THE CLINK...
GENTLEMEN, THERE IS NO NEED FOR THAT.
THESE ARE FELLOW AMERICANS. PUT YOUR GUNS DOWN.
THE WOULD-BE ASSASSIN IS UNDER LOCK AND KEY. HE'S SAFE.
UNFORTUNATELY, SAFER THAN US.
SO, WHADDYA THINKIN', BOSS?
OPEN THE GATE, MONK.
IS THERE A SECOND OPTION?
DO IT NOW.
ALL RIGHT, YOU HEARD THE MAN. OPEN IT UP!

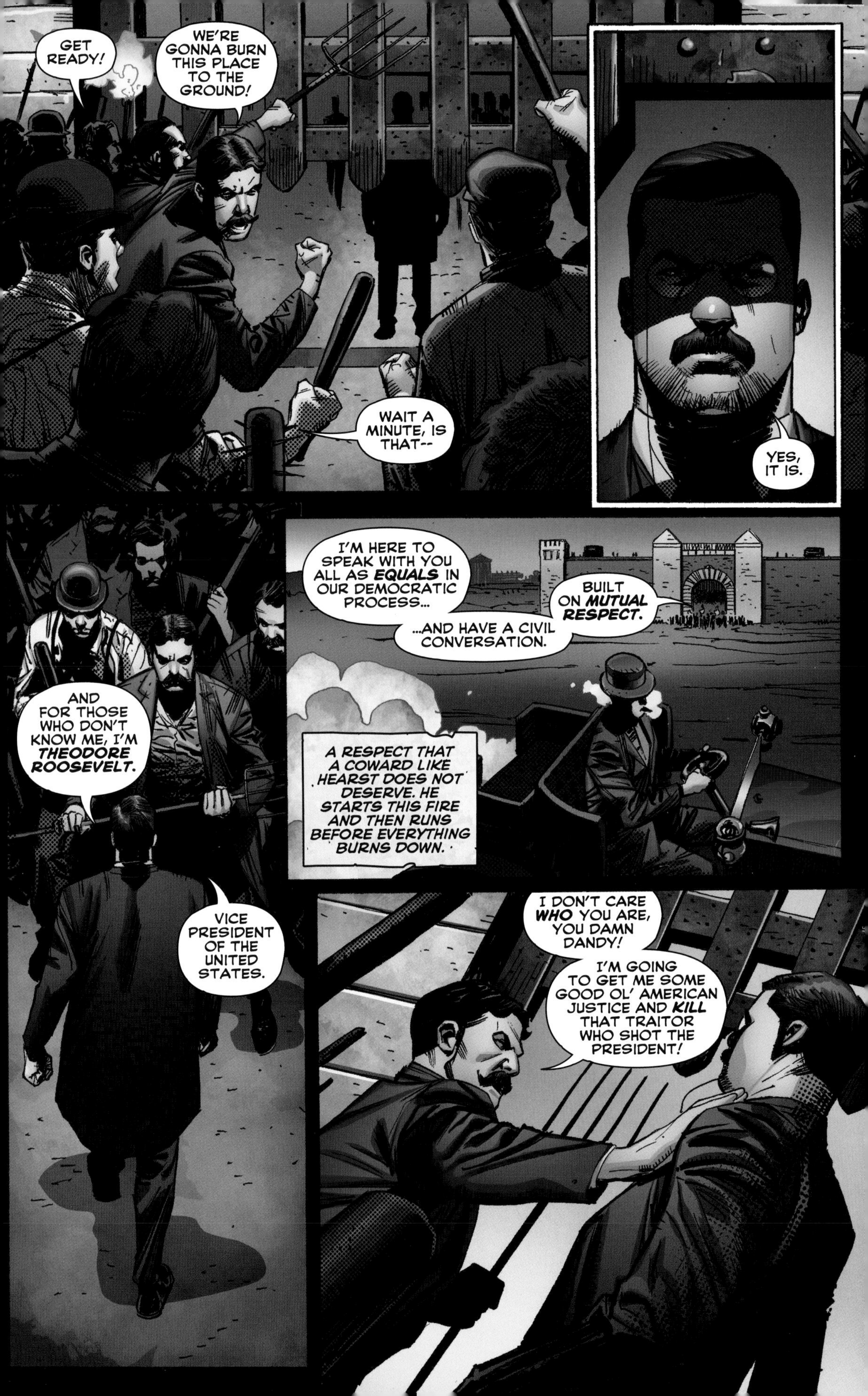
GET READY!
WE'RE GONNA BURN THIS PLACE TO THE GROUND!
WAIT A MINUTE, IS THAT--
YES, IT IS.
AND FOR THOSE WHO DON'T KNOW ME, I'M **THEODORE ROOSEVELT.**
VICE PRESIDENT OF THE UNITED STATES.
I'M HERE TO SPEAK WITH YOU ALL AS **EQUALS** IN OUR DEMOCRATIC PROCESS...
...AND HAVE A CIVIL CONVERSATION.
BUILT ON **MUTUAL RESPECT.**
A RESPECT THAT A COWARD LIKE HEARST DOES NOT DESERVE. HE STARTS THIS FIRE AND THEN RUNS BEFORE EVERYTHING BURNS DOWN.
I DON'T CARE **WHO** YOU ARE, YOU DAMN DANDY!
I'M GOING TO GET ME SOME GOOD OL' AMERICAN JUSTICE AND **KILL** THAT TRAITOR WHO SHOT THE PRESIDENT!

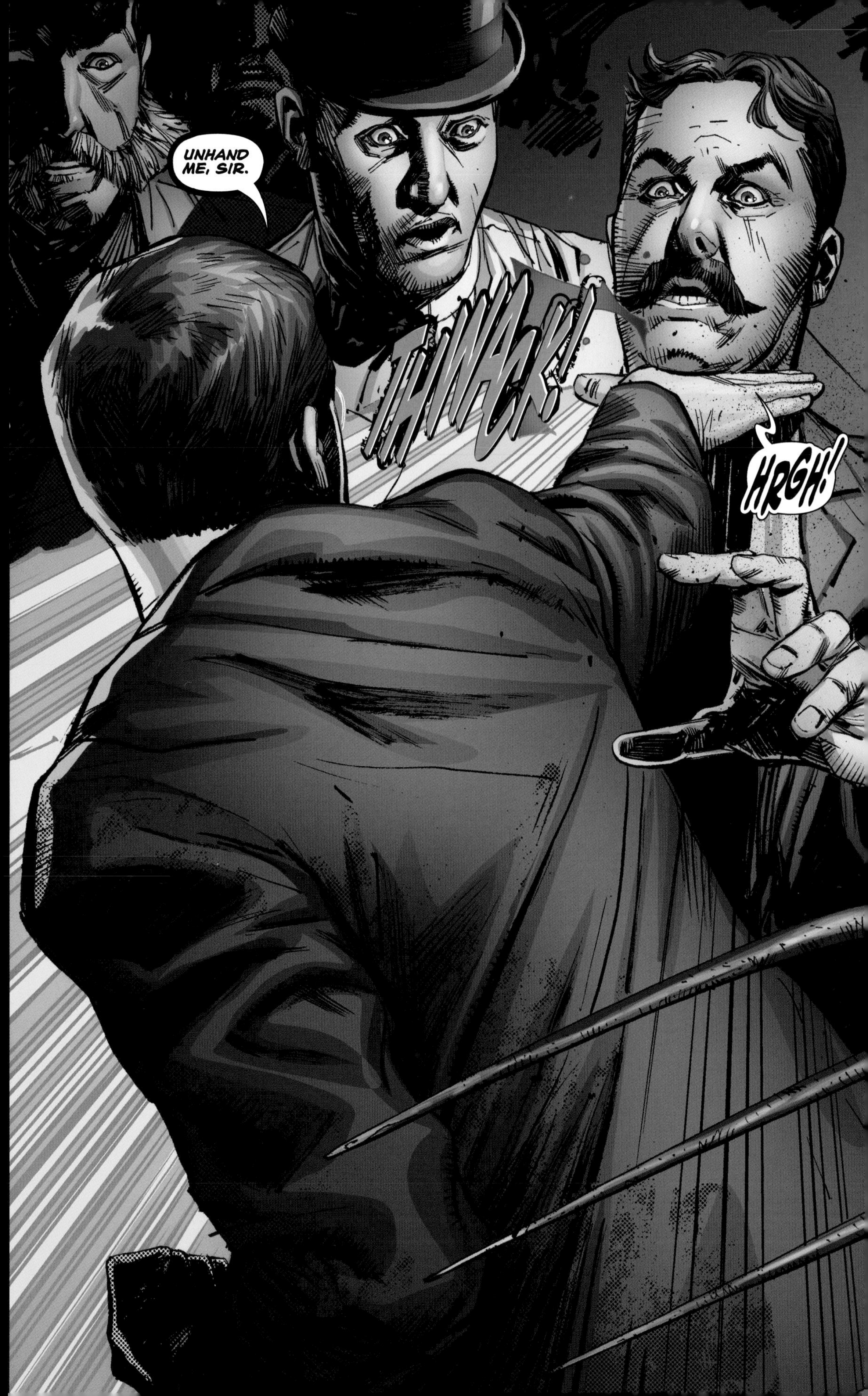
UNHAND ME, SIR.
THWACK!
HRGH!

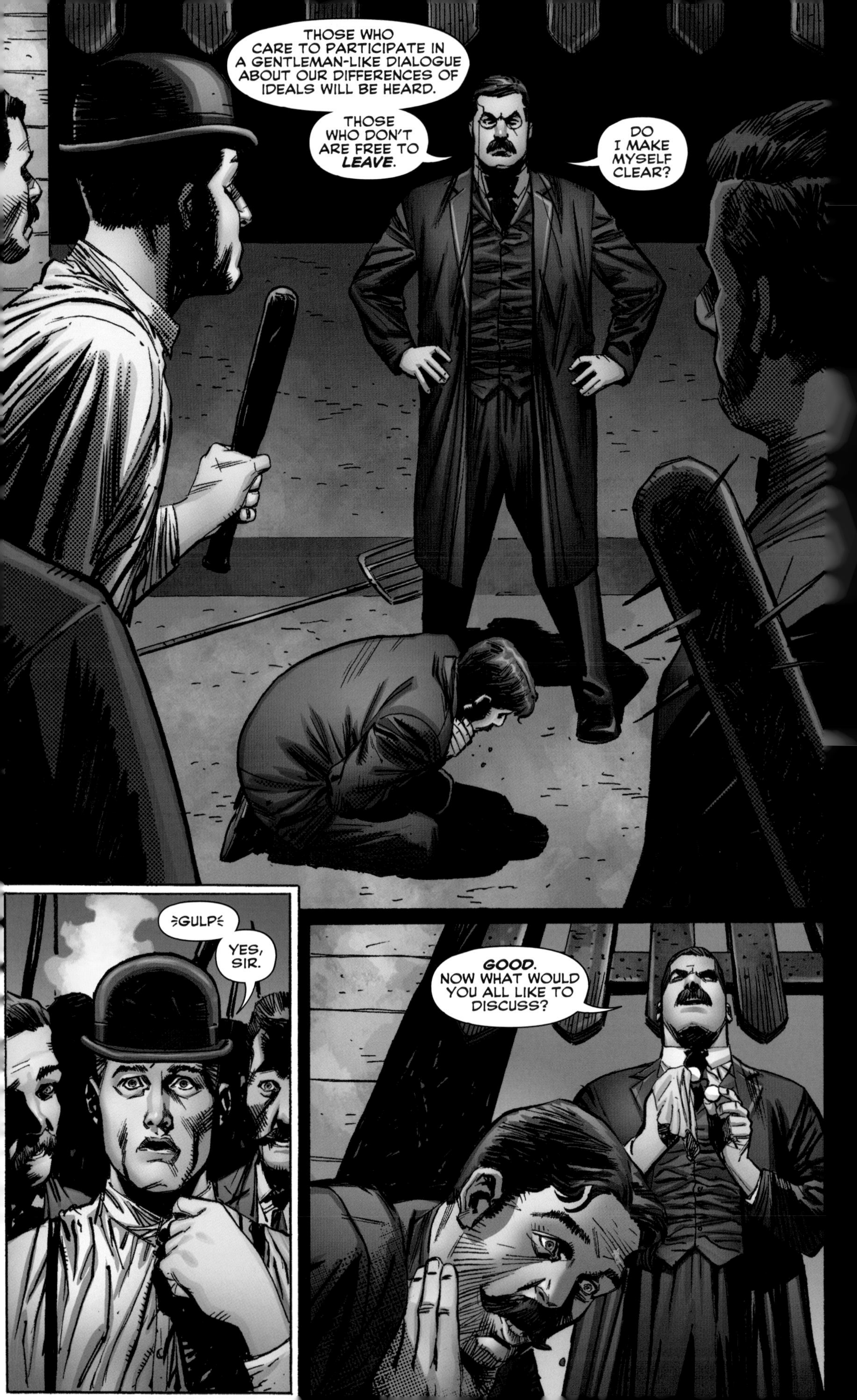
THOSE WHO CARE TO PARTICIPATE IN A GENTLEMAN-LIKE DIALOGUE ABOUT OUR DIFFERENCES OF IDEALS WILL BE HEARD.
THOSE WHO DON'T ARE FREE TO *LEAVE*.
DO I MAKE MYSELF CLEAR?
GULP
YES, SIR.
GOOD. NOW WHAT WOULD YOU ALL LIKE TO DISCUSS?

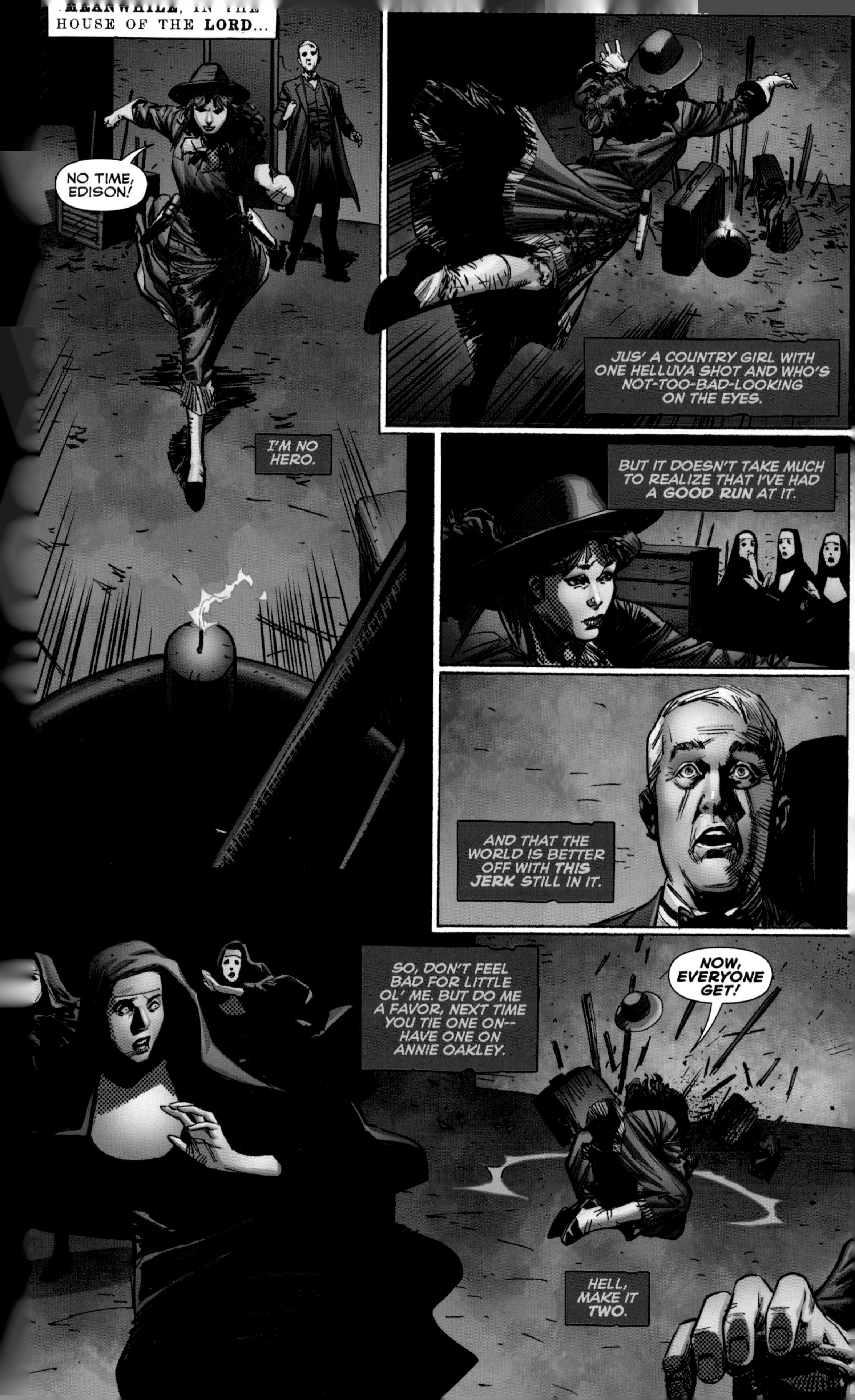
MEANWHILE, IN THE HOUSE OF THE LORD...
NO TIME, EDISON!
JUS' A COUNTRY GIRL WITH ONE HELLUVA SHOT AND WHO'S NOT-TOO-BAD-LOOKING ON THE EYES.
I'M NO HERO.
BUT IT DOESN'T TAKE MUCH TO REALIZE THAT I'VE HAD A GOOD RUN AT IT.
AND THAT THE WORLD IS BETTER OFF WITH THIS JERK STILL IN IT.
SO, DON'T FEEL BAD FOR LITTLE OL' ME. BUT DO ME A FAVOR, NEXT TIME YOU TIE ONE ON-- HAVE ONE ON ANNIE OAKLEY.
NOW, EVERYONE GET!
HELL, MAKE IT TWO.

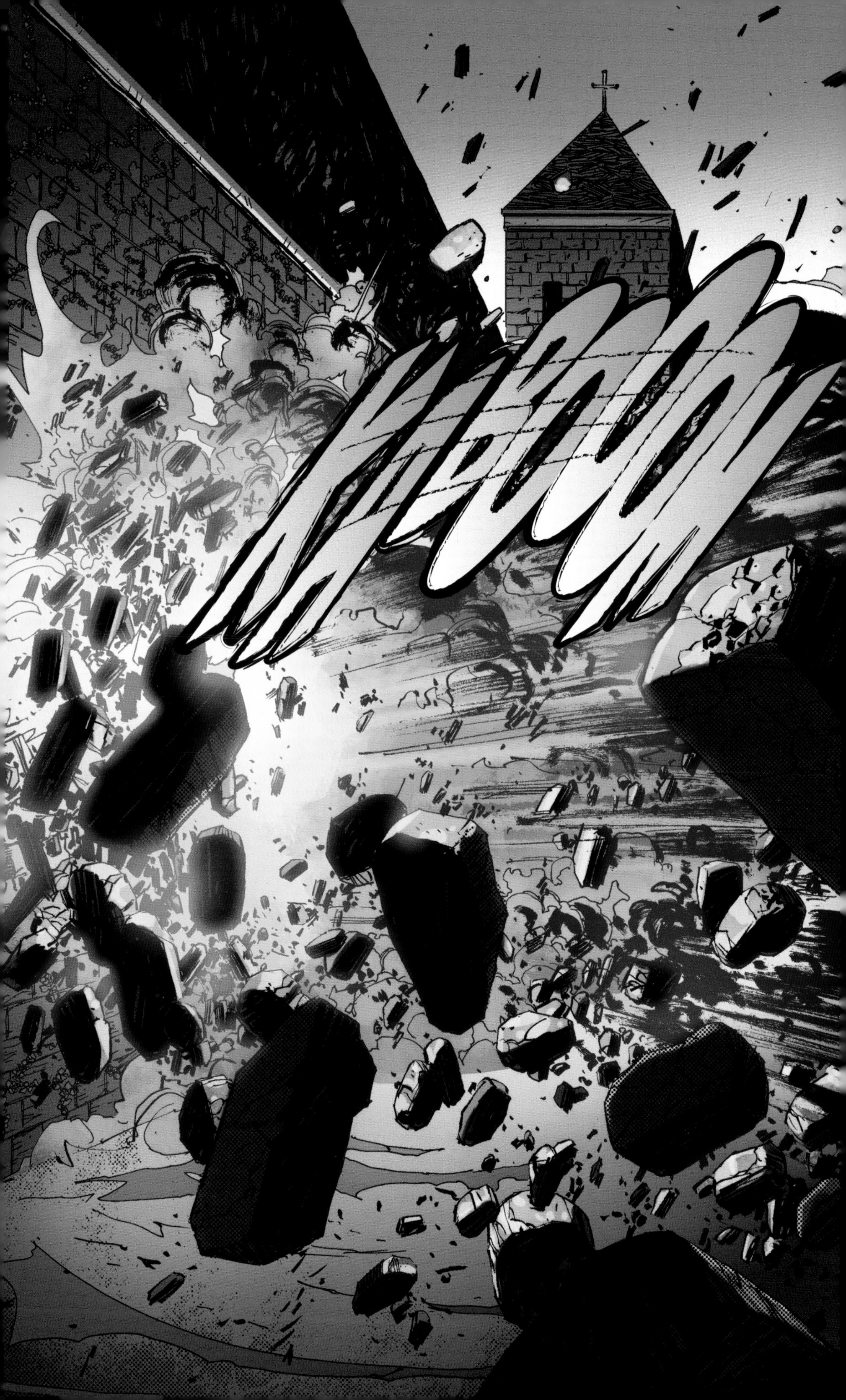

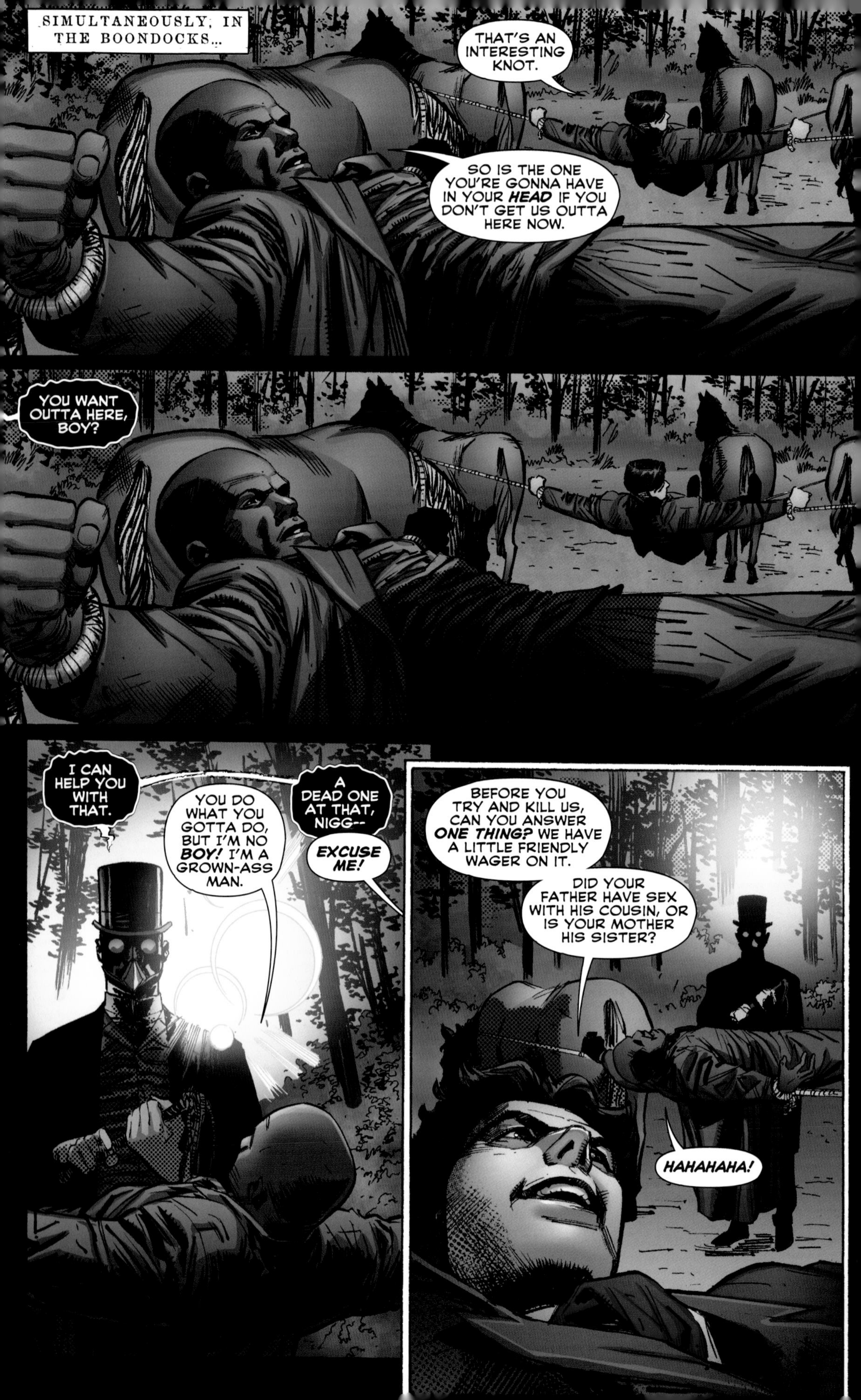
SIMULTANEOUSLY, IN THE BOONDOCKS...
THAT'S AN INTERESTING KNOT.
SO IS THE ONE YOU'RE GONNA HAVE IN YOUR HEAD IF YOU DON'T GET US OUTTA HERE NOW.
YOU WANT OUTTA HERE, BOY?
I CAN HELP YOU WITH THAT.
YOU DO WHAT YOU GOTTA DO, BUT I'M NO BOY! I'M A GROWN-ASS MAN.
A DEAD ONE AT THAT, NIGG--
EXCUSE ME!
BEFORE YOU TRY AND KILL US, CAN YOU ANSWER ONE THING? WE HAVE A LITTLE FRIENDLY WAGER ON IT.
DID YOUR FATHER HAVE SEX WITH HIS COUSIN, OR IS YOUR MOTHER HIS SISTER?
HAHAHAHA!

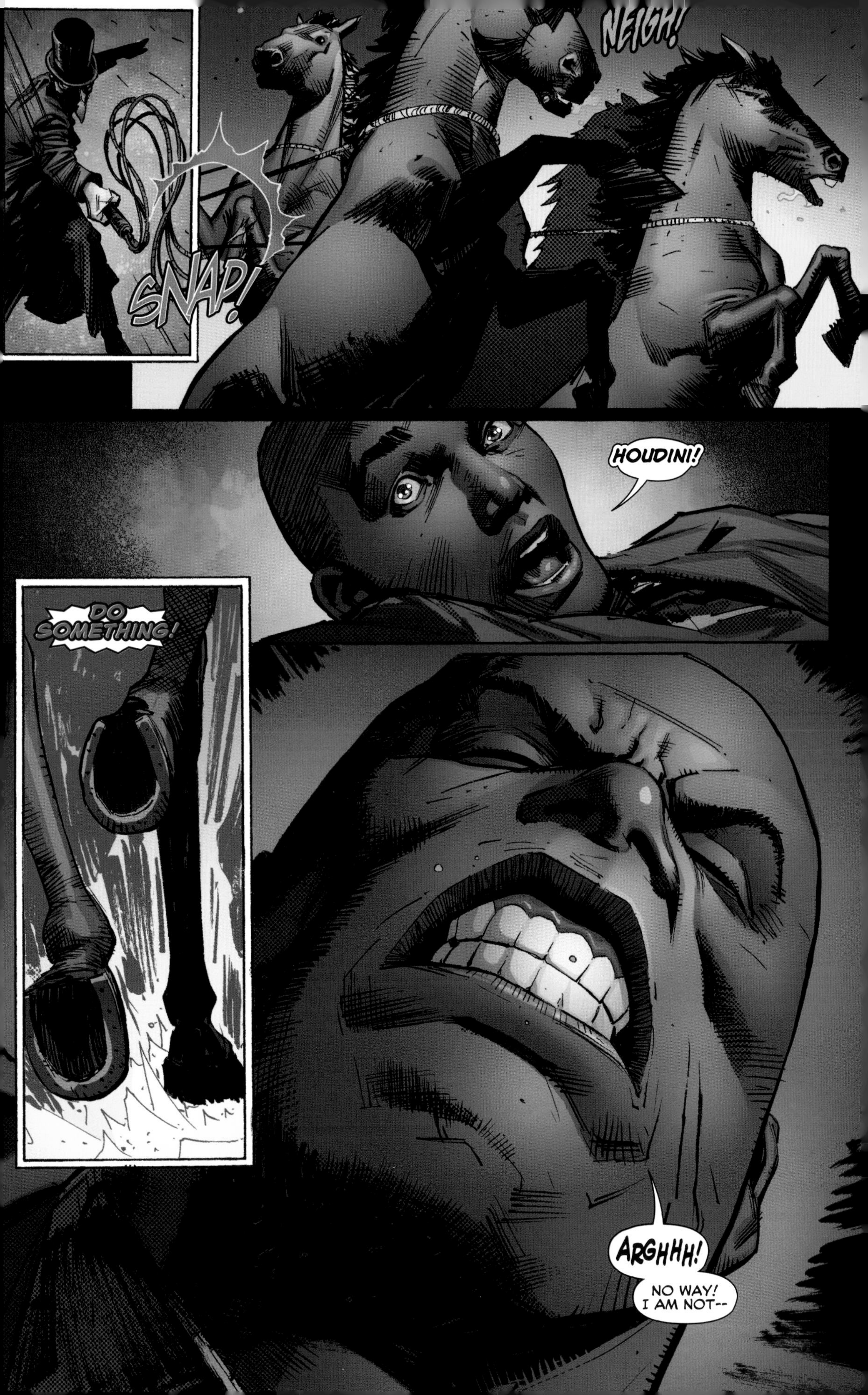
SNAP!
NEIGH!
HOUDINI!
DO SOMETHING!
ARGHHH!
NO WAY! I AM NOT--

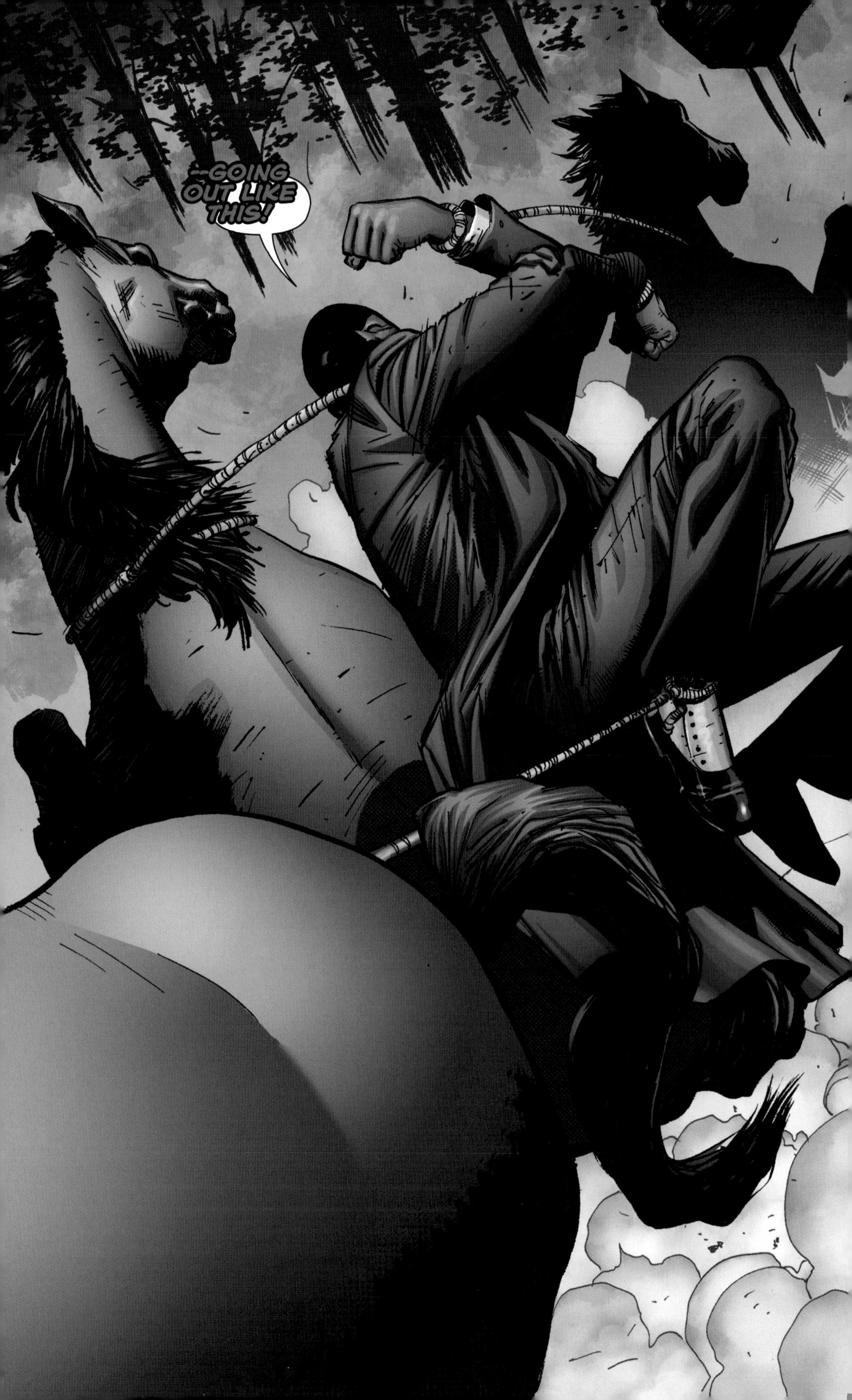
--GOING OUT LIKE THIS!

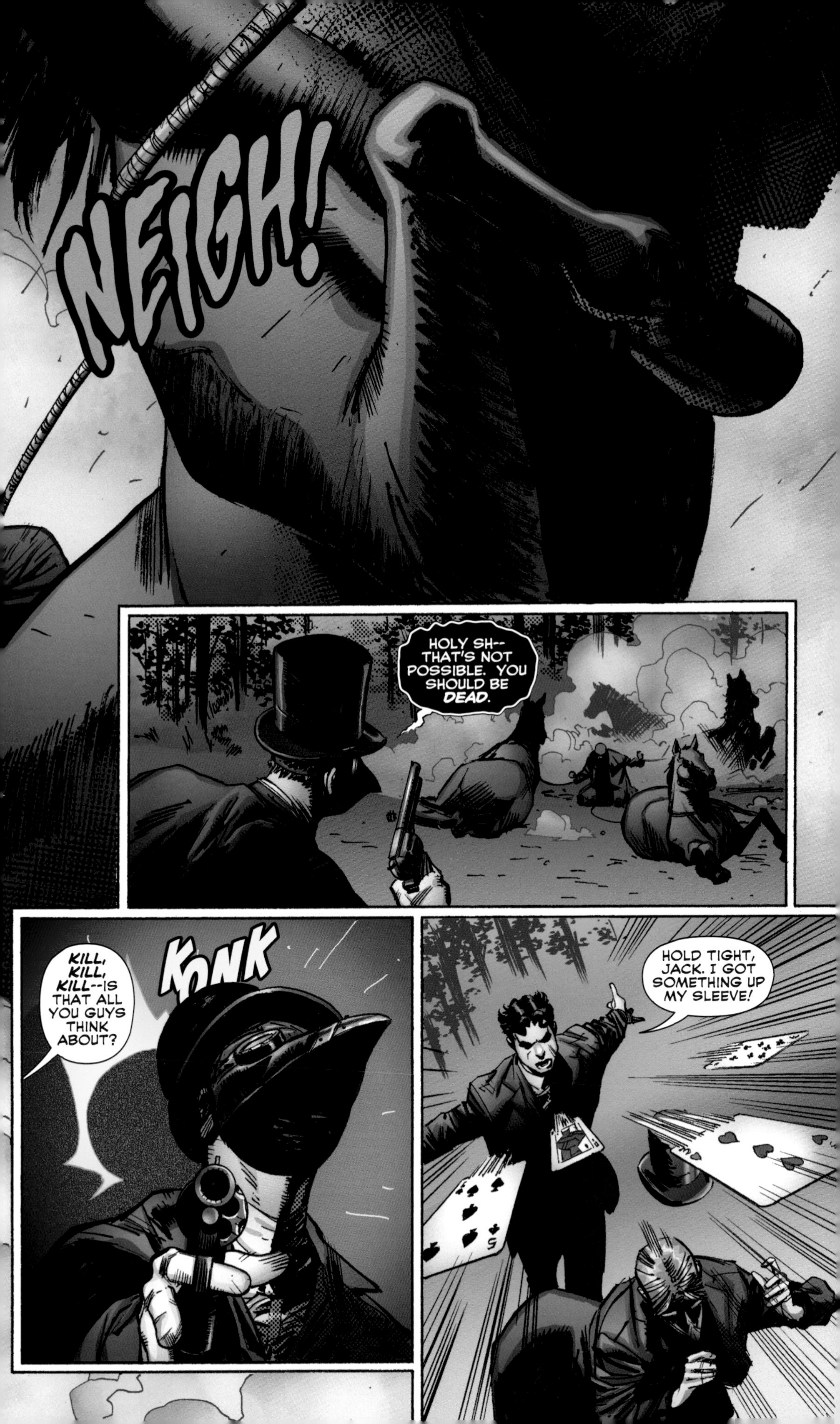
NEIGH!
HOLY SH-- THAT'S NOT POSSIBLE. YOU SHOULD BE DEAD.
KONK
KILL, KILL, KILL--IS THAT ALL YOU GUYS THINK ABOUT?
HOLD TIGHT, JACK. I GOT SOMETHING UP MY SLEEVE!

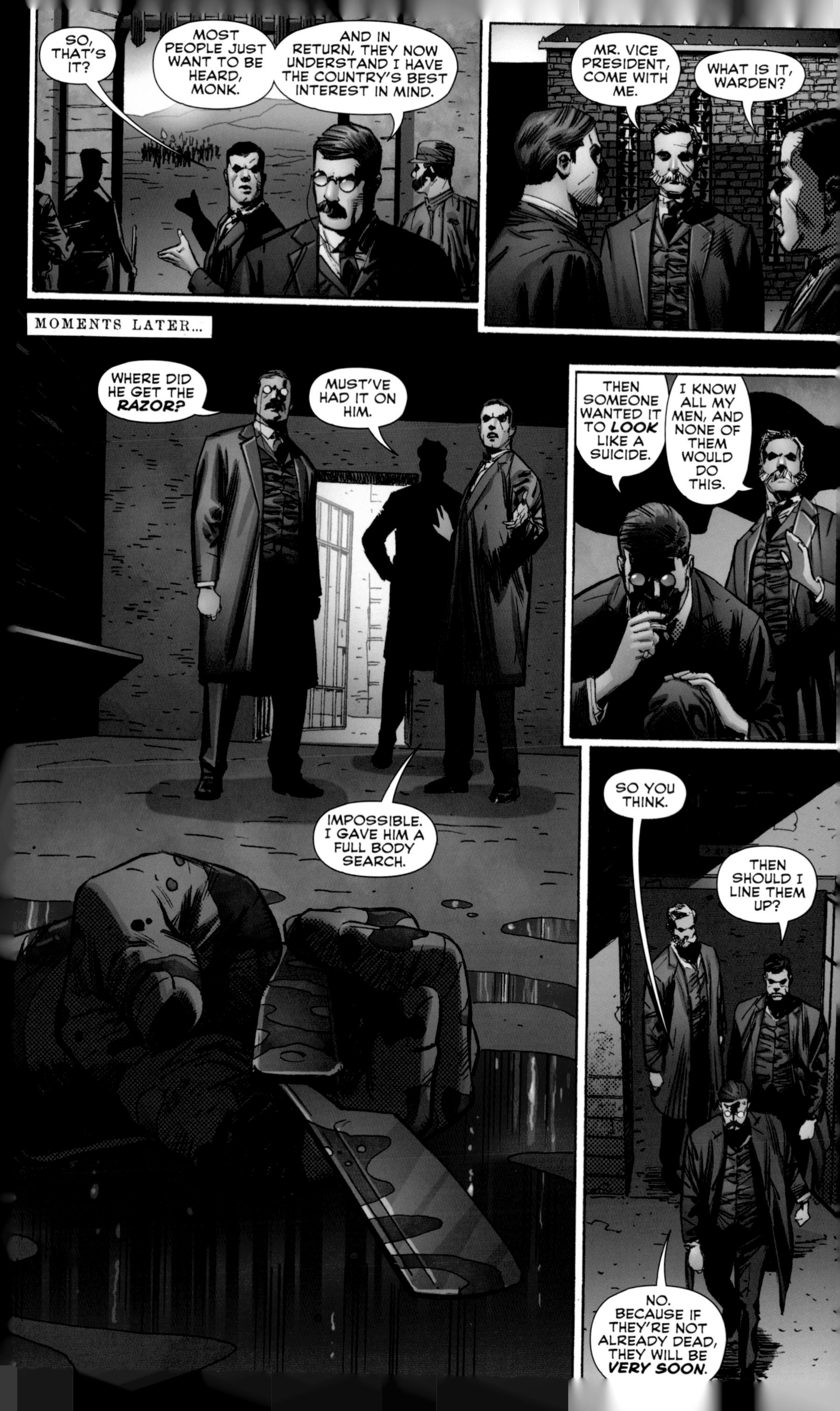
SO, THAT'S IT?
MOST PEOPLE JUST WANT TO BE HEARD, MONK.
AND IN RETURN, THEY NOW UNDERSTAND I HAVE THE COUNTRY'S BEST INTEREST IN MIND.
MR. VICE PRESIDENT, COME WITH ME.
WHAT IS IT, WARDEN?
MOMENTS LATER...
WHERE DID HE GET THE ***RAZOR?***
MUST'VE HAD IT ON HIM.
IMPOSSIBLE. I GAVE HIM A FULL BODY SEARCH.
I KNOW ALL MY MEN, AND NONE OF THEM WOULD DO THIS.
THEN SOMEONE WANTED IT TO ***LOOK*** LIKE A SUICIDE.
SO YOU THINK.
THEN SHOULD I LINE THEM UP?
NO. BECAUSE IF THEY'RE NOT ALREADY DEAD, THEY WILL BE ***VERY SOON.***

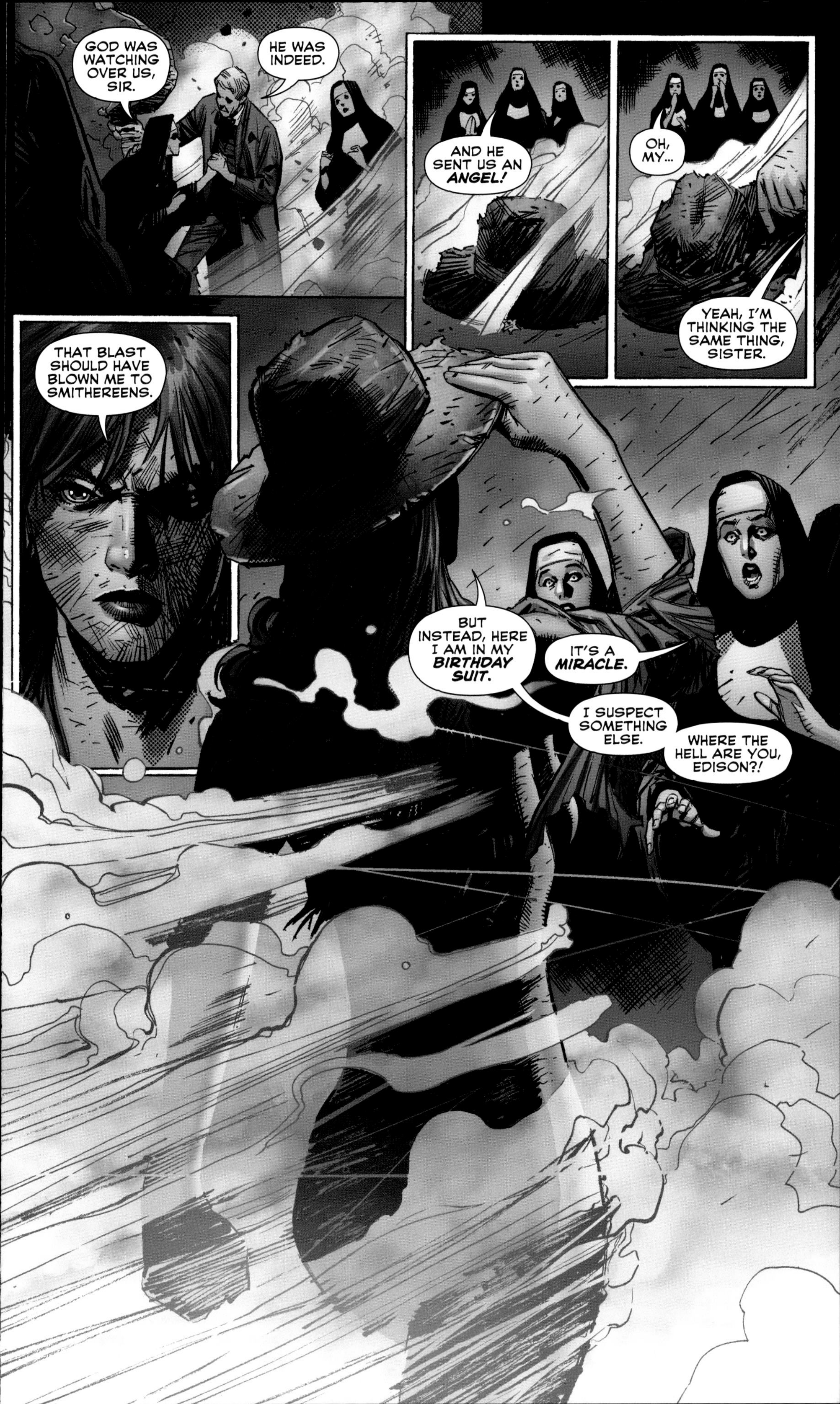
GOD WAS WATCHING OVER US, SIR.
HE WAS INDEED.
AND HE SENT US AN *ANGEL!*
OH, MY...
YEAH, I'M THINKING THE SAME THING, SISTER.
THAT BLAST SHOULD HAVE BLOWN ME TO SMITHEREENS.
BUT INSTEAD, HERE I AM IN MY *BIRTHDAY SUIT*.
IT'S A *MIRACLE*.
I SUSPECT SOMETHING ELSE.
WHERE THE HELL ARE YOU, EDISON?!

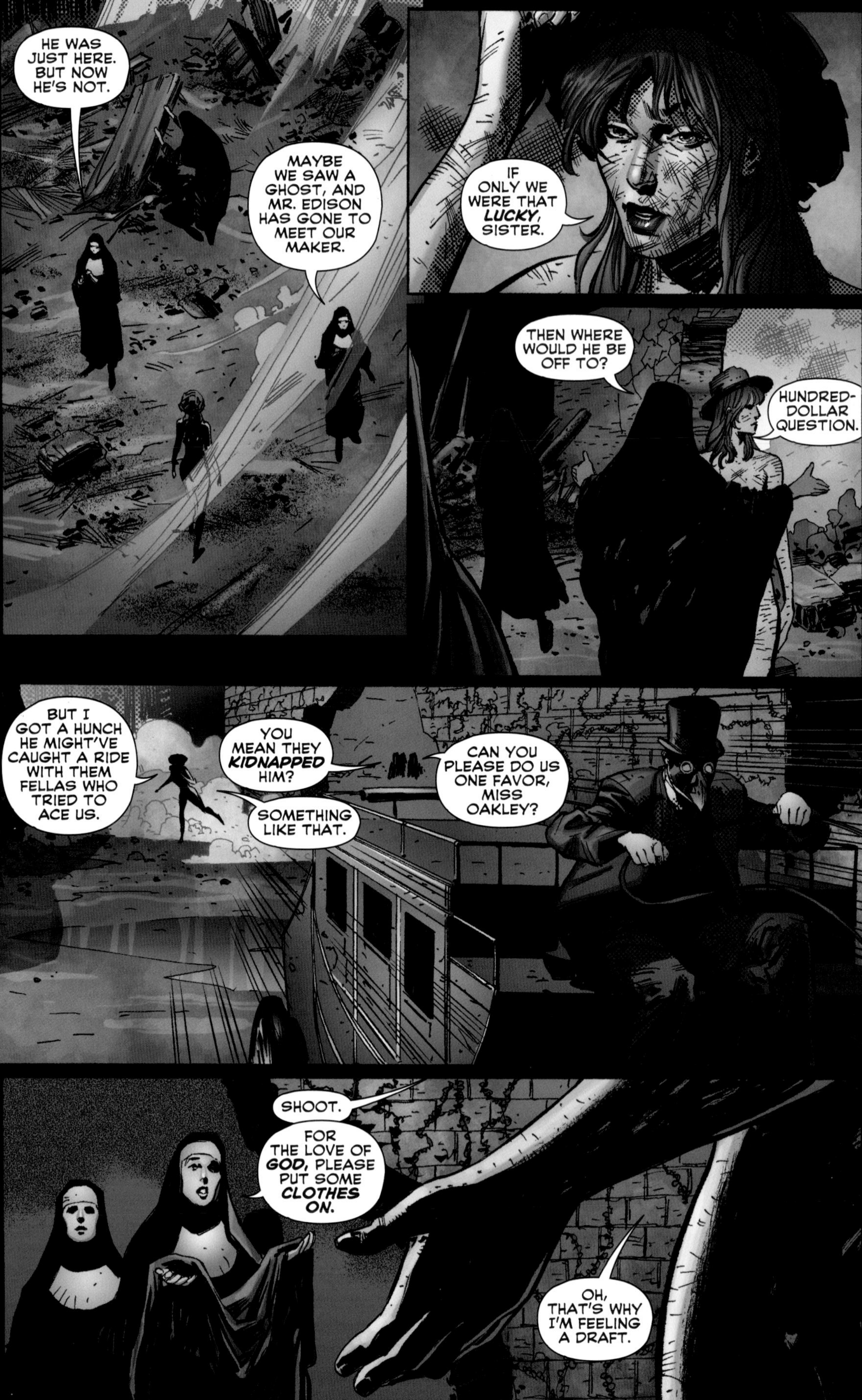
HE WAS JUST HERE. BUT NOW HE'S NOT.
MAYBE WE SAW A GHOST, AND MR. EDISON HAS GONE TO MEET OUR MAKER.
IF ONLY WE WERE THAT LUCKY, SISTER.
THEN WHERE WOULD HE BE OFF TO?
HUNDRED-DOLLAR QUESTION.
BUT I GOT A HUNCH HE MIGHT'VE CAUGHT A RIDE WITH THEM FELLAS WHO TRIED TO ACE US.
YOU MEAN THEY KIDNAPPED HIM?
SOMETHING LIKE THAT.
CAN YOU PLEASE DO US ONE FAVOR, MISS OAKLEY?
SHOOT.
FOR THE LOVE OF GOD, PLEASE PUT SOME CLOTHES ON.
OH, THAT'S WHY I'M FEELING A DRAFT.

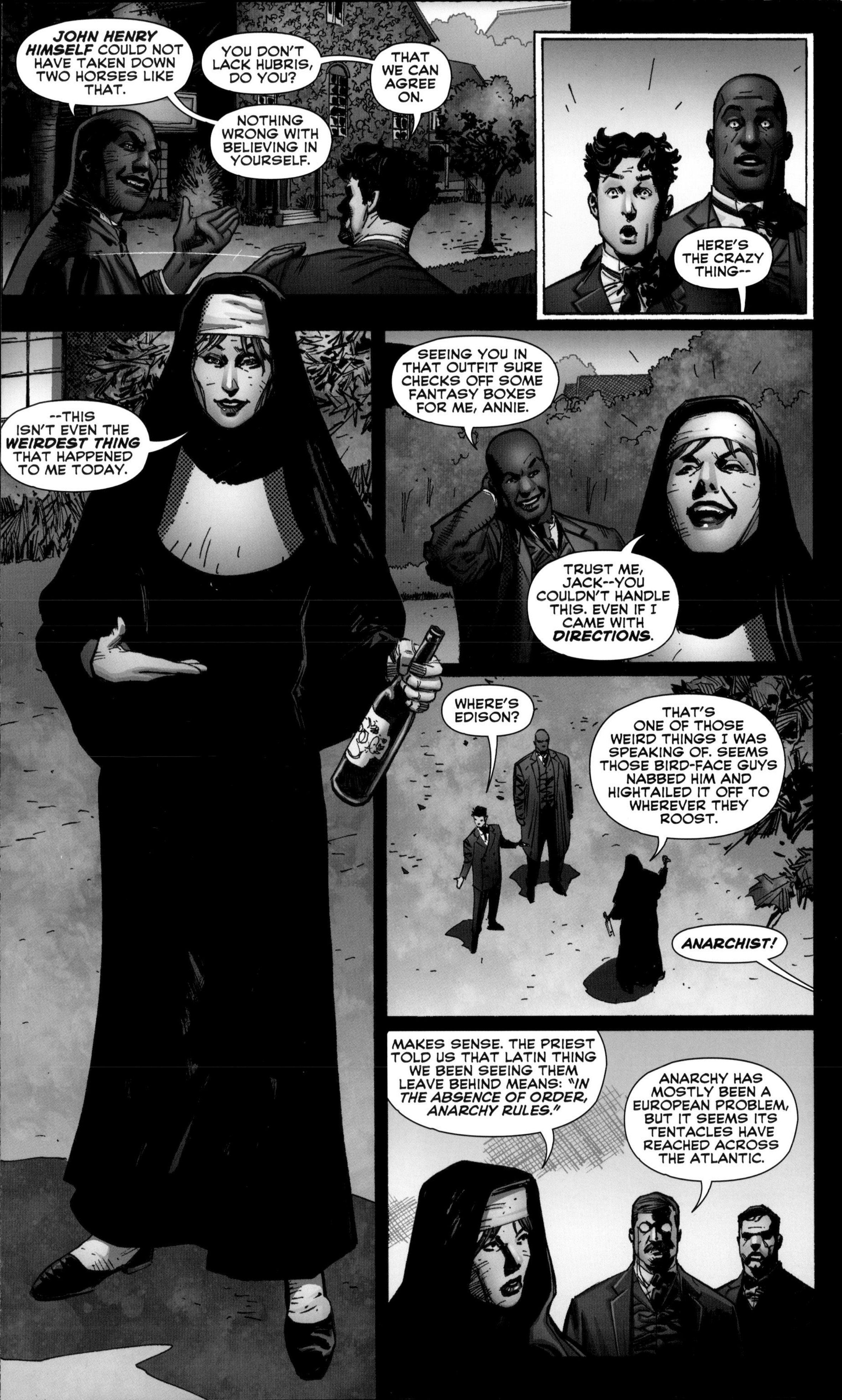

JOHN HENRY HIMSELF COULD NOT HAVE TAKEN DOWN TWO HORSES LIKE THAT.
YOU DON'T LACK HUBRIS, DO YOU?
NOTHING WRONG WITH BELIEVING IN YOURSELF.
THAT WE CAN AGREE ON.
HERE'S THE CRAZY THING--
--THIS ISN'T EVEN THE ***WEIRDEST THING*** THAT HAPPENED TO ME TODAY.
SEEING YOU IN THAT OUTFIT SURE CHECKS OFF SOME FANTASY BOXES FOR ME, ANNIE.
TRUST ME, JACK--YOU COULDN'T HANDLE THIS. EVEN IF I CAME WITH ***DIRECTIONS***.
WHERE'S EDISON?
THAT'S ONE OF THOSE WEIRD THINGS I WAS SPEAKING OF. SEEMS THOSE BIRD-FACE GUYS NABBED HIM AND HIGHTAILED IT OFF TO WHEREVER THEY ROOST.
ANARCHIST!
MAKES SENSE. THE PRIEST TOLD US THAT LATIN THING WE BEEN SEEING THEM LEAVE BEHIND MEANS: *"IN THE ABSENCE OF ORDER, ANARCHY RULES."*
ANARCHY HAS MOSTLY BEEN A EUROPEAN PROBLEM, BUT IT SEEMS ITS TENTACLES HAVE REACHED ACROSS THE ATLANTIC.

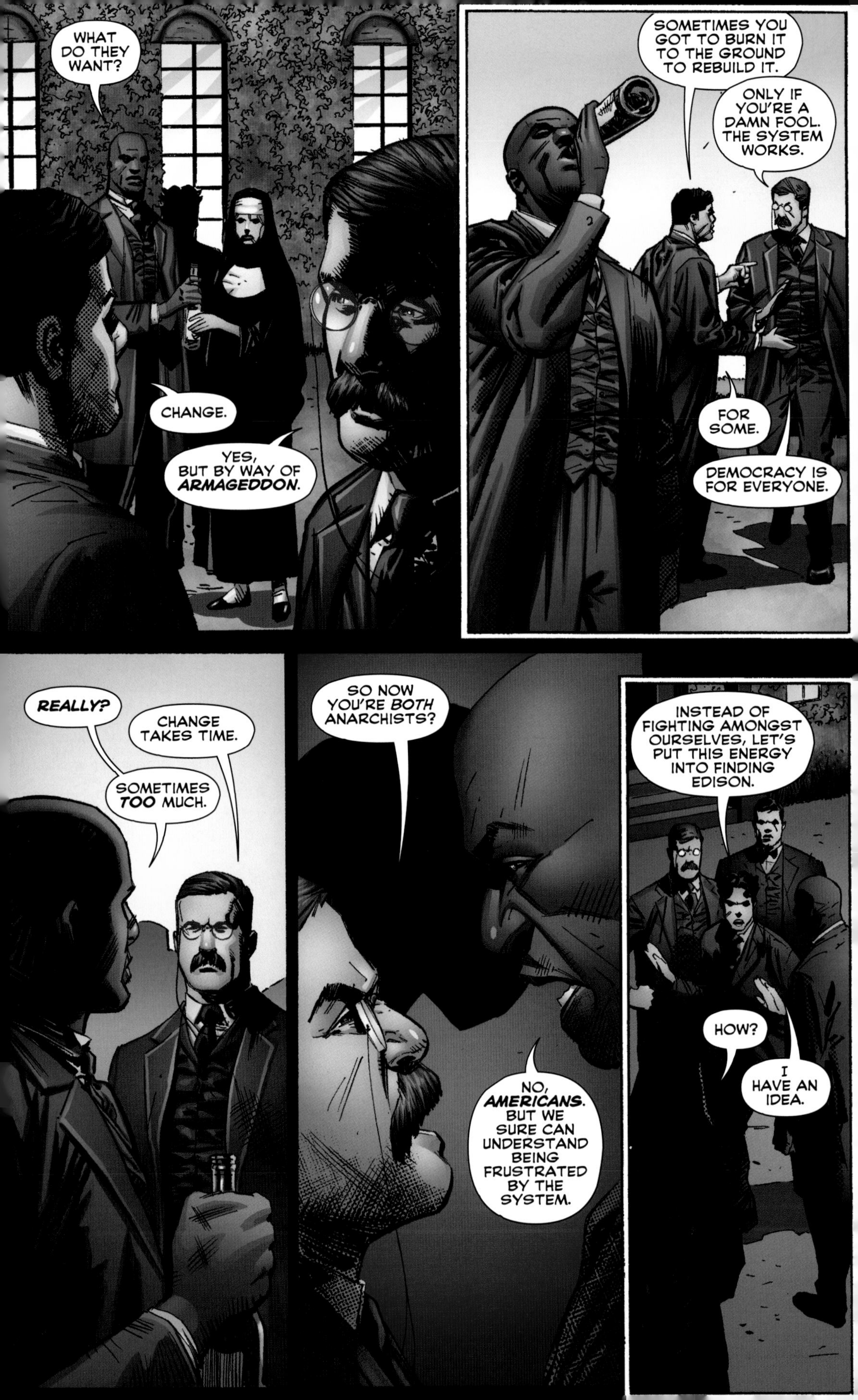
WHAT DO THEY WANT?
CHANGE.
YES, BUT BY WAY OF ***ARMAGEDDON***.
SOMETIMES YOU GOT TO BURN IT TO THE GROUND TO REBUILD IT.
ONLY IF YOU'RE A DAMN FOOL. THE SYSTEM WORKS.
FOR SOME.
DEMOCRACY IS FOR EVERYONE.
REALLY?
CHANGE TAKES TIME.
SOMETIMES ***TOO*** MUCH.
SO NOW YOU'RE *BOTH* ANARCHISTS?
NO, ***AMERICANS***. BUT WE SURE CAN UNDERSTAND BEING FRUSTRATED BY THE SYSTEM.
INSTEAD OF FIGHTING AMONGST OURSELVES, LET'S PUT THIS ENERGY INTO FINDING EDISON.
HOW?
I HAVE AN IDEA.

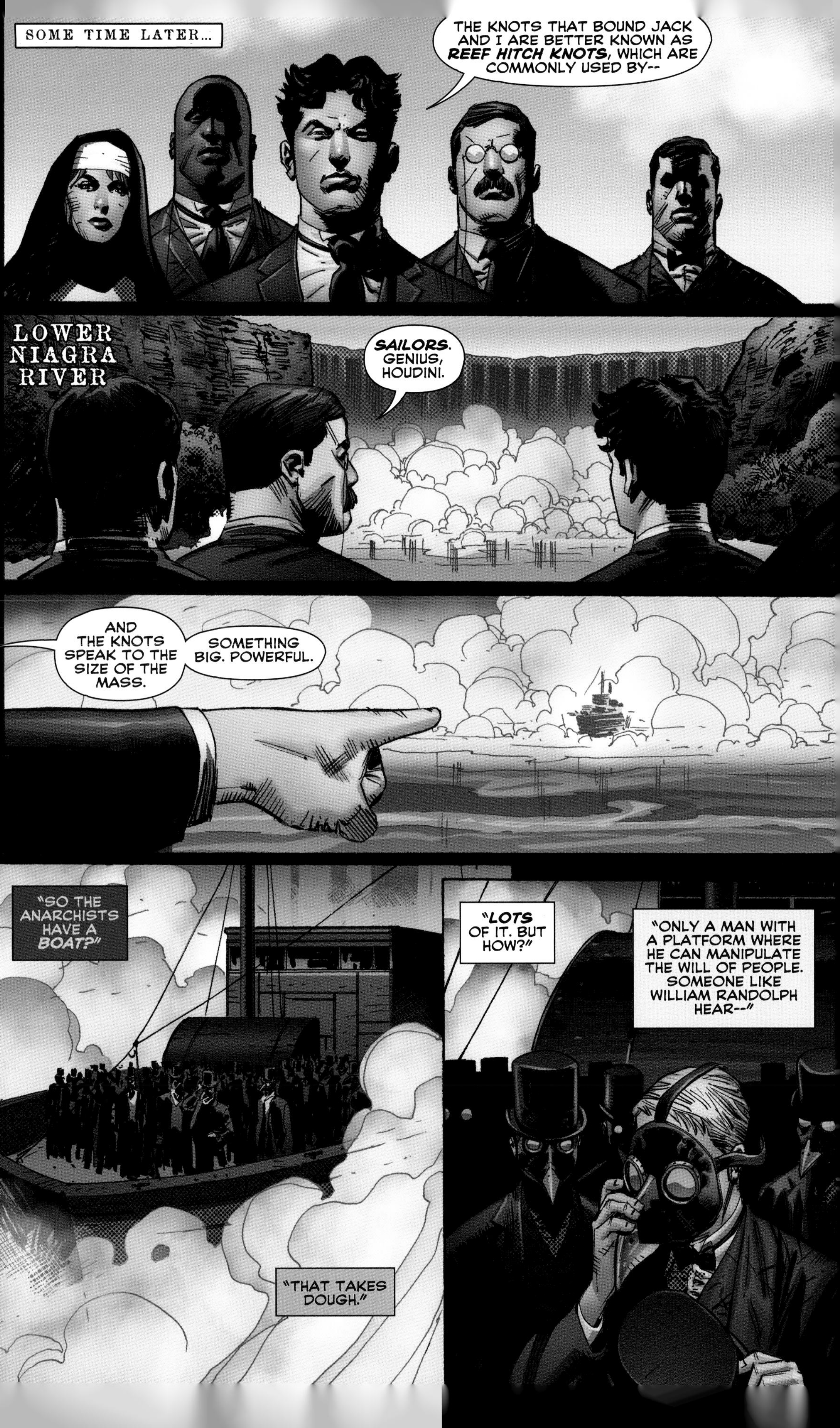
SOME TIME LATER...
THE KNOTS THAT BOUND JACK AND I ARE BETTER KNOWN AS REEF HITCH KNOTS, WHICH ARE COMMONLY USED BY--
LOWER NIAGRA RIVER
SAILORS. GENIUS, HOUDINI.
AND THE KNOTS SPEAK TO THE SIZE OF THE MASS.
SOMETHING BIG. POWERFUL.
"SO THE ANARCHISTS HAVE A BOAT?"
"THAT TAKES DOUGH."
"LOTS OF IT. BUT HOW?"
"ONLY A MAN WITH A PLATFORM WHERE HE CAN MANIPULATE THE WILL OF PEOPLE. SOMEONE LIKE WILLIAM RANDOLPH HEAR--"

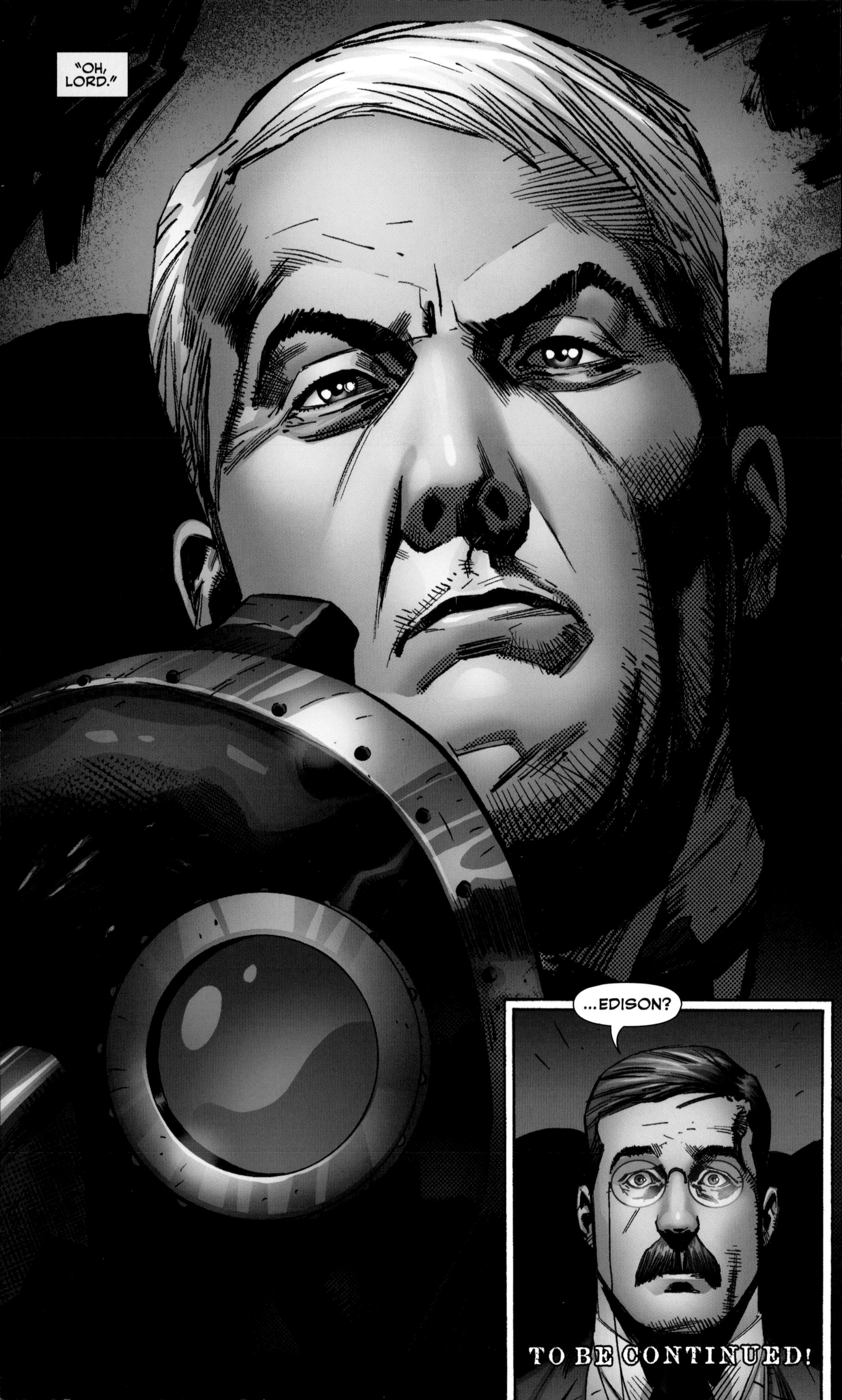
"OH, LORD."
...EDISON?
TO BE CONTINUED!

12

"MAIDEN OF THE MIST"

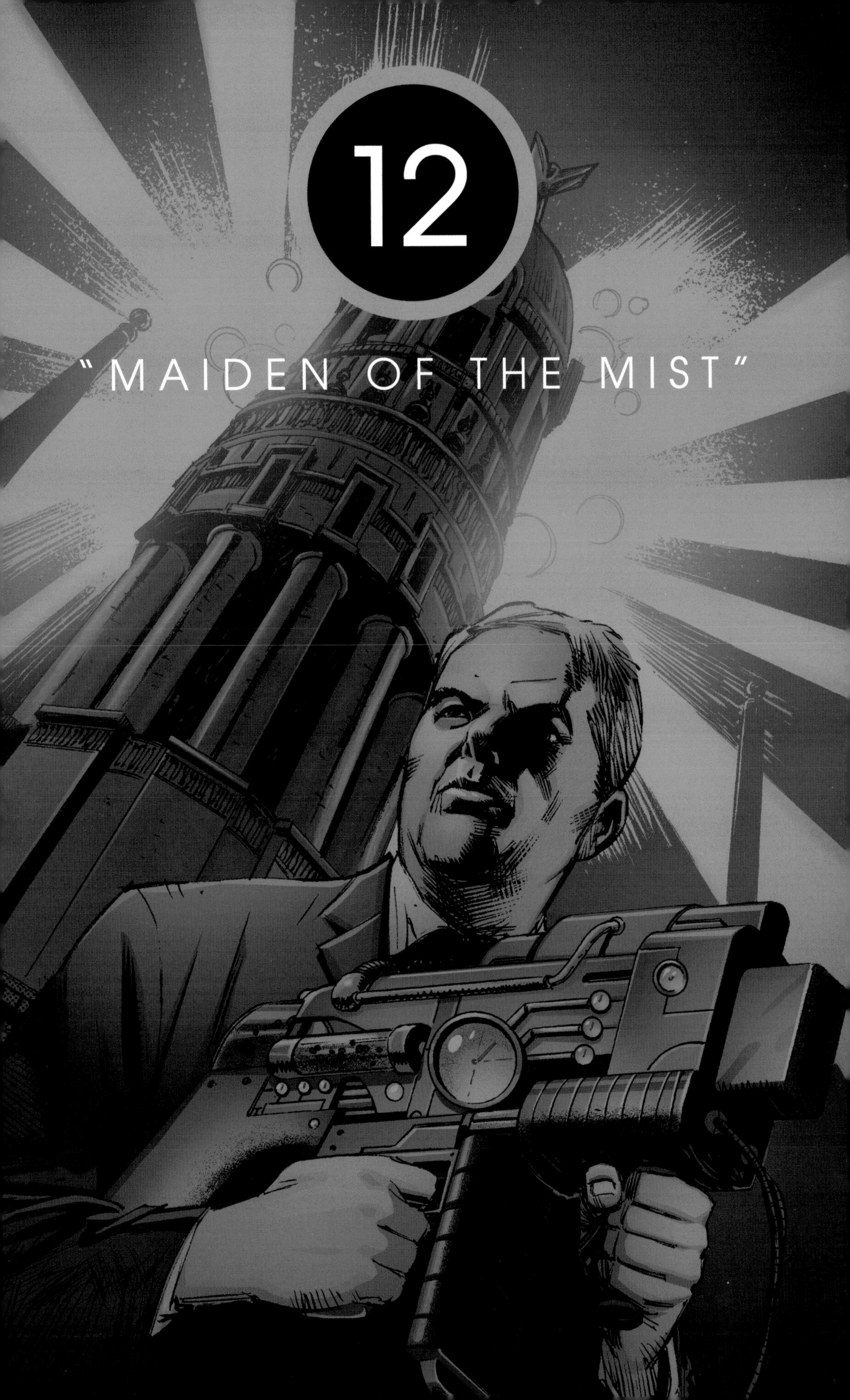

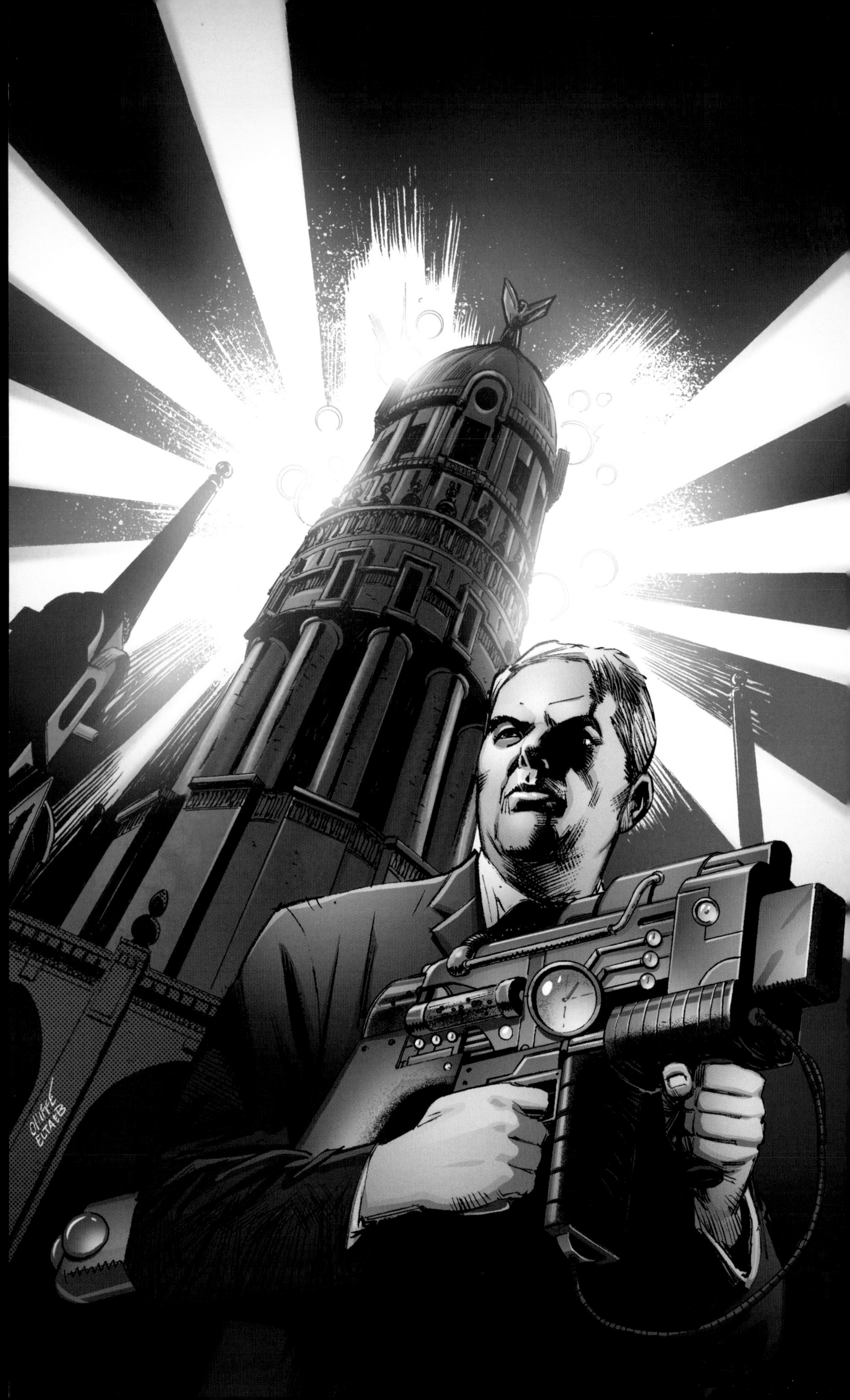
OLIFFE
ELTAEB

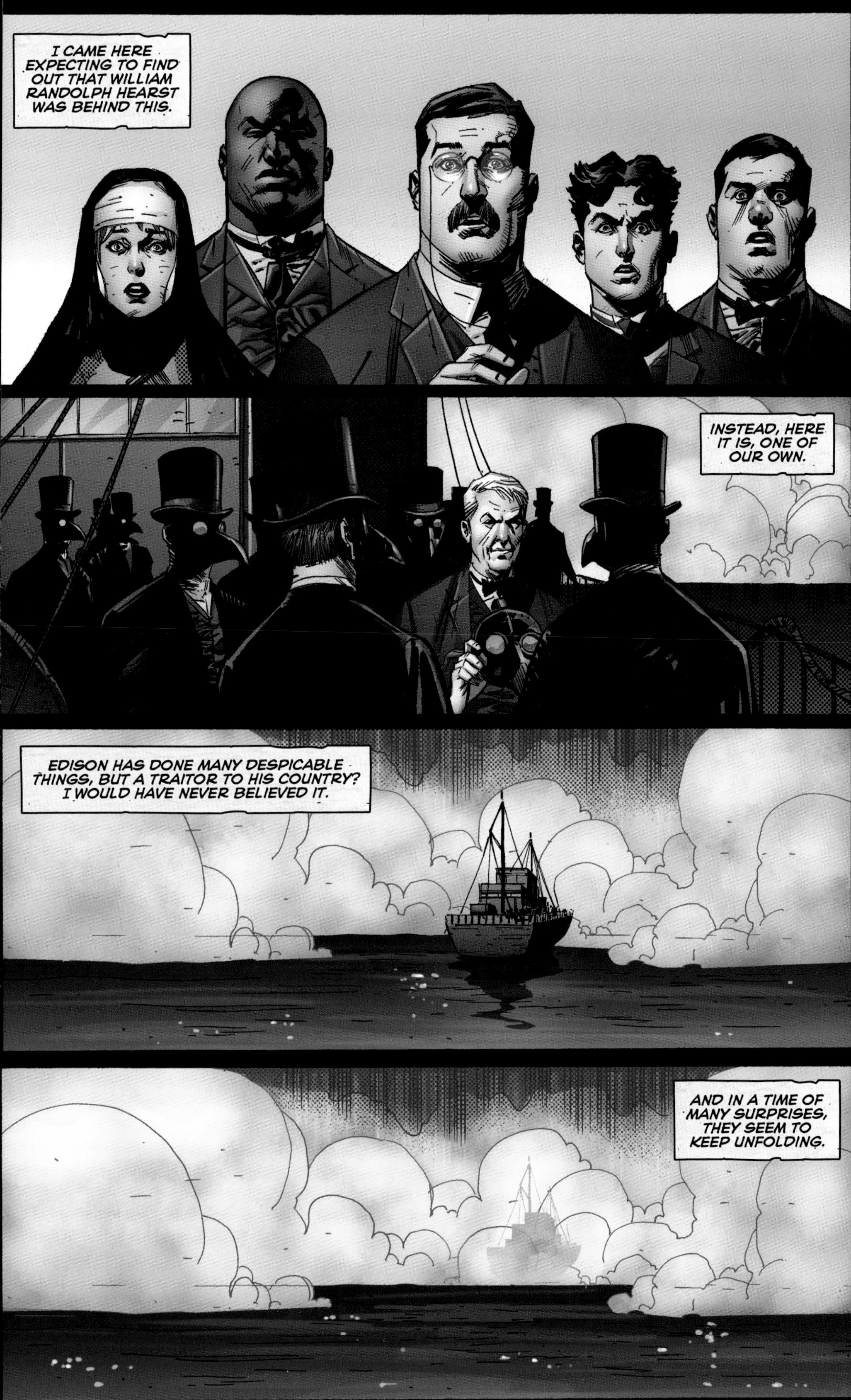
I CAME HERE EXPECTING TO FIND OUT THAT WILLIAM RANDOLPH HEARST WAS BEHIND THIS.
INSTEAD, HERE IT IS, ONE OF OUR OWN.
EDISON HAS DONE MANY DESPICABLE THINGS, BUT A TRAITOR TO HIS COUNTRY? I WOULD HAVE NEVER BELIEVED IT.
AND IN A TIME OF MANY SURPRISES, THEY SEEM TO KEEP UNFOLDING.

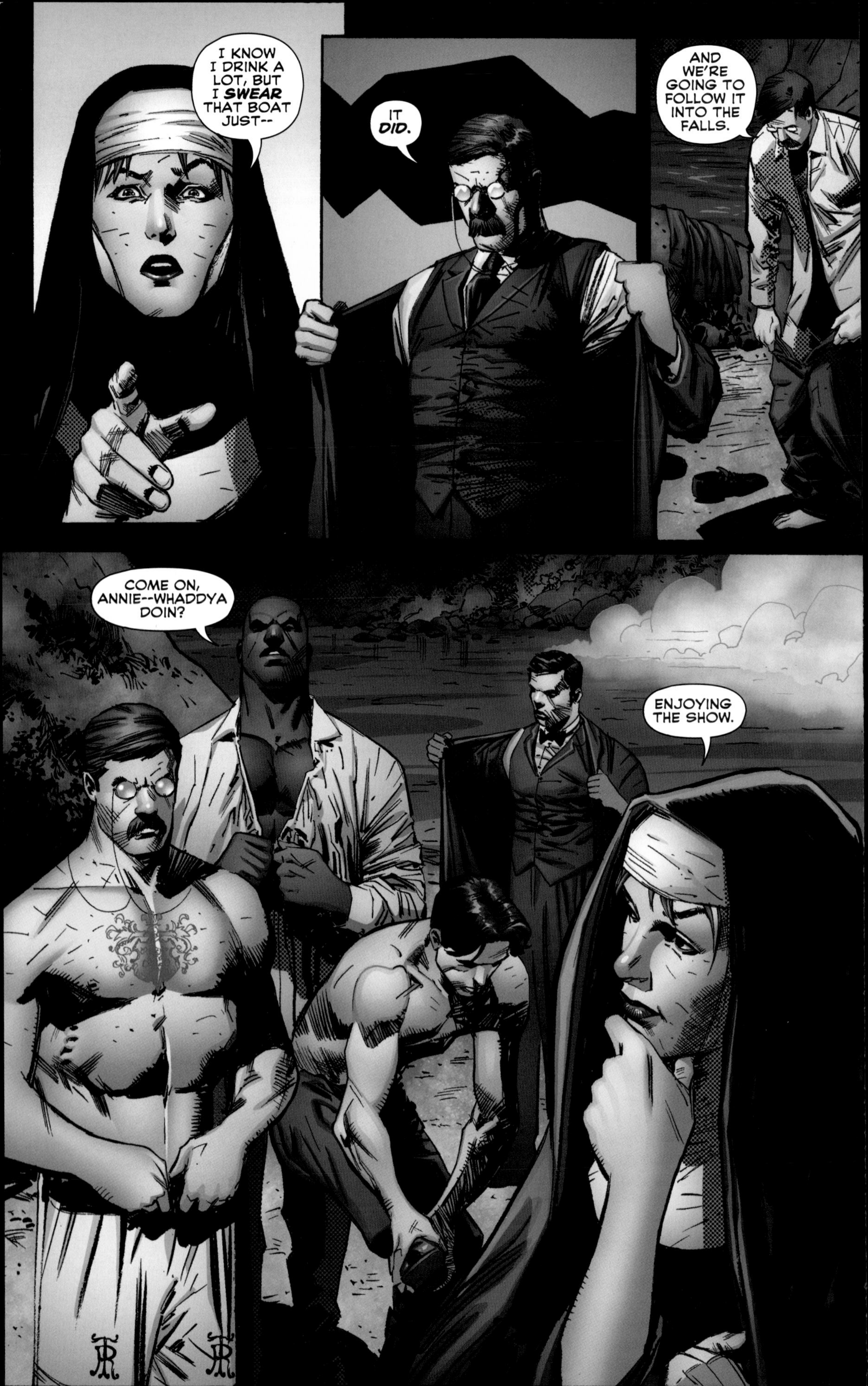
I KNOW I DRINK A LOT, BUT I SWEAR THAT BOAT JUST--
IT DID.
AND WE'RE GOING TO FOLLOW IT INTO THE FALLS.
COME ON, ANNIE--WHADDYA DOIN?
ENJOYING THE SHOW.

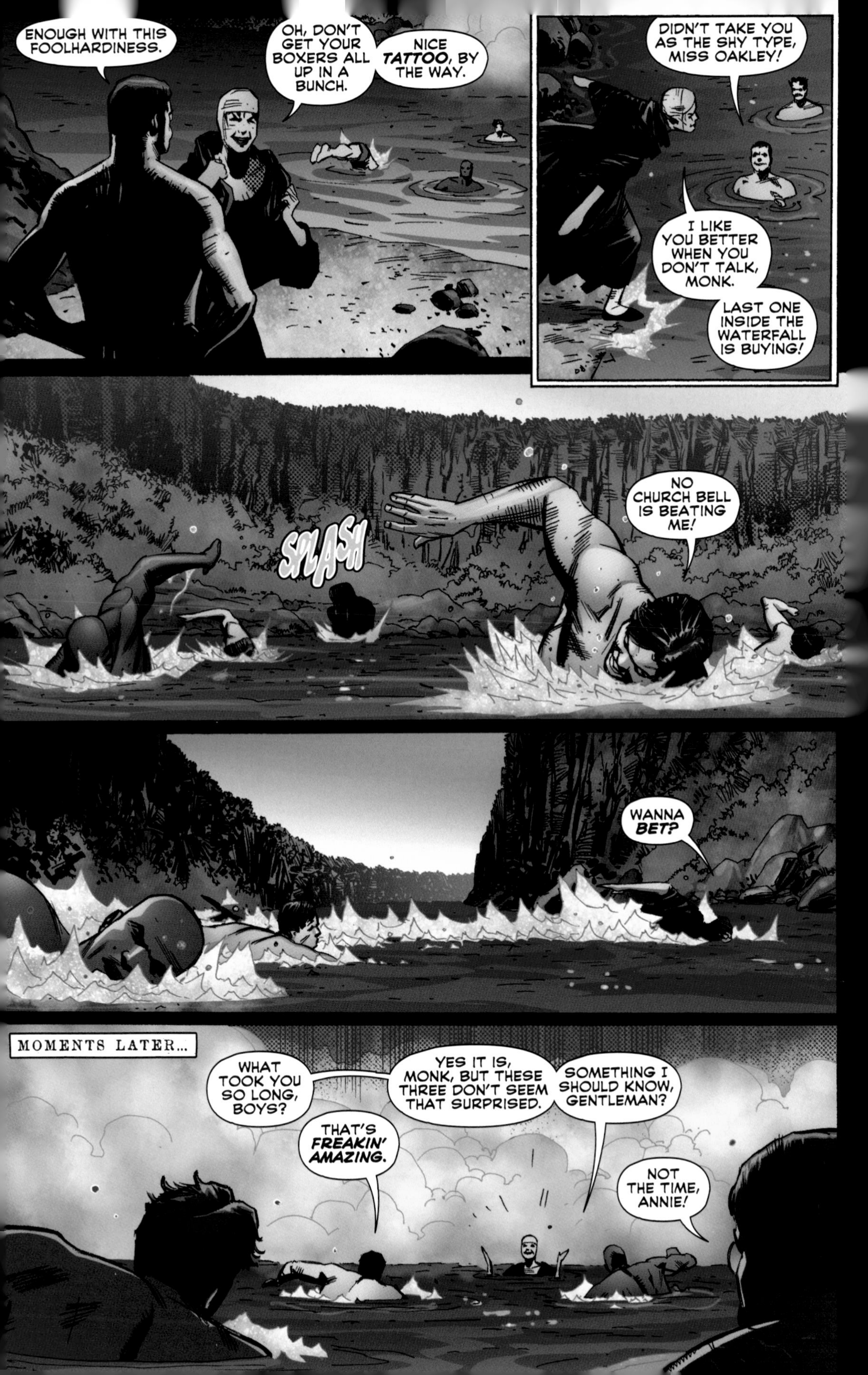
ENOUGH WITH THIS FOOLHARDINESS.
OH, DON'T GET YOUR BOXERS ALL UP IN A BUNCH.
NICE TATTOO, BY THE WAY.
DIDN'T TAKE YOU AS THE SHY TYPE, MISS OAKLEY!
I LIKE YOU BETTER WHEN YOU DON'T TALK, MONK.
LAST ONE INSIDE THE WATERFALL IS BUYING!
SPLASH
NO CHURCH BELL IS BEATING ME!
WANNA BET?
MOMENTS LATER...
WHAT TOOK YOU SO LONG, BOYS?
YES IT IS, MONK, BUT THESE THREE DON'T SEEM THAT SURPRISED.
THAT'S FREAKIN' AMAZING.
SOMETHING I SHOULD KNOW, GENTLEMAN?
NOT THE TIME, ANNIE!

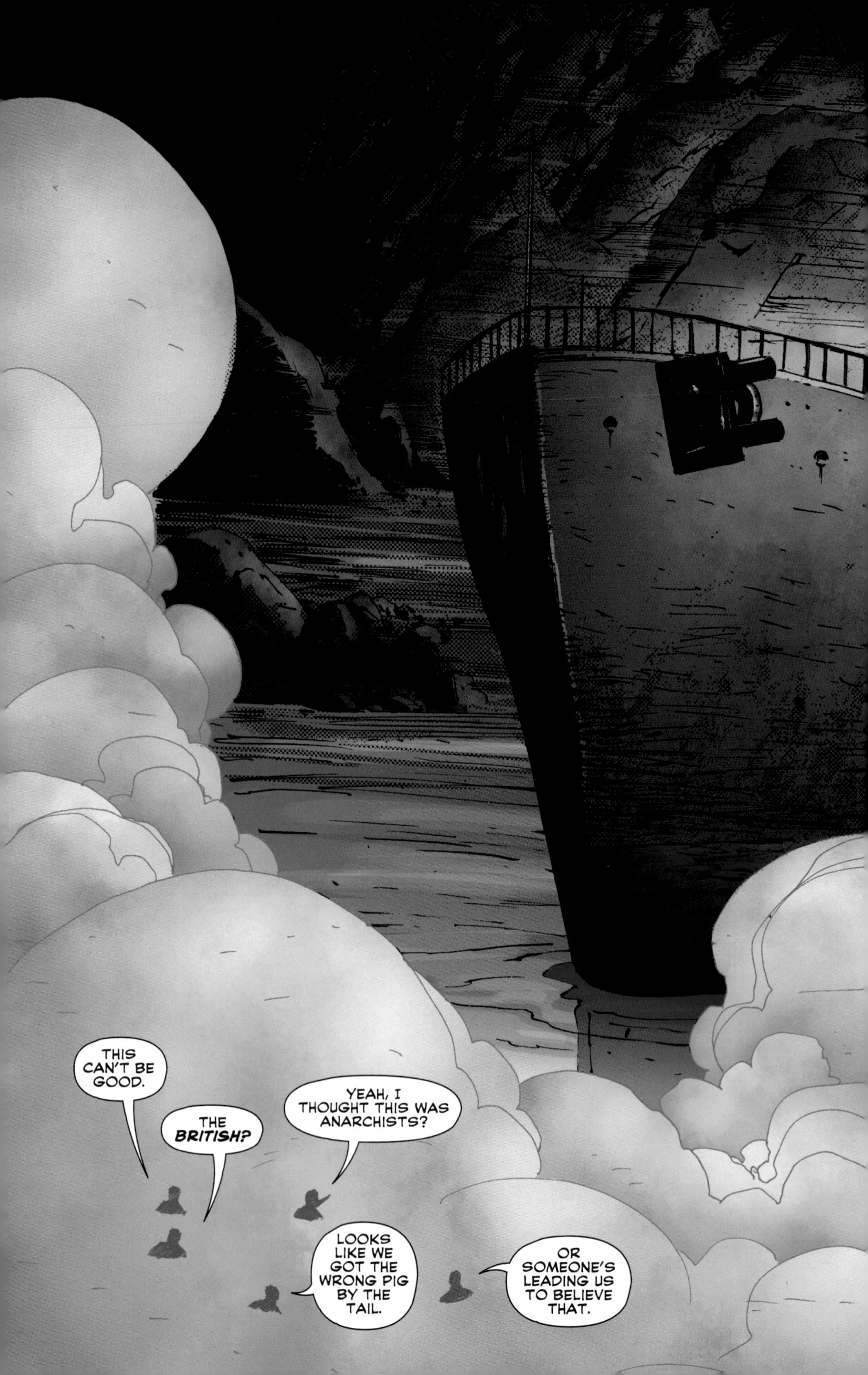
THIS CAN'T BE GOOD.
THE *BRITISH?*
YEAH, I THOUGHT THIS WAS ANARCHISTS?
LOOKS LIKE WE GOT THE WRONG PIG BY THE TAIL.
OR SOMEONE'S LEADING US TO BELIEVE THAT.

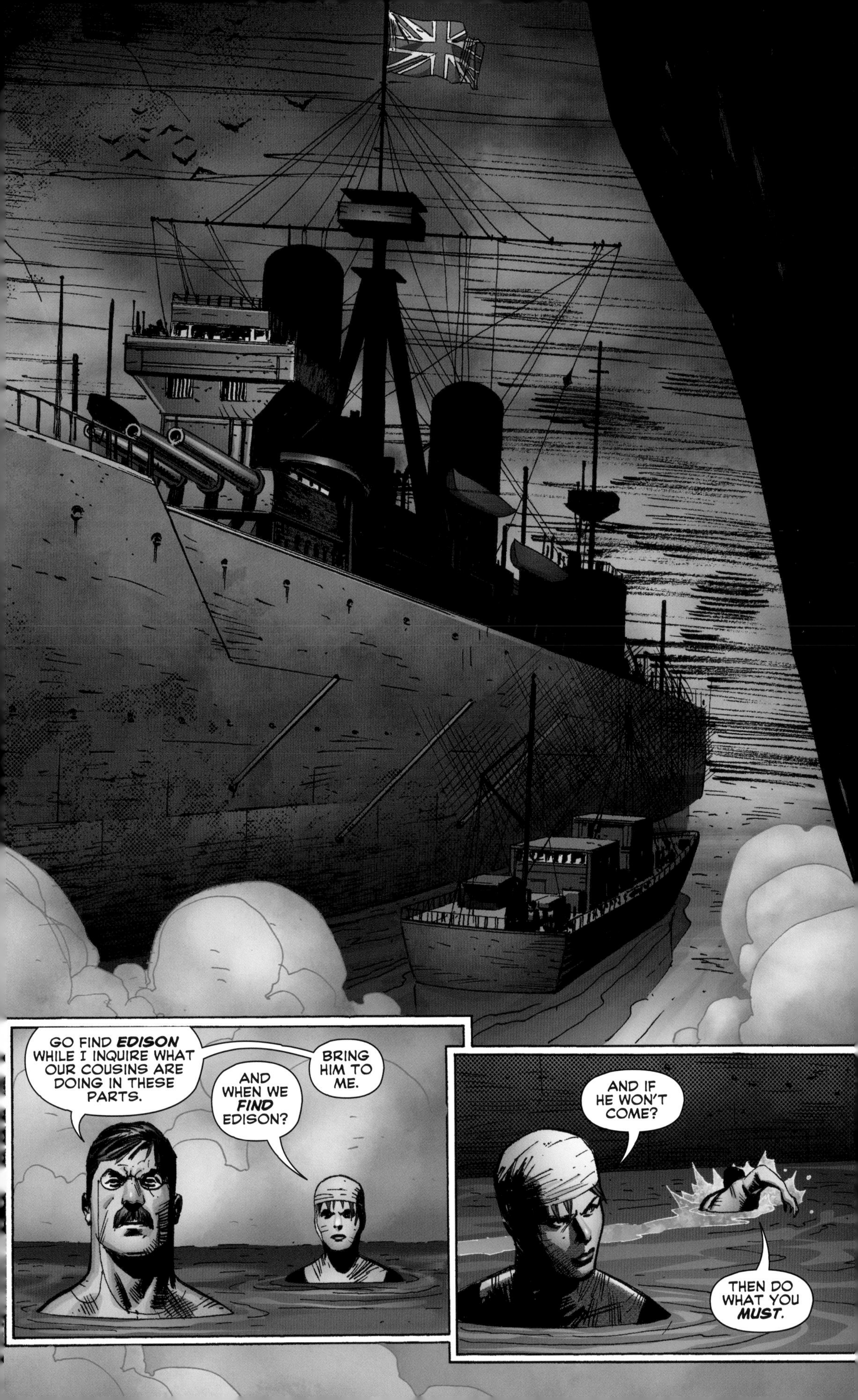
GO FIND *EDISON* WHILE I INQUIRE WHAT OUR COUSINS ARE DOING IN THESE PARTS.
AND WHEN WE *FIND* EDISON?
BRING HIM TO ME.
AND IF HE WON'T COME?
THEN DO WHAT YOU *MUST*.

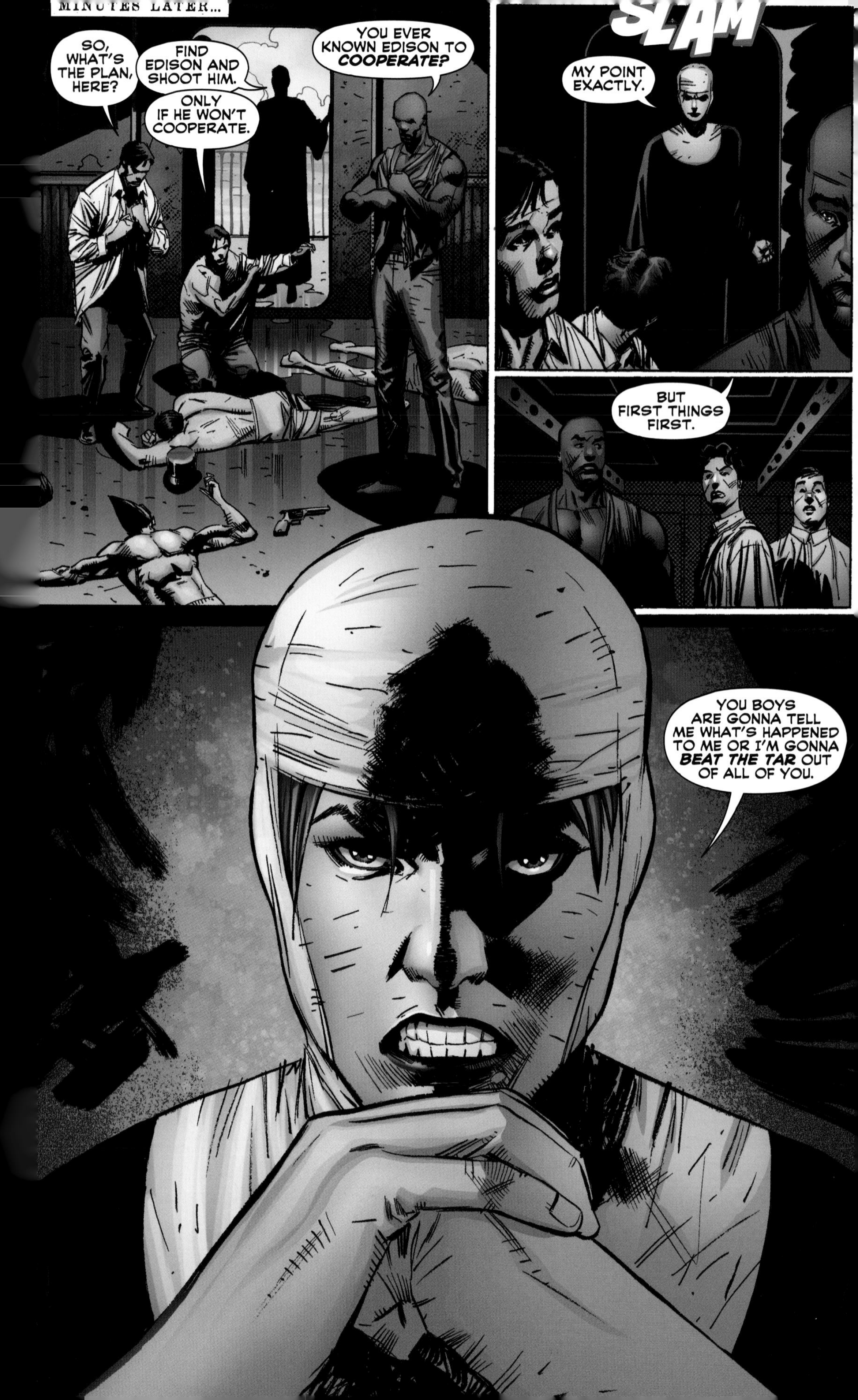
MINUTES LATER...
SO, WHAT'S THE PLAN, HERE?
FIND EDISON AND SHOOT HIM.
ONLY IF HE WON'T COOPERATE.
YOU EVER KNOWN EDISON TO COOPERATE?
SLAM
MY POINT EXACTLY.
BUT FIRST THINGS FIRST.
YOU BOYS ARE GONNA TELL ME WHAT'S HAPPENED TO ME OR I'M GONNA BEAT THE TAR OUT OF ALL OF YOU.

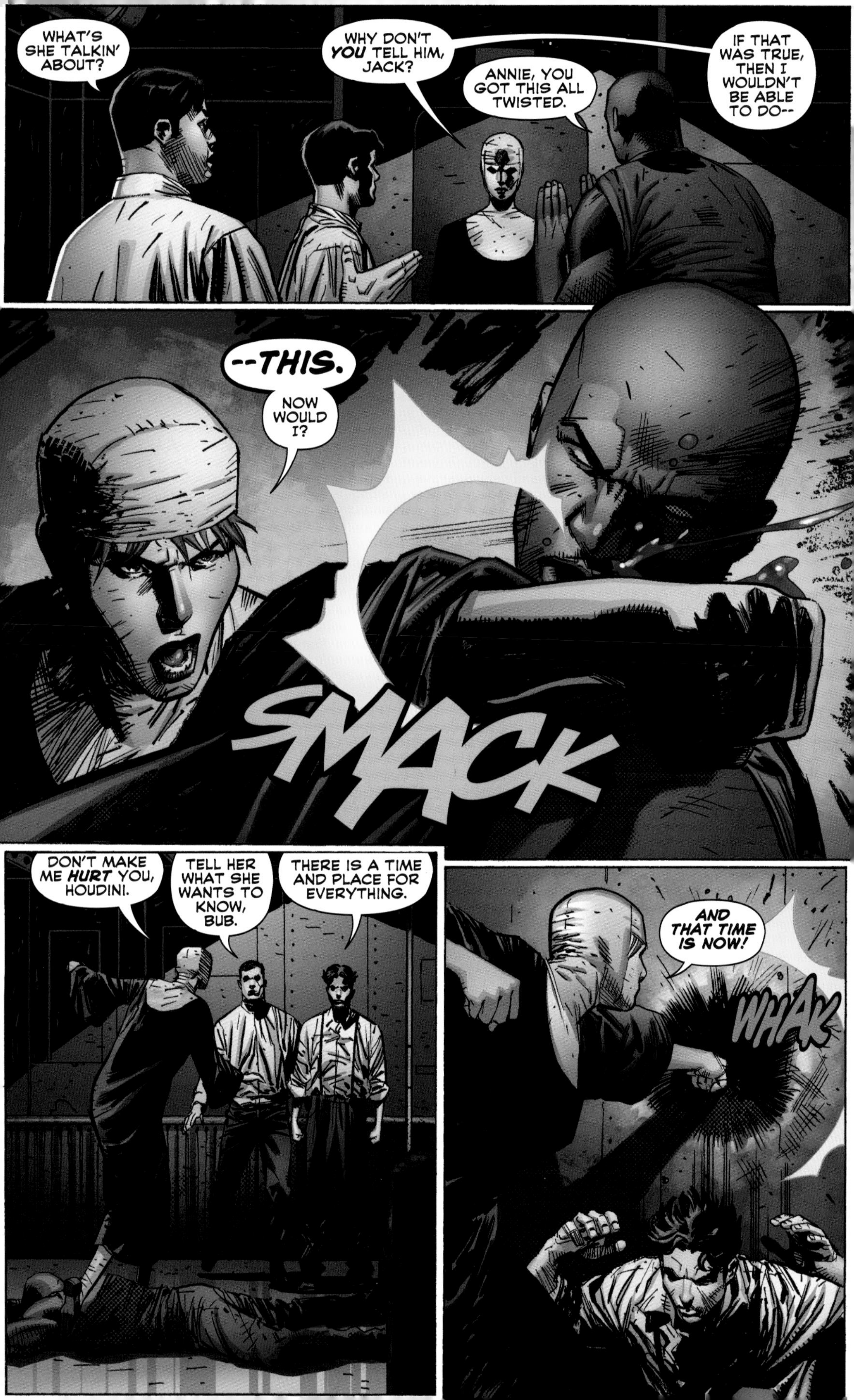
WHAT'S SHE TALKIN' ABOUT?
WHY DON'T *YOU* TELL HIM, JACK?
ANNIE, YOU GOT THIS ALL TWISTED.
IF THAT WAS TRUE, THEN I WOULDN'T BE ABLE TO DO--
--THIS.
NOW WOULD I?
SMACK
DON'T MAKE ME *HURT* YOU, HOUDINI.
TELL HER WHAT SHE WANTS TO KNOW, BUB.
THERE IS A TIME AND PLACE FOR EVERYTHING.
AND THAT TIME IS NOW!
WHAK

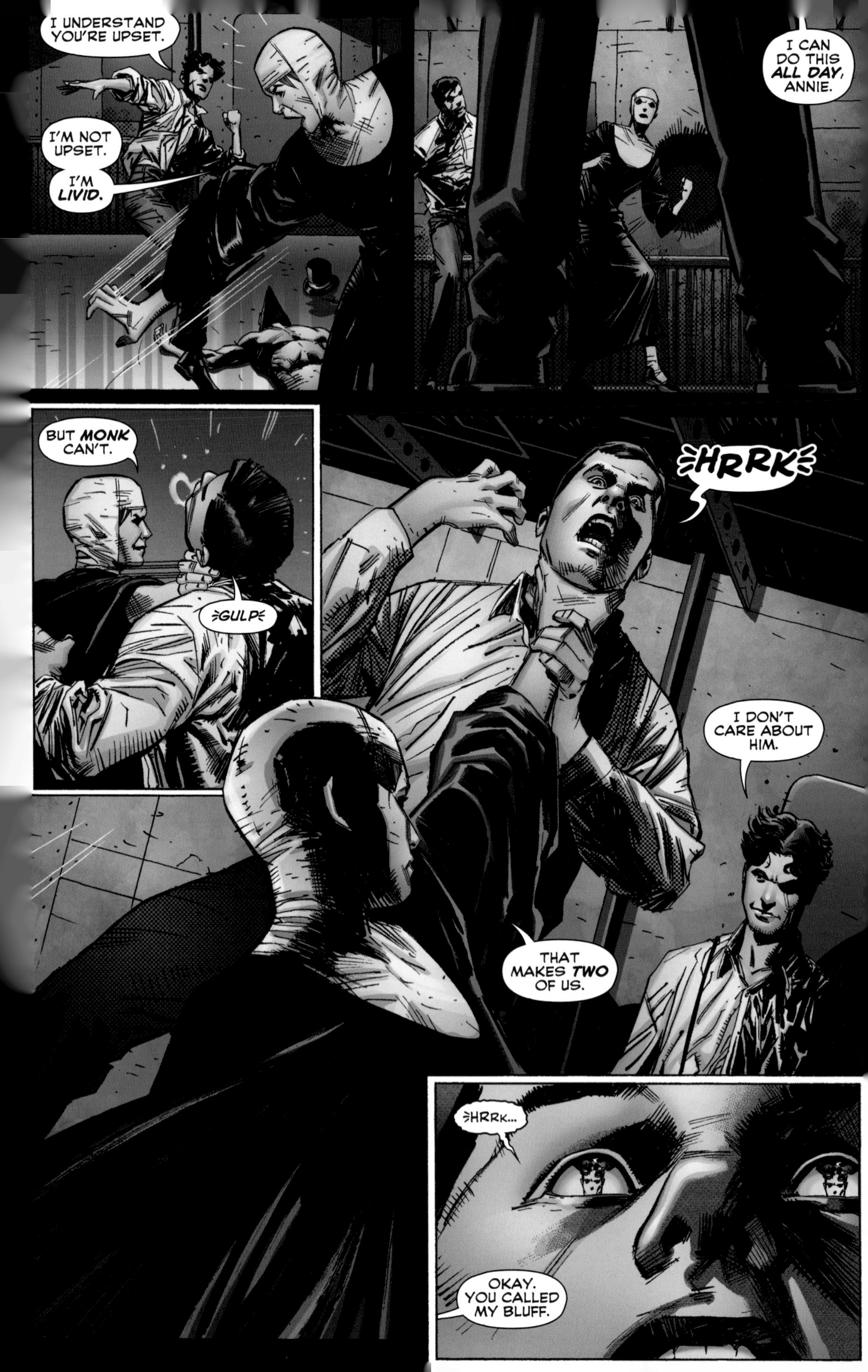
I UNDERSTAND YOU'RE UPSET.
I'M NOT UPSET.
I'M LIVID.
I CAN DO THIS ALL DAY, ANNIE.
BUT MONK CAN'T.
GULP
HRRK
I DON'T CARE ABOUT HIM.
THAT MAKES TWO OF US.
HRRK...
OKAY. YOU CALLED MY BLUFF.

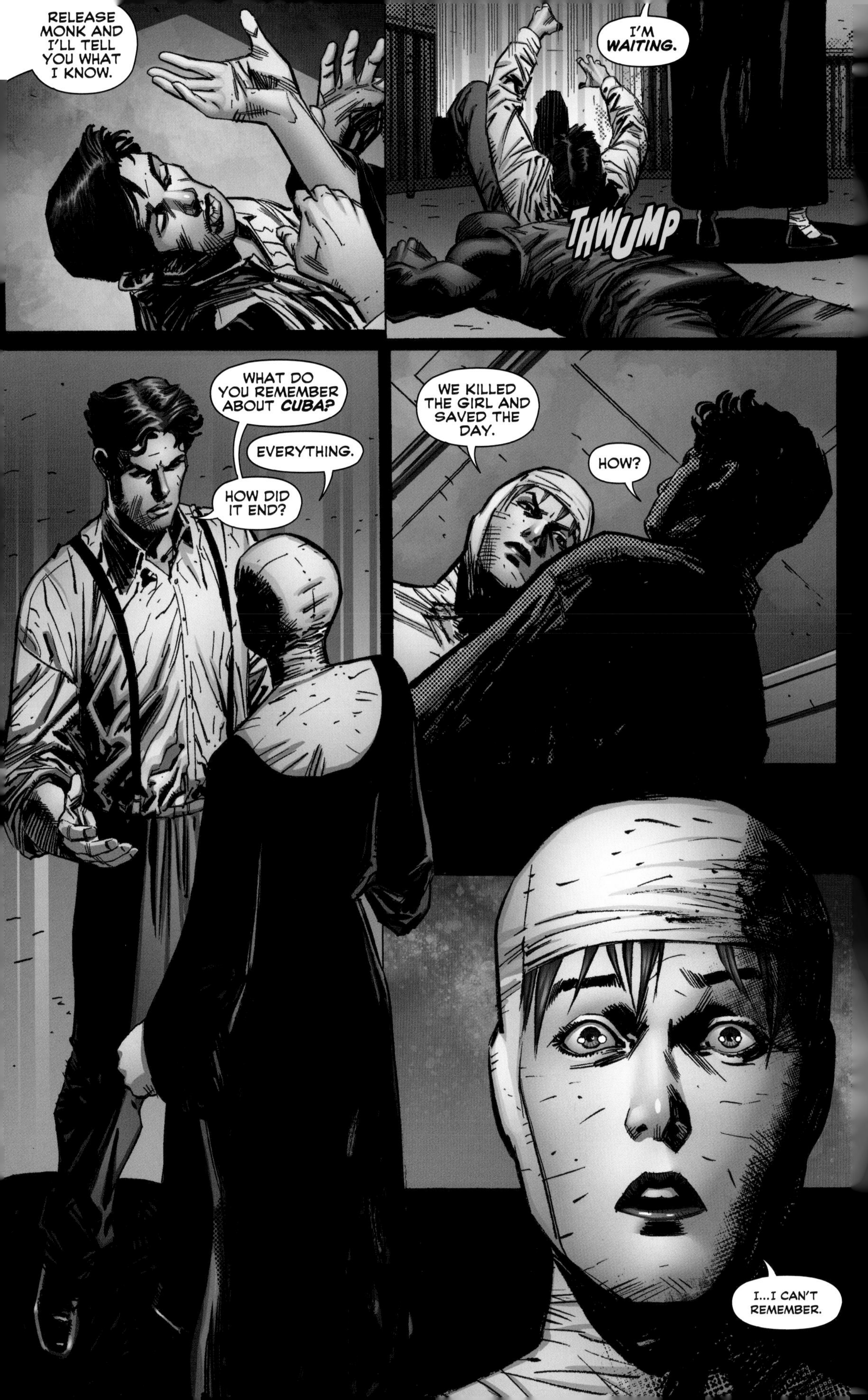
RELEASE MONK AND I'LL TELL YOU WHAT I KNOW.
I'M WAITING.
THWUMP
WHAT DO YOU REMEMBER ABOUT CUBA?
EVERYTHING.
HOW DID IT END?
WE KILLED THE GIRL AND SAVED THE DAY.
HOW?
I...I CAN'T REMEMBER.

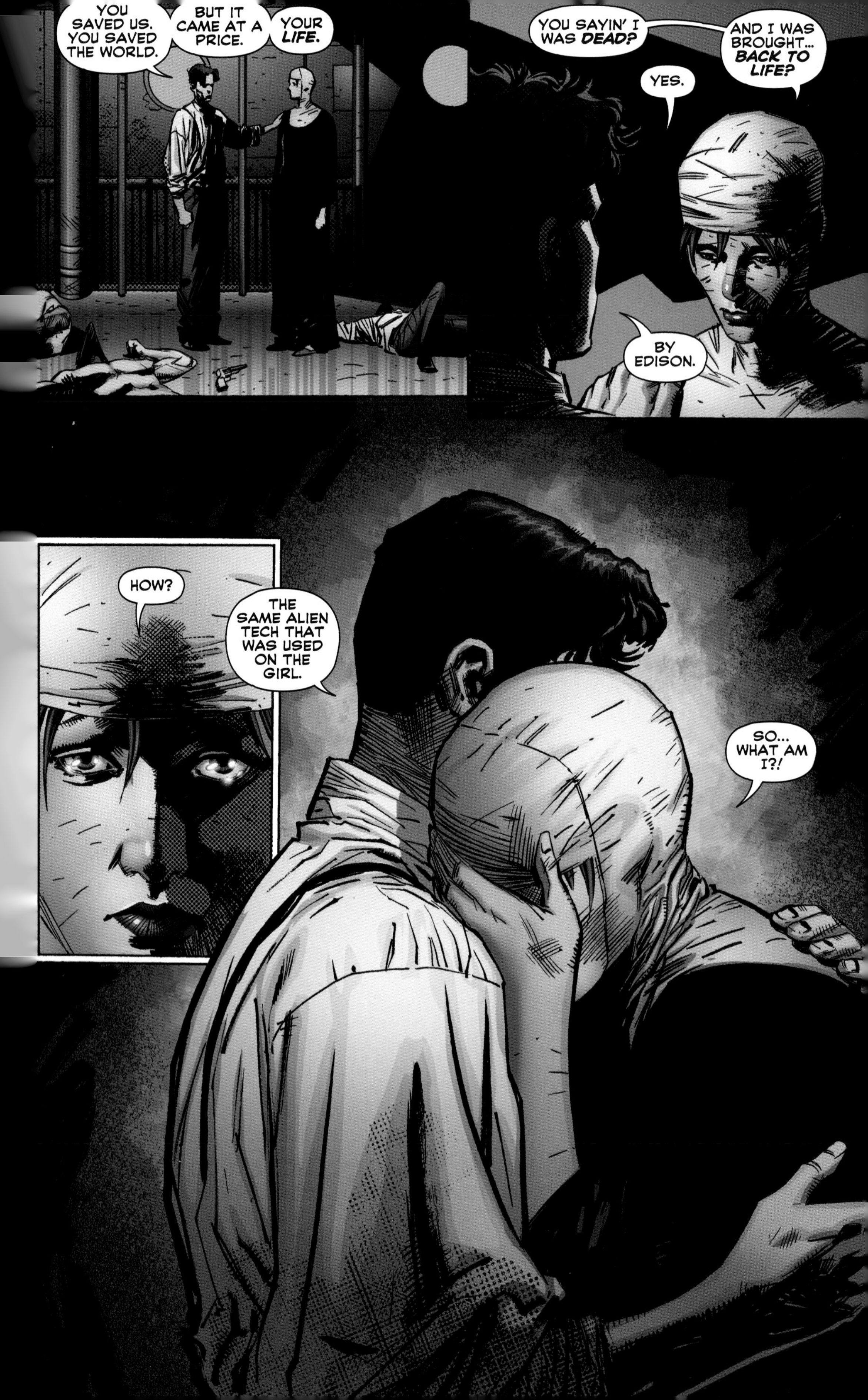
YOU SAVED US. YOU SAVED THE WORLD.
BUT IT CAME AT A PRICE.
YOUR *LIFE.*
YOU SAYIN' I WAS *DEAD?*
AND I WAS BROUGHT... *BACK TO LIFE?*
YES.
BY EDISON.
HOW?
THE SAME ALIEN TECH THAT WAS USED ON THE GIRL.
SO... WHAT AM I?!

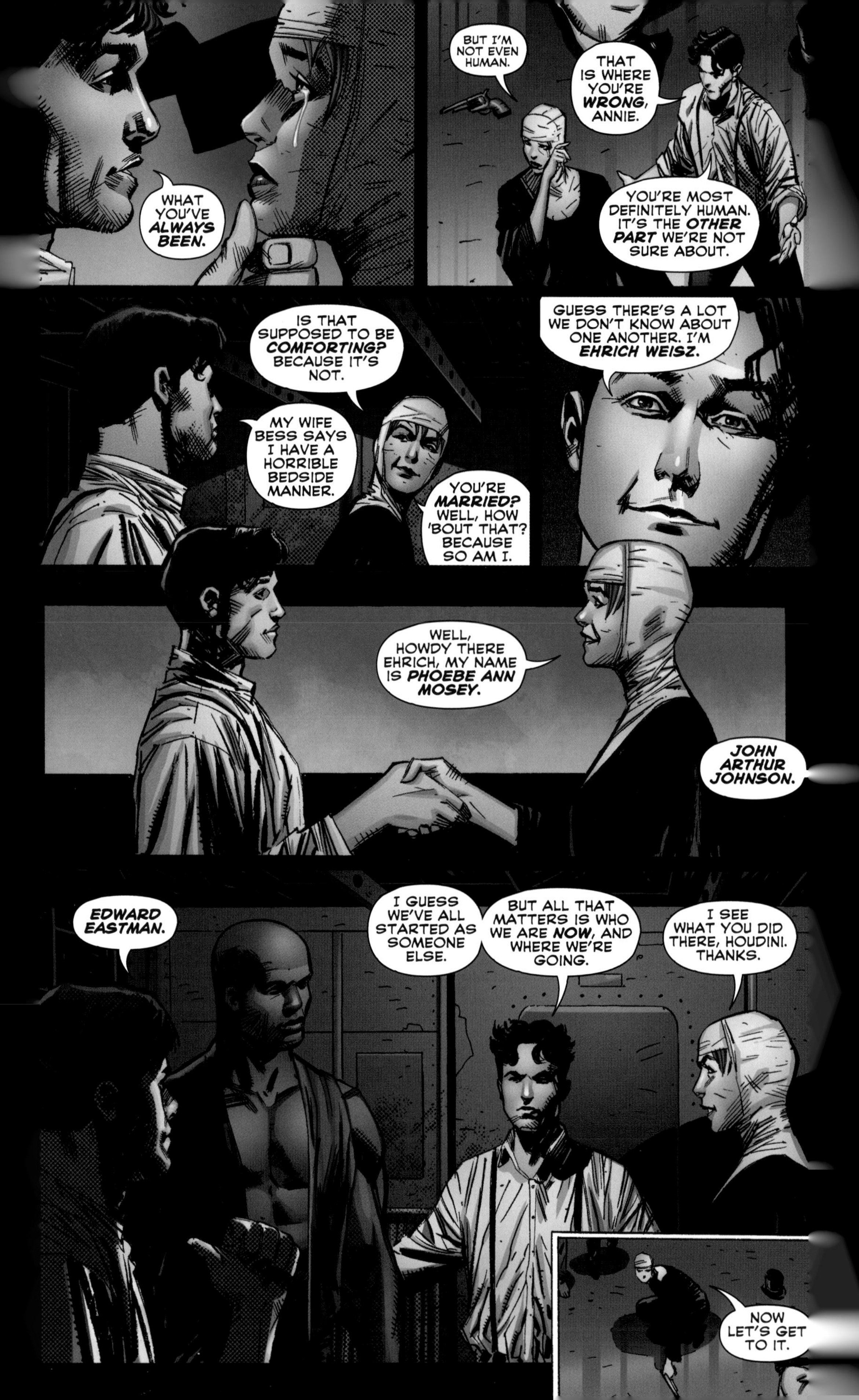
WHAT YOU'VE ALWAYS BEEN.
BUT I'M NOT EVEN HUMAN.
THAT IS WHERE YOU'RE WRONG, ANNIE.
YOU'RE MOST DEFINITELY HUMAN. IT'S THE OTHER PART WE'RE NOT SURE ABOUT.
IS THAT SUPPOSED TO BE COMFORTING? BECAUSE IT'S NOT.
MY WIFE BESS SAYS I HAVE A HORRIBLE BEDSIDE MANNER.
YOU'RE MARRIED? WELL, HOW 'BOUT THAT? BECAUSE SO AM I.
GUESS THERE'S A LOT WE DON'T KNOW ABOUT ONE ANOTHER. I'M EHRICH WEISZ.
WELL, HOWDY THERE EHRICH, MY NAME IS PHOEBE ANN MOSEY.
JOHN ARTHUR JOHNSON.
EDWARD EASTMAN.
I GUESS WE'VE ALL STARTED AS SOMEONE ELSE.
BUT ALL THAT MATTERS IS WHO WE ARE NOW, AND WHERE WE'RE GOING.
I SEE WHAT YOU DID THERE, HOUDINI. THANKS.
NOW LET'S GET TO IT.

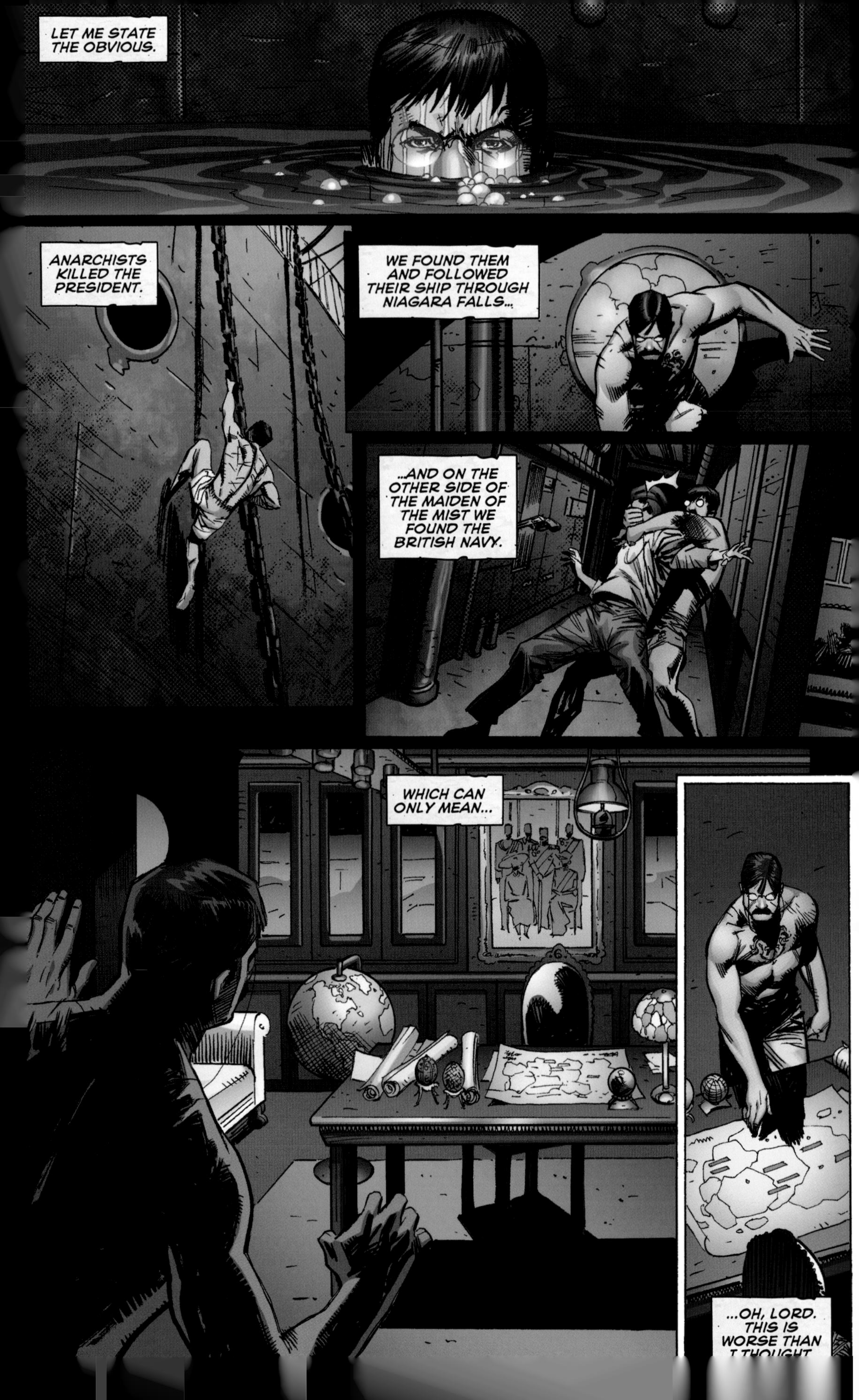
LET ME STATE THE OBVIOUS.
ANARCHISTS KILLED THE PRESIDENT.
WE FOUND THEM AND FOLLOWED THEIR SHIP THROUGH NIAGARA FALLS...
...AND ON THE OTHER SIDE OF THE MAIDEN OF THE MIST WE FOUND THE BRITISH NAVY.
WHICH CAN ONLY MEAN...
...OH, LORD. THIS IS WORSE THAN

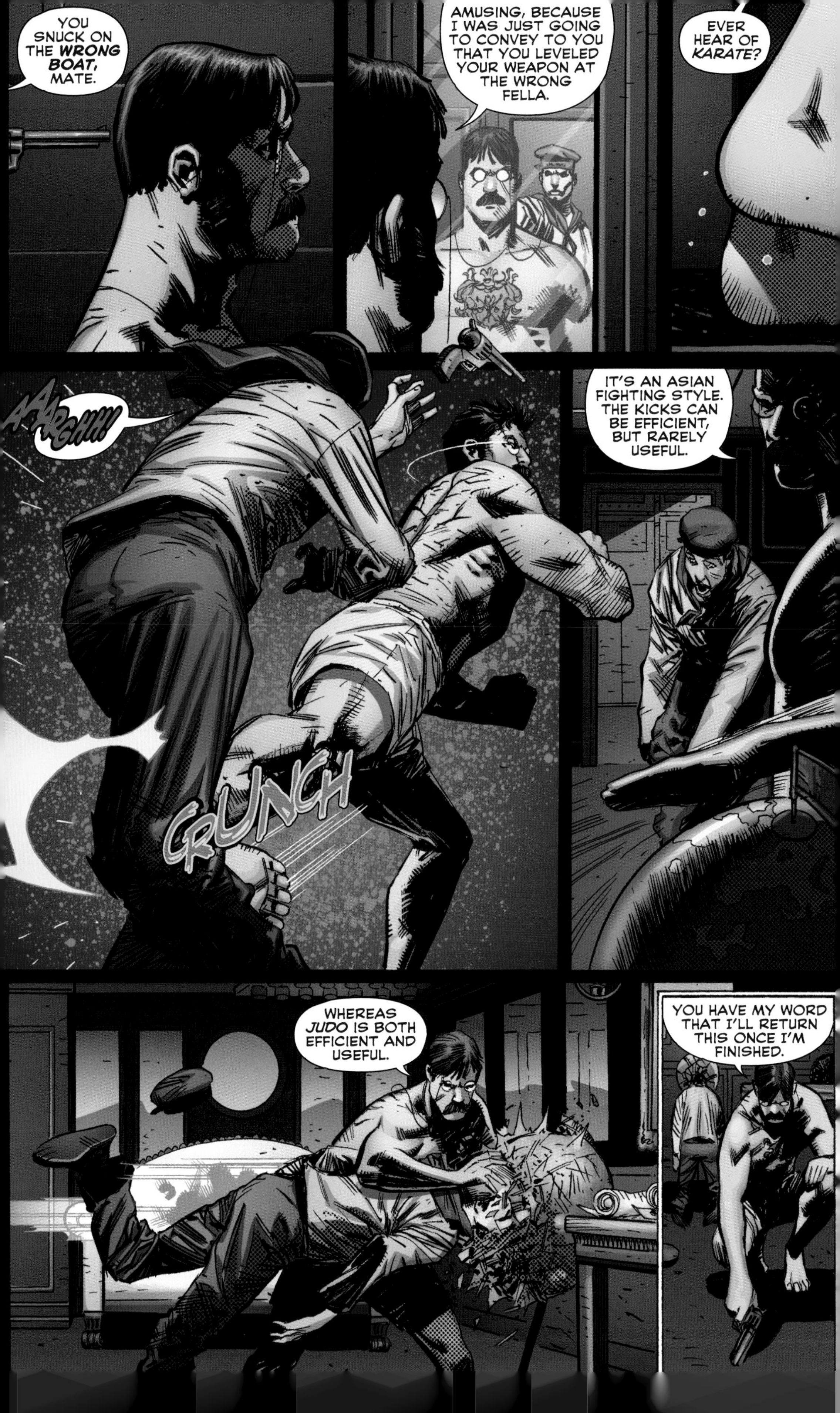

YOU SNUCK ON THE WRONG BOAT, MATE.
AMUSING, BECAUSE I WAS JUST GOING TO CONVEY TO YOU THAT YOU LEVELED YOUR WEAPON AT THE WRONG FELLA.
EVER HEAR OF KARATE?
AAARGHH!
CRUNCH
IT'S AN ASIAN FIGHTING STYLE. THE KICKS CAN BE EFFICIENT, BUT RARELY USEFUL.
WHEREAS JUDO IS BOTH EFFICIENT AND USEFUL.
YOU HAVE MY WORD THAT I'LL RETURN THIS ONCE I'M FINISHED.

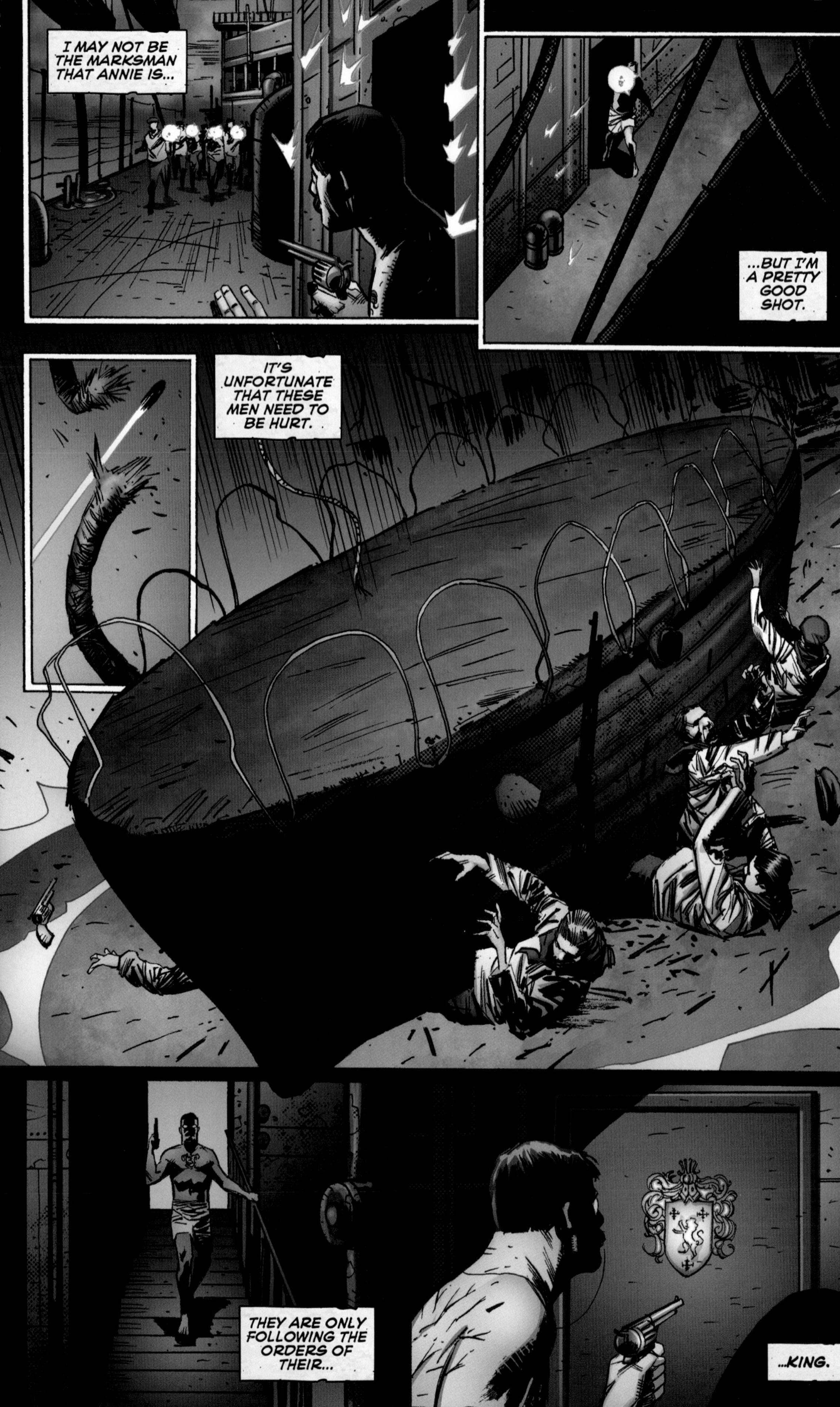
I MAY NOT BE THE MARKSMAN THAT ANNIE IS...
...BUT I'M A PRETTY GOOD SHOT.
IT'S UNFORTUNATE THAT THESE MEN NEED TO BE HURT.
THEY ARE ONLY FOLLOWING THE ORDERS OF THEIR...
...KING.

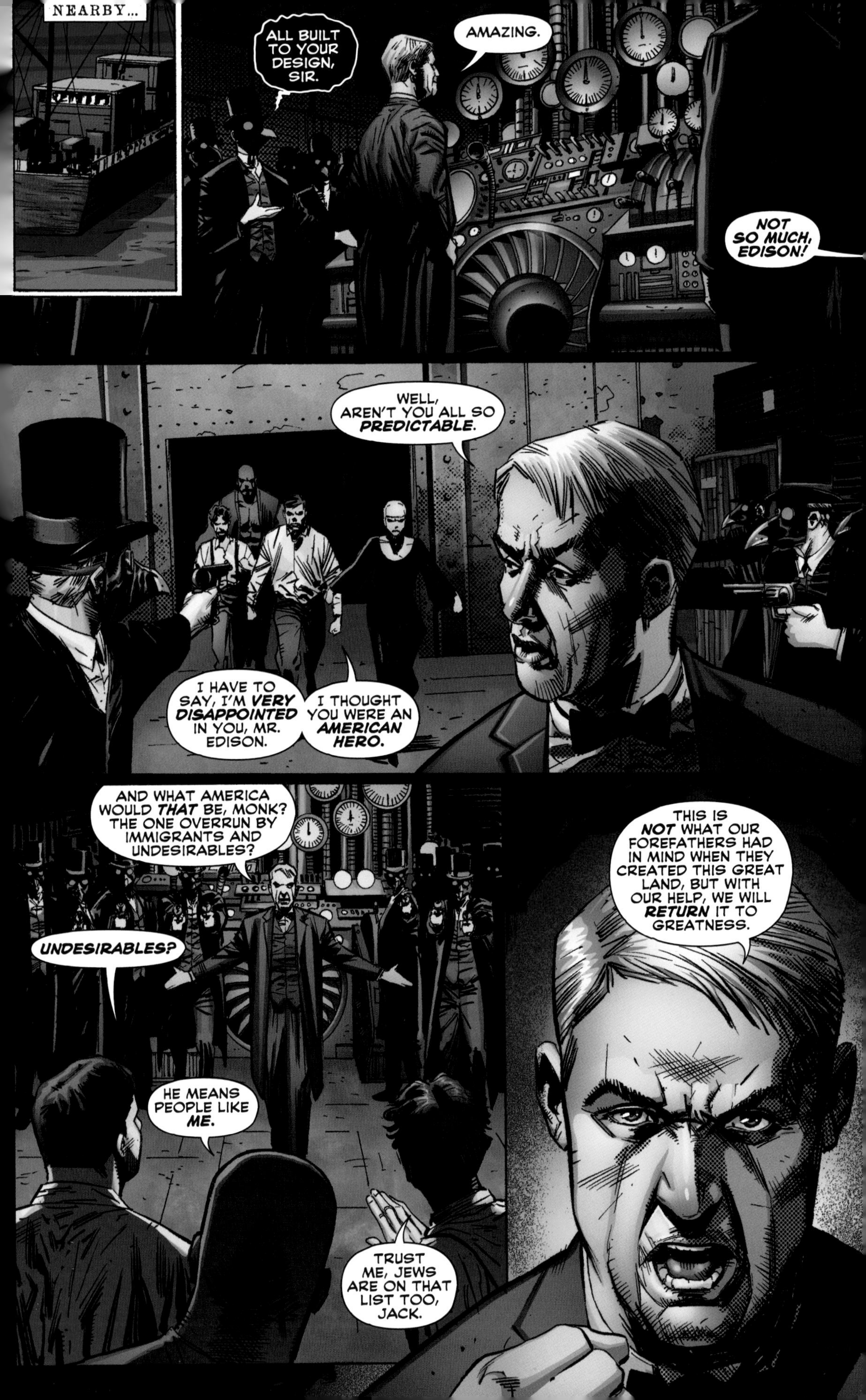
NEARBY...
ALL BUILT TO YOUR DESIGN, SIR.
AMAZING.
NOT SO MUCH, EDISON!
WELL, AREN'T YOU ALL SO PREDICTABLE.
I HAVE TO SAY, I'M VERY DISAPPOINTED IN YOU, MR. EDISON.
I THOUGHT YOU WERE AN AMERICAN HERO.
AND WHAT AMERICA WOULD THAT BE, MONK? THE ONE OVERRUN BY IMMIGRANTS AND UNDESIRABLES?
UNDESIRABLES?
HE MEANS PEOPLE LIKE ME.
TRUST ME, JEWS ARE ON THAT LIST TOO, JACK.
THIS IS NOT WHAT OUR FOREFATHERS HAD IN MIND WHEN THEY CREATED THIS GREAT LAND, BUT WITH OUR HELP, WE WILL RETURN IT TO GREATNESS.

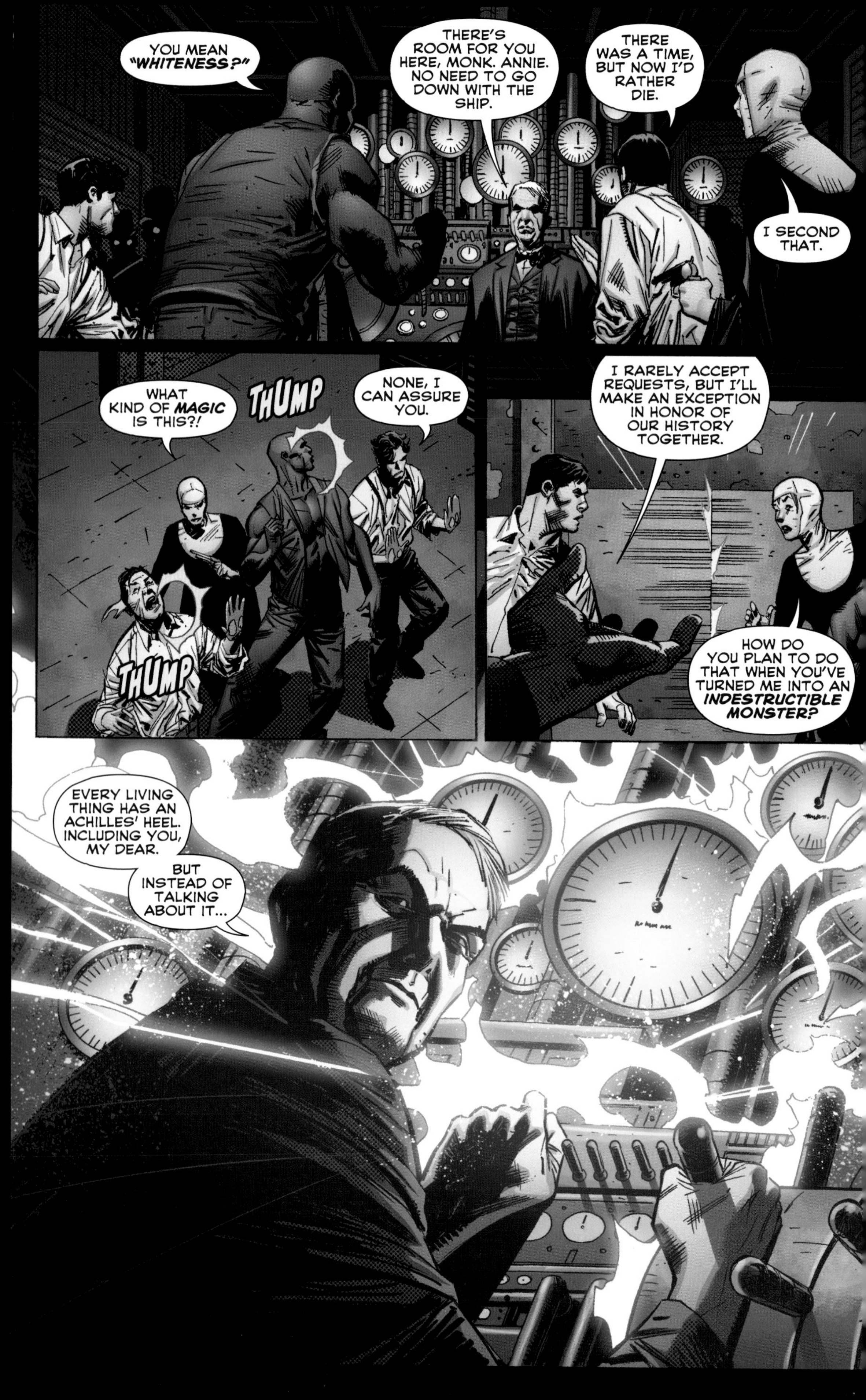
YOU MEAN "WHITENESS?"
THERE'S ROOM FOR YOU HERE, MONK. ANNIE. NO NEED TO GO DOWN WITH THE SHIP.
THERE WAS A TIME, BUT NOW I'D RATHER DIE.
I SECOND THAT.
WHAT KIND OF MAGIC IS THIS?!
THUMP
NONE, I CAN ASSURE YOU.
THUMP
I RARELY ACCEPT REQUESTS, BUT I'LL MAKE AN EXCEPTION IN HONOR OF OUR HISTORY TOGETHER.
HOW DO YOU PLAN TO DO THAT WHEN YOU'VE TURNED ME INTO AN INDESTRUCTIBLE MONSTER?
EVERY LIVING THING HAS AN ACHILLES' HEEL. INCLUDING YOU, MY DEAR.
BUT INSTEAD OF TALKING ABOUT IT...

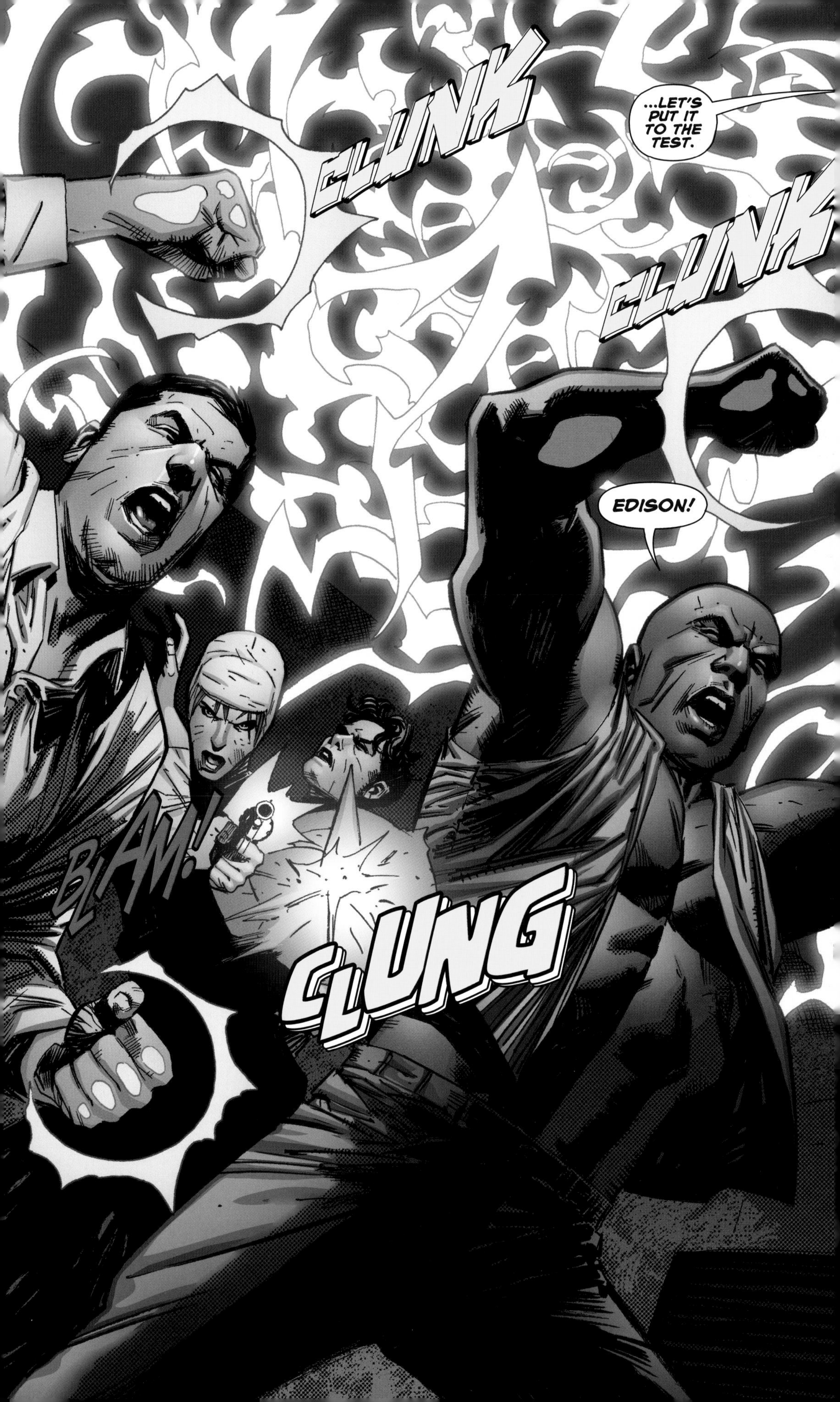
CLUNK
...LET'S PUT IT TO THE TEST.
CLUNK
EDISON!
BLAM!
CLUNG

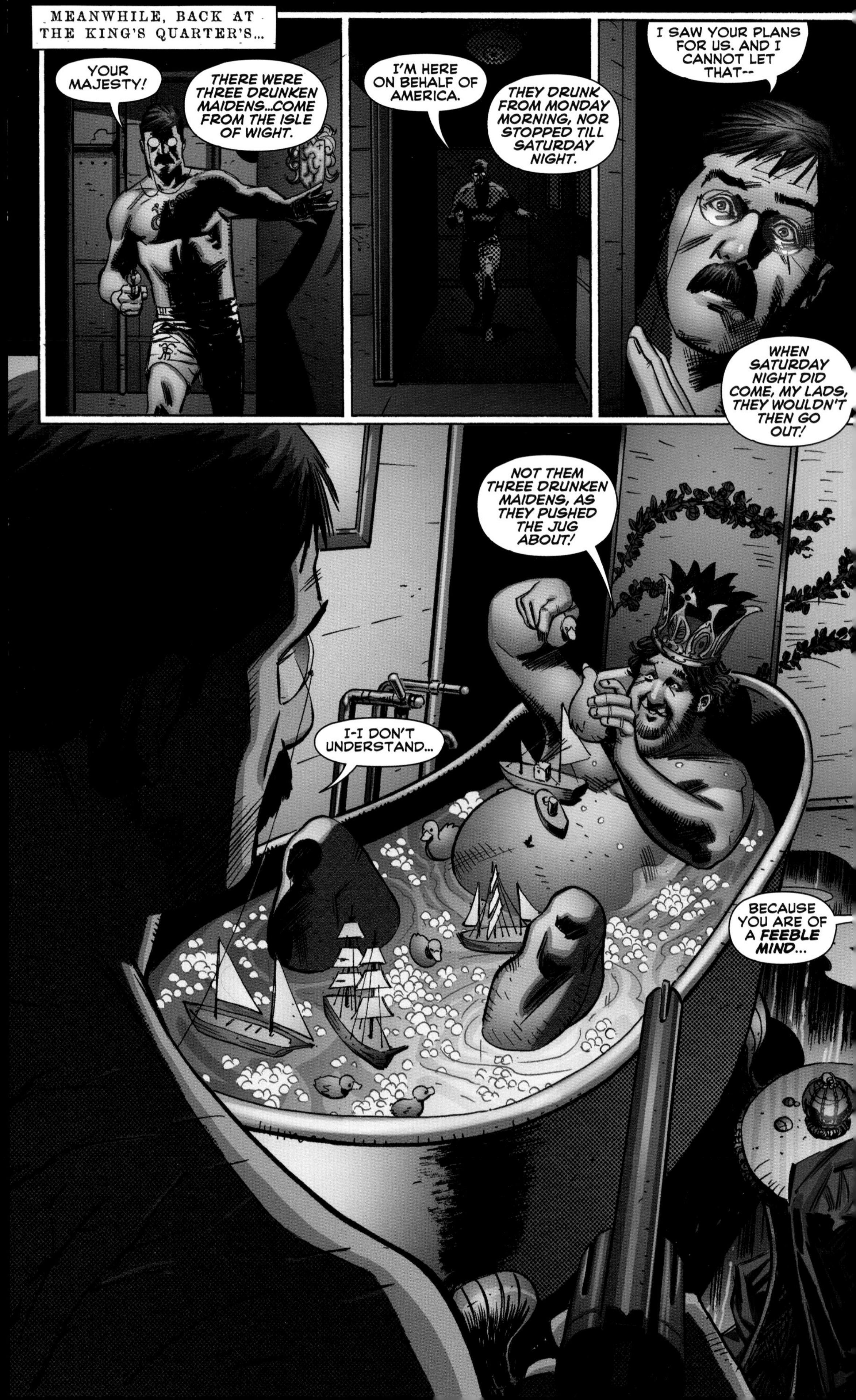

MEANWHILE, BACK AT THE KING'S QUARTER'S...
YOUR MAJESTY!
THERE WERE THREE DRUNKEN MAIDENS...COME FROM THE ISLE OF WIGHT.
I'M HERE ON BEHALF OF AMERICA.
THEY DRUNK FROM MONDAY MORNING, NOR STOPPED TILL SATURDAY NIGHT.
I SAW YOUR PLANS FOR US. AND I CANNOT LET THAT--
WHEN SATURDAY NIGHT DID COME, MY LADS, THEY WOULDN'T THEN GO OUT!
NOT THEM THREE DRUNKEN MAIDENS, AS THEY PUSHED THE JUG ABOUT!
I-I DON'T UNDERSTAND...
BECAUSE YOU ARE OF A FEEBLE MIND...

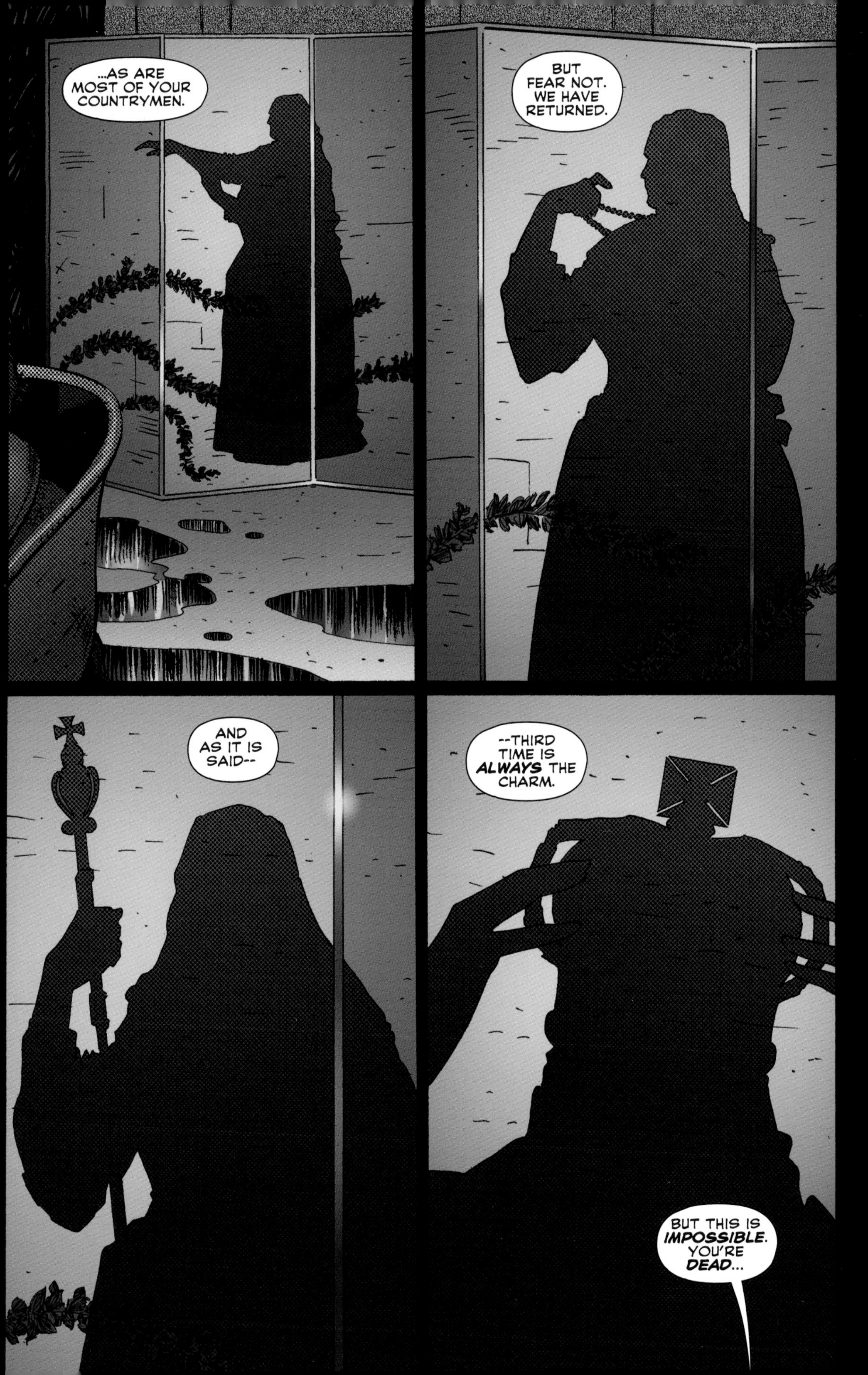
...AS ARE MOST OF YOUR COUNTRYMEN.
BUT FEAR NOT. WE HAVE RETURNED.
AND AS IT IS SAID--
--THIRD TIME IS **ALWAYS** THE CHARM.
BUT THIS IS ***IMPOSSIBLE***. YOU'RE ***DEAD***...

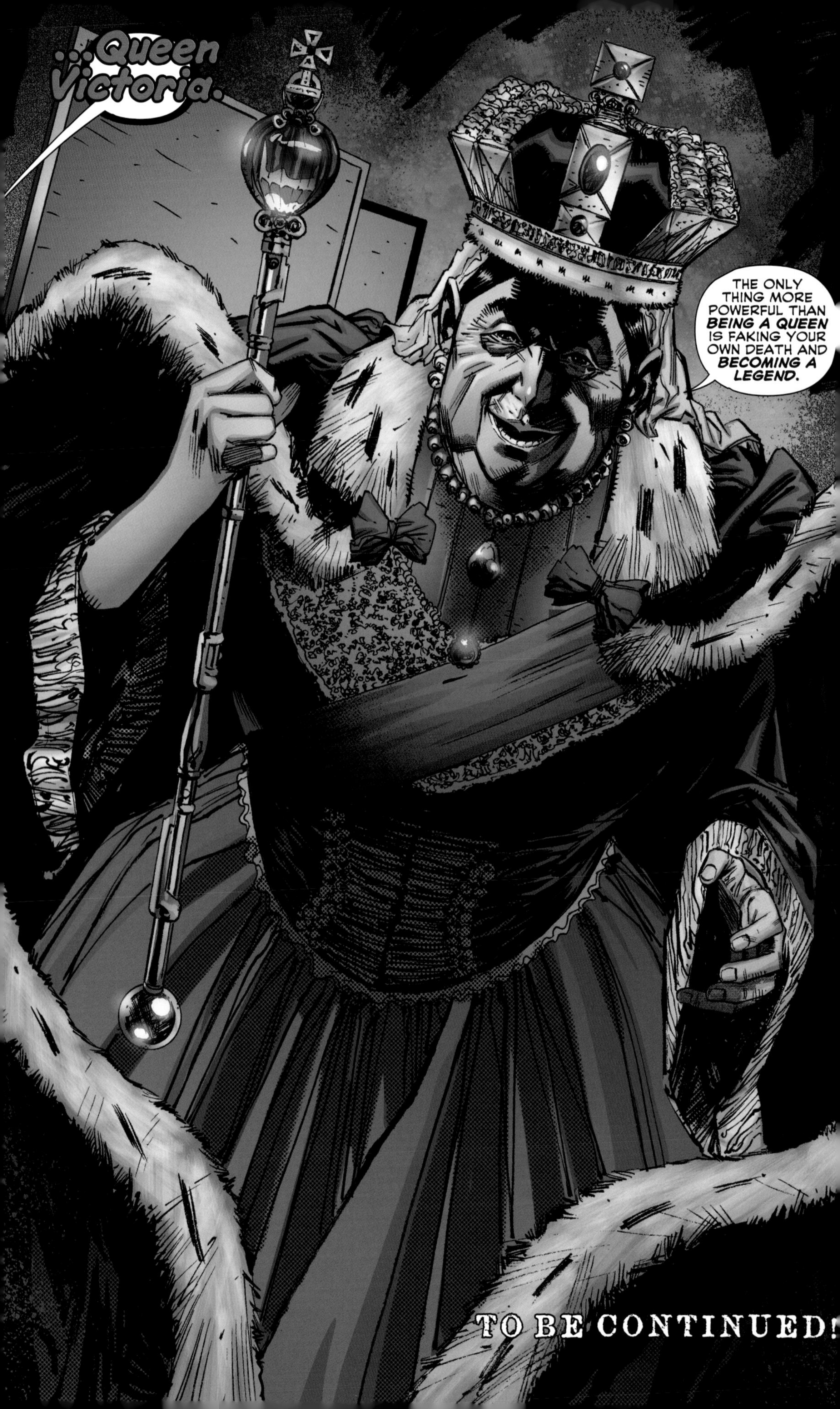
...Queen Victoria.
THE ONLY THING MORE POWERFUL THAN ***BEING A QUEEN*** IS FAKING YOUR OWN DEATH AND ***BECOMING A LEGEND.***
TO BE CONTINUED!

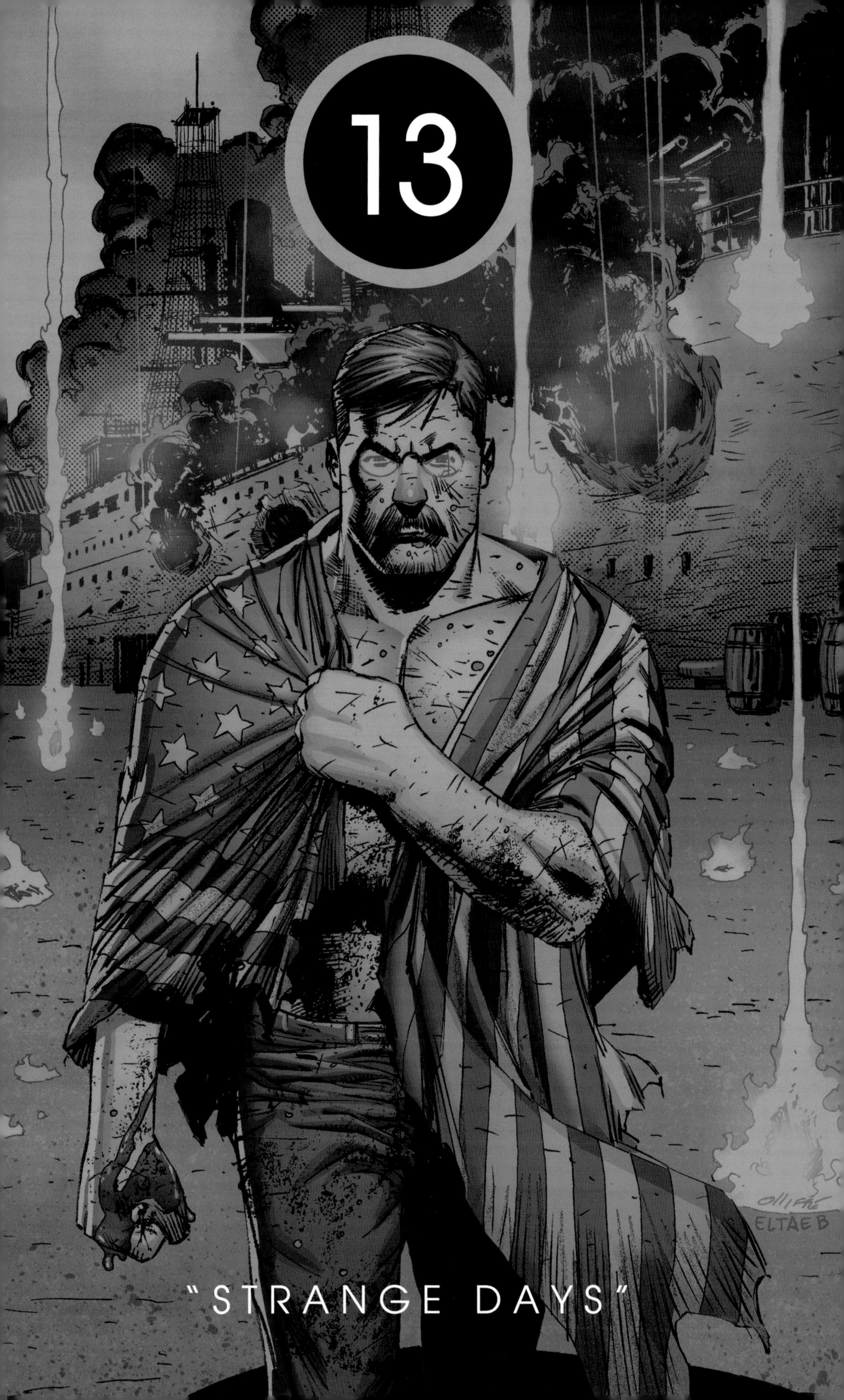
13
"STRANGE DAYS"

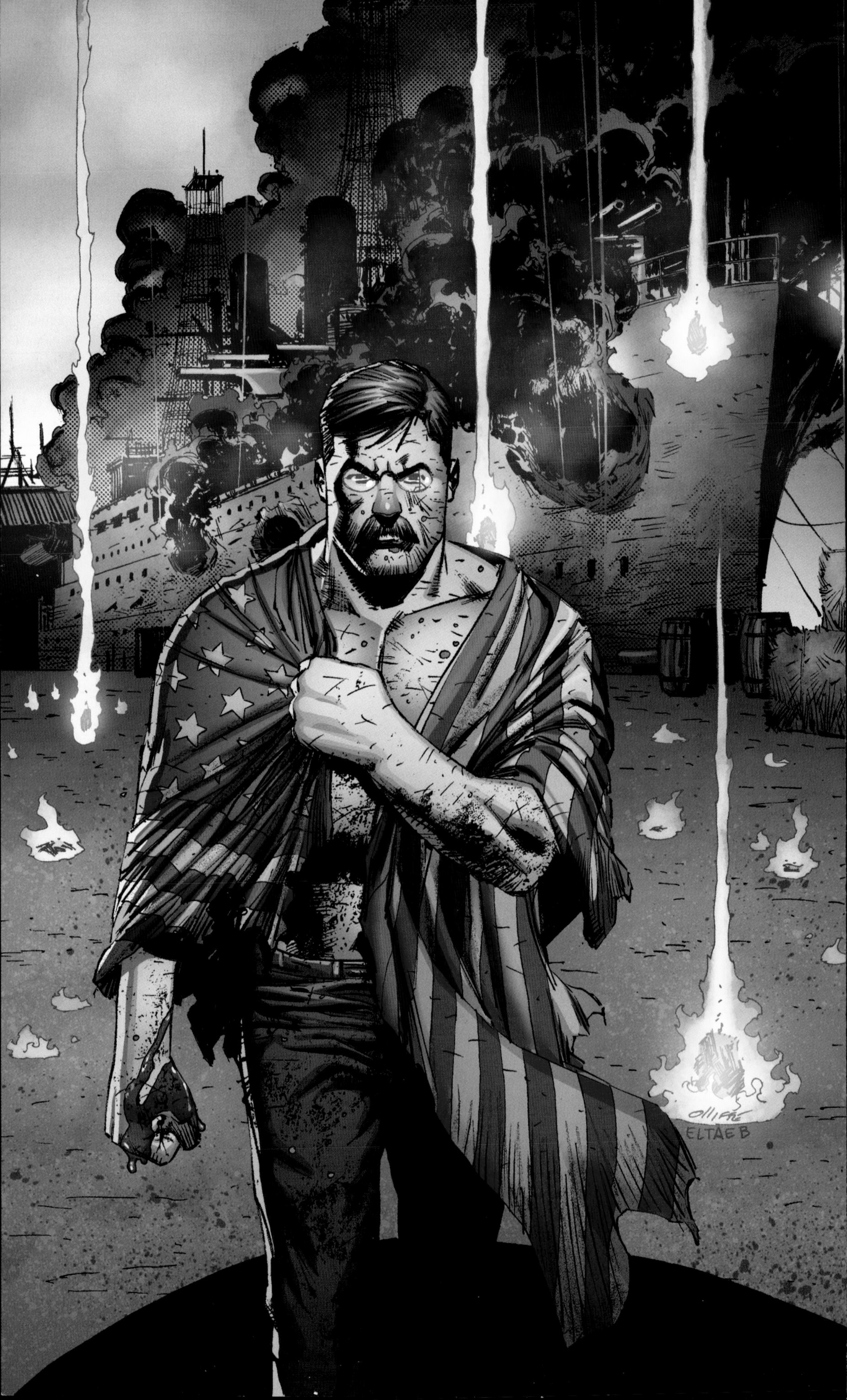

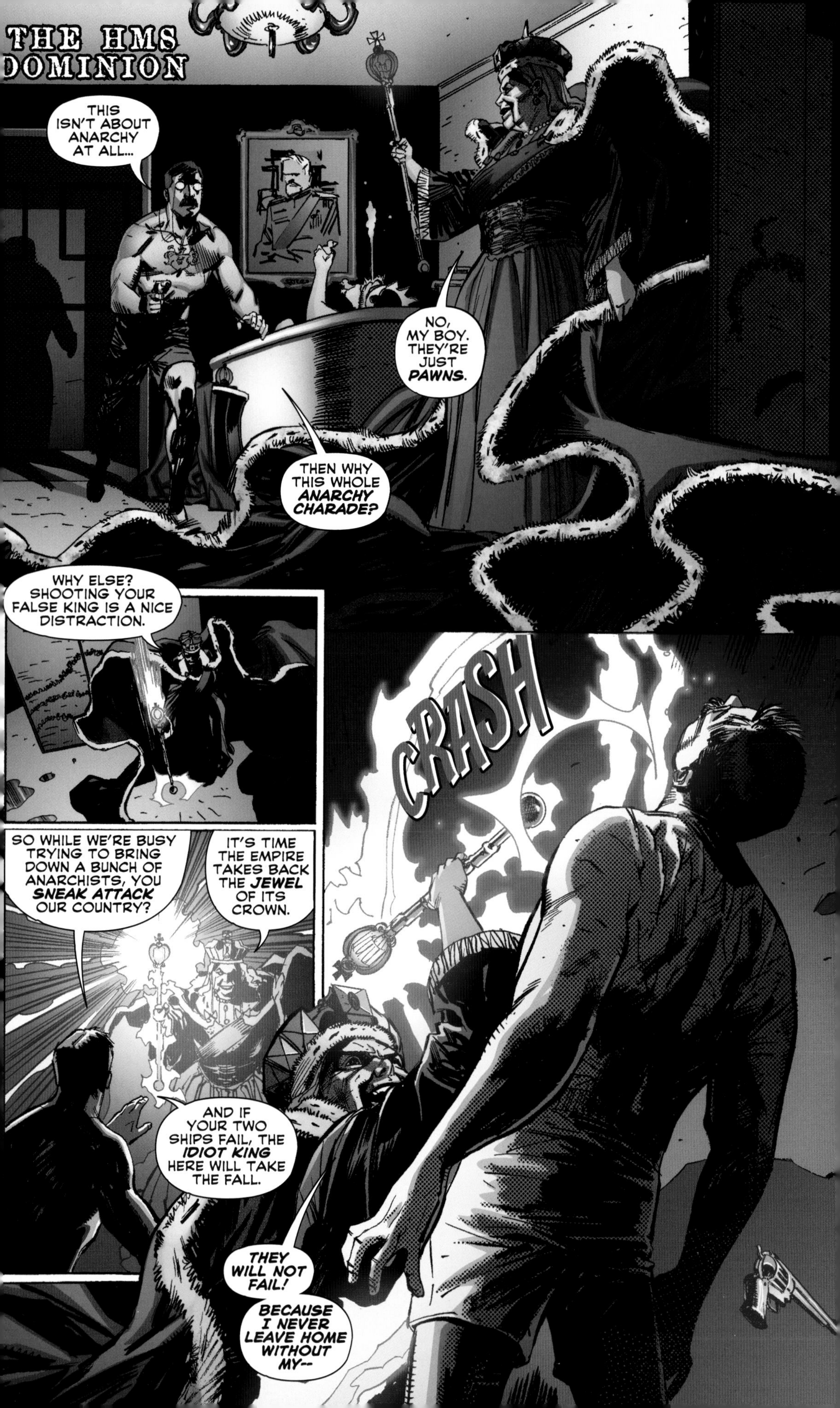
THE HMS DOMINION
THIS ISN'T ABOUT ANARCHY AT ALL...
NO, MY BOY. THEY'RE JUST PAWNS.
THEN WHY THIS WHOLE ANARCHY CHARADE?
WHY ELSE? SHOOTING YOUR FALSE KING IS A NICE DISTRACTION.
SO WHILE WE'RE BUSY TRYING TO BRING DOWN A BUNCH OF ANARCHISTS, YOU SNEAK ATTACK OUR COUNTRY?
IT'S TIME THE EMPIRE TAKES BACK THE JEWEL OF ITS CROWN.
AND IF YOUR TWO SHIPS FAIL, THE IDIOT KING HERE WILL TAKE THE FALL.
THEY WILL NOT FAIL!
BECAUSE I NEVER LEAVE HOME WITHOUT MY--
CRASH

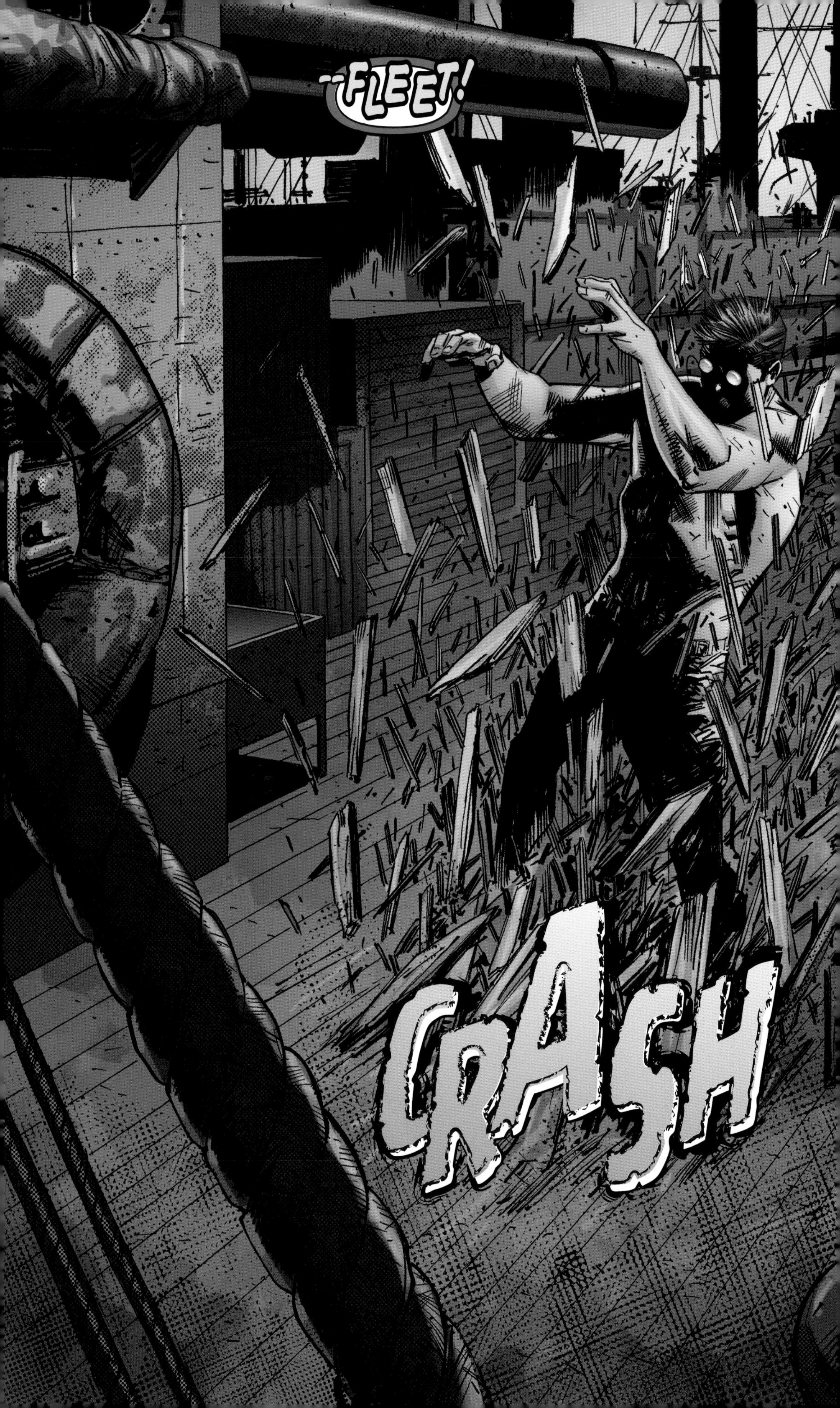
--FLEET!
CRASH

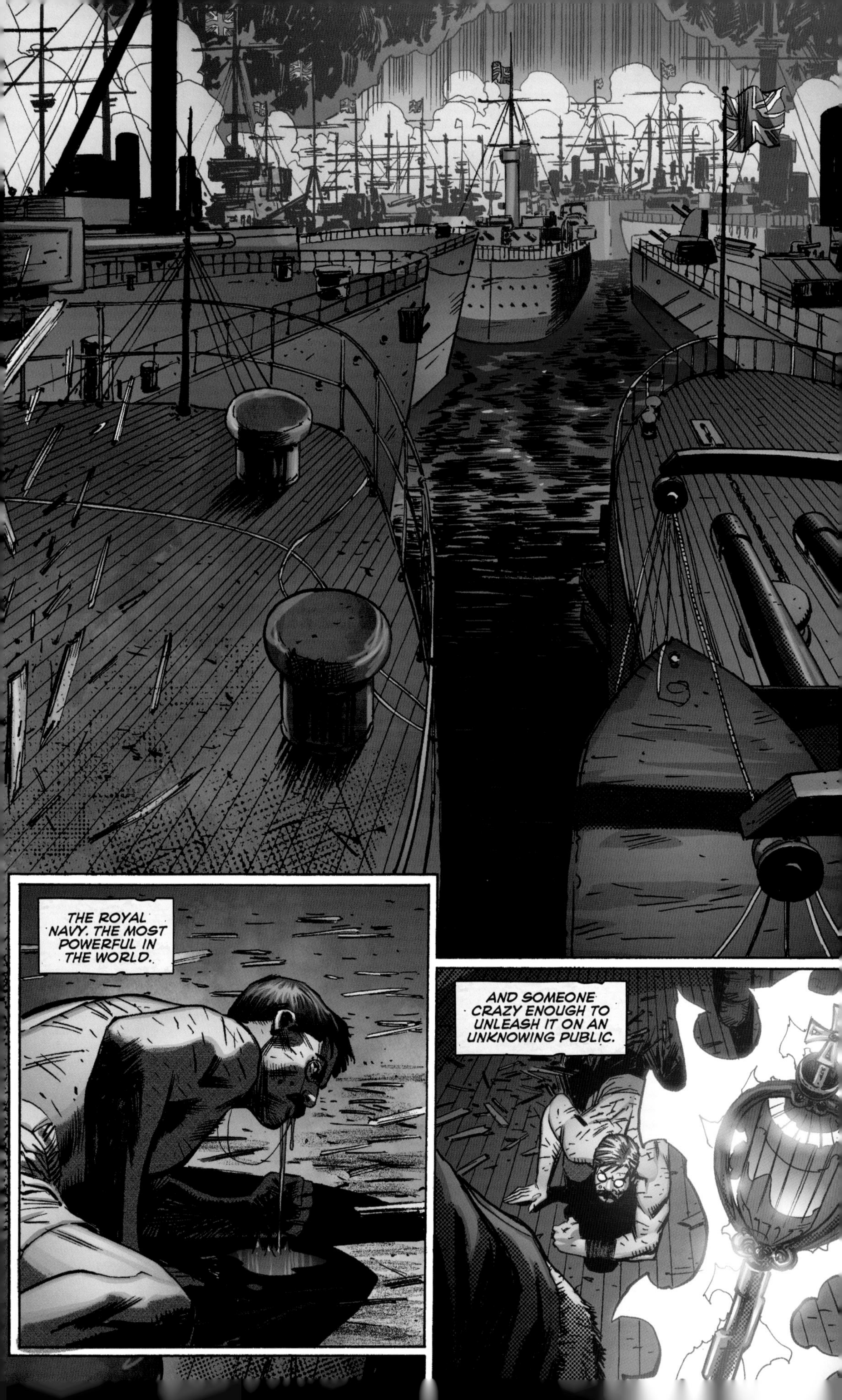
THE ROYAL NAVY. THE MOST POWERFUL IN THE WORLD.
AND SOMEONE CRAZY ENOUGH TO UNLEASH IT ON AN UNKNOWING PUBLIC.

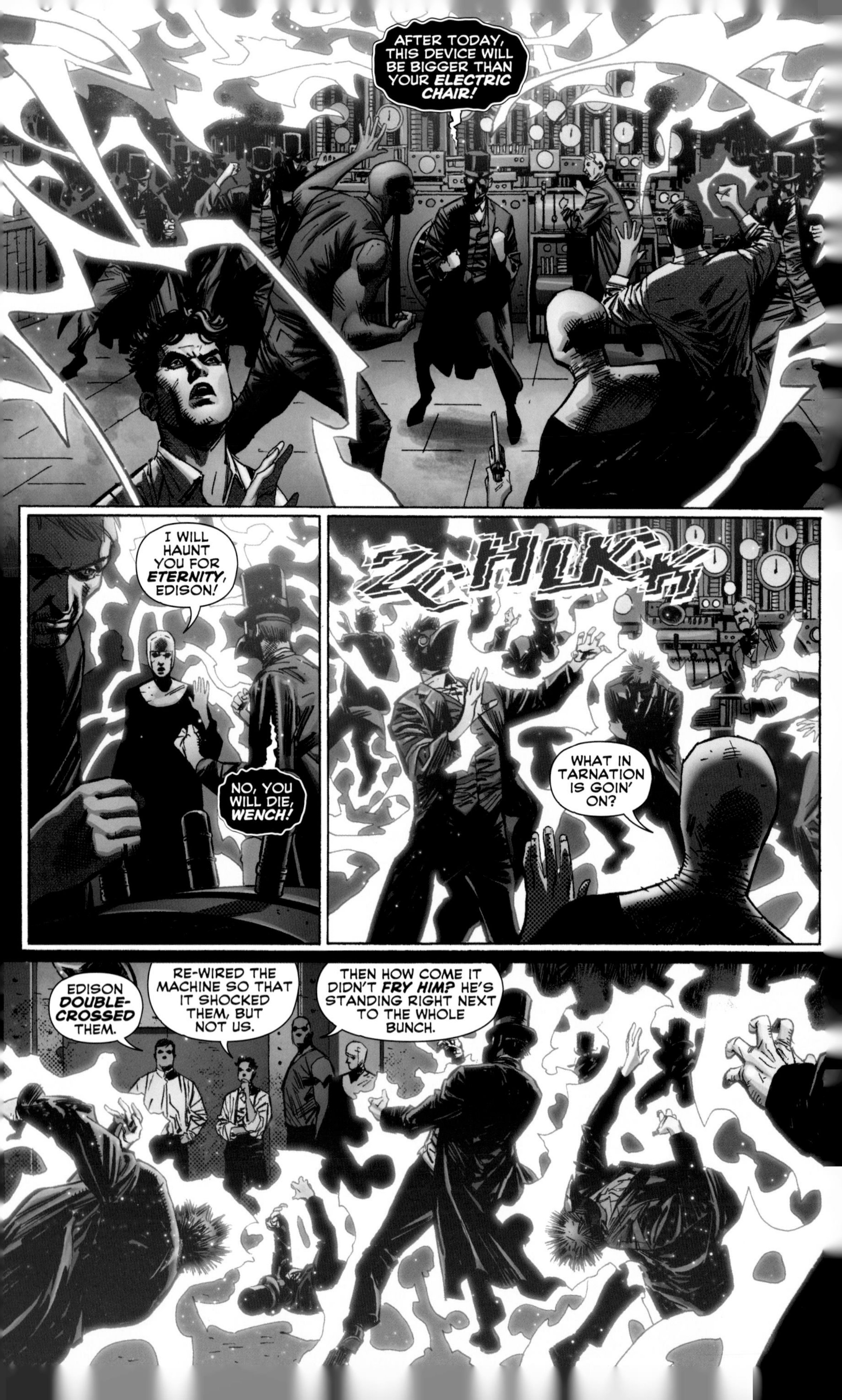
AFTER TODAY, THIS DEVICE WILL BE BIGGER THAN YOUR *ELECTRIC CHAIR!*
I WILL HAUNT YOU FOR *ETERNITY*, EDISON!
NO, YOU WILL DIE, *WENCH!*
ZZHUKK
WHAT IN TARNATION IS GOIN' ON?
EDISON *DOUBLE-CROSSED* THEM.
RE-WIRED THE MACHINE SO THAT IT SHOCKED THEM, BUT NOT US.
THEN HOW COME IT DIDN'T *FRY HIM?* HE'S STANDING RIGHT NEXT TO THE WHOLE BUNCH.

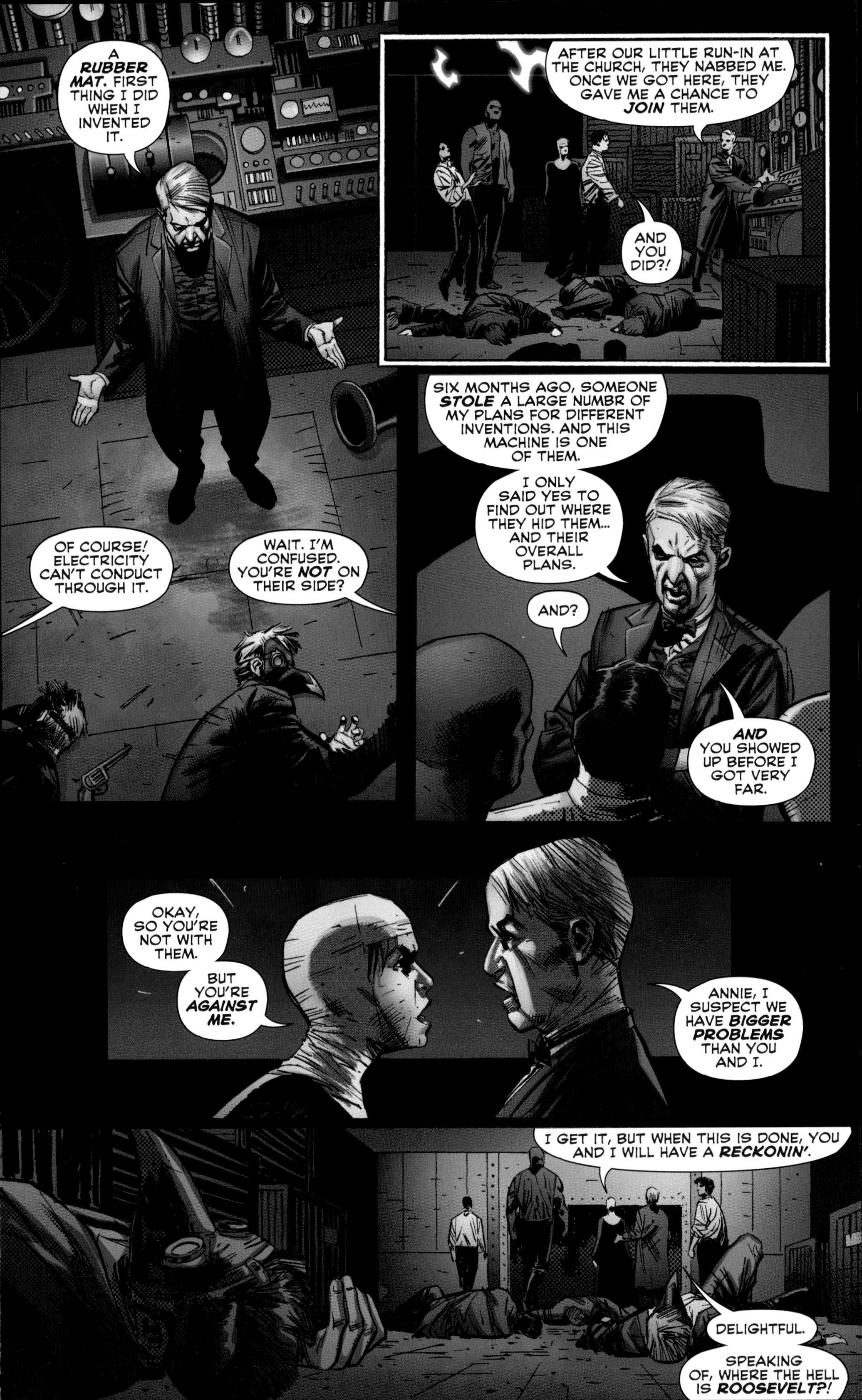
A RUBBER MAT. FIRST THING I DID WHEN I INVENTED IT.
AFTER OUR LITTLE RUN-IN AT THE CHURCH, THEY NABBED ME. ONCE WE GOT HERE, THEY GAVE ME A CHANCE TO JOIN THEM.
AND YOU DID?!
OF COURSE! ELECTRICITY CAN'T CONDUCT THROUGH IT.
WAIT. I'M CONFUSED. YOU'RE NOT ON THEIR SIDE?
SIX MONTHS AGO, SOMEONE STOLE A LARGE NUMBR OF MY PLANS FOR DIFFERENT INVENTIONS. AND THIS MACHINE IS ONE OF THEM.
I ONLY SAID YES TO FIND OUT WHERE THEY HID THEM... AND THEIR OVERALL PLANS.
AND?
AND YOU SHOWED UP BEFORE I GOT VERY FAR.
OKAY, SO YOU'RE NOT WITH THEM.
BUT YOU'RE AGAINST ME.
ANNIE, I SUSPECT WE HAVE BIGGER PROBLEMS THAN YOU AND I.
I GET IT, BUT WHEN THIS IS DONE, YOU AND I WILL HAVE A RECKONIN'.
DELIGHTFUL.
SPEAKING OF, WHERE THE HELL IS ROOSEVELT?!

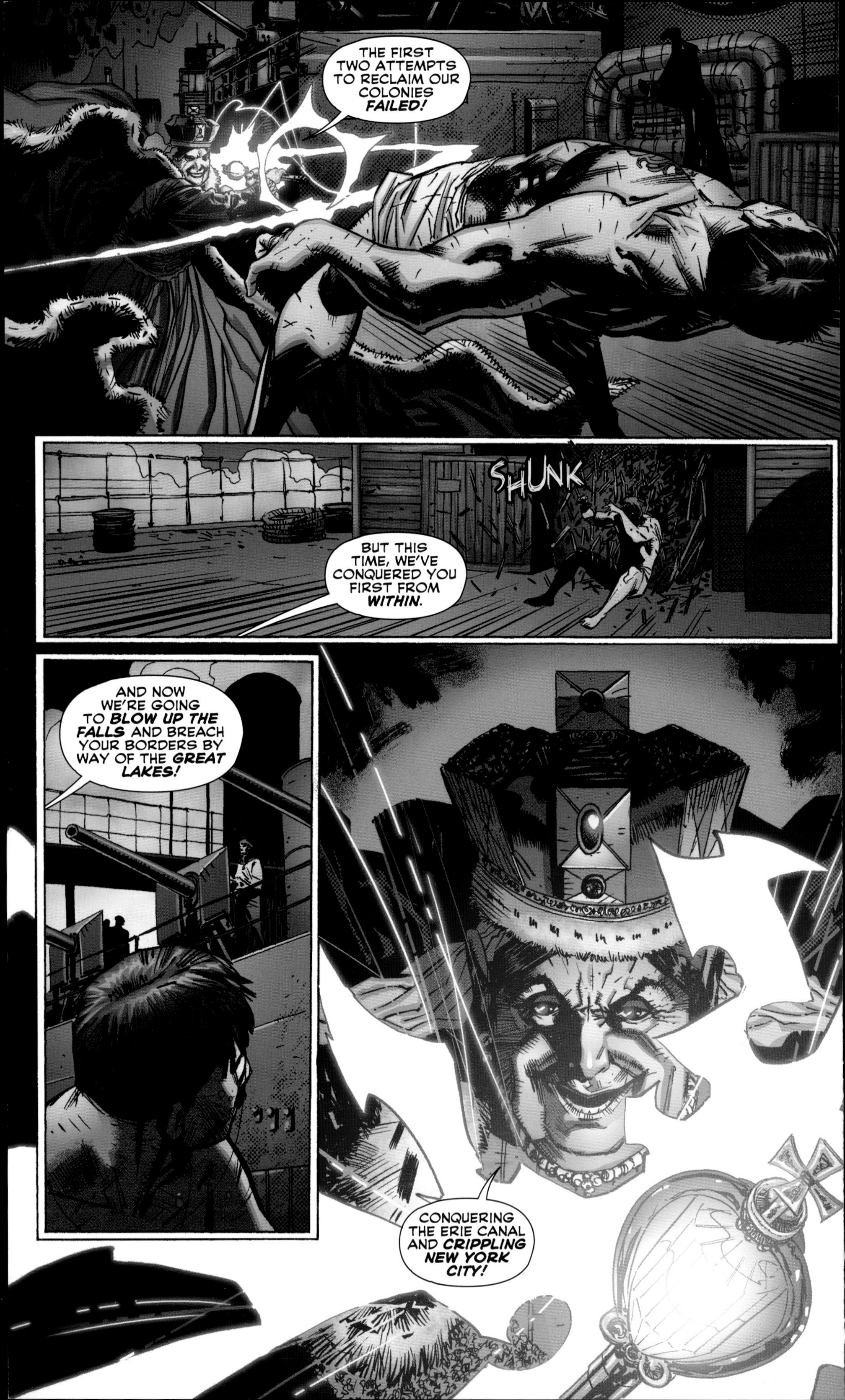
THE FIRST TWO ATTEMPTS TO RECLAIM OUR COLONIES FAILED!
SHUNK
BUT THIS TIME, WE'VE CONQUERED YOU FIRST FROM WITHIN.
AND NOW WE'RE GOING TO BLOW UP THE FALLS AND BREACH YOUR BORDERS BY WAY OF THE GREAT LAKES!
CONQUERING THE ERIE CANAL AND CRIPPLING NEW YORK CITY!

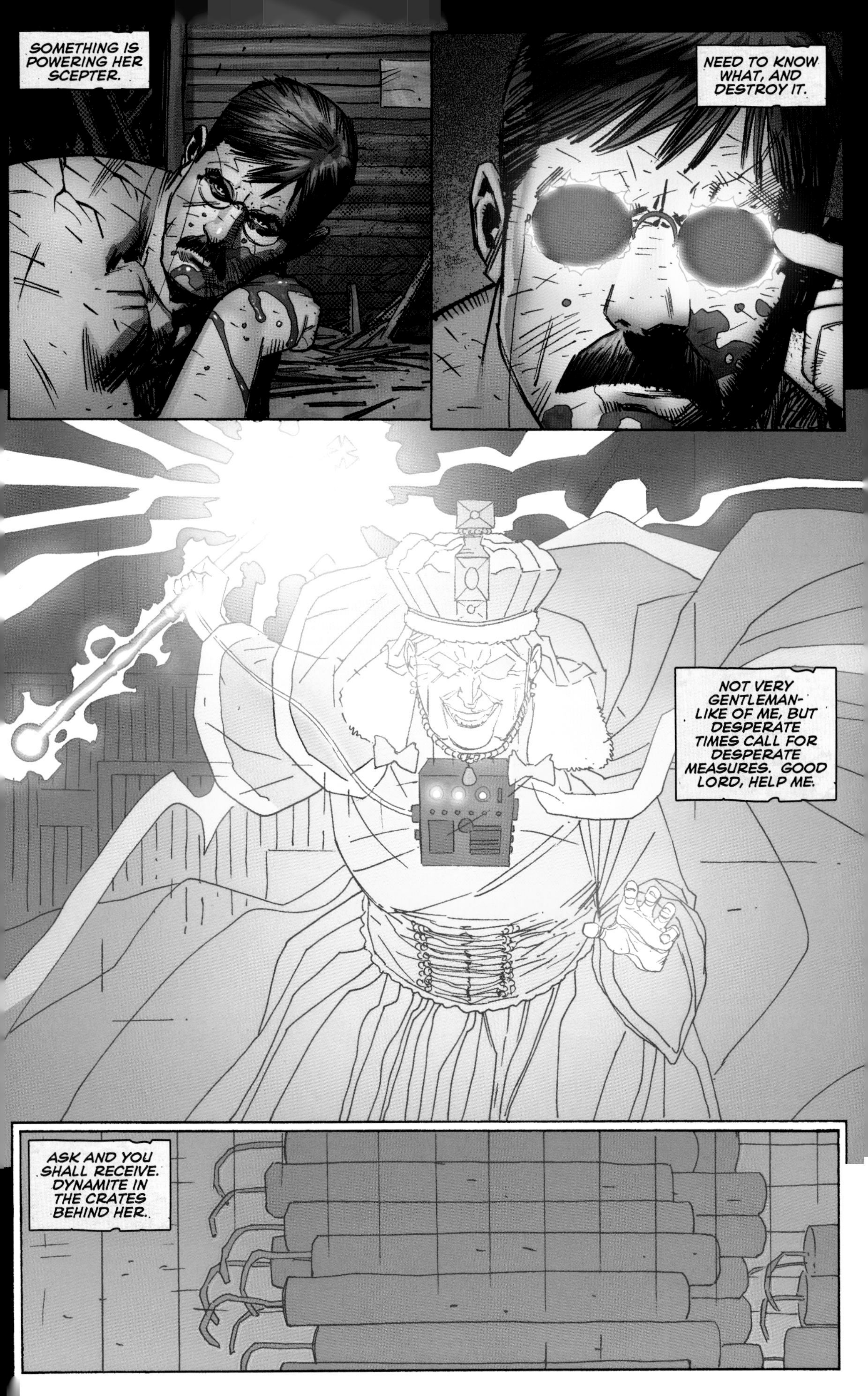
SOMETHING IS POWERING HER SCEPTER.
NEED TO KNOW WHAT, AND DESTROY IT.
NOT VERY GENTLEMAN-LIKE OF ME, BUT DESPERATE TIMES CALL FOR DESPERATE MEASURES. GOOD LORD, HELP ME.
ASK AND YOU SHALL RECEIVE. DYNAMITE IN THE CRATES BEHIND HER..

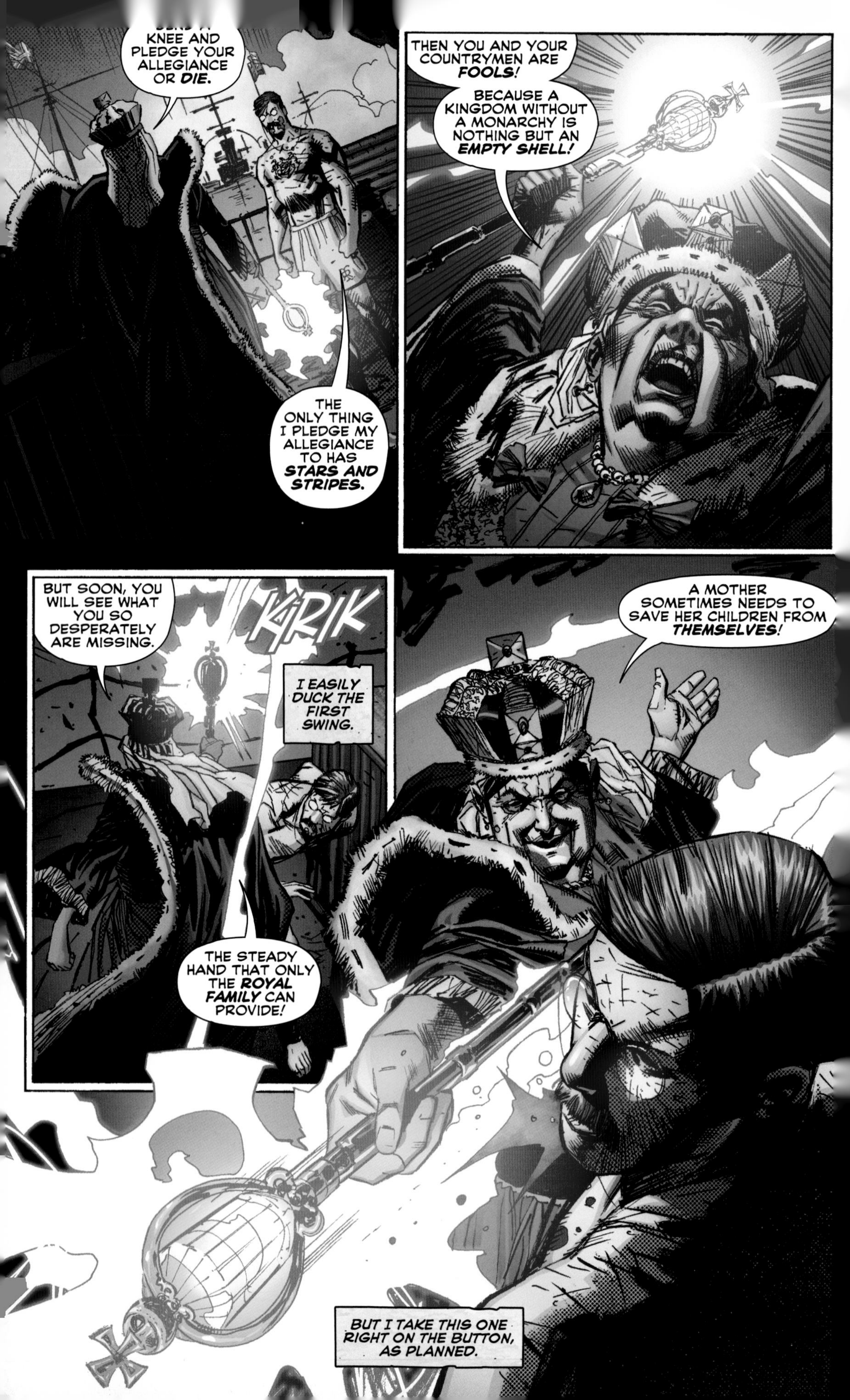
KNEE AND PLEDGE YOUR ALLEGIANCE OR DIE.
THE ONLY THING I PLEDGE MY ALLEGIANCE TO HAS STARS AND STRIPES.
THEN YOU AND YOUR COUNTRYMEN ARE FOOLS!
BECAUSE A KINGDOM WITHOUT A MONARCHY IS NOTHING BUT AN EMPTY SHELL!
BUT SOON, YOU WILL SEE WHAT YOU SO DESPERATELY ARE MISSING.
KRIK
I EASILY DUCK THE FIRST SWING.
THE STEADY HAND THAT ONLY THE ROYAL FAMILY CAN PROVIDE!
A MOTHER SOMETIMES NEEDS TO SAVE HER CHILDREN FROM THEMSELVES!
BUT I TAKE THIS ONE RIGHT ON THE BUTTON, AS PLANNED.

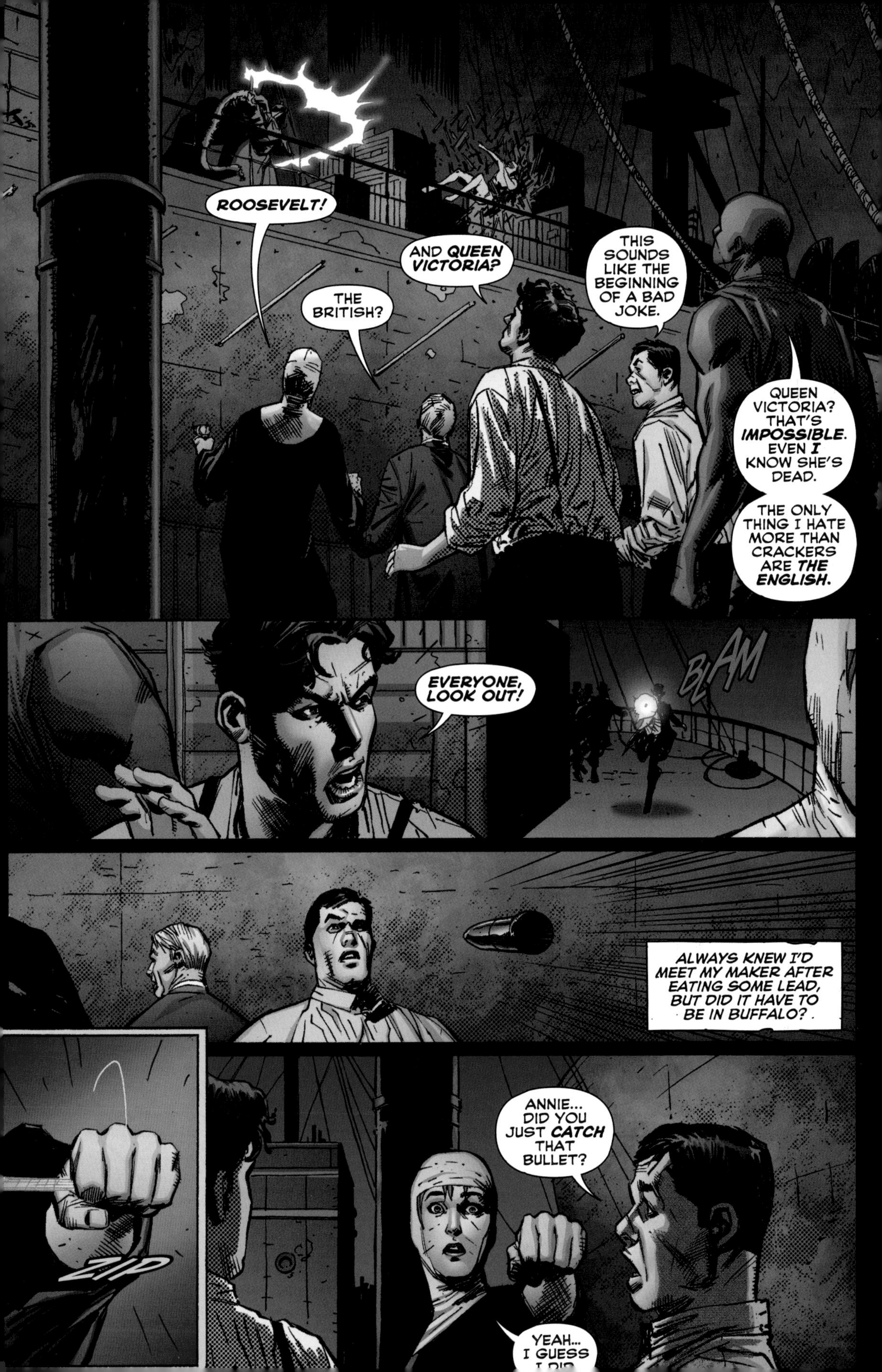
ROOSEVELT!
AND QUEEN VICTORIA?
THE BRITISH?
THIS SOUNDS LIKE THE BEGINNING OF A BAD JOKE.
QUEEN VICTORIA? THAT'S IMPOSSIBLE. EVEN I KNOW SHE'S DEAD.
THE ONLY THING I HATE MORE THAN CRACKERS ARE THE ENGLISH.
EVERYONE, LOOK OUT!
BLAM
ALWAYS KNEW I'D MEET MY MAKER AFTER EATING SOME LEAD, BUT DID IT HAVE TO BE IN BUFFALO?
ZIP
ANNIE... DID YOU JUST CATCH THAT BULLET?
YEAH... I GUESS

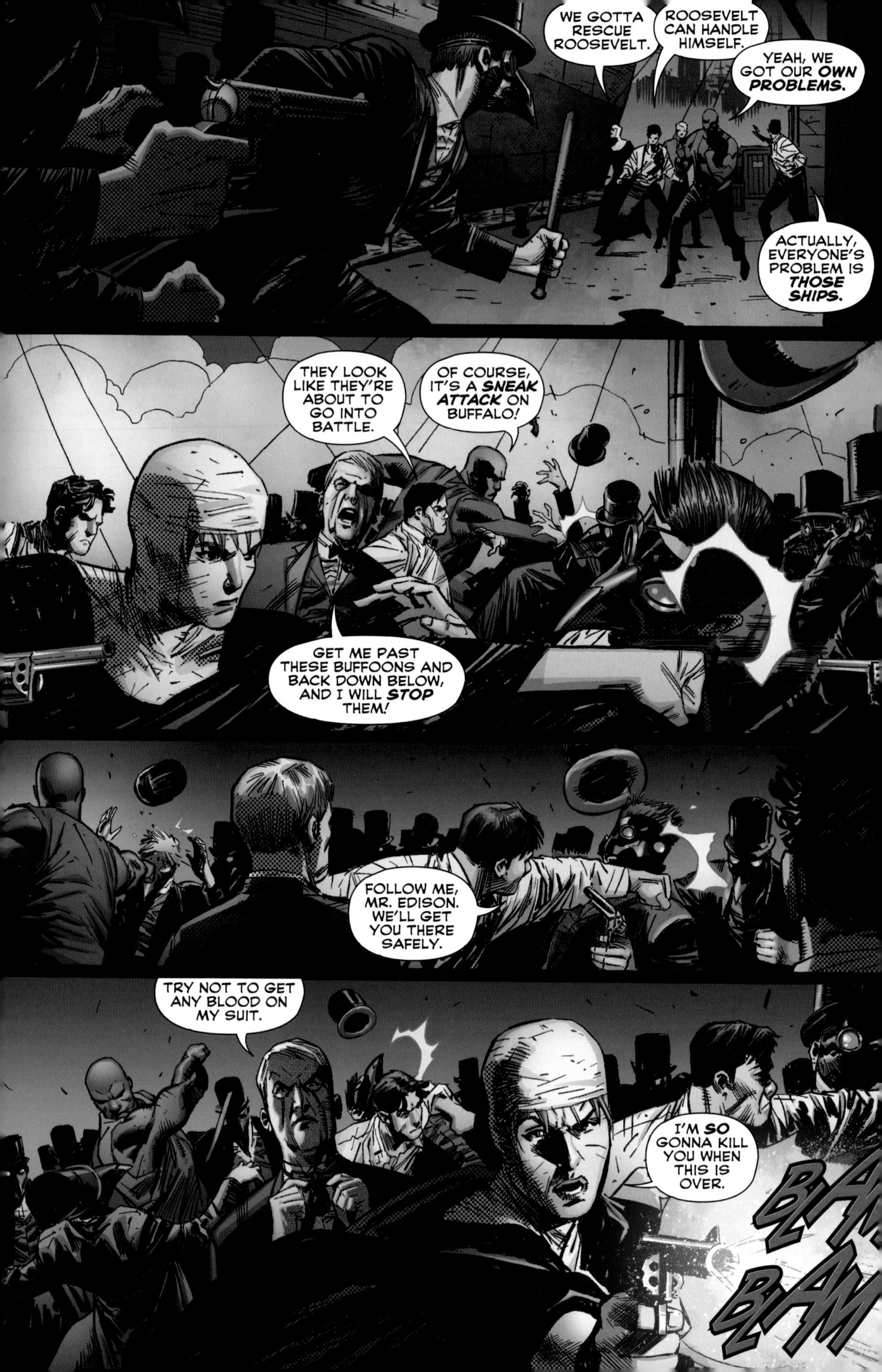
WE GOTTA RESCUE ROOSEVELT.
ROOSEVELT CAN HANDLE HIMSELF.
YEAH, WE GOT OUR OWN PROBLEMS.
ACTUALLY, EVERYONE'S PROBLEM IS THOSE SHIPS.
THEY LOOK LIKE THEY'RE ABOUT TO GO INTO BATTLE.
OF COURSE, IT'S A SNEAK ATTACK ON BUFFALO!
GET ME PAST THESE BUFFOONS AND BACK DOWN BELOW, AND I WILL STOP THEM!
FOLLOW ME, MR. EDISON. WE'LL GET YOU THERE SAFELY.
TRY NOT TO GET ANY BLOOD ON MY SUIT.
I'M SO GONNA KILL YOU WHEN THIS IS OVER.
BLAM BLAM

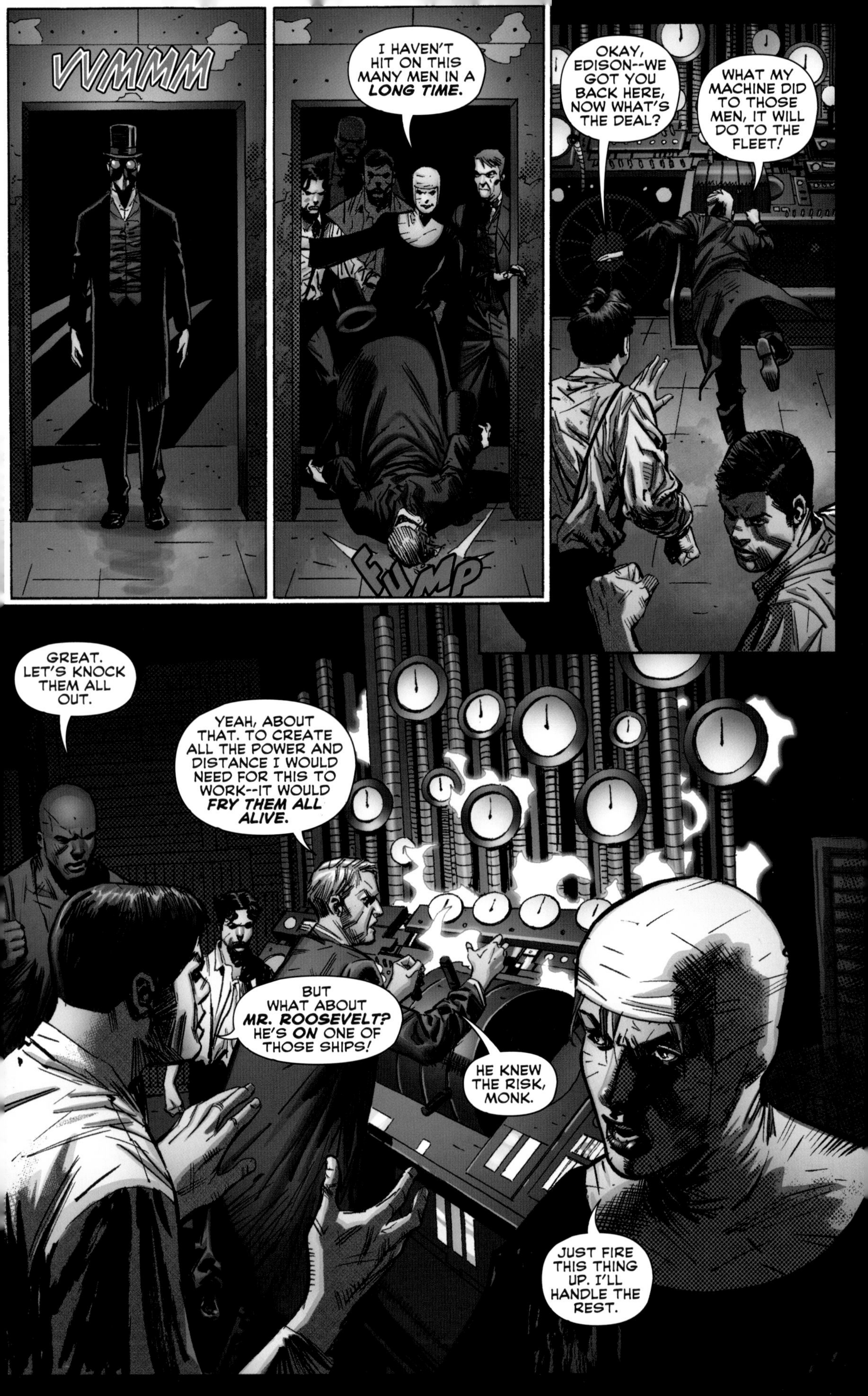
VVMMM
I HAVEN'T HIT ON THIS MANY MEN IN A **LONG TIME.**
FUMP
OKAY, EDISON--WE GOT YOU BACK HERE, NOW WHAT'S THE DEAL?
WHAT MY MACHINE DID TO THOSE MEN, IT WILL DO TO THE FLEET!
GREAT. LET'S KNOCK THEM ALL OUT.
YEAH, ABOUT THAT. TO CREATE ALL THE POWER AND DISTANCE I WOULD NEED FOR THIS TO WORK--IT WOULD ***FRY THEM ALL ALIVE.***
BUT WHAT ABOUT ***MR. ROOSEVELT?*** HE'S ***ON*** ONE OF THOSE SHIPS!
HE KNEW THE RISK, MONK.
JUST FIRE THIS THING UP. I'LL HANDLE THE REST.

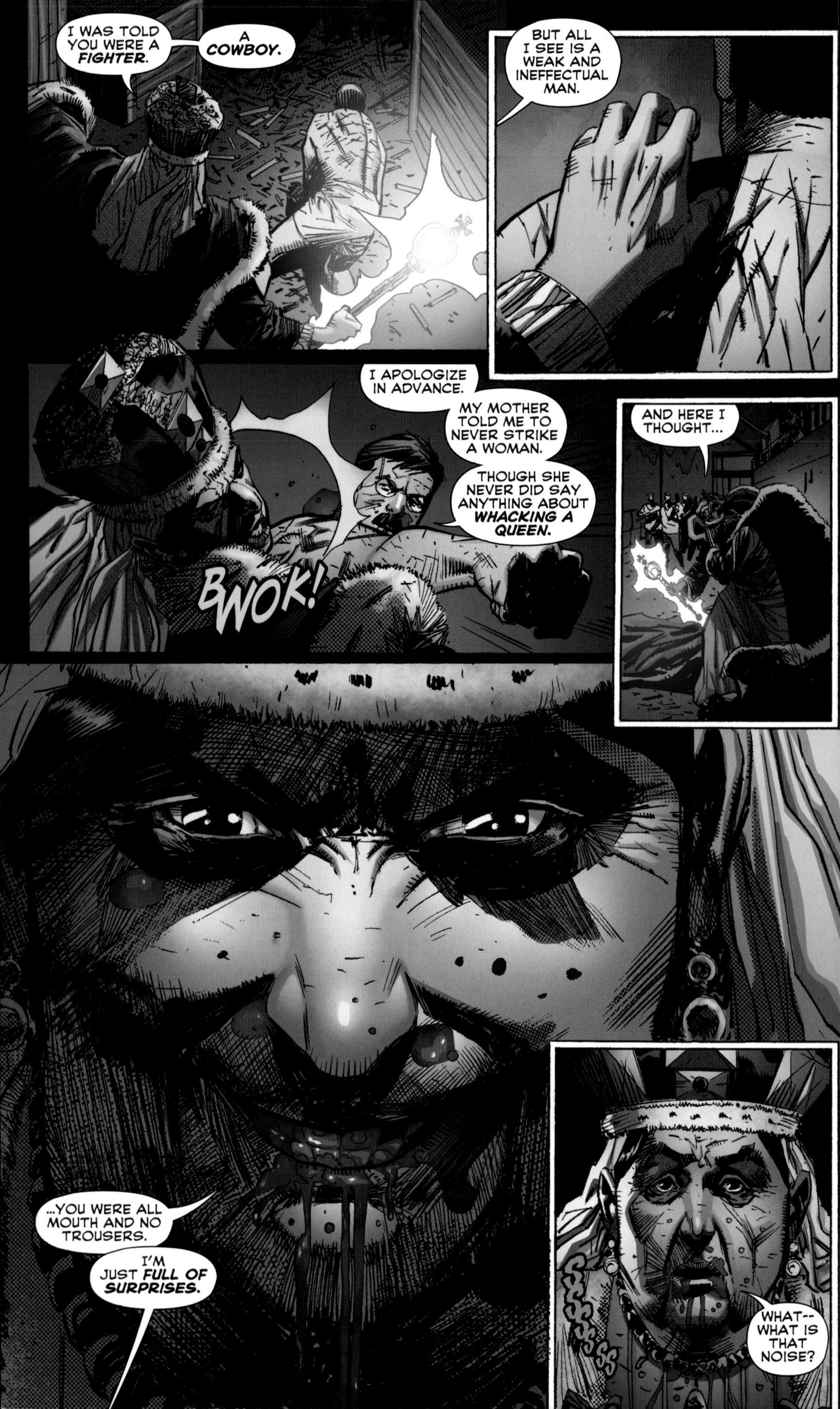
I WAS TOLD YOU WERE A FIGHTER.
A COWBOY.
BUT ALL I SEE IS A WEAK AND INEFFECTUAL MAN.
I APOLOGIZE IN ADVANCE.
MY MOTHER TOLD ME TO NEVER STRIKE A WOMAN.
THOUGH SHE NEVER DID SAY ANYTHING ABOUT WHACKING A QUEEN.
BWOK!
AND HERE I THOUGHT...
...YOU WERE ALL MOUTH AND NO TROUSERS.
I'M JUST FULL OF SURPRISES.
SSSSSSS
WHAT-- WHAT IS THAT NOISE?

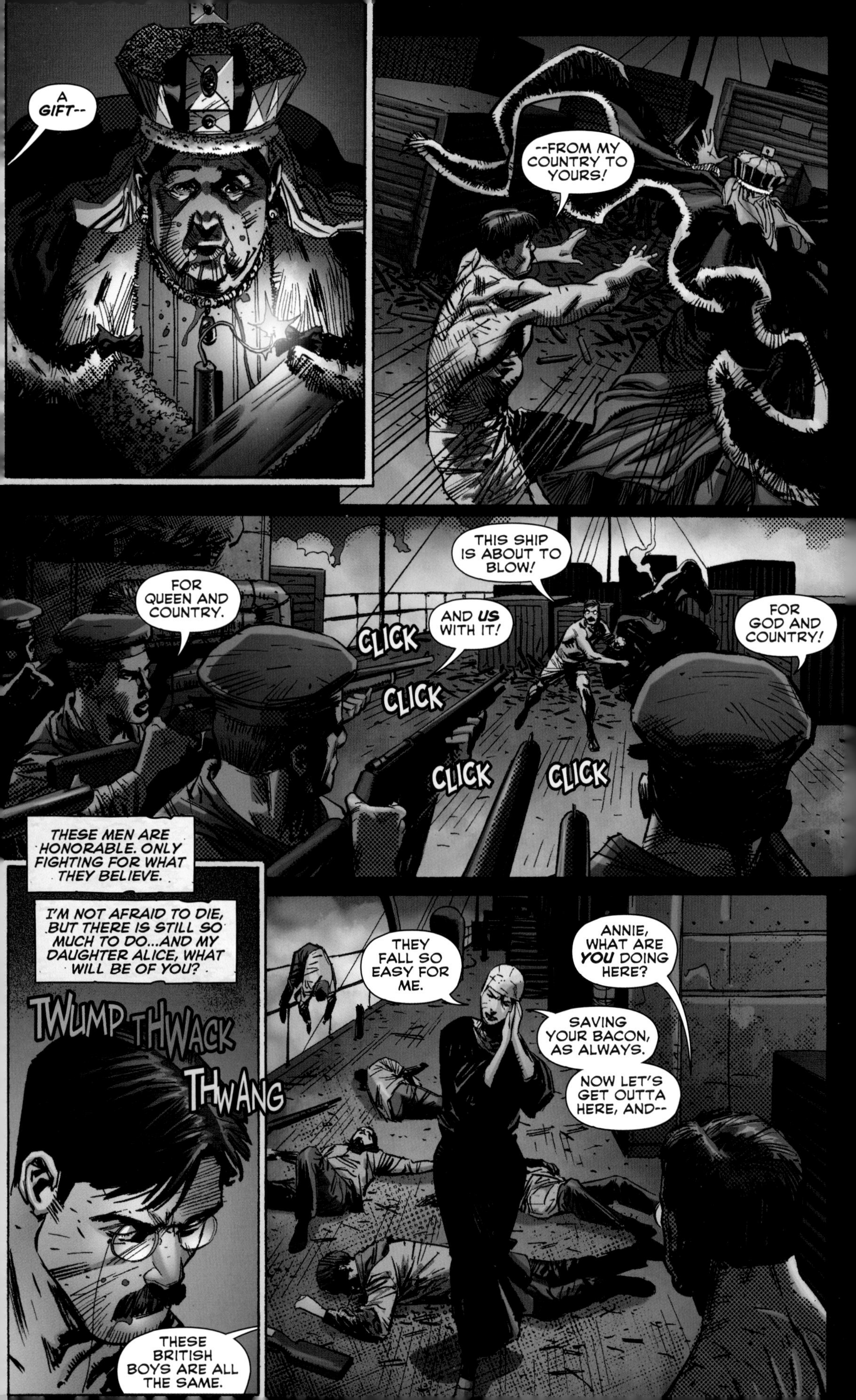
A GIFT--
--FROM MY COUNTRY TO YOURS!
FOR QUEEN AND COUNTRY.
CLICK
CLICK
AND US WITH IT!
THIS SHIP IS ABOUT TO BLOW!
FOR GOD AND COUNTRY!
CLICK
CLICK
THESE MEN ARE HONORABLE. ONLY FIGHTING FOR WHAT THEY BELIEVE.
I'M NOT AFRAID TO DIE, BUT THERE IS STILL SO MUCH TO DO...AND MY DAUGHTER ALICE, WHAT WILL BE OF YOU?
TWUMP THWACK
THWANG
THESE BRITISH BOYS ARE ALL THE SAME.
THEY FALL SO EASY FOR ME.
ANNIE, WHAT ARE YOU DOING HERE?
SAVING YOUR BACON, AS ALWAYS.
NOW LET'S GET OUTTA HERE, AND--

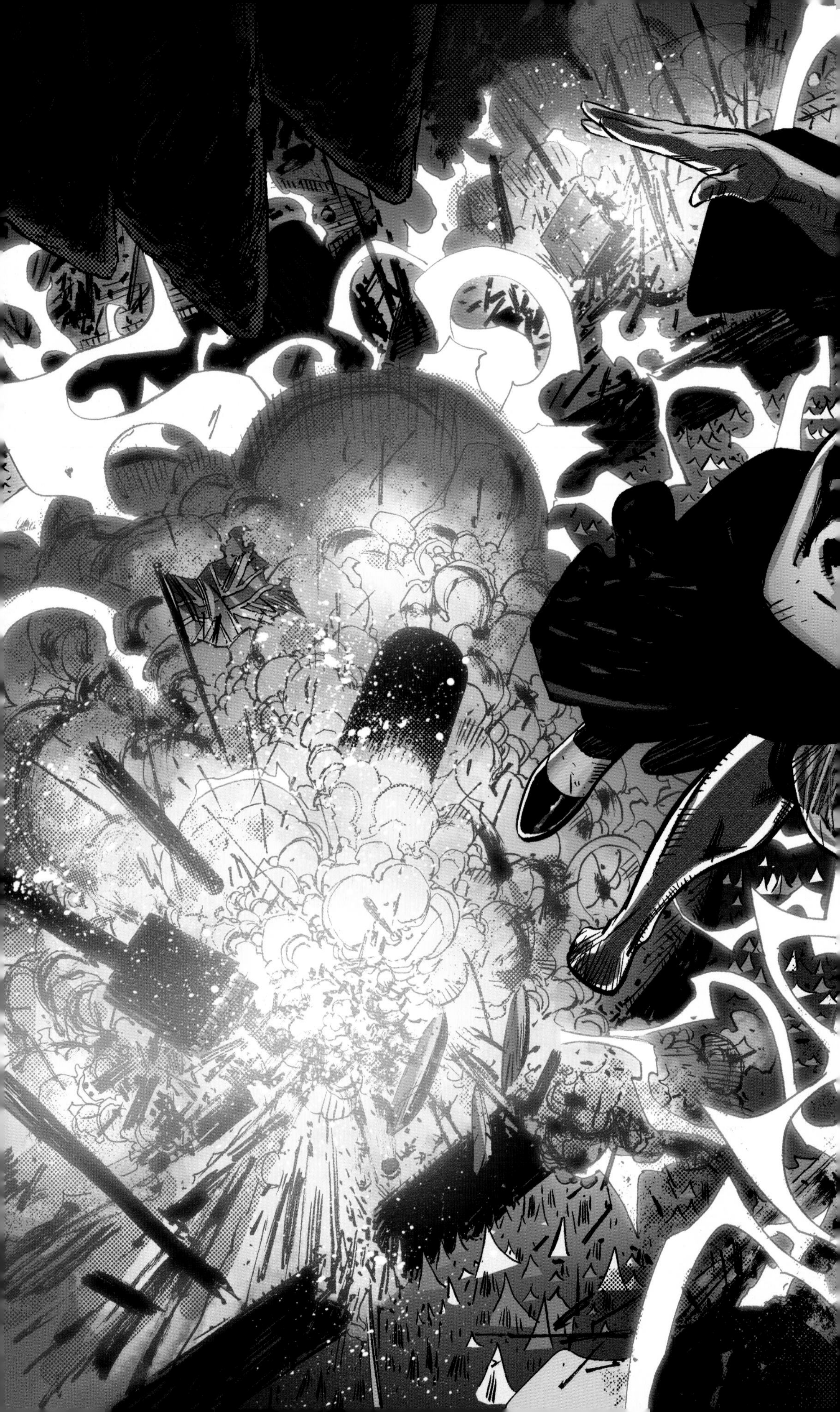

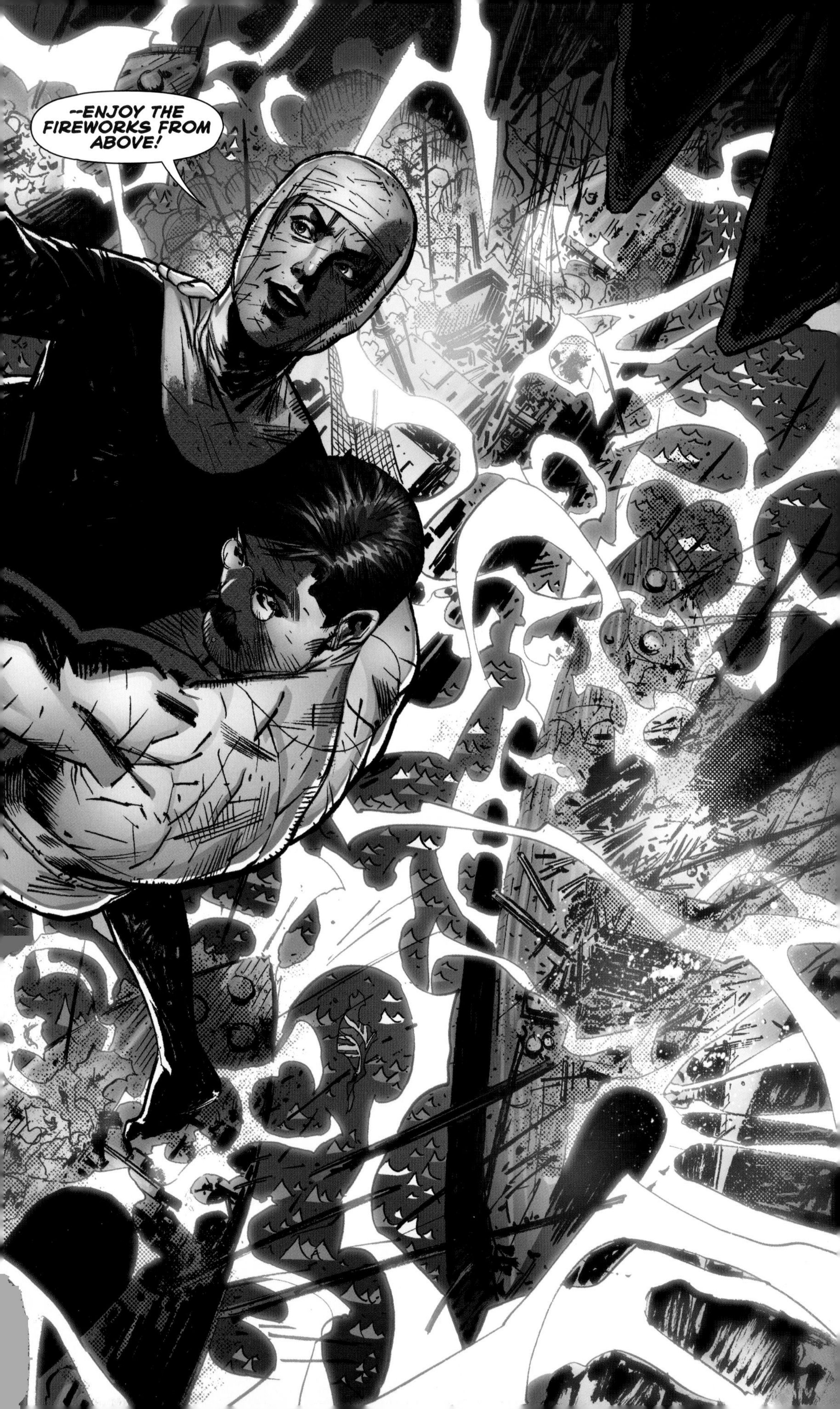
--ENJOY THE FIREWORKS FROM ABOVE!

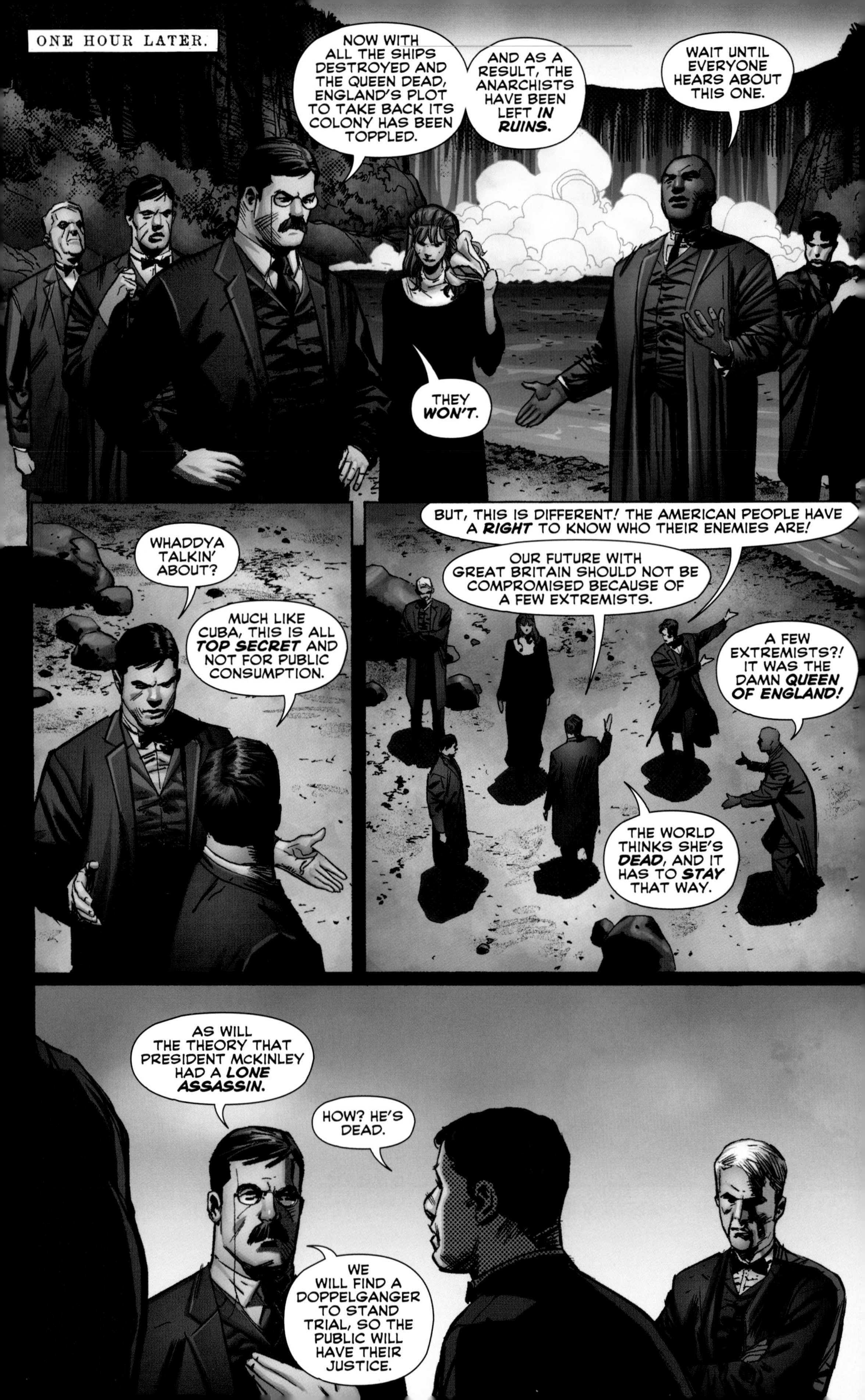
ONE HOUR LATER.
NOW WITH ALL THE SHIPS DESTROYED AND THE QUEEN DEAD, ENGLAND'S PLOT TO TAKE BACK ITS COLONY HAS BEEN TOPPLED.
AND AS A RESULT, THE ANARCHISTS HAVE BEEN LEFT *IN RUINS.*
WAIT UNTIL EVERYONE HEARS ABOUT THIS ONE.
THEY *WON'T*.
WHADDYA TALKIN' ABOUT?
MUCH LIKE CUBA, THIS IS ALL *TOP SECRET* AND NOT FOR PUBLIC CONSUMPTION.
BUT, THIS IS DIFFERENT! THE AMERICAN PEOPLE HAVE A *RIGHT* TO KNOW WHO THEIR ENEMIES ARE!
OUR FUTURE WITH GREAT BRITAIN SHOULD NOT BE COMPROMISED BECAUSE OF A FEW EXTREMISTS.
A FEW EXTREMISTS?! IT WAS THE DAMN *QUEEN OF ENGLAND!*
THE WORLD THINKS SHE'S *DEAD,* AND IT HAS TO *STAY* THAT WAY.
AS WILL THE THEORY THAT PRESIDENT MCKINLEY HAD A *LONE ASSASSIN.*
HOW? HE'S DEAD.
WE WILL FIND A DOPPELGANGER TO STAND TRIAL, SO THE PUBLIC WILL HAVE THEIR JUSTICE.

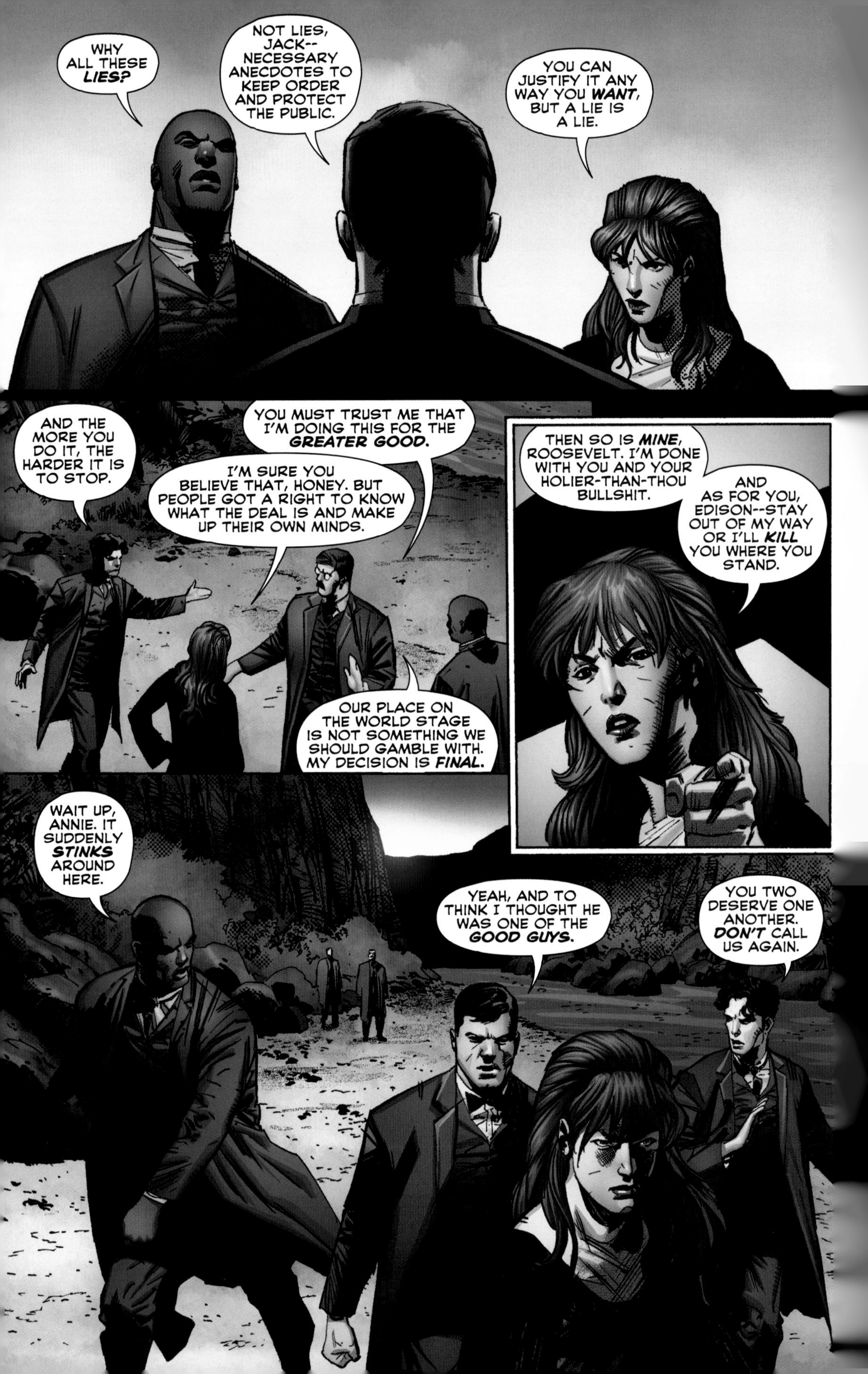
WHY ALL THESE LIES?
NOT LIES, JACK-- NECESSARY ANECDOTES TO KEEP ORDER AND PROTECT THE PUBLIC.
YOU CAN JUSTIFY IT ANY WAY YOU WANT, BUT A LIE IS A LIE.
AND THE MORE YOU DO IT, THE HARDER IT IS TO STOP.
YOU MUST TRUST ME THAT I'M DOING THIS FOR THE GREATER GOOD.
I'M SURE YOU BELIEVE THAT, HONEY. BUT PEOPLE GOT A RIGHT TO KNOW WHAT THE DEAL IS AND MAKE UP THEIR OWN MINDS.
OUR PLACE ON THE WORLD STAGE IS NOT SOMETHING WE SHOULD GAMBLE WITH. MY DECISION IS FINAL.
THEN SO IS MINE, ROOSEVELT. I'M DONE WITH YOU AND YOUR HOLIER-THAN-THOU BULLSHIT.
AND AS FOR YOU, EDISON--STAY OUT OF MY WAY OR I'LL KILL YOU WHERE YOU STAND.
WAIT UP, ANNIE. IT SUDDENLY STINKS AROUND HERE.
YEAH, AND TO THINK I THOUGHT HE WAS ONE OF THE GOOD GUYS.
YOU TWO DESERVE ONE ANOTHER. DON'T CALL US AGAIN.

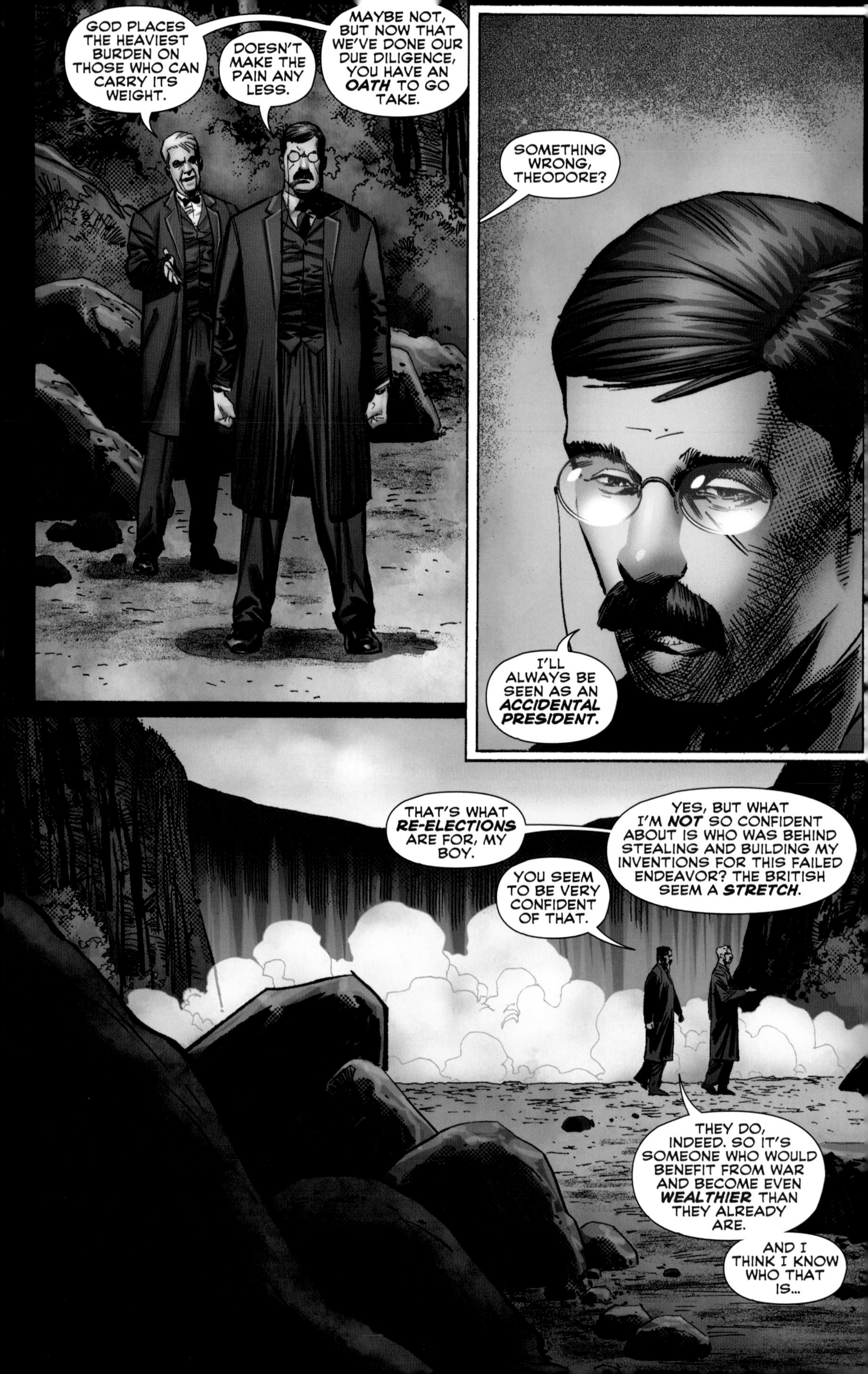
GOD PLACES THE HEAVIEST BURDEN ON THOSE WHO CAN CARRY ITS WEIGHT.
DOESN'T MAKE THE PAIN ANY LESS.
MAYBE NOT, BUT NOW THAT WE'VE DONE OUR DUE DILIGENCE, YOU HAVE AN OATH TO GO TAKE.
SOMETHING WRONG, THEODORE?
I'LL ALWAYS BE SEEN AS AN ACCIDENTAL PRESIDENT.
THAT'S WHAT RE-ELECTIONS ARE FOR, MY BOY.
YOU SEEM TO BE VERY CONFIDENT OF THAT.
YES, BUT WHAT I'M NOT SO CONFIDENT ABOUT IS WHO WAS BEHIND STEALING AND BUILDING MY INVENTIONS FOR THIS FAILED ENDEAVOR? THE BRITISH SEEM A STRETCH.
THEY DO, INDEED. SO IT'S SOMEONE WHO WOULD BENEFIT FROM WAR AND BECOME EVEN WEALTHIER THAN THEY ALREADY ARE.
AND I THINK I KNOW WHO THAT IS...

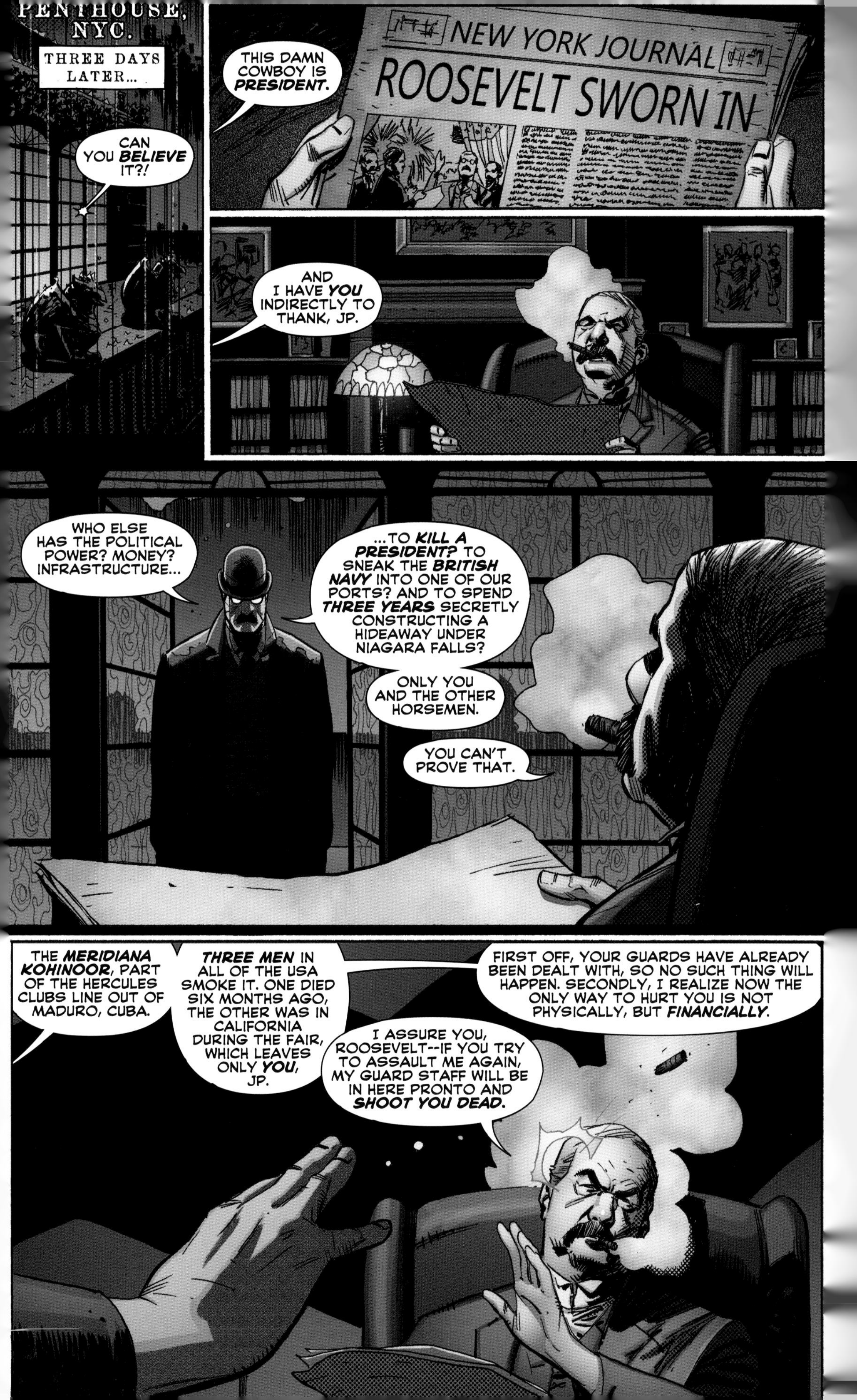
PENTHOUSE, NYC.
THREE DAYS LATER...
CAN YOU BELIEVE IT?!
THIS DAMN COWBOY IS PRESIDENT.
NEW YORK JOURNAL
ROOSEVELT SWORN IN
AND I HAVE YOU INDIRECTLY TO THANK, JP.
WHO ELSE HAS THE POLITICAL POWER? MONEY? INFRASTRUCTURE...
...TO KILL A PRESIDENT? TO SNEAK THE BRITISH NAVY INTO ONE OF OUR PORTS? AND TO SPEND THREE YEARS SECRETLY CONSTRUCTING A HIDEAWAY UNDER NIAGARA FALLS?
ONLY YOU AND THE OTHER HORSEMEN.
YOU CAN'T PROVE THAT.
THE MERIDIANA KOHINOOR, PART OF THE HERCULES CLUBS LINE OUT OF MADURO, CUBA.
THREE MEN IN ALL OF THE USA SMOKE IT. ONE DIED SIX MONTHS AGO, THE OTHER WAS IN CALIFORNIA DURING THE FAIR, WHICH LEAVES ONLY YOU, JP.
I ASSURE YOU, ROOSEVELT--IF YOU TRY TO ASSAULT ME AGAIN, MY GUARD STAFF WILL BE IN HERE PRONTO AND SHOOT YOU DEAD.
FIRST OFF, YOUR GUARDS HAVE ALREADY BEEN DEALT WITH, SO NO SUCH THING WILL HAPPEN. SECONDLY, I REALIZE NOW THE ONLY WAY TO HURT YOU IS NOT PHYSICALLY, BUT FINANCIALLY.

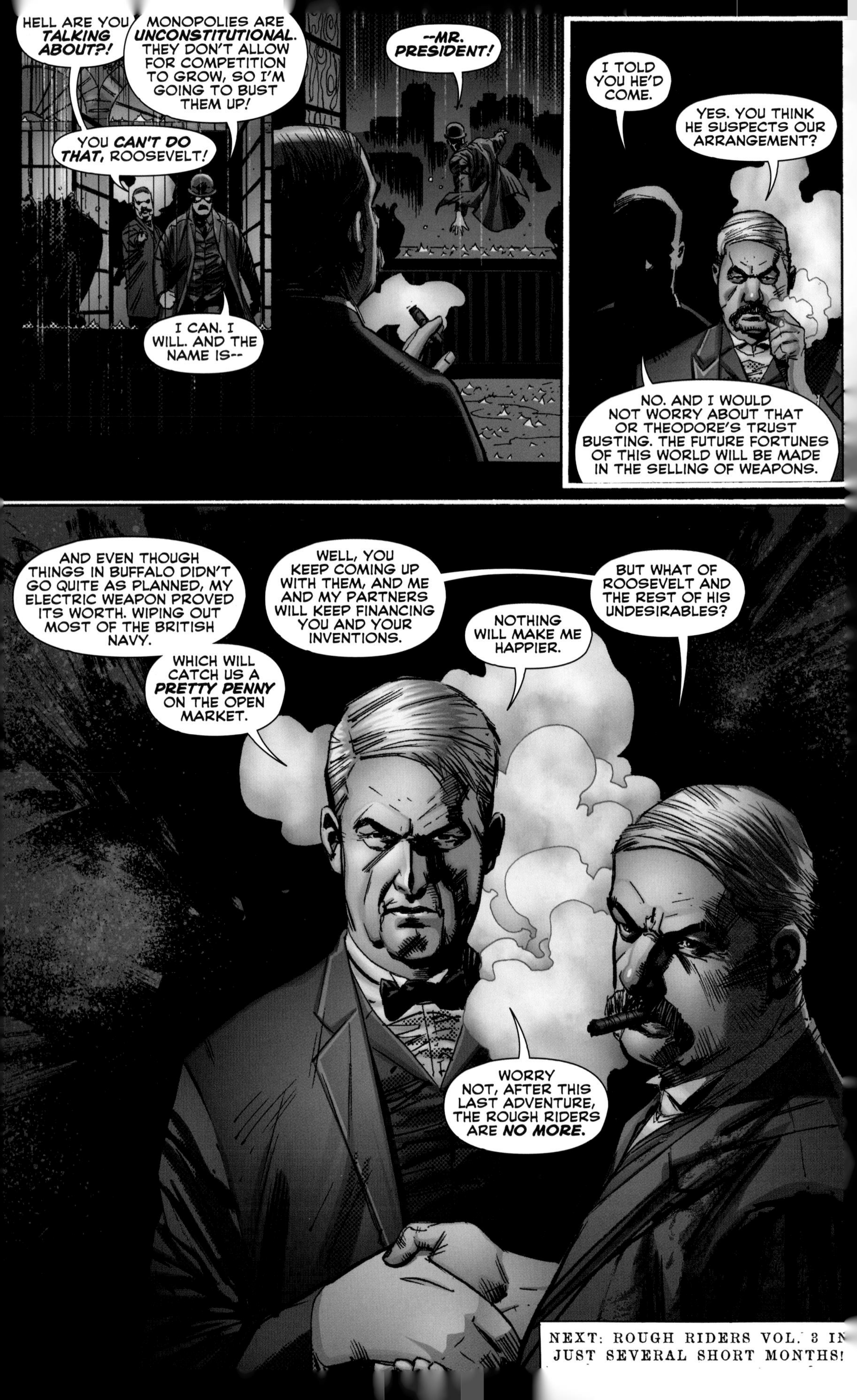
HELL ARE YOU TALKING ABOUT?!
MONOPOLIES ARE UNCONSTITUTIONAL. THEY DON'T ALLOW FOR COMPETITION TO GROW, SO I'M GOING TO BUST THEM UP!
YOU CAN'T DO THAT, ROOSEVELT!
I CAN. I WILL. AND THE NAME IS--
--MR. PRESIDENT!
I TOLD YOU HE'D COME.
YES. YOU THINK HE SUSPECTS OUR ARRANGEMENT?
NO. AND I WOULD NOT WORRY ABOUT THAT OR THEODORE'S TRUST BUSTING. THE FUTURE FORTUNES OF THIS WORLD WILL BE MADE IN THE SELLING OF WEAPONS.
AND EVEN THOUGH THINGS IN BUFFALO DIDN'T GO QUITE AS PLANNED, MY ELECTRIC WEAPON PROVED ITS WORTH. WIPING OUT MOST OF THE BRITISH NAVY.
WHICH WILL CATCH US A PRETTY PENNY ON THE OPEN MARKET.
WELL, YOU KEEP COMING UP WITH THEM, AND ME AND MY PARTNERS WILL KEEP FINANCING YOU AND YOUR INVENTIONS.
NOTHING WILL MAKE ME HAPPIER.
BUT WHAT OF ROOSEVELT AND THE REST OF HIS UNDESIRABLES?
WORRY NOT, AFTER THIS LAST ADVENTURE, THE ROUGH RIDERS ARE NO MORE.
NEXT: ROUGH RIDERS VOL. 3 IN JUST SEVERAL SHORT MONTHS!

issue 1
Photo cover

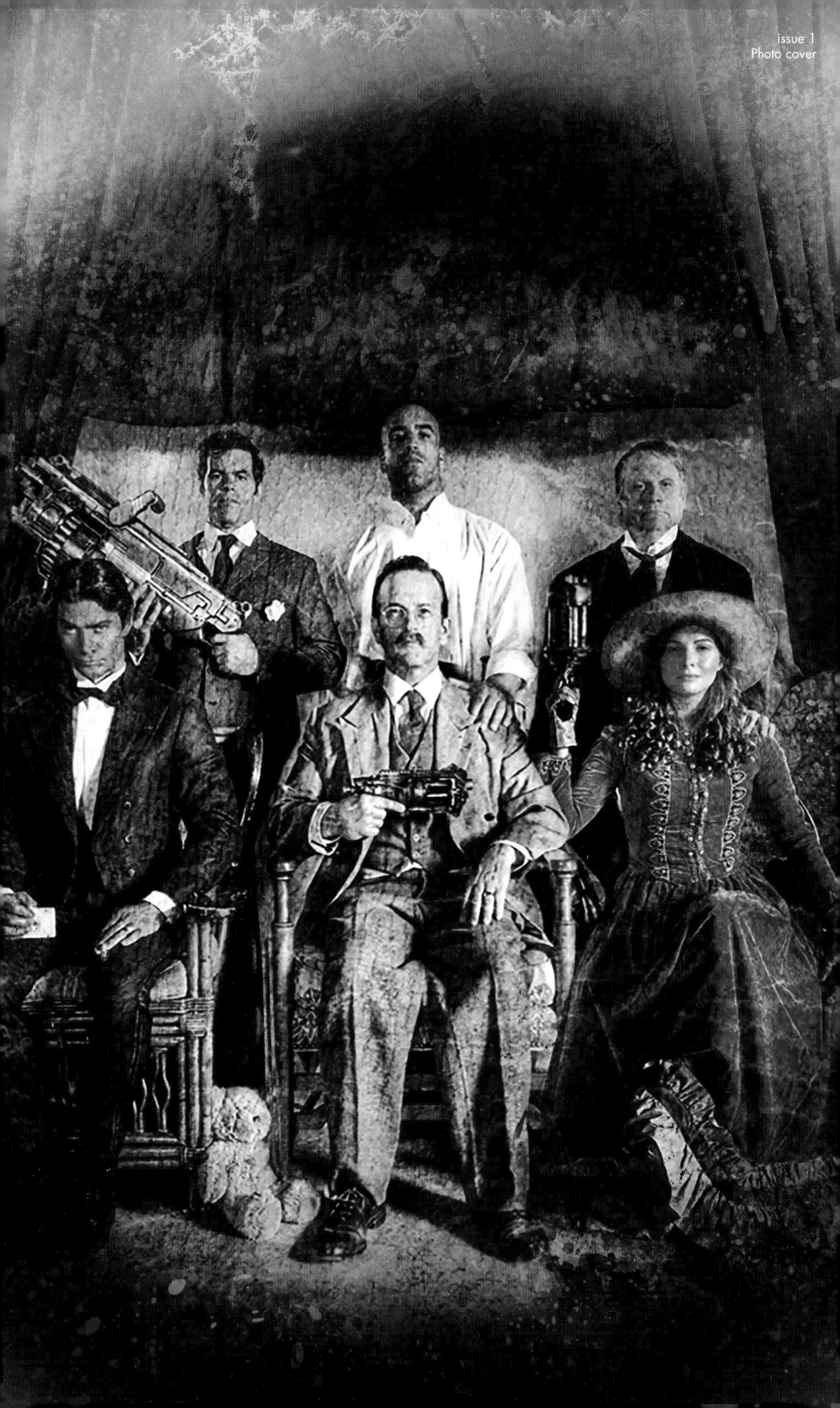

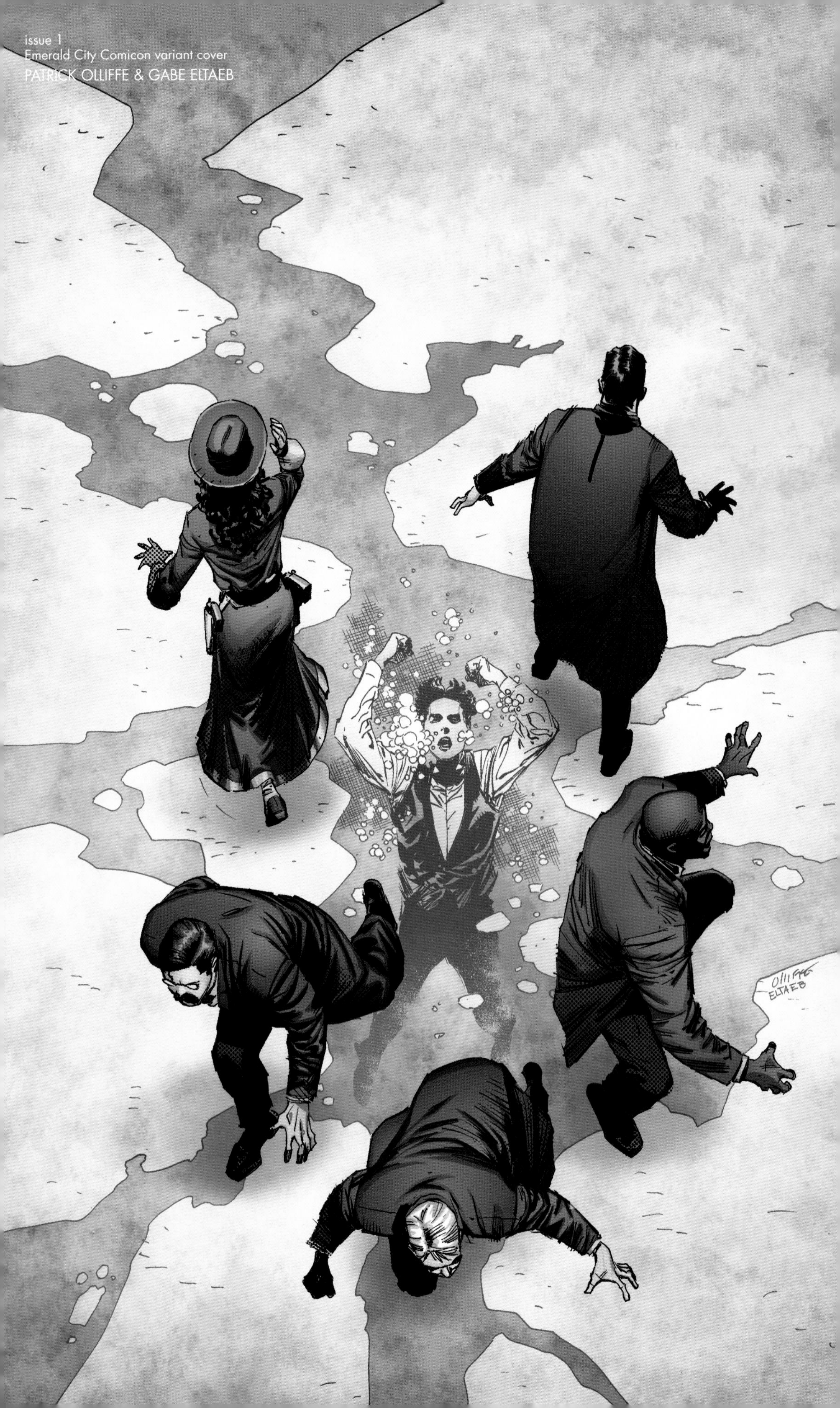

issue 1
Emerald City Comicon variant cover
PATRICK OLLIFFE & GABE ELTAEB

issue 1
ComicsPro variant cover
PATRICK OLLIFFE

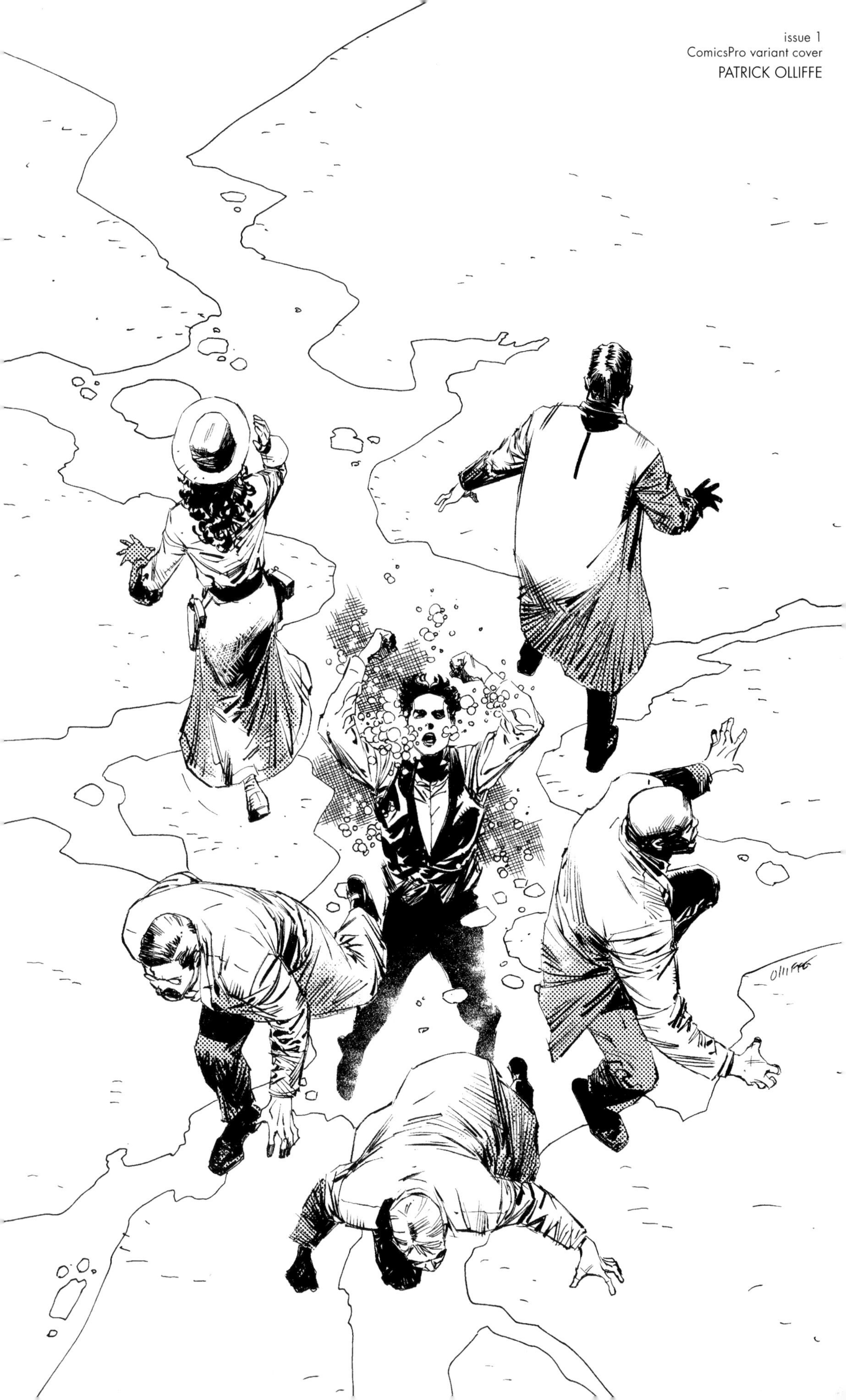

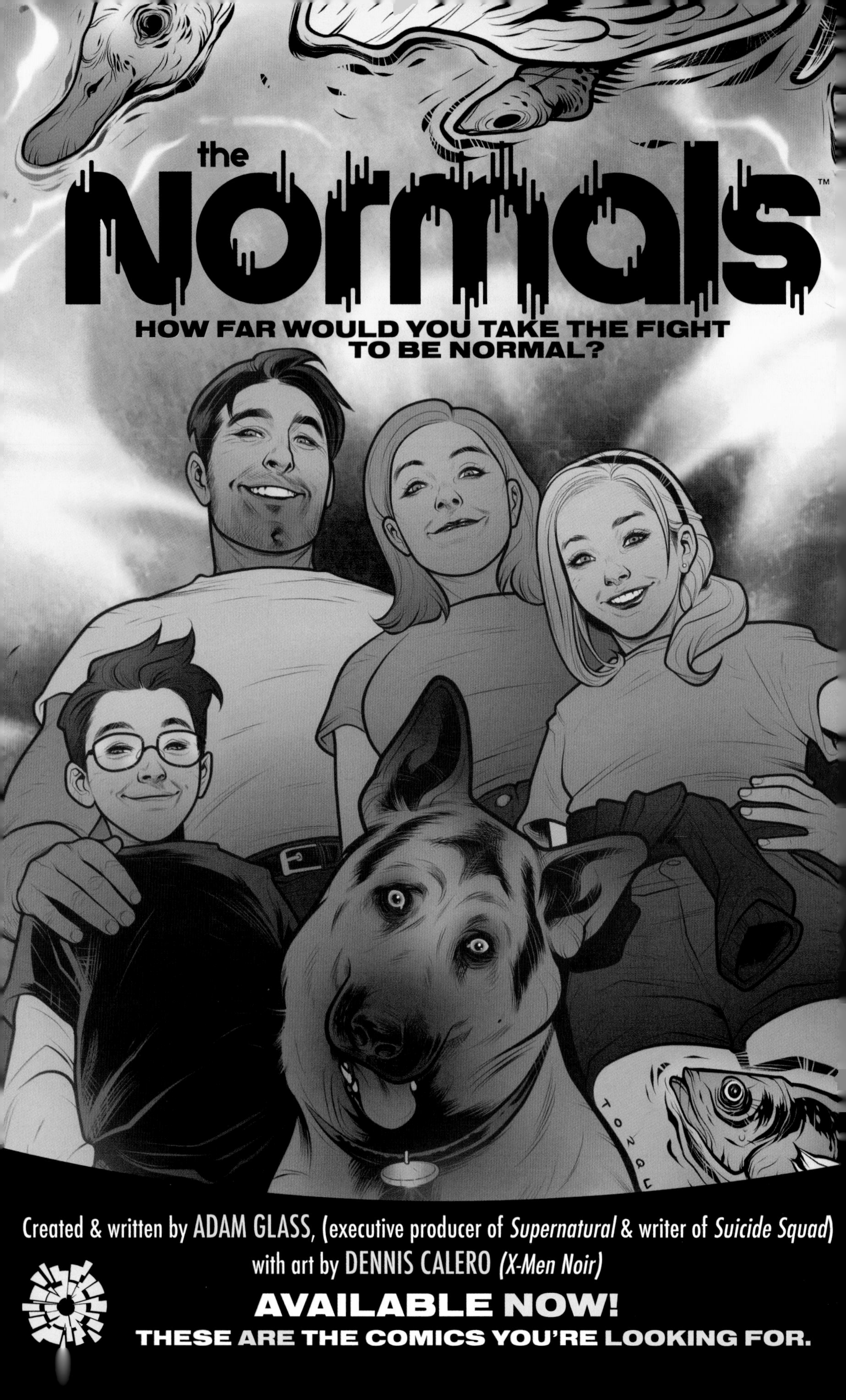
the
Normals™
HOW FAR WOULD YOU TAKE THE FIGHT TO BE NORMAL?
Created & written by ADAM GLASS, (executive producer of *Supernatural* & writer of *Suicide Squad*)
with art by DENNIS CALERO *(X-Men Noir)*
AVAILABLE NOW!
THESE ARE THE COMICS YOU'RE LOOKING FOR.

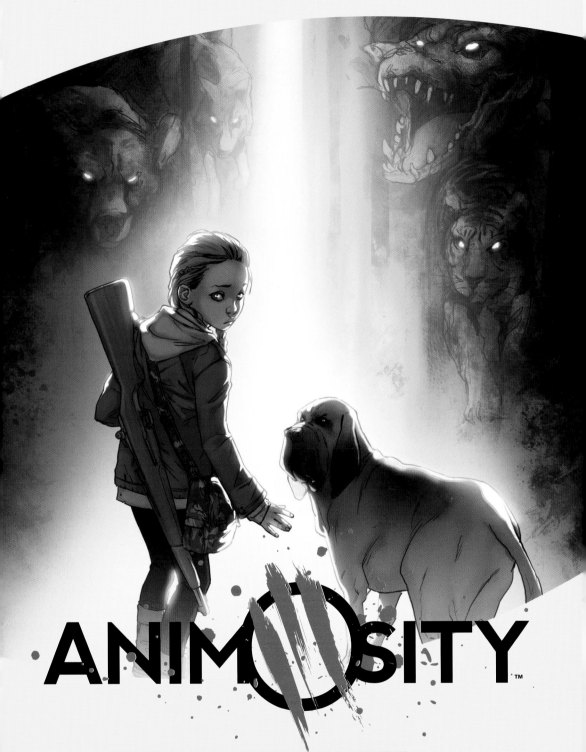

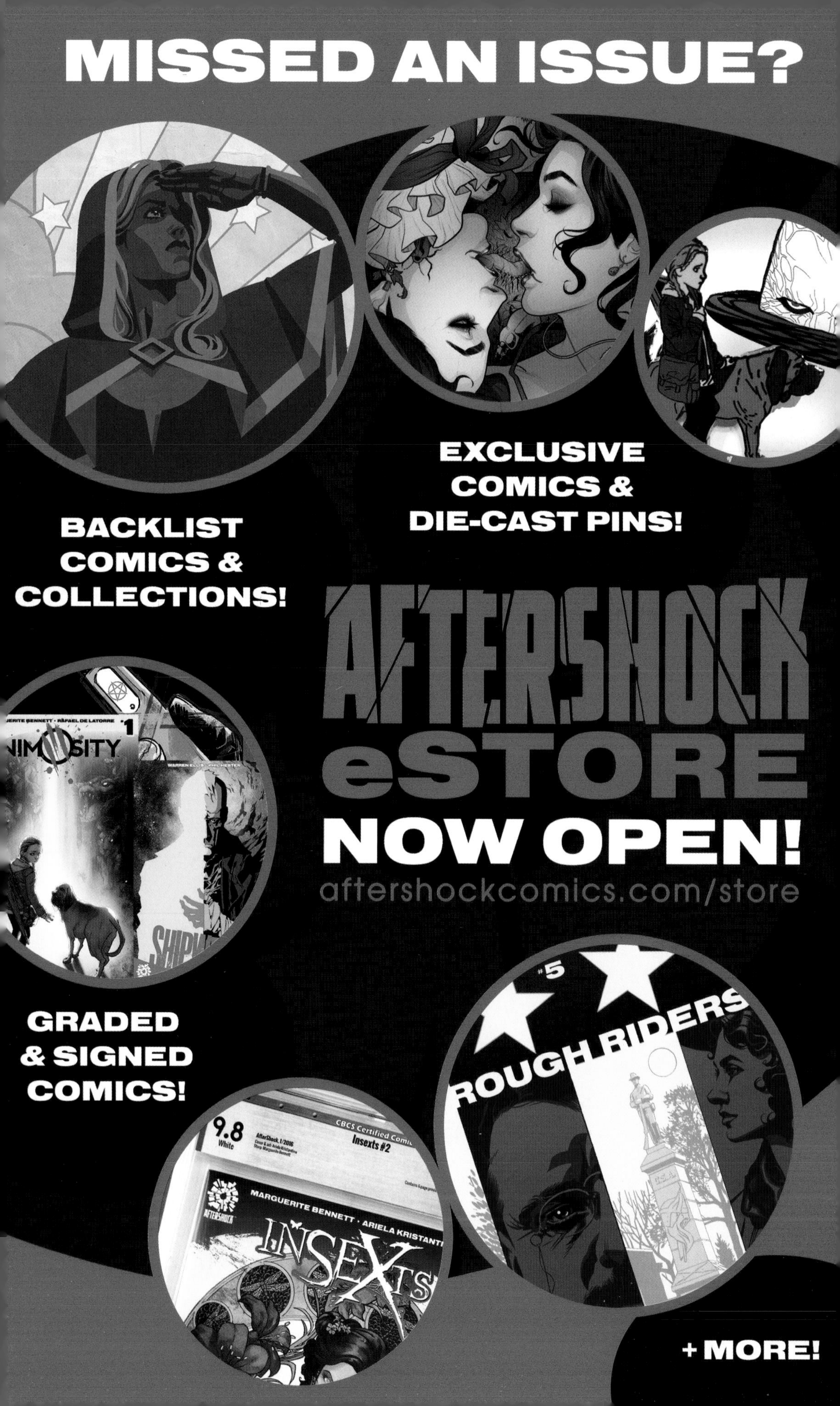
MISSED AN ISSUE?
EXCLUSIVE COMICS & DIE-CAST PINS!
BACKLIST COMICS & COLLECTIONS!
AFTERSHOCK eSTORE
NOW OPEN!
aftershockcomics.com/store
GRADED & SIGNED COMICS!
#5
ROUGH RIDERS
9.8
White
CBCS Certified Comic
Insexts #2
MARGUERITE BENNETT · ARIELA KRISTANTI
INSEXTS
+ MORE!

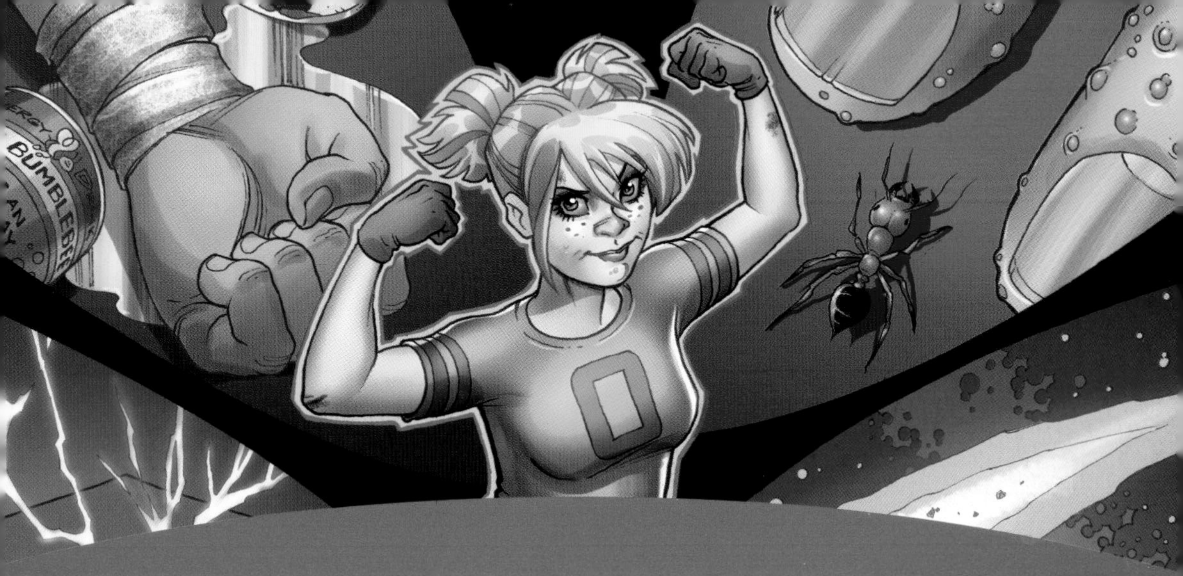

CHECK OUT THESE GREAT AFTERSHOCK
COLLECTIONS!

ALTERS VOL 1
PAUL JENKINS / LEILA LEIZ MAR171244

AMERICAN MONSTER VOL 1
BRIAN AZZARELLO / JUAN DOE SEP161213

ANIMOSITY VOL 1 & VOL 2
MARGUERITE BENNETT / RAFAEL DE LATORRE / JUAN DOE JAN171219 / AUG171130

BLACK-EYED KIDS VOL 1 & VOL 2
JOE PRUETT / SZYMON KUDRANSKI AUG161115 / FEB171100

CAPTAIN KID VOL 1
MARK WAID / TOM PEYER / WILFREDO TORRES APR171231

DREAMING EAGLES HARDCOVER
GARTH ENNIS / SIMON COLEBY AUG161114

INSEXTS VOL 1
MARGUERITE BENNETT / ARIELA KRISTANTINA JUN161072

REPLICA VOL 1
PAUL JENKINS / ANDY CLARKE MAY161030

ROUGH RIDERS VOL 1
ADAM GLASS / PATRICK OLLIFFE OCT161101

SECOND SIGHT VOL 1
DAVID HINE / ALBERTO PONTICELLI DEC161186

SUPERZERO VOL 1
AMANDA CONNER / JIMMY PALMIOTTI / RAFAEL DE LATORRE MAY161029

ADAM GLASS writer
🐦 @AdamGlass44

Though NYC will always be home, Adam resides in Los Angeles and is a TV Writer/Executive Producer of such shows as *Supernatural*, *Cold Case* and currently *Criminal Minds: Beyond Borders* on CBS. When Adam is not writing for TV or films, he's writing graphic novels. Some of these titles include: Marvel's *Deadpool: Suicide Kings* and DC Comics' *Suicide Squad*—both of which were NY Times bestsellers. Other books Adam has written or co-written for Marvel are *Deadpool: Pulp*, *Luke Cage: Noir*, *Deadpool Team-Up* and *Luke Cage: Origins*. And for DC, *JLA Annual* and the *Flashpoint* series *Legion of Doom*. Most recently, Adam finished an original graphic novel for Oni Press called *Brick*.

PATRICK OLLIFFE artist

Patrick is a veteran comic book illustrator with over twenty-five years of experience, working for such publishers as Marvel, DC Comics, Dark Horse and Disney. His long list of credits include *Untold Tales of Spider-Man*, *Spider-Girl*, *Thor*, *Captain Marvel*, *X-Men Gold*, *52*, *The Atom*, *Superman*, *Batman*, *Wonder Woman: 52 Aftermath The Four Horsemen*, *Catwoman*, *Barb Wire*, *Avengers*, *Captain America Joins The Avengers* and *The X-Men* for Disney's Marvel Press. He is thrilled to be working with Adam Glass on AfterShock's ROUGH RIDERS!

GABE ELTAEB colorist
🐦 @gabeeltaeb

Sharing his hometown of Greeley, Colorado with DC comic's Jonah Hex, colorist Gabe Eltaeb was compelled to work in comics after seeing Jim Lee's cover for *X-Men #1* in middle school. Gabe grew up in San Diego, married his high school sweetheart, Adrienne, and has three kids. Coming full circle, Gabe was hired by Jim Lee in late 2007 to work as a colorist at Wildstorm. He has colored hundreds of books for DC Comics, Dark Horse, Image and IDW since going pro in 2004. Notable titles include: *Justice League*, *Star Wars*, *Green Lantern*, *Green Arrow*, *Batman and Robin Eternal* and now ROUGH RIDERS. Gabe loves the Denver Broncos more than anyone ever could.

SAL CIPRIANO letterer
🐦 @salcipriano

Brooklyn-born/coffee-addicted Sal Cipriano is a freelance letterer and the former Lettering Supervisor for DC Comics. His previous position at DC coupled with experience in writing, drawing, coloring, editing, designing and publishing comics gives him unique vision as a freelancer. Sal is currently working with—amongst others—DC, Skybound, Lion Forge, Stela and now AfterShock! Better fire up another fresh pot!